SHADOWS SO CRUEL

COURT OF RAVENS
BOOK TWO

LIV ZANDER

INK HEART PUBLISHING

IN CASE YOU FORGOT...
A REFRESHER FOR FEATHERS SO VICIOUS

I n book one, Galantia—daughter of Lord Brisden of Tidestone—had grown up sheltered but unloved. As a young woman, she had little value to her parents, other than to be bartered into marriage. Sent away for Ammarett, the capital of the kingdom of Dranada, she was to marry King Barat's son and heir, Prince Domren, to further secure their alliance in these war-torn times.

Her journey took a harrowing turn when her entourage was attacked by Ravens—wicked beings of shadow magic with the ability to shift into an unkindness of ravens. Captured by Sebian, a pathfinder, she was brought before their leader: Prince Malyr, last surviving heir to the throne of the cursed city of Valtaris, in the lost Raven kingdom of Vhaerya.

Having been tortured and abused at Lord Brisden's command in his past, Malyr harbored vehement disdain for his daughter. In an attempt to offer her return in exchange for Raven prisoner Marla, Malyr couldn't kill or compromise Galantia to extract a sense of revenge for her father's sins. But he spared no effort to torment her with pain—and the unexpected pleasure it held for her.

After realizing that Galantia was betrothed to the man who killed his entire family, Sebian offered her a softer kind of torment, ravishing her in all ways that wouldn't compromise her value. Charmed by Galantia's innocence and helplessness, he found a strange sense of renewed worth in protecting her the way he'd failed to protect the ones he'd loved and lost.

However, Lord Brisden refused the release of his Raven prisoner. Enraged by Brisden's suggestion he take Galantia to wife and forge an alliance against King Barat instead, Malyr defiled Galantia's purity in front of witnesses, irrevocably destroying the little value she'd had and causing a rift between him and Sebian.

Faced with ruination, Galantia took matters of her survival into her own hands, offering herself to Malyr in marriage. In exchange, she would offer something he couldn't refuse: she would travel to her family feigning a visit, and free the prisoner he so desperately wanted. Reluctantly, Malyr agreed, seemingly making an effort in putting his disdain for her aside.

As the feelings of the two men for Galantia intensified, so did the rivalry between them. Worried for Galantia's well-being, Sebian didn't trust Malyr's gentler approach. Irked by Sebian's meddling, Malyr lured Sebian away onto a mission, allowing him to grow closer to Galantia during Sebian's absence and gain her heart.

When Sebian returned from the mission that had turned out to be a farce, he soon came to find that Malyr had never intended to marry Galantia. Instead, he had secured himself another human ally, Lord Taradur, promising that he would marry his daughter Lady Cecilia in exchange for his help in the attack on Tidestone.

Upon learning that Malyr's affection had been feigned to distract everyone from his upcoming attack on Tidestone, Galantia was devastated. Her heart was broken, but Malyr gave it the ultimate blow when he revealed that Sebian would never truly love her either, for his bondmate had been among the people Sebian had lost.

Realizing that there had been no love for her and never would be, Galantia shattered into a million pieces. Only to emerge from them with white wings, revealing her as a white Raven before her unkindness fluttered away...

CHAPTER
ONE

Sebian
Present Day, Deepmarsh Castle

C old, soul-rending shock froze the blood in my
veins, my senses drowning beneath a flood of
sounds and smells that stunned my mind: the
breeze of wingbeats shifting the black strands spilling from
my topknot, the pained caws echoing from the stone walls,
the stale, musky scent of dander in my nose. This couldn't
be real...

Four ravens, their feathers pale as winter, slipped
through the flight holes at the top of the wall in Cici's

chamber. Like ghosts, they disappeared into the swirl of snow and wind, their piercing cries fading into the icy oblivion.

My mind spun circles.

This could *not* be fucking real.

"What has happened here?" Asker's voice thundered somewhere behind me where he must have stood in the door, the grind of his black *aerymel* armor giving away his shifting tension. "Where is Lady Galantia?"

Gone. Galantia was gone, leaving nothing behind but a couple of white feathers that drifted in the air. What in the ever-loving fuck had just happened?

I looked over at Malyr, searching his pallid features for a smirk, a sneer, a smile—anything that would indicate that he somehow understood what was going on here while my brain couldn't explain any of it. Instead, I found his mouth agape, his bottom lip trembling as much as those fingers he raked through his long black hair before he fisted it.

Still, his bewilderment didn't fully hit me until he stared at me from wide, gray-brown eyes that narrowed with each silent passing second, until said eyes snapped to Asker behind me, and his shout shattered from the walls. "Find the white Raven! Catch the unkindness, and bring it to me!"

White Raven. Yes.

Galantia was a white Raven.

Asker's birds dashed past me, leaving a trail of shadows in their wake as they slipped through the flight hole.

"Oh gods..." Cici all but breathed in that wedding gown that should have been Galantia's—her copper mane biting against the black shadowcloth and feathers—as she lifted her shaky hand to point at the ground. "What of this one?"

I looked down.

My chest caved.

A single white raven sat quietly on the stone, unmoving, its wings closely pressed against its body, its pain-filled eyes only half open and closing more with every slow blink. Its dull, ratty, damaged feathers explained the smell of dirt, dust, and dander, but not why that bird was the size of a juvenile, at best. What was wrong with it?

"It's Galantia's *anoa*, the bird in our unkindness that carries the gift." I squatted, slowly reaching for the bird with both hands, the sick-looking thing entirely unbothered. "There isn't a trace of magic from what I can sense, almost as if—"

Malyr scooped the bird into his palm, lifting and pressing it to his chest with one hand before he covered it with the other and turned away. "I want every single fate in this castle to look at this *anoa* and give me answers!"

My skin bristled at the premise of him anywhere near Galantia's *anoa*. "Where are you taking it?"

That bastard spun and left Cici's chamber with quick strides. Just like that, as if this chaos wasn't entirely his damn fault!

"Hey!" My shout echoed through the corridor as I hurried after him, anger surging hot and fast, quickening my steps and tightening my jaw. "You don't get to just walk off with that bird. Not after all this!"

If anything, he walked faster, letting the leather lacing on the back of his black corseted vest groan under the expanse of his broad chest with each inhale. When he reached the iron-cast raven that spread its wings on the doors to his chambers, he stormed inside, letting an orchestra of noises flare up.

Wood groaned. Glass shattered.

"What the fuck are you doing?" I stepped into his

personal room and pushed the heavy door into its lock with such force, black wisps caught on the sheared sides of my skull. "Give me her *anoa*, Malyr, or by the goddess, I'll sever whatever is left of this thin thread that once was our friendship. This is all your damn..."

My voice faded under the clanking of metal.

Because Malyr one-handedly dragged a large, temple-shaped, gilded bird cage from a dark corner, many of its golden wires bent and covered in a dark reddish-brown that sure as fuck wasn't rust—it was dried blood. By the state of the cage, this must have been where he'd locked up his *anoa*, getting his bird into such a frenzy to escape, it must've cut itself on the wire.

When the cage came to a halt in front of the hearth, its embers reflecting on the glinting metal, Malyr reached the little white raven through the open door. He lowered the droopy-headed thing onto the straw at the bottom, then pushed the cage closer to the flame. A second after that, he pulled it away, only to push it closer again. He spent eternal moments finding just the right position to provide the bird warmth without running the risk of the straw accidentally catching fire.

I watched the scene with a shake of my head. How could he hurt Galantia so badly one moment, then fuss over her ailing *anoa* the next? What the fuck was wrong with his head?

"Where is its gift?" I asked again. "There isn't a trace of magic on this bird."

"How would I know?" Malyr pushed through gritted teeth as he leaned over, bracing his hands against the top of the cage in support. "I want an explanation for this. I want to know how the Brisden household has harbored a—" His gaze snapped to the five black ravens fluttering in through the flight hole above his desk, their shadowy tendrils forming the stout figure of Asker, his salt and pepper braid tousled, his beard dotted with snowflakes. "Tell me you caught the unkindness!"

"My prince." Asker bowed, his eyes nervously going from Malyr to the *anoa* in the cage before it settled back on Malyr. "I sent ten pathfinders out to find them, but... with the landscape white, the... the sky covered in gray clouds, and... the snow flurries..." A heavy swallow. "I lost them."

With a deafening growl, Malyr turned and kicked a nearby stool, sending a woven basket with all its contents to clash and shatter across his room while black tendrils of shadows webbed over his face beneath the skin. "Fuck!"

"They might yet find them," Asker blurted. "One of the pathfinders spotted the unkindness heading northeast."

Northeast.

My guts tied into a knot.

"Because it's the only direction her primal knows familiarity lies," I said, breathing against the sinking in my stomach. "She's heading toward Tidestone."

Toward danger.

"I want every pathfinder out there before she manages to reach its outskirts!" Malyr shouted. "You will track her down and bring her before me!"

"Her?" Asker made a spluttering sound as he threw his arms up. "I don't understand. Where is Lady Galantia?"

"The unkindness *is* Galantia," I said. "She's been one of us this entire time, likely without even knowing it. This might as well have been her very first shift, which left her *anoa* behind." I walked up to the cage and knelt before it, and even that didn't rouse as much as a ruffled feather from the sad little thing. Female, by the looks of it. "I think... I think she's too weak to fly."

Asker's gaze snapped my way, his brows furrowing. "How can this be? A Raven girl raised under Tidestone banners for nineteen years?"

"None of that matters right now," I barked and looked at Malyr. "You fucking bastard put her in the gravest danger. There's a Raven flying straight into Brisden's arms, and it is probably *not* his daughter. All because you can't be anything but hateful. Well done, Malyr."

His mouth tightened, the muscles in his jawline clenching until his entire body shook with rage. Well, I didn't fucking care, because there was little to no chance we would find her unkindness in this weather.

Panic seized my chest.

I can't lose her, too...

"After all this time," Asker sighed, "what could possibly have brought about this sudden shift?"

Scoffing, I rose and gave a dismissive swat at Malyr before I bit out, "Ask him. Fucking liar!"

Malyr took a strong step around the cage toward me, the shadows lashing out around him, all hate, anger, and malice. "I did what I promised her I would do!"

"Yes, you fucking broke her heart, shattering it into so many pieces, her primal forced a shift to escape the agonizing pain. You made sure I was out of the way long enough for you to make her believe you loved her. How can you be so cruel? So vicious?"

He stabbed two fingers against my cuirass with a hostility that sent a flare of heat across my skin. "That's a heavy choice of words for someone who kept the fact that he is bonded from her. I daresay you helped plenty in shattering her."

"Because you used me!" I slapped his stupid fingers off my chest. "You got rid of me. You schemed behind my back

9

—fucking snake of a friend, you are—using me as if I'm nothing more but a figurine on your map."

He barred his teeth. "Do not blame me for your choices, Sebian."

"My choices?" My primal croaked at my core, forcing me to take a step toward him, letting my chest crowd against his, as if daring him to lay his fingers on me once more. "You set me up!"

"And you made it so fucking easy," he ground out. "Did I break her heart and shatter her dreams? Yes. But so... did... you." *Thud.* Another stab at my cuirass. "You could have decided to stay with Galantia. Instead, you flew north, leaving her behind, vulnerable and unprotected. That, Sebian," *Thud.* "Was your..." *Thud.* "Choice." *Thud.*

The last stab splintered through my ribs, Malyr's words twisting a dagger in my gut, each syllable a thrust deeper into my conscience. And the worst part...?

He wasn't even wrong.

I'd known that Malyr couldn't be completely trusted with her, yet I'd left her alone with him so I could... what? Undo the mistakes of my past? Protect the dead instead of a living, breathing woman?

I'd fucking failed all over again!

Fury ignited within me, creeping beneath my skin as if it wanted to peel out of it. But it wasn't aimed at Malyr, it was aimed at myself. Too bad he just so happened to stand right in front of me...

My fist connected with his shadow-streaked face. Knuckles crunched against cheekbone. Blood rushed in my ears, drowning out Asker's shout to "Stop this insanity!"

Malyr staggered back, shadows wrapping around him like a shroud. "You fucking dare!?"

A choke of darkness lunged at me, winding around my

neck, squeezing, forcing the air from my lungs. With a roar that echoed through the shadows, I hurled myself at Malyr, my body slamming against his.

We stumbled across the room and crashed into his desk. Wood splintered. Parchment scattered. An inkwell shattered. The desk groaned under our weight until, with a loud *snap*, it caved. We collapsed onto the cold, hard floor, landing in a thudding of limbs as dust swirled out around us.

I dug my elbow into Malyr's ribs, ripping an *oomph* from him before I struggled myself out of his shadows. "You fucking backstabbing bastard!"

Another inky attack shot at me. Senses heightened, I ducked and rolled away, but it still grazed my shoulder. Hundreds of icy fingers scraped a path across my skin beneath my shirt, leaving a trail of numbness in their wake. They seeped into my flesh, strangled my bones, infested my blood.

"Stop this at once!" Asker shouted as he grabbed me by the arm, pulling me onto my feet, just as Malyr jumped back onto his, which sent a wave of shadows toward me. "In the name of the goddess, stop!"

Shadows wrapped around my neck, but it was the rising panic in my throat that choked me. Malyr was too strong for me, his shadows too relentless and twice as vicious. I couldn't beat him and win.

But I could fucking beat him to pulp before he took his victory. And beat him, I did. My fists swung as wildly as my feet jolted, landing a punch here, a gut-twisting kick there. Bone connected with bone, skin slapped against skin. Iron seasoned the air whenever my crimson fist hit Malyr's face. His blood? Mine? Didn't matter.

My fists kept pounding on him with unrelenting force, each hit an echo of my rage, my grief, my regret.

I didn't protect her. Punch.

I didn't save her. Punch.

I failed. Again! Punch. Punch. Punch.

Malyr's groan snapped me out of my fury, making me blink until red washed over my vision. Blood. Blood was fucking everywhere. Dripping from his lip. Smeared across his cheek. Webbing across the whites of his eyes, above a gushing cleft that cut across his cheekbone.

So much blood.

Not a single shadow.

I hadn't realized I'd grabbed him by the collar until I let go and stumbled backward, my lungs heaving hot air, my muscles drained from exhaustion. The fact that I had managed to beat him into such a bloody state, where he had to grab the damn cage to keep from falling on his ass, could only mean one thing...

"It's hardly fair if you stop defending yourself. Not much fun, either." Wiping my bloodied fists on my breeches, I stared at him, searching for his shadows, but there was not a single one. Had his *anoa* abandoned him? "Where are your shadows?"

Malyr laughed, the blood gurgling that accompanied the sound lending it a generous tone of impeding hysteria. He wiped the back of his hand over his mouth before he spat a blob of pink-tainted saliva through the wires of the cage. It landed in the straw, speckling the white feathers of Galantia's bird.

And there, right beside her, sat Malyr's *anoa*...

... preening her damaged feathers.

TWO

Galantia

Present Day, Tidestone

F rigid air seasoned with brine and ice bit at our feathers, the nearby clash of waves against the cliffs rumbling to our faltering wingbeats. Muscles, bones, sinews... every part of us ached with a fierceness that sucked the strength from our wings. Yet, still, we flew.

Beneath us, the land stretched out in a cerulean blanket, with purple conifers that dotted the colorful meadows here and there. How beautiful it was, how rich in color, as if a painter had dumped his thickest oils across the entire realm.

Until an updrift slapped our wings.

It ripped us sideways under piercing pain as our muscles burned, screamed. We fell from the sky, scrambling our wings to catch whatever breeze drifted us toward those trees as we sank low, lower still. Needles scraped through our feathers. Falling snow settled on our bodies, wearing us down. Our claws frantically scratched on the trunk, searching for hold.

There was none.

Our talons skittered down along the gnarled bark. The world spun into a blur until, in several thuds, the chilling blanket of snow swallowed us whole. A sudden force erupted inside us, twisting and writhing, ricocheting through us in a wave of needles that pricked our skin.

All color faded from the world.

I squinted against the blinding whiteness that seemed to come from all around me. My lungs wheezed, dragging in sharp, icy air as the cold crept through the shadowcloth of my dress. A shudder wracked through me, my head sparking with the onslaught of questions. What had happened? Where was I?

No!

What was I?

A white Raven.

A soft whimper tumbled from my lips, vanishing into the frosty air. My mind twisted and turned, wrestling with the brain-numbing echo of that answer, seeking any strand of rationality in this unraveling madness. I was no Raven, I couldn't be. I was Galantia of the House Brisden, for fuck's sake, the only living daughter of Lord and Lady Brisden!

Something tickled my temple.

My trembling fingers reached for it, pulling a single, frail, creamy white feather from my face. Nothing but a coincidence. It could have come from anywhere. A pillow, or an empty nest in the branches above, or... or...

I had nothing else, no matter how desperately I clung to the stuttering edges of my sanity, searching for comfort in ignorance. And hadn't I sworn that off? I'd spent my entire life being ignorant, and what had it gotten me?

Betrayal and lies.

Most recently, heartbreak.

There is no love for you here. Not from me. Not from him. There is no love for you anywhere. Malyr's words drifted on the whispering breeze that chapped my lips, making me clench my eyes shut against the hot flood of tears. This was all too much for my heart and head to reconcile. How could I have been so stupid?

And Sebian...

My heart clenched at the thought of him, the place where love should have bloomed now a desolate void of nothing but pain. It hurt. Gods, it hurt...

I didn't know how long I laid like this, sensing new tears run over the bridge of my nose and down the other side. Too long. What was I even crying about? A great love lost? How pathetic I was, indeed...

I wiped my eyes on the shoulder of my dress and pushed myself up to stand. Malyr might have finally broken me, but I was not dead, not yet at least. He might have failed to kill me, but the cold wouldn't. Where in the seven hells was I?

Blinking away the blur, my gaze roamed over the landscape. There, in the gray haze of the horizon, loomed the silhouette of Tidestone's outer bailey. The road from

Glosten—or perhaps, from the southern farms, it was hard to tell with the snow—carved a path toward one of the gates. I was safe.

Or was I?

I became instinctually aware of the brittle shaft of the feather still clasped between my thumb and forefinger, each second I remained still in silent contemplation driving up my pulse. Was it wise to return to Tidestone? *A Raven?* How could this even be? Did Father know? Unlikely. Mother? If she even was that...

One more glance about the endlessly white landscape. I dropped the feather, fighting my feet forward through the calf-high snow. If returning home was a smart choice, I couldn't say, but I *did* know that staying out here—with no patron, no gold, no nothing—was stupid. Neither would I return to Deepmarsh.

I trudged through the snow, each step a laborious effort, sinking into the thick white blanket. Tidestone's sturdy stone structures steadily grew larger as I stumbled and stomped, their presence a tangible reminder of the strength and resilience that had kept our family standing for centuries. But were they even my family?

Who was I?

My steps slowed with each additional question. By the time I approached the gate, where a guard stood rather close to a maid with his face buried in the crook of her neck, exhaustion gnawed on my burning muscles.

The maid's eyes snapped to me, and she quickly gave the guard's shoulder a pat, alerting him of my presence.

He turned to face me, his uniform carrying the pale green patches of Tidestone. "Who goes there?"

"Lady G-Galantia of House Brisden." Probably. "Daughter of Lord and Lady B-brisden." Probably not.

Could Father have sired me on a Raven woman? Yes, but I doubted that he would let such a child live, let alone raise it. And Mother? Had she laid with a Raven? *Was* she a white Raven? I didn't know enough about white Ravens to tell, and there would be no answers out here. "Tell Lord B-Brisden his d-daughter is at the—"

"You think any wench can just come up here and try to get behind the gates?" the guard asked with an insulted scoff. "Lady Galantia left over two months ago—"

"Don't be such a fool! It *is* Lady Galantia," the maid said before she lifted the train of her gray cotton dress and hurried over. "Oh, my lady, what happened to you? Gods, you're shaking. Gavric, call for the girls to haul hot water into the lady's chamber this instant." She glanced back over her shoulder. "Now! Or do you want her to die of the cold?"

The guard, Gavric, blinked at me, his face blank with shock for a moment. Then, with a rushed nod, he disappeared through the door in the gate, which he left open.

The maid, who I now recognized as Jana, took the shawl off her shoulders and draped it over mine, her warm touch a welcome change from the icy chill that gripped me. "Come with me, my lady. We'll have to get you into a tub and warmed up before you fall ill with fever."

Trembles wracked my entire body, turning each step inside and up along one of the winding tower stairs into a stuttering struggle while my teeth chattered along. Gods, I was so cold, so tired, and yet, my head spun with a hundred thoughts.

"Maren," Jana said to another maid we passed. "Fetch Lady Brisden and bring her to Lady Galantia's old chamber. Be quick about it!"

I followed her along the outer balcony toward the door to my chamber. "M-my Fa-ha-hather?"

"I don't think he's inside the walls, my lady." Jana opened the door to my room. "Might be with the ship builders down by the bay, last I heard. Now sit, my lady." I needed no telling twice when she helped me into the wing-back chair by the hearth. She lowered onto the hearthrug, immediately building a fire with the kindle and oak that sat in a crate beside the stone. "Just as soon as the water arrives, we'll get you into the tub."

My old wooden one, which she pulled from the back corner of my room and dragged the heavy thing behind the silk-embroidered privacy screen that stood nearby. The door swung open, letting in two young girls who carried buckets of steaming water. One after another, and in a shared effort that turned their cheeks red, they poured them into the tub.

"Don't dawdle," Jana told them before they left with the emptied buckets, then she gestured me to my feet. "Oh, how you're shivering, my lady. We'll have to get you out of this dress." Her fingers made quick work of the lacing in the front, only to struggle with peeling the black shadowcloth off me, soaked and stiff as it was. "Curse the gods, this is a strange silk. Almost as if—" Her eyes snapped toward the creak of hinges, then the maid hurried her limbs into a curtsy. "My lady."

The room cooled so quickly, even the young flames seemed to struggle in the hearth as they bit at the kindle, courtesy of Mother's arched brow that seemed solidly frozen on her stony expression. "It is *you*."

It was a sad consolation, how the disapproval in her voice didn't ache the way it used to, if only because my heart was a shattered, bleeding mess in my chest already. "Sorry to disappoint, but, yes, M-mother, I have c-come home."

"This is no longer your home. You ought to be at Deep-marsh, about to depart for Tidestone by carriage before the wedding that was to safeguard the future of our entire house." Pale green, fur-lined cotton shifted around those three angry steps that put her right before me, her graying hair elegantly pinned up and standing so at odds with that unrefined curl on her upper lip. "What have you done?"

The accusation in her tone filled my chest with a chilling tension that even the now crackling fire in the hearth couldn't warm, torturing an organ that seemed to pour into my ribcage with each aching beat. I was so sick of everyone's disdain and disappointment!

"What have I done? Me?" I fought the chatter from my teeth as I yanked on the shadowcloth, revealing the scar on my breastbone. "I have bled and hurt to safeguard the future of our entire house, only for you to abandon me to the hands of the most hateful soul that wanders this earth! Tell me, what has Father done to him to create such malice? And while we are at it, what have *you* done?"

Mother's face tightened as her cold gaze lowered to my scar, her lips thinning into a harsh line. Did she know? Did she know *what* I was?

"Out!" Mother's shout had Jana jumping before she scurried away, yet her eyes remained on my scar, harsh and ungiving. "You will let nobody enter this room. Nobody, do you hear me!?" When the door fell heavy into its lock, Mother lifted her slender fingers. Instead of settling on my scar, however, they fumbled with something on my dress. "Get out of this thing."

I looked down at her fingers, watching them pull a creamy feather from where it must have gotten stuck on the inside of the shadowcloth dress. My stomach sank deeper the higher she lifted it up between us, only for her to turn around and let it drift into the hearth.

Flames devoured my feather with a combusting hiss that matched the flare of anger that ignited at my core. "You knew," I murmured and let my eyes find hers, the heat inside me clashing with the chill of her blue irises. "You always knew what I am."

"Nobody can find any of your feathers, as unsusceptible as they might seem." She kept yanking on the fabric, letting it pool by my feet. "If anybody finds out, then we are both as good as dead."

THREE

Galantia

Present Day, Tidestone

"Get in the water," Mother said and ushered my naked form toward the tub. "You will tell me what all this is about. What of the betrothal to Prince Malyr?"

I stepped into the tub, one arm crossed over my breasts while the other covered my crotch, hissing at the way liquid heat encapsulated my feet as I mocked in the most pompous cadence I could manage, "Because he is... noah... looooard."

"Do not be smart with me," she scolded as she turned around, picking my dress up from the ground. "You will tell me everything, Galantia. What of the alliance?"

That was the least of my concerns right this moment, no matter how close Taradur's soldiers were to our borders. "Are you a white Raven?"

The way she threw an insulted hand to her sternum and spluttered in offence was answer enough. "What of the wedding?"

"I don't give a whit about the wedding!" I shouted. "Who am I?!"

"Your obstinance knows no bounds," she hissed. "Is that what you have been taught among these... animals? To abandon the few graces you possessed and forget your loyalties?"

"Oh, yes, because wanting to know why I sprouted feathers is such an impertinence. Where was your loyalty when you left me behind in that village? When you abandoned me to a man Father once flogged and tortured yards away from my bed?"

"You will tell me this instant if you failed once again, putting war at our very doorsteps."

"Failed?" Because that assumption just lay so much closer to her than the idea that we might have been betrayed. "I will not tell you a thing until I know who I am."

"Do not be so difficult for nothing," she snipped. "Your life is as much at stake as ours."

"Is it? Because, should there be war at our doorsteps, then I have wings to carry me elsewhere." How to shift, I didn't know, but it couldn't be too difficult to somehow... make it happen again, right? "What about you, Mother?

22

How do carriages usually fare against the speed of a black cloud of Ravens chasing after it?"

She stared at me for molar-grinding seconds, then pulled a wooden stool from beside the partition, onto which she lowered herself down while draping my dress over her lap. "I do not know who you are."

So much for answers...

I lowered myself into the water, my hope for answers right along with it. "Surely you must know how I ended inside a cradle donning the Brisden banners."

"Very well..." She folded her hands over the shadow-cloth, thumbs nervously fumbling with the fabric, her stare losing itself in its black weave. "That spring, I woke thinking my waters had broken overnight. It was blood," she said with the slightest of trembles in her voice. "Eight hours it took me to birth him, my son. My well-formed, handsome, golden-haired son. He was perfect, and he was... dead." Her eyes blinked in quick succession. "That was after King Omaniel stole King Barats' betrothed."

A lie, but there was no point in mentioning it when I was after my own truth. "Go on."

"When I was sent to marry my lord husband, I thought a titled woman's plight was having to bear all his children," she said. "The true plight was bearing him none. I knew that, should he return home and find yet another small grave, freshly filled-in, after war loomed over humans and ravenkind, he would put me aside or worse. But then I learned of a baby that, only two days prior, had been born to one of the kitchen helpers who tended the gardens. A healthy, red-cheeked thing with creamy-blonde hair, just like her mother."

My throat narrowed. That would mean that my birth

mother had been a white Raven, working—and likely hiding—at the Brisden household. "Me."

She nodded. "A girl, yes, but *alive*. And so, I approached the servant, offering her more gold than she would ever see in a lifetime to give you to me. One night, after I'd dismissed everyone from service who'd seen my dead son, your mother came to my chambers in secret. She left with a purse of gold, leaving a child in the cradle."

I love you so much.

Aros' voice echoed in the back of my head. The lord of House Batana, Lorn's fated mate, had told me in the Deep-marsh stables that he'd seen my birth mother speak those words to me as an infant. But how, if she'd given me away? Why was it so easy for everyone to just... get rid of me? How could she have truly loved me, yet exchanged me for a purse of coins as if I was merely a loaf of bread?

"My lord husband was not entirely satisfied with a girl, of course, but it gave him hope for a boy," Mother—*Lady Brisden*—said, and the strangest sight curled her lips: a faint smile. "I was happy. After so many years, so many graves, I finally had a baby. I... tried to nurse you from my breast, but my milk had already dried up." Another blink, followed by a sob that mangled the smile, then she rested her hand on the edge of the tub, as though she feared fainting and falling forward if she didn't. "Oh, you cried so desperately out of hunger, Galantia, each piercing screech a reminder that you were not my child, and that I... I was not truly a mother. Would never be, no matter how hard I tried. And I *tried*, Galantia, I did try. For hours, I offered milk-soaked rags, held you, rocked you, sang to you, but you just... wouldn't stop crying."

I watched a tear roll over those hairline wrinkles that had started to form beneath her eyes a few years ago. A sight so unexpected, so at odds with her usually emotionless demeanor, it dug a pit into my stomach. I could hear the pain in the echo of her words, the heartbreak over wanting to love that baby—only to be rejected.

My throat narrowed when I lifted my hand, growing tighter when I reached it for Mother's. All my life, I had lived under the weight of feeling unloved and rejected, when the bitter truth unveiled was that I, as an unknowing babe, had rebuffed her first. Had pierced her heart with the sharp edge of rejection before I could ever blame her for the same. She had wanted to love me, hadn't she? And maybe, just maybe, she had loved me—if only for a day.

But the moment my hand landed on hers on the edge of the tub, she pulled away in favor of digging her fingers back into the shadowcloth, a final sniffle giving way to another sneer. "And when I hushed you, begged you to stop crying, all this... white down appeared around you. It clung to your cradle, your bonnet, the woolen blanket that wrapped you. You contorted, mouth twisting into something... monstrous. And I knew then what you were." Her hard gaze lifted, but it was that upper lip, curled in disgust, that squeezed another trickle of blood from my mangled heart. "What you *are*."

Her revulsion, so raw and undisguised, turned my stomach, a bitter taste flooding my mouth. "I was a baby, then a girl, then a woman, and all three never craved anything more than a warm look, a kind word, a gentle touch from you. How can you be so heartless?"

She looked up, piercing me with her stare. "Bury your thirteen children, Galantia. Do it, and then see what is left to judge of my heart."

Thirteen children.

Thirteen.

25

That number sent a shudder down my spine, making me pull my steaming legs against my torso for warmth. "Where is my Raven mother now?"

"That... treacherous creature left Tidestone the day after she gave you to me. I do not know who your father is." She rummaged through the fabric of my discarded dress, pulling on the belt until the little satchel Captain Asker had given me came into view. "Your birth had been announced, your health praised by the physicians. With Lord Brisden on his way to Tidestone, eager to see his first child that had not only lived for more than a few hours, but days, I had no other choice but to keep you. Risa was hired and instructed to keep you at her breast at all times."

"She knew what I was." Mother's nod in my periphery wasn't needed to confirm. The day Risa had found a white feather in my bedding in the tavern at that village? That strange look she'd given me? Yes, she'd known. And she'd loved me anyway, more than either of my mothers ever had. "It's why you never allowed me to run, to ride, to play."

To cry.

To live.

"Any pain or emotional overwhelm could have triggered a shift, putting me on the gallows and you into a cage of flames. As it will now, if anybody here finds out what you are." She rose, turning toward the hearth. "This dress needs burning."

I only nodded, staring at the ripples on the water's surface as if I was watching my entire life the way I'd known it distort into something I couldn't even recognize anymore. Like a thousand broken pieces, and none of them fit together. Why had my birth mother given me away so easily? And who was my father?

A void expanded at my core. With my birth mother disappeared, my father unknown, and no living soul who could provide answers, how could I possibly put myself back together if I had no idea who I truly was? Perhaps a halfblood? But even then...

I squinted at a small greenish bruise on my knee as another important question formed in the back of my head. "Where is my gift?"

If I could shift, should I not have one? Or had it not manifested yet, just like it had been the case with Malyr's mother?

"I cannot say, nor do I care," Mother said on a scoff as she bundled up the dress. "Gods forbid, it was the only worry that I was spared all these years. Black magic. Evil shadows. Ungodly visions."

At that last word, my eyes opened wide as my gaze jumped to that satchel dangling toward the flames on the belt, Captain Asker's voice echoed in my memories, *"I beg of you, my lady, return my mate to me."*

Marla!

If she could see the past, like Asker had told me in the corridor at Deepmarsh once, could she also tell me about mine? Could she see my mother? My father? Explain why I had no gift—or, at least none that ever showed itself from what I could tell. I had no amplified senses, no shadows, no visions.

I had... nothing.

"No!" I jumped from the water, getting one leg stuck on the rim of the tub, nearly stumbling straight into hearth before I grabbed it. "Burn the dress if you must, but I need to hold on to this."

She reached it all toward the hearth. "I want nothing of Raven-making in these—"

I snatched the satchel and yanked it off the belt, the salt stones with deathweaver shadows trapped within them clanking inside. The sound was replaced with the *whoosh* of the fire as it devoured the dress, followed by the squeak of hinges as Father stepped inside.

His gaze swept from my toes, all the way up to my breasts before he turned around. "Gods, woman... put some cloth on her!"

"Forgive me, my lord, for not having her decent yet." Mother pulled a folded brown underdress from my old armoire, making quick work of getting me into it.

One arm. Second arm.

Then, I reached behind my back to hide the satchel while my naked foot slid into a graceful curtsy. "My lord Father."

Clearing his throat, he turned around, his brown hair not marked by a single gray strand, yet his eyes carried dark half-circles beneath them. "You were not supposed to arrive at Tidestone for another week, and now I learned that you stomped through the snow to knock on my gates? What is the meaning of this?"

His sharp tone carried every unspoken accusation. *You have failed yet again, Galantia. What a disappointment you are, Galantia. How worthless you turned out to be, Galantia.* And so on and so forth...

I held his hazel stare, unable to come up with a somewhat reasonable excuse that would wallow him in the comfort of an alliance with Malyr. After everything he'd done to me, every single Raven out there, and yes, even Malyr, why would I care if Taradur's forces slit his throat? Drove him out of Tidestone? Why would I offer assistance to any of them?

Because, as it so happened, I was in dire need of a

distraction. And what could possibly put Tidestone into greater upheaval than having to prepare for a siege?

"There is no alliance, Father," I said, clasping the satchel tightly, for I might very well have need of those spells tonight. "The betrothal was nothing but a farce, the grains so *graciously* provided by Prince Malyr nothing but Taradur's forces in disguise. They are carting disassembled siege weapons to our walls as we speak. I escaped these... gods-cursed Ravens so I may warn you."

He stared at me in shock, his pupils flicking across the room as though he was assessing the potential truth of my words and, when they proved reliable enough, he spun and marched out the door. "Ring the bells! Prepare for a siege!"

Father's footsteps hadn't even faded when the ear-shattering *ding-ding-ding* of the bells resonated in Tidestone, bringing a grin to my face. For the first time, they truly rang because of me.

Rang all fucking day long.

CHAPTER
FOUR

Galantia
Present Day, Tidestone

"Bar the inner gate!" one of the officers shouted through the cresset-lit night, the flames casting orange flickers across every set of panicked eyes that ignored the figure hushing through the shadows. "Archers! Captain Theolif wants every battlement manned with as many of you as it has crenels! Move! Move! Move!"

Hidden beneath a gray cloak and armed with a plan, I hurried along the wall until I reached the familiar hole where several stones had fallen from the mortar many years ago. I wedged myself through—only for the edge to bite into the flesh of my breast. Gods be damned, that hadn't been an issue ten years ago...

It took a bit of wiggling and deep exhales, but I finally managed myself through. My path continued behind barrels of oil that had been lined up here at some point during the day—undoubtedly to be carried up the battlements to dip and light arrows. Clouds drifted lazily over the moon, keeping me nicely hidden, even against the bit of light reflecting from the trampled snow. Still, I had to be careful...

I crouched, slipping from shadow to shadow until I reached the corner of the barbican that secured the inner bailey. My eyes drifted toward the oaken door framed into the barbican itself. The dungeons. I had an idea for the lock, but no clue if it worked. Putting it to the test out here was too dangerous. No matter, I knew a better way.

Unfortunately, it lay beyond the fire basket that crackled beside the door. It illuminated the gateway, making it impossible for me to go unnoticed by the soldier standing guard by the inner curtain wall across. A woman hushing about the inner bailey wouldn't be a sight too suspicious, but out here? So close to the dungeons? With the outer gates already barricaded and sealed? It would rouse commotion at best, and get me put before Lord Brisden at worst.

I reached into the pouch Asker had given me, past a piece of corn bread, and ran my fingertips over the smooth stones of salt before I pulled a random one out. Black, hairline tendrils of shadows slowly writhed within when I angled my palm toward the light. If I released them, they might offer me cover while I snuck across.

Or they might start killing everything and everyone in their path, including me. Too bad I hadn't been able to come up with a better plan...

After an internal prayer to the gods to not let these shadows eat the flesh from my bones, I slammed my fist onto the stone the way I'd seen Darien, the dressmaker, do it. *Crack.* Shadows poured out from between the powdered and crystalized salt. Slowly, they slithered across the ground and expanded, extending the darkness.

Taking a deep breath and holding it for extra measure, I dove into the plumes, squinting against the blackness that encapsulated me. Gods, I couldn't see a thing.

The wall!

I placed one palm against it, letting it guide me along rough stone, dips of mortar, patches of moss. Wood. Wood. Wood. Then rough stone again until—

I slipped around the corner and out of the shadows, nervously glancing over my shoulder at the guard as I stumbled backward into the looming darkness of the wall. He hadn't seen me.

With a silent exhale of relief, I continued, stomping my boots into the snow along the bottom of the wall ever so carefully. Where was it? Somewhere beneath this snow, there had to be—

Thud.

I stalled and stomped again.

Thud.

Boots dragging over the snow, I shoved it all off with the edge, revealing the hatchway that hid beneath. When I was eleven or so, the builders had added this to get kindle and wood down to the guards' and jailor's rooms faster. Or perhaps because several guards had lost their lives in an attempt to carry wood down the spindling stone stairs, slipping on the slick rock before they hit their heads or broke their necks.

After I carefully removed the chains that secured the hatch, I lifted it away. I let myself slip into the angled slide-way, making sure to lower the wooden cover while keeping one corner slightly agape. The stone chafed on my cloak on my way down into one of the storage rooms, the air inside the dungeons rank with moisture, sweat, and the scat of rodents. One jumped out of the pile of split oak on which I landed—a rat, by the size of it—scurrying into a dark corner while I skidded down the shifting pieces. So far, so good.

I slipped out of the room and checked the dimply-lit corridor, some of the oil lamps already flickering rather low for the lack of fuel.

Just like I thought, empty.

With every man, boy, and even some of the women busy preparing for a siege, there wasn't a single soul to spare to guard prisoners locked away behind thick bars of steel. Where was she?

Regardless of the silence down here, I wouldn't dare call out her name. Instead, I hurried from one cell to the next. Empty. Empty. A barrel. Empty. Stacked crates. Empty—

"Galantia," a female voice croaked.

The sound of my name sent gooseflesh across my skin, eyes going to that cell across at the end of the corridor. "Marla."

That fate better have answers about my past, considering the risk I took, should we get caught. As things stood, there probably weren't a great many alliances left Lord Brisden could exchange me for, no benefits to overlook my treason.

I crossed the corridor, but my steps grew hesitant the

closer I came to the cell and the hollow-cheeked woman who blinked at me through the tight weave of bars, her long, black hair matted in some areas, revealing bald patches in others. Squatting to her height, I reached into the satchel, retrieving another salt crystal.

"You know my name." Not only that, but she'd *expected* me. Which was promising, putting a slight tremble in my fingers as I reached the salt crystal toward the iron lock of the door. "Tell me you've seen my past. Tell me you know who I *truly* am."

She struggled herself onto her knees under groans, her shadowcloth tunic and black breeches nothing but tatters that revealed cuts, bruises, and filth. "Nobody can know who you truly are but yourself."

That... wasn't the answer I'd hoped for. "But you've seen my past?"

"For months, I've seen nothing else, until the—" A cough ripped through her words, wet with phlegm that put an audible rattle into her chest. Gods, she was in bad shape. "Until the visions stopped, and none came for a long time. Now I know why. You were captured and taken to Deep-marsh. The goddess showed me how you returned after having found your wings at last, just like she hoped you would."

I swallowed. "The goddess?"

"Your mother," she said. "The fate Lilieth."

Lilieth. A name I'd never heard before, meaningless to my memory, yet it resonated deep in my core, reverberating through my bones until my entire body shook. *Lilieth*, I said silently, shifting my tongue around, tasting her name. *Lilieth*.

Somewhere in the dungeons, metal rattled.

We couldn't stay here.

"We need to get you out of here." Did I want answers? Yes, but not at the cost of her life, or mine. "Battlements, towers, hoardings... everything's sprawling with archers, and torches illuminate every inch of wall up there. They'll shoot you from the sky the moment you take flight. I have a plan, but it'll work best if you can shift in here. Can you?"

"With your help," she said. "All we have to do is intertwine our fingers."

"Even better." I pushed the cracking salt crystal into the lock before I sealed my palm over it. "The bay will do then, saving us the climb to the cliffs. It's still quite a hike, but I brought—"

A chill bit into my palm, making me hiss in pain as tendrils of shadows rose from the edges of the lock, trying to escape. I pressed my other hand over the first, whimpering through the biting, nipping ache. What a good thing that pain and I had been acquainted, courtesy of Malyr.

Do not let go, Galantia!

The shadows kept growing, expanding, writhing free until, with a noisy *click*, the lock sprung open. *It worked!*

I pulled my burning hand from the lock and let the door groan open, staring down at that black mark on the center of my palm that seemed to burrow and bite a crater into my flesh. "Here." Ignoring the pain, I fumbled a small flask of goat's milk from my belt beneath my cloak, and pulled a loaf of cornbread from the satchel. "Eat this. You'll need your strength to fly to Deepmarsh."

Marla all but ripped the bread from my fingers, stuffing it into her mouth, even as she collapsed forward. That didn't keep her from devouring it, lying on her side, until her cough returned with more violence.

"I need you to shift into your unkindness now." I knelt, holding her head somewhat steady while I popped the cork from the flask with the thumb of the other, and let the milk wash down the bothersome crumbs. "At some point, they'll check the dungeons and find you gone. Nobody can see you roaming between the walls of Tidestone if we didn't make it to the bay by then, so I was thinking…" From where it had been folded over my belt, I pulled a large potato sack, the shadowy stains already gone from my palm. "Get your birds in here, and I'll carry you there. I checked from my window earlier, and the bay lies mostly abandoned for now while they prepare the castle for an attack from the southwest."

Nodding, she reached her hand to mine. "Help me, and I will give you what you came for."

Frowning, I intertwined my fingers with hers. A burst of shadows followed, reshaping into five black ravens, three of them mostly motionless, another croaking quietly, as though in pain, and a fifth glancing around, disoriented. I grabbed them all and tossed them into the sack, tied it shut, and carefully brought it over my shoulder.

This had been a great idea.

Galantia

Present Day, Tidestone beach

This had been a stupid idea.

A raven, as it turned out, didn't exactly have the weight of a sparrow. But five of them? They were *heavy*. By the time I'd struggled out of the wood chute, hurried through the shadows, and climbed down the slippery rocks toward the beach, they wore down on my shoulder as if I was carrying a damn ingot.

"Stop wiggling," I muttered, the snow beneath my feet

crunching against the sand as I headed toward the side of the bay where one of our docked ships would give Marla cover. "It's bad enough that every muscle in my body is still sore from—"

"Halt!" a guard shouted from where he suddenly appeared around one of the massive wooden dock posts, another guard standing by his side. "Who goes there?"

Before I managed a word across my quickly numbing lips, the other guard held his torch closer to illuminate my face. "It's only Lady Galantia."

My fist clenched tighter around the burlap. Yes, it was *only* me. Worthless, unassuming, naïve little Galantia. Most definitely not on her way to free a Raven prisoner...

"What is your business out here, my lady?" the guard asked, lifting his torch dangerously close toward the sack, studying it with eyes too curious for comfort.

I lifted my chin. "My business is my own."

"Not if Lord Brisden has all of Tidestone locking down," the other said, jutting his chin at my shoulder. "What's in there?"

Too many seconds passed, giving rise to their brows before I managed to say, "The dress I arrived in, of Raven-making. My mother is greatly offended by it and asked me to drown it in the bay."

The one with the torch only lifted his brows higher. "She sends her daughter to rid of it, in the middle of the night, instead of a maid, who could have easily tossed it into the hearth?"

A sweat pearl formed somewhere on my nape, and I sensed every darned shift of those stupid birds in the sack. One croak, and we would be done for. Well, she could possibly fly away, but still, *I* would be done for! Unless I shifted as well... But how? How had I done it? Oh gods, this was awful.

I offered a smile.

"The maids are cleaning out the privies once more before the attack," I said with a sigh. "Besides, shadowcloth does not burn. Some say it's protected by that evil magic of theirs. Probably soaked in their pitch-black blood."

"I see." The guard with the torch regarded me for another moment, then hinted a bow. Just as the flame hissed over his first step, he stalled, once more glancing at me. "Forgive me, my lady, but I would like to have a look into the sack."

My throat tied up. "Pardon me?"

He exchanged a glance with the other guard, then gave me a sheepish smile. "I've never seen shadowcloth before."

"Neither have I," the other agreed. "Heard that one touch alone will burn a human's skin clean off."

Oh, for fuck's sake...

Panic rose in my chest like a tide, threatening to drown my composure under its crushing waves. What now? Refuse to open the sack? Such resistance would only heighten their suspicion. Open the sack and attempt to convince them that the ruffled feathers inside were just part of the dress's elaborate design? Set Marla free and face the consequences?

Gallows on a cliff, with the sea stretched out behind it. A golden-haired woman's body dangling from a noose, drowning beneath salty waves.

Asker's vision formed before my mind, turning each noisy beat of my heart into time drumming in seconds between my ears. What if I'd sealed my fate? What if I couldn't simply shift and would end myself up at the gallows? After all, it had taken me nineteen years to do it for the first—

The sudden blast of a horn echoed through the cold night air. Were they attacking Tidestone? Already? Now? This night?

"I will come for you," Malyr's voice whispered between the incessant pounding of my heart.

The guard's face bleached white under the flickering torchlight before he exchanged a terrorized look with the other. "It's a call to arms."

The horn's call boomed again, louder, more insistent. Both guards turned away, sprinting from the beach and toward Tidestone fast enough the clank of metal against metal followed along.

I stood frozen for a moment, my breath a white puff of treacherous relief in the frigid air. "Malyr might get here sooner than I anticipated."

Which meant Marla could find safety behind his lines, so I hurried toward the massive wooden hull of the anchored ship. With how tall it stood and the position of the moon, it cast an ever darker shadow over parts of the beach, where I lowered the sack to the ground for the ravens to hop and wiggle out.

Shadows writhed through the night, reshaping into Marla just as she stumbled against one of the wooden posts, clinging to it for balance. "There will not be much time."

"Enough for you to tell me who I am," I said. "All of Tidestone's been called to the inner bailey for now. Please, tell me what you saw!"

Nodding, she turned until her back pressed against the looming post, the light reflecting from the snow behind us putting a faint glimpse into her eyes. "Your mother, your *real* mother, worked at—"

"Tidestone; I know that already," I said, anxiously shifting from one leg to the other as I tossed the sack into the water and wrapped my cloak tighter around me. "She sold me to Lady Brisden for a purse of coins."

Marla shook her head, and not even the darkness could hide the disbelief carved into her face in the shape of wrinkles forming across her forehead. "No, child. She didn't sell you for coins."

My mouth turned dry. "What? But... Lady Brisden..."

"On the day you were born, the premise of war already loomed over our kingdoms, with Ravens getting cursed out, refused entry to taverns, and even attacked by commoners all over Dranada," she said. "Lilieth was a fate, much like my beloved Asker, gifted to see glimpses of the future. You were but a day old when the goddess showed her your death."

My cheeks turned numb. "My death?"

"You were not supposed to live past the age of nine." A shake of her head. "It is not for us to question fate, let alone interfere. Lilieth ought not to have done it, yet, as a mother, I cannot hold it against her. The goddess knows I would have done the same, had she showed me that one winter night."

When her daughter had died...

"Asker told me. I'm sorry for your loss," I said. "But I still don't understand. Why give me away?"

"To keep you safe, Galantia," she said, her words like a soothing caress that slowly wrapped around my heart. "She saw the war and the devastating outcome, should anybody learn who you are, causing her little girl's death during the siege of Valtaris."

But that made no sense. "Why Valtaris?"

"That was where you would have lived, so you may grow and prosper alongside your fated mate," she said. Whatever did that mean? "She saw him in her visions. Saw the Raven boy you were fated to love, to cherish, to die beside as a child with him not much older. What better place was there to hide her little girl, but right beneath the nose of the man whose catapult was fated to kill her, had your mother not changed the trajectory of fate? She gave you up out of love, because she wanted you to live."

Love.

That word washed over me, my legs weakening beneath the weight of the revelation. She hadn't just gotten rid of me; no, my mother had given me away to save my life! My breath hitched as the profound depth of her love consumed me, filling the hollow caverns of my heart that had remained vacant all these years.

Not sold.

Not abandoned.

Not unwanted.

Loved!

"My birth mother..." I wiped the back of my hand over my cheeks where a few tears had broken free. "Is she... Is she...?"

"Among the stars, sweet girl," Marla said, her eyes softening around the edges. "I wasn't able to see what sent her unkindness to drop out of the sky, but the goddess did show me that, whatever she had fought off, allowed your father to escape."

"My father?" My heart gave a single whomp against my ribs. By the gods, what if I'd already met him? "Where is he? Did any of your visions show you? At Deepmarsh?"

Now that softness in her eyes turned to pity as she slowly shook her head.

"Is he..." my stomach clenched, "among the stars, too?"

"Yes, dear."

I glanced up. The night sky overhead suddenly seemed immense, empty yet densely populated with twinkling stars—each one a soul lost. Somewhere in that vast expanse, my parents shined down on me.

I was *truly* alone.

"How did he die?" I asked. "Did you see?"

Marla pushed herself off the wooden post, and that motion alone ripped another cough from her that shook the hand she placed onto my shoulder. "He, too, had been badly injured on his way to Valtaris. That was where they were headed after Lilieth left you in that white cradle. Your father choked on his own blood, and died in the throne room a messenger, with Prince Malyr stroking his forehead when he was but a little boy."

Bile rose in my throat at the image she painted—my father dying in the comfort of the very hands of the man who'd carved me up. Why him? Why did it have to be him, of all people, and not—

My breath stalled, my mind catching at the sense of familiarity of this story, as if I'd heard it before. Where had I heard it? Who had told me—

"Years before Valtaris fell, a messenger reached my parents," Malyr's voice resonated my spinning mind. *"Around his neck, he wore the pendant, stained red from his blood. Something or someone must have attacked him or his unkindness on his way to our city. He suffocated on his blood..."*

"It is of the girl destined for the younger prince," I echoed Malyr's words of that night by the creek when he'd spoken about the pendant, a salt crystal inside a socket of *aerymel.* "No. No..."

A strangled sob tore from my lips. No, this couldn't be. It was too cruel, too menacing, too fucking painful.

"Yes," Marla said in a hushed voice. "You, Galantia, are Malyr's fated mate. You were supposed to die together in Valtaris under boulders and shadows, with your little hand clasped inside his the way—"

"No." It was as if the ground beneath me fell away, the world tilting on its axis as this truth crashed over me with the brutal force of a stormy sea. "Never!"

A shout whipped from my lips, raw and unrestrained, a piercing sound of despair that echoed against the silent ship and the quiet waves. Was this a cruel joke? A terrible twist of fate? A destiny foreseen, yet so utterly, disgustingly wrong? Why him? Why this man who had caused me such pain?

My heart broke all over again.

As the pain of it seeped into my bones, my sorrow slowly gave way to a surging tide of fury, every shredded piece of the organ igniting with a fierce, indignant flame. "Never." The word hung in the frigid air. "I will not be his. Not in this fated life, nor in any other."

Behind me, the horn sounded.

"We must leave," Marla rushed.

I blinked back the last of my tears, for I wouldn't shed a single one for Malyr ever again. "We?"

"Prince Malyr *will* take Tidestone," she said. "There will be death, blood, and misery painted across its walls. Stay, and you might die in the attack. Leave, but where will you go? To Ammarett? You belong with us, Galantia. Your mother always wanted you to come home to us."

I took a deep breath, sucking the sobering chill of briny

air into my lungs. Tidestone alone was dangerous enough, but Ammarett would be worse. But going back to the Ravens? To Malyr? I just... I couldn't.

Not yet.

Maybe not ever.

I stared out to the sea where its glimmer beckoned me from the horizon, thinking back to how badly I'd wanted to fly away as a child. Somewhere far away from all this. An exotic place with strange wares and even stranger languages, but...

"My gift," I whispered. "Is it in the amulet?"

"Your parents must have found a thief to steal most of it, leaving you with little to be detected, so it wouldn't reveal itself and put your life at risk," Marla said. "Where it is, I cannot say."

It had to be inside the amulet. But hadn't Malyr told me the salt crystal had been empty? But why carry an amulet across the lands if it was worthless? Why would my father have died just to see it delivered to Malyr?

No, it was in there.

I was certain.

Another blare of the horn had me glance back over my shoulder, the walls of Tidestone brightly illuminated. "I cannot leave without it."

Not when I was this close to piecing myself back whole. For the first time in my life, everything was coming together, forming a picture of who I should have been. Who I was!

"If I don't find it, it might very well get lost in the attack," I said. "If Lord Brisden were to escape, he might even take it with him, and who knows if it will ever be in my reach again. I have to find it."

"You might die."

"I would rather die knowing who I am than continue to live, wondering," I said, and reached her my hand. "Go. Fly back to your mate."

"I cannot—"

"Go!"

Marla stared at me for another moment. She must have seen resolve in my gaze, because she intertwined her fingers with mine. Shadows followed, forming five sets of black wings that carried her out to the ocean before her unkindness drifted along the cliffs and toward safety.

I turned away, all but running back toward Tidestone. My soles slipped off the slick rock stairs on my way up to the port gate, wild energy fluttering at my core. I needed to find that amulet, but where could it be? Lord Brisden hadn't worn it since—

I slammed into a dark figure at the top of the stairs, catching hold of the low wall before I looked straight at the man himself. "Lord Bris— Father..."

He eyed my curtsy from narrowed slits. "Guards reported they found you gallivanting the beach. Not a sight too strange, given how you always had the tendency to... wander as a little girl."

I swallowed so the dread clogging my throat wouldn't turn my voice too high-pitched. "I couldn't sleep, so I decided to watch the waves."

"With a sack slung over your shoulder?" His balance shifted sideways, his inquiring gaze confirming the sack's absence. "Now that, dear daughter, is a strange circumstance... given the fact that my Raven prisoner somehow escaped the dungeons, having all of Tidestone up in arms."

I sucked in a gasp. "So, Prince Malyr isn't attacking?"

"Not yet," he said and took a step toward me, towering at least a head over me. "The gods know you were never good for much, but do not let me find out you were behind her escape."

Never good for much.

That rage at my core rekindled. "Like you just pointed out, Father, I continue to prove quite the disappointment. I'm certainly not capable of something as elaborate as helping a prisoner—"

Slap.

Pain exploded on my left cheek, spreading into my molars until their roots throbbed. My head jerked sideways and my balance toppled, making me sidestep until I crashed my temple against hard rock. It bit into my skin until my eye watered and everything blurred.

"Should I find out that you helped her escape," he growled low, "then I will personally string you up by the gallows for treason. The only reason you are not dangling there yet, Galantia, is because we happen to need the rope for the net catapults. Now go to your chamber. Your mother will lose her wits if she hears you have been wandering."

A shaky curtsy, then I hurried around him and sprinted back toward the keep. I needed to find this amulet. And once I found it? I needed to get the fuck away from Lord Brisden.

CHAPTER
SIX

Malyr
Present Day, Malyr's personal library

I hovered my marred, upturned hand in front of Galantia's *anoa*, where I'd placed the little female into a silk-filled basket at the edge of my desk. Tiny kernels rilled from the pile of grains sitting in the center of my pecked palm: a colorful mix of oats, cracked corn, ground crickets, and dried blackberries—all of it going equally ignored.

She turned her head left.

My hand followed. *"Spisa."* Eat.

She turned her head right.

My hand followed. *"Spisa, shå."* Eat, please.

The mangy-looking thing buried her head beneath her creamy-white wing, shutting me out so completely, it felt as if the heavy iron door of my Tidestone cell slammed closed on me once more, sealing me away in the cold, dank darkness. What if I'd frayed our bond to a degree it would never recover?

But was that not a good thing? It wasn't like I intended to bond myself to Galantia. No, I did not.

I should not.

I was not fit to bond.

"Stop pestering her. It will only get your *anoa* to escape your form again so he can try to peck your fucking eyes out." Sebian walked over from where he'd silently stood by the window as we waited for Asker, scooped up the little white raven with one hand, then reached the other out before me. "You know full well she refuses food from you, along with everything else. All you'll achieve here is that she'll fucking starve herself. Give it up."

My teeth ground together until they ached at the roots, the entire left side of my jaw still swollen from our fight. Whatever gentle heart Sebian carried in his chest, his iron fist made up for it in spades—no matter those bruises my shadows had left all over his neck and throat.

On my best friend.

Former best friend, apparently.

I poured the grains into his palm before I sank deeper into my chair, a fine sheen of sweat covering my forehead with how I'd ordered the maids to keep every single hearth across my private rooms generously fed to keep the bird from shivering. *Stolen,* Marla had told us about the *anoa's* gift shortly after she'd escaped to Deepmarsh, explaining the bird's poor health, her forlorn demeanor, and why I hadn't sensed that Galantia was my fated mate.

A dark chuckle escaped me.

Oh, but I *had* felt it.

Had felt a million things the moment I'd first set eyes on her when she was but a little girl—all of them equally confusing. Back then, I'd blamed it on the fever that had nearly dragged me to my grave. But when our paths had crossed again in that copse of trees, my little white dove, all grown up...?

An inexplicable force of raw want had surged within me that day, its intensity as undeniable as it had been bewildering. Her keen hazel gaze, the way my moniker had made her lift her chin. Fuck... even the cascade of her creamy hair —everything about Galantia had stirred an untamed, insatiable sense of possessiveness within me. I had wanted her in a way I'd never experienced before, *a human*.

It had been... wrong.

Until I'd heard her name.

And then it had been unforgivable.

"Shh, I'll take care of you now." Sebian lowered himself onto the elongated, red-upholstered reclining chair that stood before the window, opening his hand in offering. That was all it took for the little bird to peek out from under her wing, then slowly peck at the meal. "There you go. That's my good girl. You're so skinny, you wouldn't even feed a cat."

The sight gnawed at my insides—scratching, scraping —shadows convoluting my chest with the same density they fogged my mind. Pitch-black darkness settled onto my thoughts. Who was he to feed my mate? To care for her? A simple pathfinder? I could kill him with a single thought, having him twitch on the floor before he even realized—

You mustn't succumb to its darkness.

I closed my eyes against the echo of Mother's words, breathing down the anger in my core until reason slowly trickled back into my mind. Without Sebian, I wouldn't be alive. He'd been with me for years, and reliably so. Weak as she was, the little female needed nourishment. If anything, I should be grateful that Sebian got her to eat.

I turned my gaze away, allowing the pang of pain beneath my sternum to twist deeper into my chest. The same one that had plagued me countless times: the morning I'd found Galantia in Sebian's bed after the storm, the night when she'd first come against his tongue, and pretty much every fucking night thereafter, where she'd fallen to sleep in *his* arms.

I hadn't understood back then why the sight of her toes wedged beneath his calf had made me so... fucking... angry. Certainly not because I was jealous. No, how could I have been? Wanting a human woman for myself? Even worse, a *Brisden*? Ridiculous.

That pain in my chest?

Unrelated. Merely a coincidence.

Nothing but the Endless Ache, I'd told myself, that untied bond beneath my ribs aching for my mate. My bright-feathered *anoaley*, such a rarity that few ever met a white Raven in their lifetime, raised by the one man I hated the most. Ah, I'd been so stupid, so blinded by these fuck-ing... shadows at my core. Always shadows. Only shadows!

"Stop grinding your teeth, the sound's driving me up the walls," Sebian hissed, his hair tied into a crooked topknot, his white shirt wrinkled, his face carrying black stubbles a few days old—probably as many as she'd been gone now.

Our heads turned toward the door, where Asker shoved himself through the narrow gap, his face a strange mix between pale exhaustion and attentive exhilaration. "Forgive the del—"

"Close the door," Sebian and I said in unison, making my gaze catch with his before he added, "She starts shivering at the slightest draft."

Precisely.

My gaze dropped lower, to Galantia's *anoa*, casting a shadow over my chest. She'd fallen to sleep in his arms. Again. Well, wasn't she comfortable with him? Sebian... so tender, so caring, so gentle, so everything I was not, because all I had was darkness, always darkness, so much fucking darkness I wanted to suffocate him—

Control them!

I breathed in. I breathed out.

That Galantia had developed affection for Sebian, I'd been aware of. In fact, I'd made good use of it, hadn't I? Another chuckle that had Sebian and Asker looking at me with raised brows, as if my last thread of sanity was about to snap.

Maybe it was.

And what about Sebian's heart, hmm?

Had I expected him to be pissed with how I'd blindsided him? Yes. But not to a degree that would lay absolute ruin to our friendship with bruises, cuts, and blood. What if she was more to him than a fleeting obsession, like I'd first assumed? More than a temporary distraction to soothe the torment of his past mistakes? What if he was... in love?

With. My. Mate.

I clenched my fist around the armrest of my chair,

feeling the sting of splinters against my skin. In my own way, I loved Sebian like a brother, so naturally, I wanted him to make peace with the past and find happiness. That he might just do so with the woman destined for me, well... I didn't know what to do with that at all.

Supporting it felt wrong.

Fighting it felt... wrong, because was this not the kindest outcome for the woman I was honor-bound to care for, to protect—even if it meant protecting her from me.

"The healer gave Marla a concoction, so she is finally asleep," Asker said and closed the door. "In a few days' time, she ought to be over her cough."

I gave a curt nod. "Tidestone?"

"The returning pathfinders all report the same: they are aware of our upcoming attack and preparing for a siege."

"Galantia must have informed them." Why, I couldn't say—not that I'd given her much reason *not* to betray my plans, but it was a minor inconvenience. "It matters not. Our attack is too far advanced for Brisden to withstand it. With Marla by your side once more, Tidestone will be ours."

Sebian scoffed before his green gaze turned to Asker. "Not before I get Galantia out of there. Now that we know she truly is at Tidestone, I'll fly tonight."

My *anoa* ruffled his feathers at my core over how he wedged himself into my plans. "Your unkindness cannot brace the winds there. If anything, your ravens might endanger her at the first breeze, sending your unkindness into the line of sight of Tidestone archers."

"Endanger?" A pound of his fist against his sternum. "It was *I* who kept her safe." A stab of his finger in my direction. "*You* drove her to Tidestone in the first place. And if you show up there? She'll refuse to leave all the harder, just to make a fucking point. And then what happens during the siege, hmm?"

"Should it come to that, then she will sit the siege out somewhere safe. If she managed to endure..." *me,* "her time here, then she can most definitely endure the commotion of it in the dungeons or even down at the bay."

"Or in short, you know as well as I do that she won't come with you," Sebian said with an exaggerated laugh that made me want to choke it with my shadows.

I begrudgingly turned my attention to Asker. "Was Marla able to give you the information I asked for?"

Sebian gave me a stabbing side glance that not even my periphery could rob of its sharpness. "What information?"

"Accurately enough," Asker said and strode closer. "I managed to narrow it down to two chambers, both windows facing the way as some of the visions had showed her."

"What information?" Sebian asked again, this time with more bite in his voice, making it clear he now trusted me as much as a crow in a jewelers' market.

"The location of Galantia's chamber. I was already planning to leave for Tidestone." Not to bond, no. Merely to ensure she wouldn't end up dead beneath a broken catapult tower. She was my mate, after all. "One unkindness should go unnoticed if I approach from the ocean during the night. Their attention is entirely on Taradur for now, anyway, who is quickly approaching from the opposite side."

"Oh, really?" Sebian asked, his voice dripping with sarcasm. "Who's going to stand-in for you at your wedding with Cici, hmm? Isn't that coming up?"

Shadows infiltrated my veins, crawling up my neck and cheeks like filthy parasites. "I might just—"

"You both heard what Marla said." Asker stepped

between us, his voice gruff, throwing his hands up in an appeasing manner. "The girl was resolute to find her gift. The way I see it, she will not follow either one of you, so how about we redirect our attention to another pressing issue? Taradur will reach Tidestone soon. Lady Cecilia has been promised a wedding. In the wake of recent... events, well, she questions your sincerity, my prince, of standing by your word."

"Exactly," Sebian all but snorted. "I'll go to Tidestone. Malyr has a wedding to attend, just like he *planned* it."

"That was before Lady Galantia revealed as his fated mate," Asker pointed out. "Now that she has been found, the entire court is aware that this could change everything. A bonded deathweaver pair—"

"We don't know if she even *is* a deathweaver," I said, though her white shadows trapped inside the salt pendant could have easily gone ignored all this time. "I only ever prayed for one thing at the shrine of the Winged Keep, as you know. Given the fate our goddess has dealt me, the least she can do is grant this one thing to me."

Interesting, how I suddenly talked as if I would indeed make Galantia my bondmate...

"I can count on one hand the few bonded deathweavers that were recorded to have been fated to a Raven with a different gift," Asker said. "Regardless, once bonded, Malyr, you might gain power unequaled by *any* alliance."

My muscles tensed, old promises and new desires warring at my core. Of course, I'd always known I might meet my *anoaley*. It was fated, after all. And then I would send her far away, I'd promised myself, to live on a fine estate on the island of Lanai, with guards to keep her safe and servants to look after her every need.

But that was before...

Before I'd had her blood on my lips, her scars between my teeth, her throat in my clasp, her moans in my ear, her reddened ass beneath my palm, her tongue gliding along my blade, her cunt tightening around my cock in pleasure and pain. It was before she'd spent cold winter mornings on my lap at my desk, the both of us wrapped in a blanket, practicing her gods-awful handwriting.

That was before I fell in love with her...

"Should you go back on your word," Asker said, "Taradur might as well join forces with Brisden and march straight into Deepmarsh with him."

Yes, that was a potential problem. But what would Taradur gain by siding with the kingdom of Dranada once more? Deepmarsh was... well, wet. Hanneling Hold? A speck on the map. Even if I went back on my word, there had to be something I could offer instead? But what?

"The way I see it, you have two options, my prince." Asker paused. "Marry the Taradur girl posthaste, to ensure, in a combined effort of her forces and Marla's vision, our victory at Tidestone."

"And the second option?"

"Find a way to pacify House Taradur so they will not abandon us in this attack." He bore his eyes into me. "Then fly to Tidestone. Return the girl her bird. Do whatever it takes to let your *anoas* bond."

Bond Galantia. The sound of it alone soothed something deep within me, momentarily dulling the ache of our burdened fate.

"You can't be serious," Sebian groaned. "Hasn't she suffered him enough?"

Yes. Quite so.

The way I had scarred her, choked her, smacked her, struck her, and bit her made it all the more evident; each morally corrupted misdeed a reason why I'd stopped searching for my mate to begin with. I could never reconcile hurting my *anoaley* for my pleasure, neither could I stop liking the things I liked. My roughness was whipped into me, the desire to cause pain instead of receiving it scarred into the very fabric of my being.

Mmm, what to do?

Bonding with her would break a promise I'd once given to myself and her. But was that truly worse than breaking a promise I'd given to Father, Mother, Harlen, Naya... every Raven who had suffered because of me?

If I was a good man—a decent mate, if only once—I would reject Galantia so she may find happiness with Sebian. Bonding her would be cruel, forever tying her to the Raven prince, who had shattered her downright viciously. But then again, wasn't I already all those things in her eyes? If anything, claiming her would cradle her in the reliable certainty of what a bastard I was.

Besides, who argued fate?

"Cancel the wedding and let the Taradurs be my problem." I rose and strode toward my personal rooms. "I want every Raven with a gift suitable for war ready to depart east come morning, so they may merge with Taradur's forces. I want my crown by summer."

For that, I needed to bond.

CHAPTER
SEVEN

Sebian

Present day, Deepmarsh Castle

"Do whatever it takes to let your *anoas* bond?" I'd heard my fair share of shit advice in my life, but that one left me gaping at Asker. "You do understand that his definition of 'whatever it takes' might very well be to strangle her with his shadows until she gives in, right?"

Asker gave a slow shake of his head. "She is his *anoaley*. He would never do such a thing."

"Never do...?" Well, shake my tail feathers and call me a

peacock, in what kind of reality had he been living over these last months? "Please do explain which event in the past makes you so certain. The one where he carved her up? Oh, maybe when he jabbed through her maidenhead in front of us? Or how about when he betrayed *all of us?*"

"He didn't know who she was."

"Oh, he knew." Somewhere deep inside him, he'd known. There had been plenty of indicators in this behavior which I hadn't been able to puzzle together then, but they all made sense now. "You weren't there the day I brought her into that copse of trees looking for you. Didn't see how hyper-fixated he was on her. If I would've cut him, he wouldn't have bled, he was so frozen in that moment."

"I have known Malyr since he was a fledgling. He is... troubled, yes, but not bad by nature," he mumbled, as if even his voice wasn't convinced of what he was saying, and then more quietly, "He will do better from here on out."

Maybe he would, but I wouldn't bet my life on it, and certainly not Galantia's. "Your trust is astonishing, considering he went behind your back just the same. Mine isn't. Which is why I'm flying to Tidestone with him, whether he likes it or not."

"Ten years ago, I found you changing the wet rags on Malyr's forehead to break the fever. Five years after that, I found Malyr changing the seawater wraps on your burned arm. I am terrified of asking why you two are now fighting over a little white bird like two sparrows over a worm." Asker exhaled a long breath, folded his arms in front of his chest, and leaned with his back against one of the bookshelves. "Please tell me you did not bed Lady Galantia."

The longer he stared at me in silence, waiting for an answer he wouldn't get, the more he narrowed his eyes at me, until I just shrugged. "What? You told me to take care of her, remember?"

"Not like that, Sebian." He sighed, letting his face fall into his palm. "You bedded his fated mate, and he caught you, didn't he?"

"Caught me?" Scoffing, I ran my fingers through the *anoa's* feathers, searching for broken shafts that needed preening. "Old man, he was *there with us.*"

Now he groaned and pinched the bridge of his nose, as if sharing among unbonded Ravens was a rarity or something. "What have you done, Sebian?"

"What I've done?" Anger and annoyance mixed in my veins over how impossible it was to get into this man's good graces ever again. Not that I cared, because, why would I? "Well, where to start? I pulled a Raven off her before he could rape her. I wiped the blood from the wounds Malyr cut into her before I put salve on it. I got her away from Lorn. I watched over her at the market. After Malyr took her virginity with his fingers, I prepared her satchels of heated chestnuts for the cramps."

I listed a few more things after that, my lungs expanding wider with each one. Five years of thinking I was just a good-for-nothing waste of a man, unworthy of having a partner lifted off my chest because, wouldn't you know it, I hadn't done half bad with Galantia. I *had* cared for her. I *had* protected her.

Until that one day I went north...

"Goddess help us all, I should have known," Asker mumbled into his palm. "Should have known that something was amiss. Your... your drinking, the whoring, the irresp—"

My hiss cut through his rambling on about my shortcomings because... of course, he would keep dumping their weight straight back onto me. "I haven't been drunk in weeks."

Hadn't touched gray devil bark.

Hadn't touched another woman.

Didn't want to, either.

"Exactly." He lifted his head, giving me a look I hadn't seen in years. Not exactly soft, but... well, less sharp? "Oh, I noticed, Sebian. How you gained your weight back. How you turned down the wine at the *kjaer*. How you seemed... happy."

My mouth turned dry. That wasn't what I'd expected him to say next at all. Not that it should matter to me. Who was he to judge me one way or another?

Still, something swelled at the back of my throat, robbing my voice of strength when I said, "I was happy."

For the first time in years.

And I could have been happier still, if only I'd allowed myself to fully embrace my feelings for Galantia instead of my guilt over it. My guilt over having affection for a woman who wasn't my fated mate. But leaving behind the past wasn't the same as forgetting, or betraying, or abandoning. Something I hadn't understood when I'd gone north, leaving her behind unkissed.

"Both Marla and I want you happy, but..." Another sigh, then Asker lifted his gaze, watching me groom the little white raven. "Sebian, she is Malyr's fated mate. A bond is a precious thing under any circumstance, but in their case, it is crucial for this war, the kingdom we ought to gain, and the prince who is to rule it."

My jaws shifted because I recognized the truth of it. "It's interesting how you seem content pushing Galantia into the arms of a mate who couldn't keep her from harm, because he's the one who loves inflicting it. I never mistreated Ravenna; her death was nothing I could've prevented. Yet, for years, all you told me was what a fool I was. So irresponsible. A drunk. Useless. How you should never have allowed me to court your daughter. And I believed it."

Every. Single. Word.

Well, I was done with that.

"It is true, I said things I ought not to have said." He scrubbed his hand over his face, then lowered it by his side and looked right at me. "A father's grief runs deep. Deeper than you could ever fathom."

"Deeper than I could fathom, huh?" I held his gaze for a moment, silent understanding passing between us, then rose and carefully lowered the little raven back into her box of silk so she may sleep a while longer. The flight to Tidestone would exhaust her, no doubt. "I promised myself I'll take care of Galantia, in whichever capacity she'll let me, and I'm not going to fail a second time."

The moment I turned toward the doors that lead into Malyr's personal rooms, Asker said, "She can never bond herself to you."

"Nothing much changed then." I'd known that before, and it hadn't kept me from wanting to be with her. And now? Well, now my heart was too far gone to care. "Except for one thing: he damaged their fate to a degree that she might never bond herself to him, either."

EIGHT

Galantia

Present Day, Tidestone

I pushed the window of my room open, letting a briny gust of wind bite at my cheeks, but at least that braid I'd pinned tightly against my scalp stayed put. Far below, a fresh layer of powdery snow stretched from the wall of the keep, up along those gray stones, and all the way along the cliff that rounded the bay where the sun was slowly setting. How many seconds would a fall take before one's skull splintered on those rocks? Five? Nine?

I had no intentions of finding out and glanced down at my outfit. Brown cotton trousers I'd stolen from the male servants' quarters, a snug-fitting tunic I had shoved into the waistband so the wind wouldn't catch on the excess fabric, and the sturdiest of my old winter boots I'd managed to find... this should keep me from falling to my death. And if not? Well, then I could always shift and fly to that window to my left at the far end of this wall.

The chancery.

A room where Lord Brisden met with his officers and advisors between maps, battle reports, and strategy tables. After I'd rummaged through his and Mother's—no... *Lady Brisden*—personal rooms with no success, this was the only place left where Lord Brisden could possibly keep my amulet. The problem?

Ever since Tidestone had started preparing for the Raven's attack, a guard had been posted outside the chancery's door to oversee the constant coming and going. One who'd kept his stare on me when Lord Brisden had asked me into the room earlier, interrogating me on all things Raven. How many deathweavers did Malyr command? How many siege weapons would Lord Taradur bring? Had the Ravens mentioned any strategic details to me?

I had answered all of Lord Brisden's questions—and no surprise, none of them to his satisfaction. Not that I had expected anything different other than to disappoint him, but I took no grief with that anymore. No, I had quite enjoyed watching the anger redden his cheeks, and had offered to open the window so he may take some fresh air, like the useless but kind daughter I was. He hadn't even noticed that, upon closing the window again, I had not locked it.

Summoning every bit of courage I possessed, I swung a leg over the window's edge, my fingers white-knuckled around the frost-covered stone sill. My heart hammered an insistent rhythm in my chest as I climbed outside, each beat a reminder of the risk I was taking. The cold, harsh stone of the exterior bit into my palms, the icy sting grounding me in my reckless resolve.

With my hips angled so one knee would follow behind the other, I moved forward along the narrow stone. I loaded my left arm with the majority of the weight of my upper body, shifting my balance toward the wall. Stone scraped over the cotton covering my shoulder, and the snow along my path ached my knuckles. Gods, it was cold!

A sudden, fierce gust of wind tore along the wall, ripping at me with icy fingers, making me gasp and cling to the chilled stone. My heart stuttered in my chest as I fought a steady breath, the air sharp in my lungs. *Do not look down. Just... crawl forward.*

"I am a Raven," I muttered to myself. "Wind is to my wings what the wave is to a ship: a persistent companion, sometimes caressing, other times chastising, but always essential in the journey."

If I fell, I would shift.

If I fell, I would fly.

And would that not have been preferable instead of shoving myself along this castle in the midst of winter, one inch after another? Yes. I could soar to the chancery window, have my unkindness slip in, and shift into my human form at the center of the room...

... naked.

I let out a groan at that oversight, but continued. Without shadowcloth or enchantments like they used at Deepmarsh, there was a valid chance that I—should I be unable to shift for my return—would have to crawl along the castle wall with my naked ass rivaling the paleness of the snow. No matter. I was making good progress, even without my unkindn—

My leg slipped off the ledge.

The world pitched violently, my heart seizing in a chokehold between my lungs. With a grunt, I flung my weight against the wall, my hands scrambling over the frozen stone, my fingers clawing for hold. *Calm, Galantia. Calm! If you fall, you shift. If you fall, you fly.*

Except... I didn't shift.

Panic, raw and visceral, scraped along my throat. Why wasn't I... Oh gods, why wasn't I shifting? There was no blast of white feathers, no ocean of color, no ravens... only the sharp intake of frozen air, the piercing cold, and the heart-stopping realization that I was clinging to life on a wind-battered ledge.

I forced myself to take a deep, steadying breath. "Don't look down. Don't look down. Don't you fucking look down."

Clasping my fingers tighter around the edge of the stone to my right, I struggled my leg back up, no matter how my muscles ached, burned, tired. It found its footing on the ledge once more, giving me a moment of reprieve. What now? The chancery window was still an impossible stretch away, the distance much bigger than the one back to my room. Without being able to shift, this was much too dangerous.

Crawling retreat it was, then.

I began my torturous return to my window. With a sure grip and a bracing inhale, I pushed myself backward, my fingers closing around a protrusion in the stone, the sharp edge biting into my skin, almost unbearably. But I clung on, inch by creeping inch, moving with a deliberate slowness.

Finally, after what felt like an eternity hanging on the precipice of falling to my death, my fingertips brushed the familiar wood of my window. A sigh of relief escaped my chapped lips. I carefully maneuvered myself back through the window, only to allow my body to slip off the ledge and collapse with a *thud* on the table that stood there. How would I get into the chancery?

I stared at the ceiling, the warm glow from the crackling hearth like an inferno against my chilled cheek. Without my ravens to carry me to that window, or at least keep me from dying should I fall, there was no way for me to sneak into the chancery. Not without drawing even more of Lord Brisden's suspicion, and I already had enough of that.

If only Risa was here—the only person who might have helped me in gaining my amulet back. Unless...

Drawing a ragged breath, I pushed off the table, wincing as the world momentarily spun. Ignoring the nagging protest of my frozen limbs, I sprang to my feet and grabbed my dress from the bed. With stiff fingers, I discarded my earlier ensemble and dressed, then left my room.

A fool's errand, really.

I hurried along the covered balcony, the inner bailey lying below resonating with the barked commands of officers, the clanking of goods being moved around, and the nervous chatter of maids and stableboys alike. How much longer before Taradur and Malyr would attack? Lord Brisden hadn't dared sending scouts out—he couldn't afford to lose a single boy of fighting age to one of Malyr's scouting pathfinders.

When I reached the flower-tooled wooden door, I gave a single knock, then stepped into Lady Brisden's chamber. Was it likely she would help me? No, but I had nothing to lose by asking.

She sat before the table that held her mirror, found my eyes in it, then gave a swat of her hand toward the maid who was brushing her hair. "Leave us."

"I will see to your chamber and ready it for the night, my lady," the maid said to me with a curtsy before she hurried out the door.

Lady Brisden's reflection stared at me, its features unmoving. "What do you want?"

"Always such warmth in your tone..." I couldn't hold back that roll of my eyes as I strode toward her darkening window, where I let myself fall into the green-upholstered armchair. "I came to ask for your help. Do you remember the amulet Lord Brisden often wore when I was a child? Black *aerymel* socket, white stone?"

Yes, she did; the way she looked down as if she would rather avoid the subject—or talking to me in general—confirmed it just fine. "What of it?"

"Do you know where it is?"

She shook her head.

"I looked everywhere for it, except for the chancery because some mute, oversized guard is keeping count of everyone who comes and goes," I said. "I need that amulet, but I cannot have Lord Brisden know."

"What is the old thing to you?"

My gaze wandered to the floor, some of the brittle stones still faintly stained red from too many miscarriages and stillbirths for the lime powder to hide, the sight hollowing my stomach. "I believe it might hold my gift. If you only were to enter the chan—"

"Are you out of your mind? You would truly ask me such a thing?"

"All you would have to do is tell the guard you will wait in the chancery for Lord Brisden since you need to speak to him, but find him hard to catch," I said. "It's not far-fetched, considering his constant coming and going between meetings with his advisors and checking the hold for whatever advancements have been done in preparation for the attack. I need this amulet."

She spun around on her stool, giving me the entire weight of her offended sneer. "I will do no such thing, putting you at even greater risk."

"Me?" A laugh bubbled from my chest, it sounded distorted by the way my throat wanted to tie up. "Oh please, *Mother*, do not pretend you're trying to save anything here but your own skin." A cold, hard knot twisted in the pit of my stomach, the familiar sting of her indifference cutting deep. I rose, turning toward the door. "I shouldn't have come. Nineteen years of your loathing still didn't teach me a thing. I should have known I cannot count on you for help, should I—"

"Like when I lied for you two nights ago?" she asked, the slight but insistent waver in her voice stalling my first step toward the door. "When I confirmed to Lord Brisden that I had indeed sent you to drown that awful dress in the bay, like you told the guards by the beach?"

I looked back at her.

She had... covered for me?

My mind whirled, but my heart knew better than to stir with hope. "Out of self-preservation, and not because there's even a shred of maternal concern in you."

She held my stare for a second, a million emotions fleeting across that face of ageless beauty I had always admired so much. When a tremble hushed across her bottom lip, she swiveled around on her stool as if she meant to hide it. Well, the mirror wouldn't let her, showing me everything. Every wrinkle of... regret?

Oh, you cried so desperately out of hunger, Galantia, each piercing screech a reminder that you were not my child, and I... I was not truly a mother. Would never be, no matter how hard I tried. And I had tried.

Was she trying now?

A sudden but soft wave of doubt lapped at the walls of my resentment. For the first time, I didn't only see the harsh and uncaring woman who had loathed me so, but the mother she'd always wanted to be. Was there a trace of love still buried beneath that stoic exterior? And if there truly was, would she not help me?

I turned toward her and stepped closer, but only until the tension visibly settled on her shoulders. "If you ever had any love for me—even if it was just a shred, even if it only lasted a breath—please help me get the amulet. It holds my gift, I'm certain. I want to understand who I am and why things happened the way they did, and I won't stop until I have answers. That nearly cost me my life just now when I tried to balance on the wall to the chancery."

Her gaze lifted in the mirror, giving me a scolding look, accompanied by a single shake of her head. "Nineteen years of ensuring your survival, and you would throw it off the wall."

"I won't try again if you help me..."

Her gaze dropped again with a sigh. "Not tonight."

My heart elevated in my chest, letting bright energy stream into my core. "But you will do it? You will try to find it?"

"Tomorrow, when he is assessing the soldiers," she said. "I believe I know where he keeps it."

"Thank you..." I all but exhaled, unable to stop the way I reached for her shoulder.

But only until she lifted her hand, stopping me, making me shift back onto my heels. "You best leave now," was all she said before she dismissed me with the same swat she had used on the maid.

But she *would* help me.

In that, I found a grapple of hope and a faint caress of that love I'd always wanted from her. It had to be enough. Hells, it was more than I'd ever expected, so I turned away... only to stop.

"There isn't nearly enough time for Lord Brisden to prepare for this attack. Not a single wagonload of grains made it to the keep yet from the granarys in the north. The Ravens got their fate back." A heavy swallow. "Prince Malyr *will* take Tidestone. You should leave this place, seek refuge in Ammarett or somewhere near the capital. Betrayal or not, King Barat needs any allies he can get—even the treacherous ones."

When no answer came, I returned to my room.

The maid must have been here already with how my down blanket puffed up from my bed like a cloud, how the fire ate at the new pieces of oak, and how my nightgown hung over the privacy screen to the left. She'd also closed the window, which I must have forgotten after I'd collapsed back in here, given the lower temperature.

I slipped out of my shoes and let myself fall into my bed, loving the puff of down that caught my weight and slowly let me sink into its familiar comfort. With luck, Lady Brisden might find the amulet tomorrow, but what would happen once I had freed my gift? Each day I remained here was dangerous, but where would I even go?

I shook my head at how I was getting ahead of myself again, sensing something poke through my strands and scratch my nape. Without the ability to shift, I was stuck here, doomed to either wait for Lord Brisden to catch me... or Malyr.

When the poking continued, I reached behind me, letting my fingers find something elongated, firm, smooth and...

What was that?

I sat up and turned, finding the shaft of a feather peeking out from beneath my pillow. Was that a... a down?

I clasped the shaft and pulled it out, my guts tangling up at the sight of pitch-black vanes. A raven feather. And there, beneath the downy barbs, a tiny piece of parchment had been rolled around the shaft and tied with a blue silk ribbon. How had this gotten here? My eyes flicked to the window, then around my empty room, and finally back down to the feather.

Dread ran through me with a shiver of adrenaline that made my heart thrash against my ribs. My breath hitched, and I clutched the feather more tightly. My other hand trembled slightly as I reached for the blue silk ribbon, my fingers slipping on the smooth material before I managed to untie it. The tiny piece of parchment unfurled, revealing hastily scribbled lines.

A spread-winged raven perched on a skull.

"I will come for you," Malyr's dark threat purred through my memory, *"because you are mine."*

Liquid anger pumped hot through my veins until my cheeks itched. I grabbed this little... *gift* he must have left behind for me before he'd escaped detection when the maid had come to my room and tossed it into the fire. The feather hissed. The parchment browned. The ribbon crinkled.

I needed to get out of here.

I needed to shift.

CHAPTER
NINE

Galantia
Present Day, Tidestone cliff

The winds cutting along the cliff whipped at my face, tugging at the loose tendrils of my hair with a frosty bite, even though the clouds had lifted to reveal the lowering sun. I stared at the violent clash of waves below where they churned at the rocks. White foam rose and sank to the rumble that shook the ground beneath my soles. Was I truly going to do this? What options did I really have left?

I couldn't escape the upcoming attack alongside Moth —*Lady Brisden*—who had heeded my warning. All day, they'd readied her carriage so she may leave for the capital during the cover of the night, right after she would, hopefully, return my amulet. Ammarett, however, being the cauldron of human hostility against Ravens, would gain me no safety. And returning to the Ravens meant returning to Malyr. As much as I knew that it might have to happen one day, I wasn't yet ready to face him, the heartbreak, the court, the utter humiliation.

No, I *had* to figure this out.

With a deep breath, I stepped forward until my toe shoved a dusting of snow over the edge of the cliff, the taste of fear and freedom intermingling on my tongue. Sebian's father had tossed him over a cliff to force his first shift. And Olivar, the stableboy at Deepmarsh? The children had forced him over the edge up at the parapet walk. If they managed to fly, why would I not? All I had to do was jump off this cliff.

Simple.

Easy.

My bladder filled to bursting.

Pulling in a deep breath, I stepped back a step. Two. Five. Ten steps. That should be enough.

With a burst of determination, I lunged forward, breaking into a run—fast, faster, harder—every thump of my heart echoing in my ears, drowning out the cacophony of the waves below. The edge grew nearer, nearer—

Terror surged through me.

My boots skidded to a halt, but the momentum was too much. I slipped, my balance lost. I hit the ground. My breath whooshed out of me as I slid over the edge.

"No!" I shouted, reaching out, fingers scrabbling at the snow and ice.

They found purchase on a jutting outcrop of rock. Clinging with the strength of desperation, I hung there, my legs kicking over the gaping maw of the ocean in search of hold. A jutting boulder, a branch, or— There! My heart hammered in my chest as my toes found something solid, my ears pricking at... wingbeats?

Now they were gone.

Soles crunching over grit and snow replaced the sound, each slow, deliberate step inching toward me, driving up my pulse, making me call out, "Help!"

Black boots stepped into my vision, stopping less than an inch from my white-knuckled fingers. "Whatever are you trying to achieve here, my little white dove?"

The hair along my nape rose at the sound of the pet name. I wasn't a white dove and, by the seven hells and all the gods out there, I most definitely wasn't *his*. But then again, apparently, I wasn't an unkindness of ravens, either...

Against the pride stiffening my neck and the hate heating my veins, I looked up at Malyr. "Trying to get away from you. Now help me!"

Of course, Malyr just stood there, as if I wasn't an inch of slippage away from falling, crossing his arms in front of his black cuirass, the leather embossed with silver vines and thorns that matched his vicious personality perfectly. He stared at me for painful, muscle-searing seconds before he smacked his lips, leaned over, and clasped my wrist. In a combined effort, with my feet treading at the stone and my other hand bracing the edge, he pulled me up and against him.

I slammed into his strong chest, the scent puffing off him carrying the familiar notes of lemongrass that were as reassuring as they were painful—a treacherous mixture of comfort and chaos that scrambled my thoughts, trying to lull me with memories best forgotten.

None of it had been real.

Yanking my wrist from his hold, I swept around him and brought several feet of distance between us. "You were in my room last night."

"I once warned you not to leave your window open." Malyr shrugged and took a slow step toward me, his windswept black hair shifting in the breeze the way his black cloak did. "You found my gift, I take it?"

I lifted my chin and stared him dead in the eyes. "Found it, burned it."

"Ah." His gaze hardened with another calculated step in my direction. "How unfortunate, given how we plucked our finest-looking feather for you. And here I thought you were fond of ribbons."

"Oh, I am," I said, shifting my balance back, not liking how he slowly prowled up on me, weaving tingles of caution through my muscles. "I'm just not fond of you."

"Mmm, little white dove, you ought to leave the lying to me." His taunting smirk curled with such smugness, it made my molars grind together. "I daresay there was a great deal of *fondness* in the way you moaned my name the last time I had you beneath me. How else could I have gotten your delicious tears, hmm?"

"Because you betrayed me!" Anger flared, creeping along my cheeks until they itched. Because I'd foolishly believed him, though I wouldn't make the same mistake twice. "I should have listened to Sebian. He warned me not to trust you."

Malyr's smirk disappeared beneath the flexing of his jaw, and I only now noticed the greenish bruises under his freshly-shaven skin along one side, the cut above his eye. "I betrayed who I thought was a Brisden."

Oh, and that set everything right?

Rationally, yes, I understood why he'd done it, but understanding didn't equate to forgiveness. How could it, if it did nothing to mend the lingering pain? He'd shattered me, leaving me to pick up the fragments of my soul, my heart...

...my very identity!

"Who you thought I was doesn't unbreak me." My voice was barely above a whisper, but laced with an intensity that mirrored my rage. "Who you thought I was doesn't make me unsee what you revealed to be."

"And what would that be, hmm? What am I, Galantia?"

"A heartless bastard who knows nothing but hate."

The corners of his mouth twitched into a half-smile, as if he took it as a compliment. "Quite so." He looked away for a moment, sweeping his gaze over the turbulent sea before returning it to me. "This is your pitiful attempt at escaping said... bastard, I presume? Are you teasing me with a good chase?"

I eyed the edge of the cliff, which suddenly didn't look quite so scary anymore. "I would have preferred to find my gift first."

Arm lifting, he beckoned me to him with the curl of his finger. "Come to me."

I took a step back and lifted my chin. "I will not."

An ink-black tendril of shadows shot at me, curling around my body like icy ropes. One hard tug, and it pulled me toward him. My toes all but dragged over the snow as wind whistled past my ears. A yelp escaped me, replaced by a single choking sound as my throat slammed straight into the clasp of his hand.

He dug his fingers into each side of my esophagus, stopping just shy of pain, stepped up to me, and ran his nose along the side of my face where he growled, "Hear me, Galantia. No matter where you go, no matter what form you take, I *will* find you. You cannot outrun me. You cannot outfly me. Every path you tread, be it north, east, south, or west, I will chase after because... you... are... *mine*."

I clenched my eyes shut, shivering in the throes of his threat and the way his lips brushed over my cheek. "I'm not a white dove, and I'll never be yours."

"You will always be my little white dove." His fingers trailed down, circling the scar on my breastbone through the fabric of my woolen dress. "The thing is, Galantia, you left your *anoa* behind during your first shift. Even if you found your gift, it would go straight to your scrawny little bird... which, I just so happen to have."

My teeth ground together. Could that be true? Maybe. It wasn't like I'd counted my ravens in all this turmoil.

I looked up at him. "So you're still holding parts of me captive?"

Malyr stepped back, reached into a large satchel that rested on his hip, and pulled out a little white... Gods, that bird was, yes, scrawny, small, and... ugly. "*Anoas* are notoriously difficult to care for. They don't fare well when separated from their unkindness for too long and might just... waste away."

That sounded like another threat if I ever heard one. "Let me guess, you want something in exchange for the return of my bird. What is it? The bond?"

Of course it was. Malyr wasn't someone to bestow kindnesses without gaining something himself, and what could he possibly want from me but to amplify his powers?

He reached the bird closer, which barely lifted its

droopy head my way, then dissolved into feathers and white plumes, sending a sinking sensation into my chest. "See it as a token of my affection."

"Affection?" One word, and the shards of my heart shot up like shields. Now I knew not to trust him. "As if your hateful soul understood any of it, other than how to feign it. To deceive me."

"Deception and truth aren't always adversaries." He grabbed me by the throat once more, crowding me with his body, his lips trailing along my jawline. "Deception's most profound irony is how it can make the realest truths look like the greatest deceits."

My breath hobbled, my body trapped between his body heat and the chill of winter licking at my back. "Are you trying to have me believe that your affection was sincere?"

He pressed his thumb against my jaws, turning my head until it gave way for his nose to brush over the fine hairs at my temple, then his whisper purred over the shell of my ear, "All of it."

At that rush of his breath caressing my skin, and those words, a shiver wrecked through me with a sensual potency that carved at my bitter resolve. "Everything coming out of your mouth is a lie. There was no affection, no love. You hated me the entire time."

"How could I not have hated you, hmm? A human. A presumed *Brisden,* no less." His mouth lowered to the side of my neck, where his lips kissed a languid, slow path along my pounding vein toward my earlobe, where he rasped, "You want to know what made it worse? How I loved to spend my days with you outdoors, my mornings with you at my desk, my nights with you in our nest. You are quite extraordinary, Galantia, in a way that is not obvious, unless

someone looks closer. *I* looked closer. And what I saw, I loved."

I closed my eyes, reveling in his words and succumbing to the divine sensation of his tongue playing with my earlobe, even as I shook my head. "Liar."

"Yes, I am a liar." His breath caressed the shell of my ear before his lips ghosted hot toward my mouth. "I told myself I hated you as honor demanded. That I did not indeed betray the memory of my entire family with how I longed for you, wanted you, spent every fucking second... *obsessing* over you."

"Stop it."

My heart wasn't strong enough, wasn't nearly healed enough to protect itself from his schemes and lies. Yet... I ached for more of it, desperately searching for more pieces of true love now that I'd finally tasted it in my birth mother's sacrifice.

"I loved how curiously you watched the little girl at the cliff, loved how you cantered over that meadow, loved how you braided my hair, and loved just about any other fucking mundane moment between us." His lips prodded the corner of my mouth, gingerly at first, only to gradually demand as they tried to catch mine. "And I hated you even more for making me feel that way, *anoaley.*"

Oh gods, the way his tongue lapped at my bottom lip was absolute torture, making me ache to give in to him. "Don't call me that."

"You feel it, do you not? Even without your gift, you can feel it. We are two parts of one whole." His whisper caressed the small gap he'd worked between my lips, parting them more with each sensual lap. "From the moment I first saw you, I felt it. You and I belong together. Forever."

I fought this incessant pull in my chest that seemed to inch my balance toward him. And those gray-brown eyes... No man ever looked at me the way Malyr did now, giving me his undivided attention, as though I were the very epicenter of his universe.

"Kiss me, *anoaley*," he rasped against my mouth, his lips nuzzling mine, urging them to seal. "Let my *anoa* reach for yours. Bond with me."

Bond with me.

His words sank in, wrapping themselves around my heart like a vise. That was the only reason he had bothered coming here, wasn't it? Not to explain, not to confess his true love, and certainly not to offer an apology. I had yet to hear one of those. No... he'd come to lie.

To scheme.

To bond.

Even now, his ambitions were paramount, his motivations casting a shadow over any flicker of shame or guilt he may have had—though, there was probably none. Malyr had never loved me for who I was and hated me for who he'd thought I was, Lord Brisden's daughter.

And now?

Well, now he wanted me to bond, not because of who I was, but because of what I was to his gift—an amplifier. Nothing but a means to win this war, to win him a crown, to gain him a kingdom. A thing to be used, played, and exploited.

Never again.

I angled my head just so, letting my lips seek his, nuzzling them until he groaned. But instead of kissing him, I shifted my balance back. His mouth followed, just as planned, his lips parting wider as if he meant to devour me.

Well, he could devour this.

I spat at him, unfortunately missing his mouth by the width of a finger, but the way it hit his bottom lip was enough to make his head jerk back and his eyes rip wide open in shock. "This is the closest your mouth will ever come to mine again."

For a moment, Malyr stood frozen, visibly stunned as the spit rolled down his chin. His shock morphed into anger that bled black into his eyes, a low growl rumbling deep inside his chest as his fingers tightened around my throat.

"You want to hate me? *Fine*, have it your way." He walked me back toward the cliff until the ground disappeared beneath the edge of my heels, tendrils of shadows pulled from his eyes by the breeze. "Which do you prefer? A count from five, or a sudden push? Choose."

Turning my head within the collar of his hand, I lifted my chin at him. "I'm indifferent either way. I would rather jump off this cliff than bond myself to you."

The shadows lifted from his eyes for a moment, a fraction of a second, then his mouth lowered to my ear where he growled, "Fly, Galantia."

Then he pushed me off the cliff.

CHAPTER
TEN

Galantia
Present Day, Tidestone cliff

My heart thundered in my chest, the pulsing blood rushing through my veins a deafening roar that matched the terror gripping my very soul. Cold air bit into my skin as my hair whipped around me in a chaotic flurry. Salt seasoned my lips as the spray of waves speckled my cheeks. The cliffs rushed past me in a blur, the abyss swallowing me whole until—

A blinding flash burst from within me. Pure white

feathers erupted from every pore, catching the wind and spreading wide in an unfurling of wings. The shout of my fear morphed into the triumphant cries of my unkindness as we glided along the wind.

A strong breeze pounded our wings.

The world tilted.

Oh no!

A flurry of shadows manifested to our left, our right... all around us. Five black ravens swooped in to join our unkindness. They maneuvered closely, beating against the onslaught of the biting wind and tumultuous air currents, their bodies absorbing the gist of it. Malyr?

Down, a voice croaked somewhere inside us, just as five more black ravens joined. *Land on the beach, sweetheart, or the currents will pull you out to sea.*

Sebian?

We lowered, guided by the black vanguard of ravens. They swooped, soared, and spiraled, skillfully maneuvering so the gusts would shift us in the right direction.

The scent of salt, seaweed, and wet sand grew stronger, the whispering roar of the waves louder. The ravens flanked our landing, wingtips occasionally brushing against ours. Our formation scrambled, each bird individually picking their spot on the beach below. As we touched down, the graininess of the sand beneath snow chilled our feet until the blinding surge of magic returned.

A painful chill pin-pricked at my bare soles, making me gasp just as I slung my arms around my naked body. I'd done it! I'd shifted and flown down here!

"Goddess, help me, did all your things fall into the bay? Your shoes?" Sebian was still shifting out of shadows and feathers as he fumbled with the ties of the black cloak he wore over his brown cuirass, his topknot tousled, and his cheeks and chin generously dusted in black stubble. "You'll catch a damn fever. Here, take this." He quickly draped the cloak around my shoulders before he barked over his own, "I saw you push her off. Are you insane? She could have been pulled out to sea."

Malyr only turned his back on Sebian, crossed toward the rock a few steps, and shoved the tip of his boot through the bare shrubs that slept along the outline of the alcove. "But she did not."

Sebian made an annoyed sound in the back of his throat. "Freeze to death, then."

"And you truly think that wasn't a possibility she considered before coming out here?" Malyr pulled a familiar brown bundle from between the shrubs, and tossed it into the snow by my feet, making it clear once more that he'd been spying on me. "Not only did she stash away three of these in the vicinity, knowing full well that she would be naked after her shift, but she actually licked her finger and held it up in the wind to analyze the drift, determining just where she *might* land."

I leaned over and peeled the contents of the bundle from the cowhide that had kept it all dry: a warm brown dress, boots, and a large woolen scarf.

The latter I wrapped around my upper body and neck once dressed, then I handed Sebian his cloak. "What are you both doing here?"

"Getting you out of here before the attack," Sebian said and grabbed my hand. "Come. Follow my ravens, and I'll bring you to our camp."

"What camp?" I stared down at how he intertwined his scarred fingers with mine, and quickly pulled away from their hold before he would... I didn't know... make me shift.

"No. I can't leave. Not until I have my amulet, and I'm so close to finally getting my hands on it."

"Fuck the amulet." He gave an aggravated swat at the air, only to drag the same hand over black bruises that speckled his throat wherever the stubble couldn't hide it. Shadow-marks? "It's not the most important thing right now."

"It is to me!"

"Until you're dead under rock and debris." Jaws shifting, he looked at Malyr. "If you meant to contribute something to convince her to leave instead of just standing there, then now would be a good time to do so."

Malyr folded his arms in front of his chest, eyeing me for long, silent seconds, his eyes their usual gray-brown once more. "You said you were close to getting your hands on it. How close are we speaking?"

"Why does that even matter?" Sebian asked. "There'll be plenty of time to look for it *after* the attack."

"Sieges have a habit of making things forever disappear beneath rubble and boulders," Malyr said. "And that is only if the remaining servants don't steal the amulet, along with other jewelry, before they flee the stronghold once the slaughter starts. There is still time."

Sebian took a step toward Malyr, his elbows angled wide enough it made his back appear impossibly broader. "If you're seriously considering to let her walk back into Tidestone, Malyr, then you're a shitty fucking mate."

Malyr's eyes narrowed to dangerous slits, sparking with a raw intensity that rivaled the savage gales whipping around us. "You must know."

"That was low," Sebian countered, "even for you, and that sure as fuck means something."

They stared at each other, the energy between these

two men filled with mutual aggression, the air growing thick with a tension I'd never felt between them. Ever. Their animosity was palpable, making my gaze draw back and forth between Malyr's bruises and those shadowmarks on Sebian's throat. Dear gods, had they fought? Because of me?

Or... over me?

Treacherous tingles coursed through my chest, but I internally swatted them away. Gods, I was a silly girl, indeed...

"That decision is for neither of you to make." I stepped between them, taking a deep breath because that next words would physically hurt my mouth to say. "But Malyr is right; the risk of forever losing it is too great."

"There you have it." Malyr gave Sebian a smug grin and shrugged, then looked at me. "Where exactly is the amulet? You found it?"

"Not exactly..." I shook my head, which caused him to hiss low, which could only mean he once more had an ulterior motive here. "Why are you so eager for me to get it? What is it to you, hmm? Another... how did you put it, token of your affection? Like my *anoa*?"

"Would that be so hard to believe?"

Sebian scoffed. "I'll chance a guess here, you can't bond her without her gift, can you? Probably tried your hardest to get it to tie up there. Clearly without success."

I looked at Malyr, not surprised in the slightest, but apparently, my heart wasn't numb to his self-serving motives yet with how it clenched. "Such affection..."

A brief flicker of something crossed his face—Discomfort? Shame?—but it vanished as quickly as it had appeared, replaced by a hard, steely expression which he bore into Sebian. "Tell me, Sebian... Why are you here again?"

"Apparently to make sure you're not forcing a bond on her while she's still absolutely clueless about how to reject it." Sebian stepped up beside me with a swath of his body heat that blanketed my side. "That's why you're suddenly behind this idea of her getting her gift, especially since everyone expects her to be a powerful deathweaver. Am I on to something here?"

A deathweaver.

Excitement and fear coursed through me in equal measures. To possess such a gift, commanding over shadows that drove fear and respect into many... I'd never imagined to have such power.

"None of this makes his concern about losing the amulet any less valid," I said, though I clearly had much to learn if I wanted to avoid getting stuck with Malyr for the rest of my life. "I already knew the only reason he wants to bond is so I can amplify his gift."

"It is not the only reason..." Malyr once again lied with a nonchalance that should have been struck dead by lightning right there as he stepped in front of me.

"Pray tell, Malyr, what is your reason?" I asked. "Something selfless, I presume."

"I have three reasons, all utterly, wretchedly, *unforgivably* selfish." Malyr leaned into me, running a nail over my scalp the way he'd done at the *kjaer*, sending a heated shudder across my skin. "If you turn out to be a deathweaver, then the pair of us commanding shadows together would make us a force to be reckoned with. We could drown entire continents in our shadows, and blacken the skies right along with it. Here's the thing, though, little white dove..." He slowly ran his finger through my hair, twirling a strand around his digit before he let it uncoil on my scarf. "I do not believe you to be a deathweaver."

My entire body shivered under the blanket of his nearness and dreadful anticipation. Whatever my gift was, I wanted it—*needed* it, like a piece of a puzzle to complete the image of my being.

I huddled closer to Sebian, pretending my heart still beat this incessantly for the thrill of my flight alone, and not because of Malyr's sheer presence. "Where is your wife?"

Malyr let his gaze stroll lazily over my form. "I am looking at her right now."

"I'm not your wife," I snarled.

"You will be so much more once we are bonded."

That certainty in his voice ruffled my feathers. "You said there's still time. How much?"

"Whoa, whoa, whoa!" Sebian took hold of my arm, turned me toward him, and gently sidestepped us away from Malyr for a poor semblance of privacy. His palms ran up and down my shoulders, the motion bringing memories of the many nights I'd fallen to sleep under his touch. "I don't want you to go back to Tidestone, sweetheart. My unkindness circled our army before coming here, and they are nearly here."

That fact made my toes curl inside my boots, but the lack of time couldn't be helped. "Tidestone is my home, and I know every corridor, every face, every shortcut. All I'll have to do is find Lady Brisden before nightfall. I'll be swift."

"So will be this—"

When his attention shot up along the cliff, I glanced up, but couldn't see anything out of sorts. "What's wrong?"

"Nothing. I just thought..." He stared for a moment longer, then shook his head and let his eyes connect with mine once more. "Tidestone won't stand for long."

I looked up at him, reaching to cup his stubbled cheeks, frown lines cutting deep craters of concern between his soft gaze. "My gift is a part of me. If I want to find out who I am and why things happened the way they did, then I need to get it back."

There was a tremble in his long exhale, as if it carried a dozen unspoken attempts to talk me out of it. "I understand that. It's just..." His forehead sank against mine as his eyes closed, but it only pronounced the worry carved into his features all the more. "I'm terrified of losing you more than I already have."

I stood there, frozen, my heart beating in sync with the tumultuous waves that washed against the nearby ships in the bay. There were so many things I wanted to ask him. Why hadn't he told me he'd been bonded to his late mate? And the affection he'd shown me? Was a bonded Raven capable of loving someone else, or had it all been a lovely lie we'd both wanted to believe?

I had no answers and not enough time to ask, but the way his fingers clutched my arms, as though fearing I might otherwise disappear...? Those stuttering breaths in the space between us? The way his eyes held mine captive? That concern for my well-being was sincere.

That was real.

With a final, deep inhale, he lifted his head, his gaze sweeping to my lips before they found mine again. "I could go with you."

"And get killed before we even step through the first gate?" With his long black hair and those burn marks on his hands, there was no hiding the ravens in him. "This is something only a white Raven can do."

"Just promise me you'll come back." His palms glided up to my cheeks, his thumbs circling there very so gently.

"There's a lot I have to say to you. I expect you to hold me to it."

"I will," I said, offering him a smile before I turned toward Malyr's cold, unmoving face. "You said I have time?"

His hard gaze flicked back and forth between Sebian and me, and a swallow visibly bobbed down his throat. "Once you have the amulet, seek shelter in the dungeons. As much as it pains me to say, it truly is the safest place to be. Stay away from the walls and the towers, *especially* the ones with the net catapults. Those will come down first." He suddenly placed his hand on my face, letting an intense but brief chill flare across my skin that had me jerking back. "Should you cross paths with any of us—"

"Shh, he only marked you with his shadows," Sebian said, lifting his hand to thumb over the dissipating sting. "Make sure you never hide your face from any of us, sweetheart, but most Ravens should sense his magic on you. Should you run into Lorn... well, keep running. She didn't take the news about you two being fated too well."

"She can have him," I said and looked at Malyr, giving him my sweetest smile. "When are you going to attack?"

In that moment, the haunting toll of Tidestone's bells echoed across the beach, cutting through the cold winds and prickling my senses.

The Ravens were coming.

Malyr smiled back. "You have one hour, *anoaley*."

ELEVEN

Galantia

Present Day, Tidestone

T idestone's walls echoed with chaos and mayhem. Servants scurried like mice running from a flood. Soldiers clattered past me, their heavy boots stomping out an erratic, discordant rhythm. I pushed myself through hallways that had transformed into crowded chutes of frenzied activity, cloaked in haste and desperation. Where was Lady Brisden? Had she left without retrieving the amulet?

And if she had, should I really be surprised?

I hurried toward the stairs that would take me to our private chambers, the air thick with the scent of fear, sweat, and anxiety. It clung to me, sucking the warmth from my body despite the exertion of my pace. Above it all, the ominous thrum of impending danger resonated, like a tumultuous orchestra of clanging metal, shouting voices, and the low murmur of hurried prayers.

"Lady Brisden?" I asked whichever face I passed until I finally shoved myself in front of a soldier, bringing him to an abrupt stop. "Lady Brisden? Where is she? Have you seen her?"

"No, my lady," he said and hurried off.

My heart pounded, keeping time with the hurried rhythm of my boots against the stone floor, each frantic beat a ticking clock. It had taken me at least fifteen minutes to reach the castle. If I couldn't find her in the next half hour, I might—

Skinny arms clutched at mine as a maid all but stumbled into me. "Oh, my lady, I finally found you! What's this on your face?"

"Have you seen Lady Brisden?" I blurted, not bothering to explain my shadowmarked face. "Where is she? I have to find her."

"It was she who sent me to find *you*. She came looking for you in your chamber earlier, but you weren't there." She glanced around nervously, her eyes wide with fear, her fingers trembling as she reached into the pockets of her apron, only to bring forth a small package carefully wrapped in cloth. "Find my daughter, she said. Find my daughter and give her this, or I'll have a guard string you up outside for the ravens to feast on."

I grabbed the package and quickly unfolded the cloth,

my pulse pounding in time to each flicker of light reflecting on the socket of black polished *aerymel*. In its center sat a white stone of salt, nearly translucent in some areas and wrought with cloudiness in others.

My core lifted.

The amulet!

The moment the maid turned away, I grabbed her shoulder. "My mother? Where is she?"

"I don't know, my lady," she whimpered, her eyes glistening with unshed tears before she tore away. "She left for the stables, last I saw."

The stables. A long, unexpected exhale left my lungs. *She'd escaped...*

I quickly put the amulet around my neck. With my gift trapped inside it, my next destination was clear: the dungeons.

The clamor of the castle raged around me as I made my way toward the bailey. Shadows danced and flickered along the stone corridor, more ominously the faster night fell.

A bloodcurdling sound pierced the air as I stepped into the chaos of the inner bailey, like a distant thrum. My heart lurched as the earth beneath me trembled, the castle itself moaning in protest. What was that? Ravens had to be trying to invade the cas—

A rough hand grabbed my waist, yanking me off my feet. "Got you!"

"No!" I yelped. "I'm one of you! I'm one of you!"

A Raven!

The man slung me over his shoulder, turning my world upside down as the constant shift of his chainmail bit into my lower ribs, the seam of his cloak shifting over the ground at his hurried strides. His *pale-green* cloak. A Tidestone soldier? But... no. That was all wrong!

"Let me go!" I writhed, twisted, and kicked. "I command you to let go of me!"

"I'm afraid I cannot, my lady," he ground out, carrying me through the turmoil of frantic soldiers. "I am under order to bring you before you father."

My blood froze.

No!

Anyone but him!

With desperation fueling me, I grabbed the soldier's helmet, ignoring the sharp edge that bit into my flesh. I tugged it backward, and he stumbled, his grip loosening momentarily. I arched my back and swung my legs, using my momentum to roll off his shoulder.

The world spun.

My back collided with the cold, unyielding ground with a force that knocked the breath out of my lungs. Yet I kept kicking, shoving myself over the dirt-packed ground and away from him.

He lunged at me. "Get back here!"

The world around us shuddered violently. A crash echoed. A blast of wind hit me like a furious gale. Men screamed. Chunks of stone and debris rained down, burying the soldier under a tomb of rubble alongside others, his outstretched arm twitching eerily for one breath, two, three.

It stilled.

With my heart pounding like a drum in my chest, I got to my feet, brushing stone dust from my face as I took in the damage. Was that... parts of a catapult tower?

No, no, no.

It was too soon! Too soon!

Chaos escalated, the sense of danger palpable in the air as I weaved through the rushing bodies, my breath harsh in the chill of the evening. The scent of smoke mixed with the distinct tang of iron and bloodshed. Hurrying past the fallen debris and those trying to unearth the injured soldiers, I managed to squeeze through to the barbican, my eyes fixed on the oaken door.

The dungeons!

If the door was unlocked, I would have to figure it out. Even if not, I could always hurry along the wall back toward that—

Something slammed into me.

No, not something. *Someone.*

I staggered sideways, finding myself in the arms of a frantic Lady Brisden, her eyes filled with terror. "Quick! We must get you out of here somehow!"

"What?" My mind scrambled to process her words as a wave of dread crashed down on me. "What are you still doing here? Why didn't you escape the attack?"

"He had you shadowed," she said as she ushered me away from the dungeons, her green dress a mud-speckled mess. "Brisden knows, Galantia. He knows what you are. Worse yet, he believes you might be Prince Malyr's fated mate. Every soldier of the house guard was ordered to find and capture you."

The air seemed to freeze in my lungs, the way the soldier had tried to snatch me earlier now explained. "What of the carriage?"

"The moment I learned of Lord Brisden's discovery from my maid, I abandoned the stables to find you," she said. *What had she just said?* "The carriage is lost to the Ravens now. They swept into the outer bailey like a swarm of blackness drawn from the hells themselves, killing everyone. You must fly, Galantia. You must leave from here an find your own before our guards capture you."

The weight of her words landed heavily in my chest. Lady Brisden, who'd never shown me any love, had abandoned the carriage—her only way of escape—to... warn me? The thought rattled me to my core, stripping away the icy layers of bitterness I'd built around my heart for her.

"Galantia!" She took hold of my shoulders and shook me out of my stupor. "Lord Brisden is having ships readied and the bay will bustle soon, but you cannot stay here, either!"

With a blink, I snapped back to the present, my mind clearing with a sharp inhale. No, I couldn't stay here. Definitely not to play sitting duck in the dungeons.

I glanced upward along the walls, finding only nine out of ten catapult towers fully intact where soldiers scrambled to reload the nets. *"Stay away from the walls and the towers, especially the ones with the net catapults,"* Malyr's voice resonated in my head.

"I need to get to a high place. It's the only way I know how to get myself to shift, but it can't be any of these," I said with a jut toward the catapults. "Our personal chambers are too far back toward the ocean and among the first places where soldiers would look for me."

Lady Brisden nodded, her pinned-up hair a torn mess. "The bell tower!"

No sooner had she spoken the words, did she usher me back toward the inner bailey. Together, we pushed and maneuvered through the turmoil, our pace rapid as we neared the chapel. Its steeple, topped with a bell tower, shot up into a sky darkened by black clouds. No, not clouds...

A massive unkindness.

One raven fell from the sky, growing big, bigger, only to drop beside me with a heavy *thud*. Its wings still fluttered around the arrow protruding from its chest, uselessly pushing the bird over the ground before its muscles seemed to first lock up, then stiffen into stillness.

When we reached the chapel's entrance—the doors lying in pieces and massive protruding splinters on the ground—a strong hand clamped around my arm. "Halt!"

"No!" I screamed, lashing out blindly, but the grip only tightened, yanking me backward.

Lady Brisden's eyes widened before she lunged at the man. "Run, Galantia!"

The soldier twisted away from me to backhand her, metal gauntlet meeting her cheek with a *clank*, ripping a pained cry from her.

My stomach clenched. "Mother!"

She stumbled back. Her upper body swayed. Her knees buckled. The last thing I saw was how she lost her balance before the soldier once more built himself up in front of me.

He reached for me, but his hand never landed.

Instead, tendrils of darkness snaked out from the shadows, wrapping around him in a deadly embrace. The soldier convulsed, his scream swallowed by the black cocoon that constricted him tighter and tighter until his armor creaked under the force. Crimson oozed from within, glistening under the sheen of the rising moon.

My gaze shot to the Raven woman approaching from the right, one side of her long hair shorn, her black robe shifting with shadows. A deathweaver.

She gave me a curt nod. *Malyr's marks.* She must have recognized them on my face.

The same luck didn't extend itself to Lady Brisden. The Raven's shadows did, however, sprout black fingerlings that snaked toward her, over the ground, around pieces of wood, through a puddle of... blood?

"Not her! You will spare her!" I stepped in front of the Raven, then quickly reached my hand toward hers, my fingers splayed wide. "Can you help me shift? This is how you do it, is it not?"

Her attention lingered on Lady Brisden behind me for another moment, then she intertwined her fingers with mine, giving me the focus of her stare. "Staying on the ground too long gets a bird killed, so you best hurry, white Raven!"

Yes, I had to hurry!

Closing my eyes, I dug deep into the recesses of my mind, searching for that bright energy. Where was it? Where— Ah! There, it brimmed, right at my core, flickering in sparks of white. *Please make me shift,* I pleaded with it. *Please, make—*

"Hurry!"

I jumped at the Raven's shout, my muscles trembling from how I tensed, as if it might get them to reshape into my wings. "I'm trying, but..."

Nothing happened.

"Find your primal where it sits in your heart," she said. "See how it spreads its wings, ready to be fr—ugh!"

The jerk of her hand pulled me forward before our fingers parted. My eyes snapped open, finding the woman twitching on the ground with an arrow protruding from the base of her skull. *Phhwt!* Another arrow embedded itself in her back.

Against every single tendon in my body stringing tight, I whipped around, taking in the hell that had descended all around me. Oh gods...

Archers lined the battlements, firing their deadly rains of arrows into the teeming unkindness of Ravens that shadowed the moon. Where arrows met their mark, birds fell from the skies, each hitting the ground with a heavy *thud* that echoed before being swallowed by the cacophony of screams and clashes. Ravens retaliated with gleaming black swords and even blacker shadows, their figures dancing between the piles of fallen soldiers and rubble.

"Galantia!"

I looked back at Lady Brisden, only for my blood to drain from my cheeks at the sight. *No. Please, no...*

That crimson puddle I'd spotted earlier? My eyes wandered to the bloody source: a gushing wound surrounded by tainted shreds of green silk, a large wooden splinter protruding from its center where it had stabbed through Lady Brisden's thigh during her fall.

"Gods, no..." I knelt by her side, warm blood soaking my dress and dampening my knees. "We need to get you off this thing."

"Leave me," Lady Brisden hissed through gritted teeth, her hand pressing on the wound. "You must flee. Now!"

"No, I can't leave you." My hands shook as they hovered over the splinter, the reality of what she suggested crashing down on me. "I... I have to—"

"Leave!" Her stern glare, the same one she'd given me a hundred times, locked onto mine. "Do not make me watch you die... My heart can't survive it a fourteenth time." With a sudden surge of strength, she pushed my chest, shoving me backward. "Go!"

I inched back toward the chapel, my entire chest a strangling knot of emotions. My gaze lingered on her until her outline blurred behind the rise of tears. Then I tore away, turned for the chapel, and hurried inside. It was dangerous, shifting in this chaos, but being found by Lord Brisden would be far worse.

I turned left, toward the tower's staircase, each footfall

overwhelmed by the moan of wood, the rumble of rock, the clang of metal against metal. Stone dust grated under my boots, dislodged by the trembling flagstones beneath. Up I went, taking two steps at a time, then three. The scent of old wood filled my nostrils, mixing with the staleness of dust and debris. Fast! Faster!

My legs burned from the effort, each new step a piercing bite into my muscles. The world spun around me, a whirling dervish of stone and debris. The only constant was the continuous upward spiral of the stairs, a lifeline I clung to with desperation.

The ground beneath me shifted.

Convulsed.

Tilted.

I pitched sideways, my hands instinctively reaching for the wall. My shoulder hit the stone first, my temple followed, sending a shockwave of pain through my skull. A shower of sharp pebbles and debris cut into my skin. My knees buckled under me, and I collapsed onto the ground.

Something small but pointed struck my eye. I snapped it shut with a yelp, instinctively curling up as another wave of rubble cascaded down. A soul-rending groan echoed around me, the very air vibrating with it. I rounded my spine against the assault, folding my arms over my head as the world seemed to cave in around me.

Because it did!

The stone beneath me shifted and cracked, and then...

... silence.

I was buried in the dust and rubble, my nostrils filled with a choking cloud of stone dust, the collapsed bell tower turning into my tomb.

No...

No, this couldn't be the end.

My trembling fingers blindly found their way to the amulet that hung from my neck, the salt crystal cool against my skin.

"Please..." I murmured in the silent tomb, pressing a knuckle into the salt crystal until it cracked against its *aerymel* socket, shattering into shards. "Let me be a death-weaver so my shadows can get me out of here."

But there were no shadows.

Only a gaping emptiness at my core, an abyss that seemed to devour me from the inside. It pulled at me, sucked at my being.

Swallowed me whole.

CHAPTER
TWELVE

Malyr

Present Day, Tidestone

The taste of copper hung heavy in the air, an acrid testament to the swath of death that whirled through the castle on pitch-black wings. A savage symphony of screams and clashes echoed around Tidestone, its fear-strung melody utterly... intoxicating.

I crossed the outer bailey toward the barbican, my gaze jumping from one fear-painted face to the next. Soldiers.

Stewards. Stableboys. Where was that bastard? Where was Brisden?

Bones crunched beneath my strides, the squelch of entrails underfoot bringing a smile to my face. This was revenge, this was retribution, this was the outpouring of a lifetime's accumulated wrath.

And it was glorious.

My gift pulsed beneath my skin—scratching, scraping —writhing with the need for bloodshed and death. I let the darkness surge from within, shadows extending like tendrils, sliding through the chaos. They coiled around those pitiful soldiers within reach, binding them, enveloping them in a web of darkness the way a spider would wrap its prey in silk. Oh, how lovely they screamed...

I pulled them behind me like an eerie funeral procession, a grim garland of trophies, nothing but lifeless marionettes in a morbid puppet show that dragged over the ground on shadowy strings. Goddess, spare my rotten soul, it was beautiful!

"Oh, come on, love. Don't be so coy," Lorn cooed nearby at a soldier who quaked by her feet, a smile curving her painted mouth. "Let me have a look at those pretty eyes of yours."

She grabbed his face, digging her nails into his skin, letting little black offshoots slither into the gaping, screaming cave that was his mouth. This, she enjoyed best —letting her shadows burrow through the cavities in his skull. They clogged his nose, tied up his throat, infested his brain until, with a squelch and a blood-curdling scream, they wiggled out from around his eyeballs. *Pop* went the first, then the other, blood and brain matter oozing out of every orifice the man possessed in his head.

She leaned over the soldier's jerking corpse, letting her

tongue lap at the dark red blood that trickled from his empty eye socket before her eyes flicked to me, a twisted grin splitting her face. "Delicious."

A perverse thrill swept through me at the sight, like an echo of the bloodlust we shared, the urge for revenge that bound us, if not much else anymore.

Arrows whistled.

I burst into my unkindness, dodging the deadly projectiles with ease before I reshaped from the inky mass of birds. "Archer on the battlement!"

To my left, Sebian moved with lethal grace, nocking a shadowy arrow onto his bowstring. His eyes, reduced to focused green slits, locked onto the archer perched upon the parapet. The bowstring thrummed. The dark missile flew true, stabbing through the archer's eye socket. He stayed upright for a moment, frozen. Then, slowly, he dropped to his knees before the weight of his lifeless head sent him tumbling forward to land on another corpse.

I raised a brow at Sebian. "Well aimed."

"Shut up, Malyr," Sebian grumbled, but he couldn't hide that twitch of a smirk. Whatever differences he and I had over Galantia, in battle, we were inseparable; and while maybe not friends, but always allies. "You better pick up speed so we can make it to the damn dungeons and get Galantia out of this chaos."

A low vibration thrummed through the ground beneath my feet, the sudden shift in equilibrium snatching my attention. Somewhere, muffled by the cacophony of battle, stone crumbled with the rumble of a distant thunderstorm. My eyes flitted to the horizon, where one of the looming catapult towers teetered precariously, a cloud of dust mushrooming around its base before it collapsed, though only partially. *What in the skies...?*

Cold dread seeped into my gut, replacing the prior excitement with a sudden, jarring concern that had me exchange a look with Sebian. It was too early, too soon for the ballistas to bring down these darned catapults. What had happened?

More arrows whistled.

Thrusting my hand out, I released a blast of shadows so forceful, it rippled through the air, striking the battlement like a physical force. Archers stumbled backward, their screams echoing as they flung over the wall.

"Fucking bastards," Sebian shouted, sending shadowy arrows through the faces of whichever archers had remained upright.

A gnawing, debilitating pain seized my hand. I looked down at it, my skin going pitch-black, as if devoured by a malevolent rot. My fingers gnarled and locked up, pain shooting up my arm like tendrils of liquid fire. My wielding hand needed time to recover.

"We need to get rid of those archers." A shift and a handful of wingbeats thrust me forward several feet before I commanded through the unkindness, *Clear the battlements with me!*

That was where I reshaped, drawing my black *aerymel* sword from its sheath. I swung the blade at the soldiers up there, just like Father and Asker had taught me during countless hours spent in the courtyard of Valtaris, each violent strike buying my hand time to recover. Bodies fell all around me, their screams piercing the tumultuous noise that rose from the inner bailey, bodies crumpling onto the blood-soaked wood.

Something caught my eye.

Nothing but an innocent gesture down in the inner bailey near an iron portcullis: an arrogant toss of the head.

A head shrouded with brown hair, its longer strands in the back curling against the richly embroidered pale green cape that clothed the man.

I'd seen it before.

Too many times.

And if the man turned around to face me now, he would stare at me from hazel eyes that still haunted my dreams.

Lord Brisden.

"That him, huh?" Sebian walked up beside me with his bow in his hand, narrowing his eyes in the direction of my gaze. "Fighting our way over there will take time... more than we have."

"Not if you give me cover from up here."

"Any moment now, it'll be a tomb down there," he said. "It can't be much longer until the ballistas take down the towers. You'll have to fly across the bailey and pray to the goddess that not a single arrow finds its way into your ravens."

Each scar on my body began to throb—every lashing, every humiliation, every depravity forced into me in the lightless depths of his dungeons resonating in a furious symphony. Oh, how long I'd waited for this...

A wicked grin spread across my face, the pure, unadulterated anticipation of what was to come making my skin prickle. I would kill him... but not here, not now. A laugh rumbled in my chest. Goddess, no, not anytime soon.

But I would capture him.

Revenge like this ought to be—

The ground beneath me shuddered violently, a shockwave of tremors rippling through the stone battlements.

My gaze snapped toward the catapult tower that had partially collapsed earlier, the rest of it now surrendering to gravity. It crumbled, stone blocks shearing off before they burst in a rain of death and destruction. The groaning cacophony of splintering timber and grinding stone filled the air, a discordant tune of impending disaster. The airborne debris slammed into the walls, tearing through the battlements like battering rams.

One particularly massive piece made impact with the base of the chapel tower. An ear-splitting *crack* echoed across the bailey, the entire structure swaying ominously before it fell. The bells tolled through the chaos.

Just as well.

I looked at Sebian. "We see this through?"

A curt nod. "Til' the end."

"Give me cover!" I roared before I burst into my unkindness.

We took flight, plunging downward into the chaos of the bailey before pulling up, gliding over the clash of swords toward Brisden. Close. We were so fucking close. All we needed was—

Something moved the air.

Ropes tangled around our wings, our beaks, our feet, catching us in its merciless grip. A collective screech echoed from us as the weight of the net pulled us to the ground. Claws ripped. Beaks pecked. Wings brushed against each other.

Trapped. We were trapped!

Wings turned into shoving hands.

Claws turned into kicking legs.

I tugged, yanked, and twisted, detangling myself from the net. I wriggled out, casting it off to the side just as a deadly shadow fell over me.

A sword whistled through the air.

I rolled to the side, narrowly avoiding the strike. Gritting my teeth against the persistent agony in my hand, I thrust my palm out, a surge of shadows exploding from it. They collided with the attacker, sending him sprawling backward to the blood-soaked ground.

Another soldier ran toward me, his sword held high for a strike. It never cut through the air, his efforts and life snipped short when a shadowy arrow punctured his neck, and another protruded from his chest.

This place was a grave.

One I needed to escape.

My eyes found Brisden again. I scrambled to my feet, dashing toward him alternating feet, wings, and swings of my sword, my quick shifts fueled by years of hatred. I was so close. So fucking close!

Until a merciless stab punctured my heart.

The brutal onslaught struck without warning, forcing my *aerymel* blade from my grip. What was this pain? A sword through my middle?

Staggering, my hand shot to my chest as I looked down at myself, sinking to my knees. No, there was no sword. There was... nothing. Nothing but profound agony. Bottom-less grief. An acute sense of loss.

"Malyr? You have to get up!" Sebian appeared from shadows writhing beside me, his knees sinking into the mud. "What the fuck is going on with you? Get up!"

Dread. Fear. Panic.

It slammed into the very fabric of my being, wrapping around my heart and lungs, pulling tight until all air rushed out of me. I glanced back in the direction of the portcullis, toward Brisden, but whatever rage I'd harbored only moments ago had been swept away by this... *something*. Something I'd never felt before, but... it seemed like the beginning and end of my very being.

"Galantia," I choked out, the name searing through me,

carving its path into my very core where my bond hummed a chaotic tune.

Sebian's gaze followed my line of sight. "What are you talking about? Galantia, *what?*"

The pain within me did not dissipate, nor did it escalate —it fluctuated, like a rhythmic torment playing its haunting melody in sync with my pulsing heartbeat. It wasn't just pain; it was a warning.

It was the bond.

"Something went wrong," I said. "I think she released her gift."

"We have to find her!" Sebian shot to his feet before he grabbed my arm and yanked me onto mine. "You have to find her, Malyr! Where is she? Where!?"

My gaze tore through the chaos, trying to find her creamy hair in this ocean of darkness and despair. "I... I don't know."

Sebian glanced back over his shoulder toward where she was *supposed* to be. "The dungeons?"

"No," I said with a certainty that baffled me. It wasn't something I knew, but rather... sensed. An instinct. "She never made it there."

"The bond, Malyr," Sebian said. "Listen to the bond in your chest. Where is it pulling you?"

I closed my eyes, focusing on the pain, the panic. Screams of men, twangs of bowstrings, whistles of arrows —it was too overwhelming. The chaos around me was too much, drowning out any internal focus.

"What the fuck is going on with your shadows?" Sebian asked, his eyes fixed on the writhing plumes that flickered from between my armor pieces.

Startled, I followed his gaze, noticing the unusual movements of my shadows. They all seemed to flutter in one direction like candle flames bending to the will of the wind, bending toward... toward...

"The bell tower!"

Without another word, Sebian and I burst into motion. Shifting between forms, we weaved through the chaos—dodging deadly slashes, parrying strikes, felling those who dared block our path. Every stroke of my sword, every beat of my wings, was guided by one thought. *Anoaley.*

We reached the ruins, the lower part of the tower still mostly intact. A large portion of the debris had slipped to one side, a heap of fallen stones and timber jutting out into the chaos of the bailey. For a moment, we both stood, taking in the disastrous sight before us and how my shadows drifted through the cracks, toward the inside on their own accord.

"She's in there." My shadows knew. "She's trapped."

The way was blocked for us from here.

But not for my ravens.

One quick shift, then we hopped and squeezed through the gaps in the ruins, slipping past broken stones and twisted beams, our black feathers ruffling with each arduous movement.

And then we found her.

Nestled within a makeshift cave formed by several large boulders, the remnants of the staircase offering some protection, lay Galantia, her once-vibrant hair now dulled by dust. A gaping wound slashed to one side of her forehead.

She's breathing, Sebian's unkindness said nearby. *Her heart's beating fine.*

I shifted back into my human form within the cramped space, the ceiling pressing low above us, the cold stones biting against my back. Galantia lay before me, her chest rising and falling in shallow rhythms that barely stirred the dust around her. My shadows drifted from me, slithering toward her. They caressed her, encapsulated her, streamed around her—no!

Into her.

Beside me, Sebian shifted out of shadows and darkness, his whisper barely stirring the air between us as he asked, "What is she?"

What I'd always hoped she would be.

My very own void.

THIRTEEN

Galantia
Present Day, Tidestone

I woke with a hole in my chest.

An aching, chasmal, endless crater.

Was I... in my chamber? Yes.

The sun wove honeyed warmth through the ornate windows, my muscles aching beneath the linen that lay smooth against my body. How long had I slept? How had I escaped the rocky tomb?

"Prince Malyr used his shadows to lift the debris off

you," a soft, familiar voice said nearby as if in answer. "It allowed Sebian to carry you to safety. It is midday, a day after the attack. The fighting stopped many hours before the sun rose."

I glanced around my room.

Marla sat in an armchair beside my bed, her legs propped up on a stool and a book lying upside down on her lap. Her black hair spiraled atop her head in beautiful, pinned-up braids. Still, the dark shadows under her eyes gave away the sickness she'd been through, the hardship, the many months spent in captivity.

"Presume I don't have to ask who won." Not with how she looked rather comfortable, my room and the balcony that lay behind my door eerily quiet. "What happened to the amulet? My gift?"

"It once again rests with your *anoa*," she said calmly, "as it ought to."

I pushed myself up to sit and let my fingers brush over that abyss in my chest that seemed to hunger and churn beneath the creamy cotton of my shift. "What am I?"

Marla closed the book, propped it behind her lower back on the chair, lowered her feet to the ground, and leaned forward slightly. "You, Galantia, are a void."

A void.

I expected something to surge within me—excitement, exhilaration, maybe even a strange sort of pride—but instead, my shoulders slouched.

I wasn't a deathweaver, feared by all. Not a pathfinder, able to enjoy the delicate nuances of the air. Not a fate, able to find excitement in glimpses of visions. Hells, I couldn't even knit a damn shadow scarf. In the grand scale of things, I felt as though I had been gifted nothing.

Quite literally.

Marla chuckled, rose, and grabbed the metal carafe from the nearby table, from which she poured into a wooden cup, her black dress simple with no adornments. "You are disappointed."

"Is it so obvious?" After all, I'd balanced along a damn wall, had been pushed off a cliff, and, most recently, nearly been squished beneath boulders. And for what? Exaggerated heartburn? "What do voids even do, other than remove shadows?"

"Nothing."

"Exactly..." They did *nothing*, like I had all my life, with no shadows of my own, no agency. "Does it always hurt like this?"

"After a lifetime of being deprived the shadows it craves, your void is starved, child. Now drink." She handed me the cup of water, then brushed her hands up and down her arms as she glanced out the window over the snow-capped cliffs that reflected the rich sun. "Voids are rare, Galantia. So very rare, blessed with the gift to undo darkness—also to wield it, should it turn out you can indeed mirror the shadows of others."

I quickly swallowed my final gulp of water. "An echo."

"Yes, an echo," she said with a nod over her shoulder back at me, a soft smile curving her lips. "My Asker told me you read up on all the gifts. It will prove helpful during your training."

"Training," I repeated, quite liking that word. "Presume we're not talking about knitting, sitting straight, or the mastery of the curtsy."

Her smile lifted higher, almost resembling a grin that made deep wrinkles appear over her cheeks and around her lips as if she'd enjoyed a lifetime of laughter. "We have yet to figure out just how deep your void is, or the potential variation of your gift. The only way to do so is have you use it under guidance."

"Wield my gift." Oh, I *really* liked the sound of that one, sparks of energy tingling my fingertips. I'd never wielded much beyond an embroidery needle. "Guide me, then. I'm ready."

"No. What you are, is bruised, with a nasty cut on one side of your forehead requiring a bit more healing," she said with a sigh. "But even then, as a fate, I have no shadows for you to absorb. There is, however, one particular death-weaver who has enough shadows to spare, it would feed four voids a lifetime."

My stomach clenched. "I'm glad Malyr saved me, I truly am, but I have no interest in being anywhere near him."

"All night, he spent beside you, guarding over your sleep until other responsibilities called him away," she said, as though he'd done so out of concern for me, and not how I could benefit him. "He is your fated mate, Galantia."

"And Aros is Lorn's fated mate. If she manages to avoid the bond and reject her *anoaley*, then so will I."

"You have been dealt a fate wrought with hardship and pain, a price our goddess wants you to pay for another chance at life," she said. "And with that, I mean the *both* of you."

"I'm not oblivious to the hardships Malyr endured." But ones suffering in the past could not excuse every misdeed of the present. "Maybe fate made a mistake."

"Fate is woven with precision, not chance; every thread perceived woven wrong is nothing but an essential right in the complex tapestry of a life." Marla tortured her upper lip between her teeth for a moment. "Yet, your mother's interference was like a tug on a web too intrinsically spun for me to grasp completely."

Mother.

That word sent a subtle rise of dread through me. "Lady Brisden. She, um... she..." A heavy swallow, then I placed the cup on the bedside table. "Did she succumb to her injuries?"

Marla shook her head, but it held a certain surprised reluctance. "I know nothing of injuries, nor could I, for she was neither found among the living nor the dead."

My core lifted at the possibility of her survival. "Maybe she escaped?"

"Perhaps," Marla said. "Lord Brisden escaped on one of the ships. She might have boarded alongside him."

After he found out about what I was, my existence nothing but living proof of her betrayal? Was that likely?

Linens shifted with a soft rustle.

I looked down at the floor beside my bed. There, in a makeshift camp of down and cotton, surrounded by a collection of small pillows seemingly gathered from all around the castle, lay Sebian. He'd spread about his limbs in a manner that appeared anything but comfortable, strewn haphazardly over the wrinkled blankets—a testament to a night of restless sleep, as was the ashen tone of his usually tan skin.

"He, too, insisted on staying with you, not once leaving your side." Marla slowly walked around my bed, only to squat beside him. "Time will tell why fate wove him into your life as strongly as she did." She gently shook him by the shoulder. "Sebian. She is awake."

Sebian stirred, his sleep-heavy limbs pushing him up to sit. His emerald eyes locked with mine, and he smiled a genuine, heartwarming smile that sent a flutter through my insides. Gods, I'd missed seeing it.

Marla rose and turned toward the door. "I will find Prince Malyr and let him know you woke."

"He eyed the door to the dungeons earlier," Sebian said. "If he's not up here, maybe you'll find him down there."

Marla shook her head. "I hope not, for I would worry about the state I might find him in."

Sebian waited until she left my room before he rose and sat on the edge of my bed, his narrowed gaze undoubtedly assessing the wound on my head. "How you feeling, sweetheart? Got a headache? Nausea?"

I reached for his stubble, loving the way it gently scratched over my palm. "Just sore. Thank you for getting me out."

"I wish I could take all the credit, but, um... we wouldn't have found you without Malyr." His smile faded, quickly replaced with a heavy seriousness. "You scared the shit out of me, sweet thing. Both of us."

"Lord Brisden found out I'm a Raven and sent the house guards after me," I explained. "I tried to get out of Tidestone before they'd catch me, but then the entire tower just... crumbled on top of me."

"Yeah, one of the ballistas went off prematurely when a rope somehow caught fire without anybody noticing quickly enough and burned through." He brushed a stray lock of hair from my face, tucking it behind my ear, his touch lingering, as if he was gathering the strength to speak. "Look, I had a lot of time to think after you fled Deepmarsh. I should have told you that I bonded myself six years ago." His throat bobbed. "I should have told you about my fated mate instead of leaving you unkissed, unknowing about what held me back. For that, I'm sorry."

Despite the weight of his words and the sorrow in his tone, something light came over my chest at his earnest apology. "Will you tell me about her now?"

He stared at me for long moments, his face an ever-changing canvas of emotions, before he nodded and waved me to him. "Come here."

He eased himself down onto the bed, the straw crunching beneath his weight. Extending his arm, he invited me into the familiar hollow of his side, his features softening as I gingerly shifted against him.

My head easily found its way to that spot on his chest where I'd fallen asleep and awoken countless times, all tension falling away from my muscles. The solid plane of his body, the warmth radiating from it, the faint scent of leather clinging to his shirt... everything felt so wonderfully familiar, so soothingly safe.

I let out a soft sigh, easing into the solace that only Sebian offered. "What was her name?"

"Ravenna."

I'd heard that name before. "Asker's and Marla's daughter?"

"Uh-huh."

That explained the tension between him and Asker, the coldness that cast over them whenever they were in each other's presence. "What did she look like?"

"Mmm, let's see." His arm settled on the small of my back, thumb drawing circles up along my spine. "Well, she um... she had black hair." When I gave a playful nudge at his chest, he chuckled, making my head bounce as the deep sound rumbled beneath me. I'd missed that, too, terribly. "She was a tiny thing. Barely reached my chest, but goddess forbid something piss her off, because I could hear her bickering over miles."

"Was she a fate?"

"No, a weaver. Every night, she um... she created a fine web of shadows around me, muffling out the sounds and smells. To this day, I still have some of her salted spells."

"They help you rest your senses."

"Mm-hmm." He nuzzled the top of my head, inhaled, then gently moaned, as if he enjoyed my scent as much as I loved his. "She was a little older than me. It was she who found me when I tried to nurse Malyr and Lorn back to health in my family's hut. She'd grown up in the palace, so she recognized him."

"That's how Asker reunited with Malyr."

"Exactly. Hmm... what else?" He thought for a second. "Ravenna laughed a lot, and I enjoyed making it that way. There was still so much more to discover about her, but I never got around to it. We... we'd been bonded for less than a year when she died."

Forcing a swallow down my dry throat, I reached up, my fingers light brushing against the area over his heart. "Malyr told me your unkindness was attacked on your way to the camp, making you miss your watch."

"It had to be a great owl with how it knocked my primal unconscious, making me shift and just... drop out of the sky." The brush of his fingertips slowed, his chest lifting high before it stuttered through the exhale. "When I woke, I was dizzy, disoriented, with a terrible pain in my chest. I soared through the night and straight to the camp, but when I got there... when I spotted Prince Domren where he stood behind my bent-over sister—"

When another stuttering exhale whispered noisily past his lips, I curled my fingers into his chest, holding on to him tighter. "If you'd rather not—"

"No." Sebian's eyes found mine, his glistening gaze

filled with such agony, it sent shivers cascading down my spine as he said, "You deserve to know what happened that night."

FOURTEEN

Sebian
Past, a burning forest

It started in my calves, that violent tremble that rooted me to the blood-soaked ground before it crawled higher. It dug into my thighs, wrapped around my torso, twisted along my arms until the wood of my bow stuttered against the leather sheath on my hip.

I clenched my eyes shut.

Not real.

The stench of singed hair and feathers climbed into my nostrils. Someone screamed with a violence that stirred the bile in my stomach, high-pitched and strained, as if the vocal cords were about to snap. The air clung, wet and sticky, to my fingers.

I opened my eyes, nausea rising in my throat as the infernal nightmare continued before my eyes. Long black hair. A red ribbon gathering the strands at the top of her head. A silver earring shaped like a teardrop dangling from her lobe. In front of me, the world tilted and warped around Zaima's listless body, my little sister going in and out of focus as her heart thudded strangely.

No, not her heart.

The *laol* stone on her necklace jumped with each thrust of the man hunched over her backside, *clanking* against the barrel over which he'd draped her. Her heart was... quiet. Why was it so quiet?

My upper body swayed.

Not real. Not real. Not real.

My ears twitched at the crack of a bone—a rib, maybe. Flesh tore under crackles and wet gulps as the man forced himself deeper into her body. Dark red cape, maybe purple. Chest piece embossed with beastly eyes, one to each side. They stared at me.

After a final grunt, the man stepped back. Zaima's body slipped off the barrel and out of sight. She didn't scream, didn't cry. I should have caught her; I should help her up, but...

My feet wouldn't lift.

Seconds passed. Minutes? Hours? I just stood there for what felt like eternities. Stood there and did... nothing, my body entirely frozen.

But I had to pick her up, get her off the cold ground. She always caught fevers way too easily...

I strained every muscle, propelling myself toward her.

Tears blurred my vision as I swayed past shifting tree trunks, everything around me moving in stuttering frames and twitching motions.

Metal clanked against metal.

Flames roared.

Something bumped into me, sending me stumbling sideways into a flare of heat. My legs snapped like twigs beneath me. My knees hit the ground.

Ahead, a shrouded figure sprinted toward me, his glinting sword held up high. Cold sweat doused my entire body beneath my fur-lined armor as I conjured a shadow dagger. I aimed at the head, but it hit the soldier's stomach instead, making him drop his sword and cleave through his shoulder before he collapsed forward to the ground.

"Zaima." Glancing around, I lifted my arm, warding off the flames beside me. Where was she? Where was—

My eyes locked on her motionless body, my feet pushing me up to stand before they stumbled toward her. "I'm here. I got you."

I carefully slid my arms beneath her body. Still, her broken rib ground noisily as I lifted her.

"I'm sorry," I said as I turned. Turned again. Turned a third time, my entire world painted in fire that engulfed the huts and corpses that littered the ground. Here and there, distorted figures moved about. Human? Raven? "Where is Ravenna? Have you seen her?"

Zaima didn't answer.

"I have to find her." Had to keep my vow. "Did you see where she went? Did she shift and flee?"

No answer.

The world around me dulled, all sounds muted, as if a heavy curtain settled around my senses, giving focus to that dread rising in my stomach. No, Ravenna couldn't have shifted, not without help. And if she'd shifted with help?

My heart beat faster, mercilessly pounding alongside that ache in my chest as if... as if... No, it was nothing. Just a few broken ribs from my earlier fall. Maybe a damaged lung. I had to find her. I had to get them both out of here.

With my sister draped over my arms, I stumbled north, toward the sea-sawing line of conifers. Behind those, lay our hut. It wasn't far.

But it seemed endless.

Zaima's weight pulled me from one side to the other. I sidestepped left, I swayed right. My foot caught on something. I stumbled forward to the sound of metal clanking and the twitching flutter of wings.

I looked down at the net of chains that pinned a dying raven to the ground. It blinked at me, once, twice. Then it blinked no more, its beady eyes as black as its plumes—aside from that roaring red and orange center.

My gaze trailed to the all-consuming fire across from it, my vision blurring and warping through the haze. Heat billowed out of a hut in scorching waves, the flames twice as tall as me, gorging on the roof—*our* hut.

No...

A raw, animalistic shout ripped from my throat, the sound swallowed by the cacophony of crackling flames, the heat searing my face and stealing the air from my lungs. The chains. The nets. What if they'd trapped Ravenna in there? I had to... had to...

"I have to put you d-down," I stammered with the same violence my arms trembled and shook as I sat Zaima down as gently as I could, propping her against a tree. "I have to f-find Ravenna. Stay there. Real quick. Ju-ju-just... stay there."

The moment I straightened, her body slumped, shifted,

then fell sideways into the snow, her eyes vacant, staring at nothing. She'd get cold. She had to be cold, but...

"I have to save her." I spun toward the hut, each stuttering step sending waves of tingling weakness through my legs. "Ravenna? Ravenna!"

Another bout of weakness.

I hit the ground, and my chin knocked against something hard. A metallic tang spread across my mouth. Scrambling, I clawed my way back up. My lungs seared with the smoke, each ragged breath a brand against my insides. *Save her.* If she was in there, I had to save her!

My world narrowed to the blistering inferno. Holding my arm up in front of me to shield myself from the fire, I lunged forward, elbowing my way through the curtain of leather. Inside, a crossbeam moaned, the structure groaning and hissing in protest. The snow clinging to my armor hissed with the flames.

Smoke choked my throat as I weaved around flames and collapsed crossbeams, my skin screaming against the relentless heat. The world spun, my vision blurring and wavering through the suffocating haze. Chains clanked.

Beneath. My. Foot.

Then I smelled it, the biting stench of charred flesh and singed hair—maybe feathers—a savage retch clawing its way up my throat. *No. No, no, no, no—*

Biting pain tore through my wrist, shooting up my arm like a bolt of lightning. Lowering it, I stumbled backward, my gaze going to the plumes of smoke puffing from my bracers.

Fire.

I was on fire!

"No!"

My fingers scrabbled with the leather fastenings. I staggered back, away from the fiery hell in front of me. It followed, biting into my skin and eating its way up my arm. The scent of sizzling flesh joined the charred stench of my surroundings.

My own flesh.

My stomach twisted, bile rising. My fingers, slick with sweat, pulled on the leather straps, yanking on the bracers. *Get it off me, get it off me, get it off me!*

A strangled scream clawed its way out of my throat. I stepped backward and a chill licked at my back. The world tilted, and my balance right along with it. I hit the ground, everything going black to the sound of a hiss.

"Sebian."

My eyes opened to the cloudy sky, the blackened branches above me swaying with the wind. Grayish snowflakes drifted down on me, settling on my face, bringing with them the scent of charred wood, smoke, and... something else. Why was it so silent?

Pain.

Goddess, the pain.

It was everywhere—in my chest, at my core—but nowhere more than my arm. A roar of agony coiled around it, spreading down along my ribs. My fingers... They wouldn't move, wouldn't respond.

"Sebian, say something." Malyr's face appeared above me, frown lines between his brows, his open black strands dusted in gray snow. No, not snow. Ash. "We have to get you to a healer. See if we can save that arm."

Arm?

I followed Malyr's gaze over the soot-covered right side

of my cuirass. Beside it, a remaning leather strap of my bracer hung pitifully around my upper arm. Shoulder, biceps, elbow, underarm, knuckles, fingers... My entire fucking arm lay steaming beside me, the skin blistered down to the exposed flesh, oozing blood and who knew what else.

A sickening lurch buried in my stomach, every nerve ending along my arm screaming in torment, but it had nothing... *nothing* on the sudden stab beneath my breast-bone. "Ravenna."

Malyr's lips narrowed, pressing together before he hooked his arm under my good one, and pulled me up. "Come on, we have to get you to a healer."

"No, I... I have to... have to get Ravenna out of... out of..." The forest spun around me, faster when I glanced over my shoulder at my hut. Nothing remained but a blackened frame and smoking crossbeams. "Where's Ravenna?"

Supporting most of my weight, Malyr walked me toward a clearing. "She's not in there, Sebian."

Good. That was good. "Zaima?"

"She's not there anymore, either," Malyr said. "We only just found you. The others already carried your sister away."

They took her away.

I waited for relief to infuse my chest.

It didn't come.

Instead, a black heaviness expanded at my core, slithering around the pain that kept stabbing beneath my ribs. "So Ravenna escaped? Where is she?"

I clenched my eyes shut, letting Malyr guide my wobbly steps as I sensed for our bond. But it didn't pull me in the direction in which we were going.

It didn't pull at all.

It only hurt.

Hurt so fucking badly.

A keening wail sliced through the quiet forest. It was the raw, desperate cry of a heart shattering, a sound that spoke of soul-crushing despair and unbearable grief. It echoed in the chilly air, rising and falling in a broken rhythm, mixed with choked sobs and unintelligible words.

A pang of dread squeezed my heart as I opened my eyes, gaze catching on the source of the sound: a woman kneeling in the snow, her arms frantically moving about over the blackened body by which she wept. But she was not just any woman.

Marla.

Because Asker stood beside her, his hand resting on his mate's shoulder, his stare fixed on the ground. Until it lifted.

Then, it fixed on me.

My stomach twisted violently, a wave of bile threatening to work its way up my throat. "Wh-wh-where is Ravenna?"

Asker stood tall, his body trembling harder the longer he stared at me, his brows pulled taut over red-rimmed, glistening eyes.

"You..." He stormed toward me, drawing his arm back. "She's dead because of you!" His fist shot forward, slamming straight into my face. "You left her unprotected! You left *all of us* unprotected."

I stumbled back. The world distorted. There was a dull *thud*. My body quaked. Pain gnawed at my entire arm like shards of glass dragging over the blisters and pustules.

"Get away from him and sort yourself out!" Malyr shouted.

"You left her to die alone like the irresponsible, drunk,

good-for-nothing you are," Asker barked down at me under spitting rage, his cheeks as red as his eyes. "Pregnant! Unable to shift, she burned, Sebian. They burned her down to nearly nothing, and where were you!? You're still swaying, even now! I'm going to—" His fingers clasped around my throat, yanking me up by it until my feet dangled off the ground. "I should kill you for—"

A blast of shadows kicked Asker back.

I dropped to the ground.

And so did Asker. There he stayed, pounding his fist against his temple as he cried. Marla cried louder, harder.

Tears streamed down my cheeks, clogging my throat until salt mixed with bile. I retched onto the white ground under sobs, my chin dipping into it each time I rocked back and forth, back and forth, back and forth, the agonizing pain in my chest all-consuming.

I hadn't protected her.

Hadn't saved her.

I'd failed.

CHAPTER
FIFTEEN

Galantia
Present Day, Tidestone

A single tear slipped from the corner of my eye, tracing a wet trail down my cheek and soaking into the fabric of Sebian's shirt where my head still rested on his broad chest. The hardship he'd gone through, the self-blame, the guilt he must have endured all these years... The aching truth of it all touched me, but it was the fact that he'd shared it with me—the intimacy of being so open and vulnerable—that made me feel closer to him than ever before.

"Ravenna was already dead when you woke, wasn't she?" Just like his sister had been when he'd watched her body getting raped, likely putting him in a state of shock. Heavens, chances were he'd had a concussion. "That was the pain in your chest, wasn't it? The pain of having lost your bondmate?"

"Yeah." His voice was choked, heavy with emotions. "I didn't realize it then. Fuck, it took me months to figure it out, and years to make peace with that. Five years, to be exact. And the tension between Asker and me wasn't helping."

"He still blames you?"

"Yes." There was a brief pause. "Actually, as of recently, I'm not sure anymore. Before the attack, he had a vision that showed me leaving a nearby tavern, but he had no time to give it much attention. And I *had* come from a tavern before my unkindness got attacked, but I wasn't drunk. Did I like my cup of wine now and then? Sure, but not before a watch. Never."

My thoughts trailed back to Asker's stern remarks, and how Malyr had told me the night of the *kjaer* that Sebian had been drunk most of the time. Maybe he'd heard Asker accuse him of it so many times, that Sebian had succumbed to it, just to prove his father-in-law right and reinforce his own guilt?

Swallowing hard, I blinked away new tears over the tragedy of that, my hand lightly tracing the lines of his scars beneath his shirt. "Why were you there?"

"Ravenna couldn't keep anything down in the mornings because of the... the baby." That last word carried a sort of forlorn reverence. He'd lost so much that night—his mate, his unborn child, his sister, mother. Everything. "She wasn't far along. We'd only found out two weeks prior when the pregnancy wouldn't let her shift anymore. Before my watch started, I decided to get her some of her favorite pie, hoping she might have better luck with that."

"Which is why he thought you'd spent the night at the tavern, drinking."

The stubble on his chin caught on my hair as he nodded. "When I told Asker of the attack, he brushed it off as a lie. Marla... well, she was too grief-stricken to care. Until she saw the truth in a vision about a year ago, but it was all too late then."

A deep ache formed a knot in my stomach. The enormity of Sebian's suffering was almost too much to comprehend, and all this time, he'd hid it behind smirks and smiles. It made sense now why he'd struggled to be with me fully. How could it not?

But as the weight of his tragic past settled heavily on my shoulders, a disquieting uncertainty prickled at the back of my mind. What *had* he felt for me? Lust, obviously —he'd never lacked that. But what about affection? What about... love?

I listened to the steady beat of his heart, trying to find courage in it. "Sebian?"

"Hmm?" A quiet rumble, a subtle encouragement in the silent room.

"Now that I know everything, where does that leave us?" I asked. "Because I'm telling you, I'm done begging for scraps of affection, just to find out they were nothing but hollow bones to begin with."

His large hand slowed those circles it drew on my back, letting me know that my question had his attention. Silence stretched, the world waiting with bated breath.

Gradually, he shifted underneath me, pulling back just enough to glance down at me and meet my gaze.

"I spent the last five years unattached because I didn't think it was right to be with someone, or maybe I thought I didn't deserve to have someone. I don't know." His fingertips brushed down along my temple, caressing my cheek before his thumb played with the corner of my mouth. "With you, it just... happened, and I'm done fighting it."

Warmth spread through me at his words, yet it wasn't enough. "And what exactly is it that happened?"

One corner of his mouth tugged into a lopsided smirk, his gaze wandering to my lips. "Going after those bones, sweetheart, aren't we? Checking if there's some meat on them."

I lifted my head off his chest, loving the way his hand pressed down on my back, as if to ensure I wouldn't bring another inch of distance between us. "I want to hear you say it."

"I'm just a peasant who finds himself at court. You want pretty words, sweetheart, hmm?" His thumb feathered over my lips, tugging the bottom one away slightly before it dipped inside, swiping along the wet, warm flesh. "If that's what you need, you have to find yourself a well-spoken prince. I just so happen to know one."

My heart pounded the back of my throat. "I don't want him."

"Yes, you do. You can always refuse to act on the urge of your bond, but you can't deny the urge itself. But be that as it may, I'm not someone who murmurs honeyed endearments, Galantia," he rasped as he lifted his head, letting our breaths mingle. "I'd much rather show you."

"But I need to—"

His full lips captured mine in a heart-rending kiss that

stalled my pulse, infusing my blood with such desire, I shook uncontrollably in the ungiving clasp of his arm. His fingers tangled in my hair, trembling with the same desperate intensity as his breath against my mouth. I opened for him, allowing his tongue to lap at the inside of my mouth, stoking flames of longing deep in my belly. Gods, I'd wanted this kiss for so long. So long!

The world melted away under the searing intensity of his kiss, stripped of all pretenses. His lips moved over mine with a tenderness that was achingly sweet, a quiet affirmation of something more. The heat of his mouth, the way he held me so close against his warm body, told me more about his feelings than words ever could.

This was no meaningless gesture, no fleeting carnal craving. It was a silent vow, a pledge that seeped into my veins and echoed in my heartbeat. His fingers tightened in my hair, holding me close, and a soft moan escaped me as I clung to him, lost in the potent mix of hope, desire, and an emotion that felt suspiciously like love.

"There," Sebian breathed as he pulled back, staring up at me from glistening eyes, hard breaths fanning over his parted lips. "How was that, hmm?"

A smile curled my lips as I cupped his cheek, running a nail over his stubble. "Scratchy."

"Is it?" His chuckle banned all earlier sorrow from his tone. "Malyr flies much faster than I do. I had to decide: shave or keep up with him. I'll get rid of it tonight, hmm?"

I nodded. "Please do."

"That kiss was long overdue, and there will be a lot more in the future, if you'll have me. But just for the record, because I'm not going to risk your doubt again over three fucking words," he tugged the back of my head, pulling my mouth back to his as he rasped, "I love you."

Another kiss, almost savage in its intensity. I gasped into his mouth, my heart pounding in my chest like a wild drum. His taste, his scent, the raw emotion vibrating between our lips—it was like an inferno that consumed me, burning away all doubt and fear.

He loves me.

Truly loves me.

A deep clearing of one's throat sounded behind us, followed by Asker's baritone. "Prince Malyr needs Lady Galantia by the north-eastern cliff."

Sebian sighed and glanced around, but made no attempt at shifting me off him. "She's recovering."

"He is aware, but this is an urgent matter," he said. "We made a discovery."

CHAPTER
SIXTEEN

Galantia
Present Day, Tidestone

After Asker left, I quickly dressed. Sebian led me outside into the quiet chill of the balcony, but it took me less than three steps before they slowly faltered.

"Not a single catapult tower remained standing." My gaze wandered along the outer wall, parts of it crumbled, a shaky hand pressing to my stomach when my attention landed on a small, lonely shoe down in the inner bailey. A child's shoe. "Did Malyr spare anyone?"

Sebian gave me a pinched look. "You know the answer to that, sweetheart."

Yes, I knew. Benevolence wasn't a part of Malyr's personality.

My breathing turned flat as if my lungs refused to pull down the scent of bloodshed that tainted the air. Maids who had brushed my hair, girls who had brought kindling for fire, stewarts who had cleaned my chamber pot. Unless they'd escaped, all these people were now lying somewhere in heaps of bloody limbs and pale faces. Maybe black faces.

"How many died?"

"Too many. At the same time, not even a fraction of what Asker feared he might lose of our army, so there's that." Sebian took my gloved hand, slowly leading me down the spindling stone stairs so my feet wouldn't get caught in the train of my brown, fox-lined winter dress. "Two hundred and sixty something Ravens, most of them ripped from the sky by nets or arrows during the first wave of the attack."

We emerged from the stairs, stepping into the inner bailey. "I meant how many humans."

He took me in for a moment, inhaling a long breath before he said, "Again, too many."

A cold, hard knot formed in my stomach, spreading icy dread through my veins. Throughout the attack, I'd had nothing on my mind but my amulet. I hadn't given a single thought to how this place might look after, the ground speckled with blood and feathers, the air disgustingly sweet. So this was what war looked and smelled like...

I hated it.

Despised it.

"Come on, sweetheart." He turned me toward the northern gate. "Let's get out of here. At some point, we need to get some shadowthread into your dresses so we can practice your shifts."

"We should head through the gate by the port."

He shook his head and continued on, broken shields and weapons littering the ground here and there. "No, we shouldn't."

"But it's faster. We could take the stairs—"

"Do not go there, Galantia." His command was sharp, but his gaze immediately softened when it met mine. "Not for a few days, do you understand?"

The stench of smoke hung heavy in the air, filling my nostrils and turning my stomach. "It's where you put the bodies."

The way his jaws tightened was answer enough. "How's that void of yours feeling, hmm?"

"Strange." My fingers lifted, mindlessly stroking over that aching hole right beneath my chest. "You know the feeling when you didn't eat all day?"

"All too well."

"Like that, but three times worse, like a constant churning in the belly that sends a cramp through my stomach every now and then," I explained. "Except, it's in my chest. It seems to be getting worse, too."

"Because it is," he said on a sigh, glancing around the white landscape before he stopped, took my hand, and turned me toward him. "Your void is drawn to shadows, sweetheart, but *particularly*, Malyr's. That discomfort in your chest? It'll get worse the closer you get to him while you're unbonded, especially while your void is starved like it is, so let's fix that real quick. Be a good girl for me and close your eyes."

I did as I was told. "What are you doing?"

"Giving you some of my shadows." He let our fingers intertwine and stepped closer, lowering his forehead against mine before he whispered in the space between us, "I'm not a deathweaver, sweet thing, but whatever I have to offer is yours."

Something fluttered in my chest. "How do I absorb?"

"You already are," he crooned. "It's not so much that you have to learn how to absorb them, but when and how to stop. If you're not able to wield them and absorb too much, they'll kill you from the inside, do you understand?"

A sigh slipped from my lips, my body melting into his as if drawn by an unseen force. His strong arms wrapped around me, lending me support as I swayed, the pain in my chest easing, if only slightly.

Sebian nuzzled my temple. "Alright, I need you to stop now."

Languid heat flooded my veins, turning me sluggish. "How?"

"By closing your void," he said. "This is how my grandmother once explained it to me, okay? Imagine it's a container of sorts. It can be anything you want, as long as it can hold shadows. You got something?"

"Mm-hmm."

"What kind? Tell me."

I focused on the rendering before the black backdrop of my mind. "A box."

"What box? Wood? Metal? Color? You need to *see* it. Truly, see it."

"It's glass." Sparkling in shades of white, silver, and the lightest blue. "Translucent glass."

"Close it."

I focused on the box, trying to close it, but gods... It felt so good, how his shadows filled that sense of emptiness I'd carried for years. All my damn life! I wanted more. Needed more of—

"Alright, I need you... I need you to stop, or you'll drain me empty," Sebian ground out. "Close your glass box, sweetheart."

I hummed in bliss as the shadows soothed over the pain. More. I wanted more!

"Now, Galantia!" Wrapping an arm around my waist, he pulled me against him, pressing my body tightly against his. "Close the fucking box!"

With a start, my eyes snapped open, my chest heaving. "I'm... I'm sorry."

His hard breaths filled the silence, ragged and broken, swirling together in the space between us before it puffed up in heated plumes. "We'll have to practice that a bit more, hmm? Are you feeling better?"

I nodded. "A little."

"A... little," he echoed, a strange tension settling on his features before he tugged me back into motion. "Where does this lead? What's over there by the cliff that can possibly be this urgent?"

There was a strange roil in my stomach. "The gallows."

"Gallows on a cliff, with the sea stretched out behind it. A golden-haired woman's body dangling from a noose, drowning beneath salty waves," Asker's vision resonated in my clouding mind.

Shadowy figures by the cliff's edge materialized into three distinct forms—Asker, Marla, and Malyr. They stood motionless around the skeletal silhouette of the gallows. Nothing more than three tall structures looming before the backdrop of the endless sea, one beside another, with empty ropes swaying on two of them whenever a spray of saltwater from the crashing waves hit. But on the third?

A body dangled there.

Cold sweat settled on my forehead. One moment, I held Sebian's hand, and the next, my fingers slipped from his as I stumbled toward the woman hanging from the creaky rope. No, this couldn't be.

My shaky hands lifted to her boots, fingers turning black from the thick, black goo that smeared across the brown leather.

"Tar," Sebian said, who'd walked up beside me.

I forced my gaze up. Tar covered the green train of her dress, the blood-stained bodice, the blonde tresses that clung to the ornate embroidery like sticky cobwebs. Here and there, white down fluttered in the breeze as if it wanted to drift away, but couldn't.

No. No, this was impossible.

My gaze lifted higher, to those graying strands, the hairline wrinkles, those regal features that had gone near-translucent. "Mother?"

The rope creaked in answer.

Muscles failed, and I sank to my knees, my upper body swaying with the corpse as I kept clinging to those boots. "Oh gods... Gods, no..."

How he'd gotten there, I couldn't say, but Malyr knelt beside me, giving a little tug on my shoulder. "Come he—"

I threw myself at Sebian's legs, clinging to them as if the wind might otherwise truly pull me out to sea. "He killed her!"

"Shh..." Sebian sank to his knees and pulled me into his embrace, hushing me and holding me so tightly. "I'm here, sweetheart. Everything will be alright."

"Asker found her like this earlier." Arms crossed behind

his back, Malyr stepped back into view, his jaws tense enough that the valleys beneath his cheekbones filled with dark color. "I presume our suspicions were correct, and this is Lady Brisden?"

No, this wasn't Lady Brisden. How could it be? If it was, then she would sit in a carriage heading for Ammarett, coldly frowning at the heavy pelt draped over her lap. She certainly wouldn't hang from the gallows because she'd come back for me.

No, this woman had sacrificed herself to keep me safe and ensure my survival. And what did you call such a woman?

I nodded, the back of my throat filling with salty tears, overflowing from my eyes as if years and years of sorrow poured out of me. "Yes, this is my mother."

CHAPTER
SEVENTEEN

Malyr
Present Day, Tidestone dungeons

The wooden crate crashed against the claw marks on the damp, dark stone, erupting in a cacophony of splinters and echoing groans that reverberated off the walls. Fragments whizzed through the air, one slashing across my cheek, searing the skin with a hot burn.

I shouted—a raw, guttural roar that clawed its way out of my throat—my arms flailing wildly, hands clasping around anything within reach to smash and destroy. And if this damned dungeon wouldn't happen to support an entire fucking wall of the castle, then I would lay ruin to the cell the way Brisden had laid ruin to me!

"Fucking... escaped!" A burst of shadows erupted from my core, slamming against the walls with an ear-splitting growl, the stone shaking and trembling under the force of my wrath until mortar dust rained down from the cracks. "This pretty Raven boy is going to catch you and string you up by your balls. I'll even put a hook through your cock for good measure, and shove nails up your ass!"

The shadows recoiled, then came crashing back over me, a whiplash of my own rage, ripping my legs out from underneath me. My spine slammed against the cold, hard ground with a sickening *thud* as darkness seeped back into me, sullying me, tainting me to the fucking core in a sludge that no amount of scrubbing could ever remove.

A groan wrenched itself from the depths of my lungs, only to morph into a long, drawn-out laugh. It echoed. This place was laughing back at me.

That sounded insane.

My laugh morphed into a chuckle—a hollow, dissonant sound that scraped my parched throat. Nothing about me was sane, or right, or whole, or decent, or clean.

Not anymore.

I lay there for I didn't know how long, sprawled across the ground, the dank air heavy with the scent of mildew and months of sorrow. My heart thudded in my chest, gradually quieting to a murmur. My breaths followed suit, slowing but not deepening, as though even the air refused to get close to something as filthy as me.

I shouldn't have come here.

A flicker of sensation surged within me—a bright speck

of nothing at my core, resembling something akin to light with how my shadows shifted outward.

I knew this feeling; had first met it in this very place as a naïve boy, and later in that copse of trees as a man too broken to care. But I cared a great deal now, drawn to it like a crow to fresh carrion.

I wanted more of it.

Needed more of it.

I pushed myself off the ground, my shadowcloth robes torn in places. My boots scraped against the stone floor as I followed a corridor that echoed with century-old shouts for Harlen. The winding stone stairs loomed ahead, each step a fight against the past clawing at my heels, refusing to let me go.

And maybe I would have collapsed on the stairs, waiting for Asker to find me and drag me out, wasn't for how that sense of brightness lured me up into the light of the barbican. *Where is she?*

I lifted my hand, watching the plumes of shadows writhing between my fingers. Fated gifts called to one another, but none so quite as intensely as a void called to shadows. My little dove beckoned them, bent them, made them bow toward the gate on the left like a compass needle straining north.

Brushing the dirt off my sleeves, I left through the open gate, letting the shifting of ground seashells change into the crunch of snow. Three days ago, Galantia had set fire to Lady Brisden's pyre, if only because the ground was too frozen to bury her the way humans did. After that, she'd retreated to her room, grieving, sleeping, crying...

All while in Sebian's arms.

A mental picture that clawed at my insides—scratching, scraping—but not quite as violently as the memory of how she'd thrown herself at Sebian's feet in front of the gallows instead of into my arms. Ah, where had this gone so utterly wrong?

When I had carved my sigil into her flesh? When I had choked her with my cock, my shadows, my hand? Or perhaps the day I'd ripped through her maidenhead with my fingers? When I'd told myself that I hated her, and that I needed to shatter her heart?

Mmm, so many possibilities.

The farther I ventured into the dormant orchard of perfectly lined trees, the more the bond ached in my chest, urging to be tied. And perhaps I would have already lured her into it, if only she'd left her room and ventured away from her lover. Like she had now, finally offering me—

My feet stalled.

There she stood, my beautiful *anoaley*, her hair even brighter against the backdrop of snow and her cheeks peachy from the cold. A shame I couldn't see the color of her lips through the grayish haze that bled over my vision with how she'd pressed them to Sebian's.

Kissing him.

Darkness shifted at my core—scratching, scraping—a shroud of obscurity enveloping my mind, choking out the light of clarity, blurring the edges of reason. How dare he kiss my mate? Intertwine his fingers with hers? Preen the brittle strands of her hair as he raked through them in a show for *everyone* manning the walls to watch!? I was going to fucking—

Control yourself!

My breathing flattened. Nothing but a reflex to take in less air, leaving more room for my shadows to lash at my ribcage with a violence that made sweat pearl around my temples. They'd been... vicious ever since she'd released her gift.

More so than usual.

I folded my hands behind my back, carefully breathing past the jealousy over a situation of my own making. I understood that, though my shadows, however, did not, threatening to overwhelm me—to make me do something truly regrettable.

To my best friend.

Maybe to my mate.

I couldn't let either happen.

In a blast of shadows, Sebian shifted and flew off, his senses oblivious to my presence. Strange, but a welcome opportunity, nevertheless.

Galantia turned and headed back toward the gate, toward me, until her eyes caught mine, widening as her feet froze to a halt. "Why are your eyes pitch-black?"

My breathing flattened further, a rush of dizziness slamming into my mind. Maybe I shouldn't have sought her out in this state, when my control already balanced on the thinnest of threads, shadows bleeding into my eyes. But that brightness...

Lands. Titles. Crowns. Kingdoms. I would give it all up in exchange for one day of reprieve in its serenity. Fuck... a moment. A minute. A breath.

"Your void is still starved." I breached the distance between us with a hurried step, desperate to siphon into her, to rid myself of this oppressive darkness. "Let me pour my shadows into your void, and—"

"No." Galantia shuffled backward on a sharp intake of air. "I don't want your shadows."

The bond yanked painfully in my chest at her rejection, my *anoa* flapping his wings, stirring up my shadows until they poured like liquid tar over my thoughts. Had I not suffered enough, goddess? Had I not sacrificed enough of my feathers, praying, pleading, *begging* you to give me my very own void, only for her to reject me!?

I stepped toward Galantia, following her retreat until her back bumped against the trunk of a tree. Before she managed to slink around it, I lifted my arm and grabbed a low-hanging branch to the right and shifted my hips to the left, caging her in.

I stared down at those trembling lips, and how the thinnest threads of my shadows drifted from my mouth into hers, pleasure spreading across my entire body. "The pain in your chest has to be severe."

"Still preferable over getting stuck with you for the rest of my life," she said, her voice breathy, telling me she was no less affected by this... symbiosis between us. "You tried to trick me into bonding."

I pressed myself against a body I remembered had reddened so nicely beneath my rough hands, only now noticing how hard I was, my cock pulsing. "Surely that cannot surprise you as much as you pretend it did. As we already established, I'm a bastard."

One who'd botched this so completely, I would never be anything else in her eyes. Why would she ever willingly give me this bond? Because she would take pity on me? Because she would dare to love me? No... I was beyond redemption.

Then why not take it?

Either way, I had her hate. But I'd much rather have it along with that brightness...

"Open up for me, little white dove." I lowered my face to hers, shrinking the distance between our lips until the air crackled with overwhelming energy. "Take my shadows, swallow them down."

"Malyr, please... you're scaring me when your eyes are like that." She tilted her head ever so slightly, slowing the flow of my shadows into an excruciating trickle as she eyed me up and down. "Your face is bleeding, your clothes are torn. You're filthy."

Filthy.

Hot shame washed into my veins, searing into my hands; the heat so unbearable, it erupted as my fingers wrapped around her throat, collaring her to the tree. Yes, I was filthy. Sullied, with no conscience. So why pretend I had one now?

I took a deep breath, filling my lungs and forcing my shadows through the gap between my ribs. They rushed out of me, slamming through whatever feeble barriers she'd erected against me at her core, and straight into her void.

They poured, and poured, and poured, and... Goddess, help me, I needed more of this. Needed this expanding brightness at my core, the lifting of these fucking shadows!

Galantia's little hand clawed into my side but did not push. "Please, just let me go..."

Never.

My bond yanked toward hers, tugging at my core, straining toward her with the same desperation my shadows poured into her, making me feel lighter, freer than I had in years. Fuck... a lifetime.

How could I give up on that?

How could I deny myself?

I pressed my body against hers until my cock throbbed at the friction, my entire being focused on that pulsing tether between us, so fragile but growing stronger with every shadow I poured into her. The sensation was intoxicating, a torrent of need and yearning crashing through me, drowning out everything else—her writhing, her wiggling, her plea for me to stop nothing but a faraway whisper.

Until she placed her palm onto my chest. "I said stop!"

Something stabbed into my chest, clawed at my shadows, and ripped a lump of them straight from my ribcage. My vision cleared, all sludge melting from my thoughts, leaving nothing behind but clarity.

Painful, agonizing clarity.

This wasn't right...

She slipped away from me, stumbling back a few steps before she lifted her chin in that defiant way of hers. "You know, I came out here because someone told me you went this way. I came out here so I could thank you for saving me the night of the attack." She spun around and stomped toward the gate, but not without glancing back over her shoulder with a snarl. "Now stay away from me."

A burn spread across my face as if she'd smacked me, shame bleeding into my veins. Owls, enemies, vicious winds... on my life, nothing would ever harm her.

Except for me.

Just like I'd feared.

CHAPTER
EIGHTEEN

Galantia
Present Day, Tidestone

T he winter sun barely clambered over Tidestone's high walls at midday, casting long, lazy shadows across the inner bailey. All around me, builders chiseled away on the sandstone ashlar with utterly monotonous *ding-ding-dings*, forcing little cutouts into my childhood home: flight holes to accommodate the constant arrival of ravens now that Malyr held the stronghold.

I shuffled my boots, trying my hardest to ignore the

rusty hue still staining the dirt and how it conjured memories I kept pushing into the darkest, deepest recesses of my mind. Crushed bodies, dying ravens, Mother dangling from a—

No, no, no. Too raw. Too painful.

Too damn distracting.

I forced my gaze upward to that cloudy salt crystal sitting at the center of Sebian's palm. "Ready."

"Remember to keep that box shut, sweetheart." Sebian's fist slammed down on the crystal with a loud crack, releasing the shadowy tendrils of whoever had offered them up so I may practice. "Do not absorb them. Resist."

I braced myself, watching the cloud of living ink spill toward me. Nearby shadows always did that, as I'd learned during a week of practice, drawn to my void like water to the edge of a fall. And that wouldn't even have bothered me so much, wasn't it for how my gift longed for even a single drop of it with the urgency of hells' parched soils...

Do not absorb them, Galantia!

With gritted teeth and trembling limbs, I breathed through a pain that blurred the lines between physical and emotional torment. I closed my eyes first, then my box. I locked it, threw away the key. Tossed the entire damn thing into the ocean of my imagination for good measure.

Sweat broke out on my forehead.

My chest curled.

"That's my girl." Sebian's praise came with a waft of his body heat, scented with the comforting traces of pine needles and the tickle of his breath caressing my temple. "Open your eyes, sweetheart."

I lifted my lashes to the sight of Sebian's smile, so bright and sincere, it coaxed a flutter deep within my stomach.

Damn him and those utterly charming dimples on his freshly-shaven cheeks.

I smiled back. "Did I do it?"

He lifted his palm between us, presenting me with those shadows that flicked in all directions, as though uncertain where to go. "I'd say that's a good fucking job."

"I have a good teacher," I said, my face close enough to his I could see that tiny scrape on his jaw where he must've nicked himself with the shaving knife. It didn't take long, however, for my periphery to register the sudden motionlessness around me. I looked over the bailey, finding dozens of eyes locked on me, and even a handful of ravens watched from where they perched on the rails that rounded the balcony. "Why is everyone staring?"

"Voids aren't a common sight these days," Sebian explained, reminding me of how, not too long ago, they'd been hunted and slaughtered. "Suspicion runs deep, sweetheart. Ignore them. They're just a bunch of idiots who probably fear you'll go after their shadows next."

Hmm, perhaps there *was* more power in being a void than I'd first assumed?

The way my cheeks bunched toward my eyes at that thought ripped a *tsk* from Sebian, before he said, "You're not planning to go all renegade on us, are you?"

His tease had me grinning. "Maybe."

He scoffed and stepped back, pulling three more crystals from the satchel tied to the belt beneath his brown cuirass, which he placed on a row of stacked wooden supply crates. "I'll shatter all three, but you'll *only* absorb the shadows from the one in the middle using your *left* hand. You're right, that one proves to be way more reliable in channeling your void. Ready?"

Shuffling caught my eyes, drawing my gaze to the

balcony on my left, where the sight of a figure leaning against a stone column hardened my stomach. Ugh... why was *she* here?

"Lorn's watching me."

"Yeah, I noticed her hushing along the balcony for a while now. Ignore her, too," Sebian said, as if that was such an easy thing to do, given how she'd attacked me—*twice*—and stared at me now. "She's trying to size you up."

Oh, sizing me up, was she? Well, that might not have worked out well for me a few months ago, back at Deepmarsh, when I'd known nothing, been nothing. But I was a Raven, same as her. Did I have powerful shadows like Lorn? No, I didn't *have* them, per se...

Apparently, I *ate* them.

"Ready," I said.

"Remember," Sebian crushed the salt beneath his fist in quick succession, "only the ones in the middle."

I waited as the shadows from the crystals bloomed into thick, swirling blackness, and raised my open left palm at it. Then, with a courage I was proud of, I opened my box, ripping the lid right off. My void gaped at my core, yanking any and *all* shadows into its unquenchable maw. The sudden suction knocked a crate off, and a communal gasp echoed all around me.

I looked at Lorn.

How was that for sizing me up?

She held my gaze for a second or a minute, her eyes flat with an odd disinterest that chipped away at my victory. Her red lips curved into a mocking, half-hearted smile. With a roll of her eyes, she turned away, disappearing into the heart of the keep. That... that was not what respect looked like at all.

Sighing deeply, Sebian shook his head. "That's one way

to challenge her for sure... one of the strongest, most ruthless deathweavers we have, who also happens to be obsessed with Malyr."

"I can absorb her shadows."

"And you might just do her a favor with that. Less work for her if her shadows clog your lungs faster than your void can take them in. Why would you do that when I asked you to ignore her?"

Because Lorn was a cold-hearted predator, and they smelled fear like bloodhounds. "She needs to understand I won't let her scare and push me around anymore."

"And you need to understand you're holding a gift that most don't trust, are the fated mate of the most powerful deathweaver, who also happens to be our prince. Not to mention, King Barat probably knows by now that you are the key to amplifying Malyr's gift," he said. "I don't have enough arrows available to mark the many people who think you shouldn't be alive. And what you did just now...? Well, that makes it tough on me to keep you fucking breathing."

My molars ground together, the way his ears visibly twitched, making it clear he heard it. "Isn't this why we're practicing? So I can keep myself alive?"

"You want to stand up for yourself and wield your power? Fine. It's giving me cold sweats, but... whatever." He stepped up to me and cupped my cheek, his eyes fixed on my mouth. "Can you at least, for fuck's sake, sweetheart... meet me halfway and not taunt death, hmm?"

I placed my hand on his, unable to hold his concern against him now that I knew how much he'd lost, and how caring for me might just return him some of his self-assurance. "Fine."

"Fine." He grabbed me by my scarf, pulling me against

him until his smirk was inches from my mouth. "I have something for you."

"What is it?"

"I told you I'm a simple man, so..." His fingers sank into the leather pouch on his belt, pulling a clanking bracelet from it with several chestnuts strung onto leather, which Sebian brought to my wrist. "I can't promise you riches or lavish things, but I *can* promise that we'll never starve so long as there are chestnut trees around."

My heart gave a couple of additional beats at the gesture alone—the fact that I had my very first, true courting gift. "Those have to be the prettiest chestnuts I've ever seen."

"Years of practice," he said as he tied the leather string shut. "Are you aware you cleared the entire damn bailey?"

My gaze flicked from one abandoned half-carved flight hole to the next, the grin that spread across my lips probably of pure mischief. "They're probably scared."

His breath kissed my lips, sending a lovely flutter through my core, more violently when his hand settled on my hip. "Terrified."

His lips descended onto mine in a heated kiss. His tongue explored my mouth, sending sparks of energy through my body. Tightening his grip on my hip, he pulled me closer, deepening the kiss as he walked me away from the center of the bailey.

"I love you," he panted, his body pressed against mine. "Love you so much."

"I love you, too," I whispered, the words tumbling from my lips before I could even think, but it made them no less true.

I had loved him before he'd went north.

Loved him a bit more with each day.

Crushed seashells crunched beneath our steps as we slipped beneath the balcony, where he walked me backward against one of the stone columns. Sebian's hands glided over my body, our breaths turning to panting as he pressed himself against me.

"Fuck, sweetheart, I didn't touch you in so long," he groaned, kissing a path from the corner of my mouth, along my jaws, and down the side of my neck. "You're healed. I want you so badly."

My mind dizzied with pleasure, numbing my senses with the raw need vibrating off his body. "Sebian..."

He growled, grinding his hard cock against me through the fabric of our clothes. "Yes, sweetheart?"

I gasped, arching my back and pressing my clit over the length of his flesh. "We're outside."

"So?" His lips moved hungrily against mine in time with the rocking of our hips, each movement setting off a tingle of pleasure that threatened to consume me. "Remember the night of the storm? When I made you come just by humping you like this, hmm?"

"Yes," I moaned into his mouth, gripping his arms as our movements grew frenzied.

"I love rubbing myself on you like this until I come," he rasped with another roll of his cock against me, the friction against my clit sending wave after wave of pleasure reverberating through my core. "Come with me, sweetheart. I want to fucking soak my breeches with my cum when you fall apart."

My breath hitched, his words fanning the flames of my desire until I was burning with need. His hands moved to my hips, fingers pressing into me as he kept us in perfect rhythm. I closed my eyes, giving myself up to the sensations completely...

"That's a fucking good girl." His breathing grew more labored with every roll of his cock against me, intensifying the pleasure until it spread, heated. "I'm about to come in my pants, sweetheart."

The pleasure crested, cold air streaming into my lungs. It broke against the heat in my core, where it seemed to splinter, sending a million shards to slice at my insides. All tenderness wilted away under the flare of a sudden pain, right in my chest. It gnawed on my ribs, burned into my scar, scraped away the air in my lungs until I gasped.

By the seven hells, what was *this*?

"Whatever you two are practicing right this moment," Malyr drawled nearby, his voice roughened by something that sent a shudder down my spine, "I daresay it has little to do with handling your void, little dove."

NINETEEN

Galantia
Present Day, Tidestone

Arms crossed behind his back, Malyr walked toward us, dressed in fine black robes, his air of royal composure so at odds with the wild flickering of shadows that swathed him. They danced low all around him, as if someone had doused him in oil and set him on fire, feeding black flames that flickered and stretched toward me.

Toward my void.

Of course, that treacherous thing answered in flares of pain that tugged violently beneath my ribs, almost as if it wanted to escape through the gap in my bones. Too many sliced through me, violent enough that I lifted a hand to my sternum, as if I could calm it.

I could not.

Sebian stared down at my hand, frowned up at me, then released me from his embrace, fully facing Malyr. "Actually, she's done pretty great today."

Malyr scoffed. "That's not what I heard the builders say when they hurried past me, mumbling about an *uncontrolled* void."

I dug my nails into my scarf, all but pinching myself to distract from the pain that swelled beneath. "It's not uncontrolled."

Malyr's eyes caught the motion of my fingers, which had me drop my hand to my side, but unfortunately, not quickly enough to keep one corner of his mouth from lifting into the most infuriating smirk. "How about you show me, hmm?" A lift of his arm, then he slowly curled two fingers, beckoning me to him. "Step into my shadows, little dove."

Dread spiraled through my belly.

A challenge.

My eyes went to those black plumes that played around his long open strands, the sight alone sending tingles into the strangest parts of my body. Was it worth the risk of losing control of my void over proving him that I wouldn't? No. That would only further motivate him to get me to bond so he may gain more power.

"Like Sebian pointed out, I did quite well today," I said. "Your concern is misplaced. I knew exactly what I was doing just now."

His smirk died at the way he ran his tongue over the

162

upper corner of his teeth, his disappointment over my refusal to be taunted palpable. "Whatever is it you have been doing? It clearly left you... aching."

Heat stained my cheeks and my heart pounded an inconvenient rhythm against my ribs. Wasn't it already bad enough that this void kept bothering me? Now he had to notice how his presence alone flared it up?

I flicked a loose strand of hair over my shoulder with as much aloofness as I could muster, then stared him dead in the eyes. "*Rejecting shadows.*"

And you... Words I didn't say, but I made certain he saw it, there in the slight lift of my chin. His stare didn't even waver, my proud declaration landing with seemingly no impact at all.

"Ah..." His posture remained regal, elegantly so, which, somehow, only caused that twinge in my chest to wring taut a couple more turns. "Your void is still starved, given how it pulls on my shadows." His attention shifted from me, to the small salt crystals that littered the ground, and finally to Sebian. "She has to be sucking you dry."

My stomach sank. Was I?

Sebian shifted beside me, and his jaws right along with him. "We're managing."

"If barely," Malyr mocked. "You didn't hear me walk up on you just now, did you? I haven't seen you shoot a single arrow in days, either. I wonder why."

I looked at Sebian. "What does he mean?"

Exhaling deeply, Sebian crossed his arms in front of his chest. "What *exactly* is it you're trying to say, Malyr? She's improving, isn't she?"

"She might improve faster if she practiced with me."

"Well, you weren't exactly around, were you?" Sebian

pointed out. "You've been busy doing... I don't know, princely stuff."

"If you are referring to how I made certain that the fallen Ravens received a proper funeral on individual pyres," Malyr said, *two hundred and sixty-seven of them,* and started organizing a *drif* so we may celebrate our victory here, then yes..." His ears twitched as if it took his facial muscles great effort to pull the corners of his mouth into something that barely resembled a smile. "I have been doing *princely* stuff, but I have time on my hands now because the remaining ships will take us exactly nowhere until spring."

"So... no rush, then," Sebian said.

"As long as her void is starved," Malyr said, his eyes briefly setting on the bracelet on my wrist, "it will be hard for her to focus on mastering it. Other things will go neglected, such as her unkindness."

"I'm trying to shift," I said.

"Yes, yes, I spotted you two holding hands quite a lot, though none of it causing a single one," Malyr said, sending another flare of heat into my cheeks that made my jaws clench. "You are aware that there are only so many tall buildings between here and Ammarett to shove you off, I take it? Besides, an uncontrolled void is useless at best, and a liability at worst."

"Useless?" That heat in my cheeks spread to my lips, making them purse around a huff of annoyance. "I *can* control my void!"

Malyr's brow lifted at my shout, as did his arm. "So you say, yet you have shown me nothing." The prince once more gave me a come-hither motion with two fingers. "Come and prove it."

His shadows expanded sideways, slowly creeping to his

left and right in writhing tendrils. They morphed and thickened, gradually forming towering walls of black around him, undulating with a life of their own, leaving merely a gap—an eerie pathway—leading straight to him.

"She's been at this since daybreak," Sebian said beside me, as if he, too, doubted my progress. "It's probably better if she gets some rest now."

Yes, yes, it would be.

I walked up to Malyr anyway, my feet propelled forward by pride, or maybe it was stupidity. The two weren't always easy to tell apart, but I refused to let Malyr's challenge go unanswered. Might I lose? Sure. But if I refused, then I'd already lost.

I stepped into his shadows.

A cage of pure blackness weaved shut around me, isolating us within its confines, the only source of light trickling down from a small opening overhead, barely enough to cut through the all-consuming darkness.

"What are you doing?" I looked around, disoriented, and with my pulse racing, the outside world abruptly muffled as if we stood submerged under a deep, dark ocean. "Let me out."

Malyr grabbed me by the neck and yanked me against him, the impact letting all air whoosh from my lungs, his voice a menacing growl against my ear. "Why don't you just sit on his cock out here in the open so the entire court may snicker behind my back!?"

I flinched at the violence in his voice, those shadows that dripped over his eyes. His grip was iron around my neck, his body hard and unyielding as he held me close. I could feel the thunderous rhythm of his heartbeat, his labored breaths burning my temple, the tremble of his hand against my spine. Whatever he'd been hiding under the shadows, the noble decorum, and the fine consonance of words now poured out of him as pure malice and rage.

"Like they snickered behind mine when you shoved me to my knees during the feast?" I barked back, for he had no claim on me. "Announce another one for the sake of a better audience, Malyr, and I might just consider your suggestion."

Not even the shadows could hide how his eyes flicked across my face as though determining if I would truly go through with that threat. "You wouldn't dare."

"No, I wouldn't," I confessed with no small regret over the fact that my heart would never allow such vengefulness. "Because I'm not cruel like you."

"Not cruel, you say?" His hand slipped from my neck into my hair, fisting my strands until the roots ached. "Do you have any idea what it feels like to see his treasures on your wrist? The lips of my *anoaley* pressed to his?"

Probably the same way it had felt when he had kissed Lorn in front of me, almost as if a part of me had known then. "You didn't seem to have an issue with the concept of sharing when you gave me to Sebian."

"I don't see much sharing being done here," he hissed. "Did you let him fuck you, hmm? Are you writhing on his cock at night when you should be with *me?*"

"What hypocrisy, considering how Cici had come out of your chambers with her hair looking tousled, right before—"

"I never touched that woman."

"Maybe you did, maybe you didn't. But you sure as fuck dressed her in *my* wedding gown!" I shouted, not believing a word he said. "What I do with Sebian is *my choice.*"

"The illusion of choice is a comforting lie that we succumb to while fate guides our every step. Trust me. I tried to avoid fate for years, only for it to end up in my arms." He yanked on my hair until my head tilted back enough for him to lick from my collarbone to my earlobe, where he whispered, "I'm not sure if you have taken note, but my shadows are growing restless, and that's never a good thing." His lips lingered against my skin, his breath caressing my neck like a winter breeze until I shuddered. "Open your void for me. Let me siphon them into you."

I clenched my eyes shut, focusing on the light blue and silver glimmer of a glass box standing in the center of blackness. I couldn't let his shadows pour into me, turning me into a brainless, moaning thing like they had in the orchard.

"Does it anger you that I didn't turn out to be a death-weaver?" I asked. "You have to be disappointed."

"On the contrary, Galantia, I am utterly *delighted*."

"I don't believe you for a second."

"I don't give a damn what you believe." He nuzzled the side of my face on a trembling exhale that sent a spark of energy into my core. "Open your void. Let me in."

"No," I ground out. "I will ne—mmm..."

A rush of shadows seeped through my clothes and into me, like slick oil spreading on water. Dark tendrils prodded and probed at the edges of my focus, seeking cracks in the delicate material of my resolve. They pushed and pressed, testing the resilience of my mental barrier, chiseling hair-line cracks into the glass of my core. One slip of focus and my void would gape open.

My entire body trembled, but I refused to succumb. I sucked in a lungful of air, sealing it behind my clenched lips. *Do not absorb. Reject.*

"So starved for my shadows," Malyr crooned, and the darkness intensified, invading my senses with a force that felt like a physical blow. "Swallow them, little dove, until you are sated. Open up. Let me in. Take as much of me as you need."

"Do not absorb," I mumbled to myself, clinging to the fraying ends of my determination. "Reje—"

Malyr's lips crashed onto mine with feverish intent, letting his tongue slip into my mouth. His kiss sent waves of pleasure radiating up my spine and around my body, igniting an insatiable fire in my core that blazed deep within me. My skin tingled and trembled with anticipation as the heat between my legs surged into an uncontrollable need.

Glass cracked.

I gasped.

"You are losing your impressive focus, little dove," he rasped, stroking his hand between my legs, letting the fabric of my dress shift over my clit. "I just want to siphon into you."

Something shifted inside me.

It was a tug—a wrenching sensation in my chest, much like the one in the orchard—as if someone had tied a rope around my heart and was attempting to yank the organ out. I whimpered, a hand instinctively clutching my chest. Was this... the bond?

Panic surged.

Summoning the last bits of my mental strength, I searched the deepest, darkest, most primal parts of my core. *Shift,* I commanded into it. *We need to escape! Now!*

A familiar tingle crept under my skin. In a blast of white shadows, we fluttered up and up, higher and higher toward that cone of light, leaving the darkness behind.

CHAPTER
TWENTY

Galantia
Present Day, Tidestone

W e soared over the cerulean-frosted landscape, our wings beating against the biting breeze with the same desperation our little hearts beat beneath our feathers. Our sharp eyes scanned the vastness beneath us, diving toward the forest, where we weaved around trunks and thorny underbrush, only for a white burst of tingles to ruffle our feathers until—

My feet hit the ground, sending me stumbling forward through the ankle-high snow. Something caught my toe. I careened sideways over a root or whatever hid beneath the white powdering, arms flailing for balance. My fingers scratched over rough bark, making me curl my knuckles until I finally found hold on the wide, thick trunk of an oak.

Limbs heavy, I leaned my shoulder against the tree, my chest lifting and falling rapidly. I closed my eyes, the remnants of Malyr's touch still burning my skin, his shadows still writhing at my core—a grim entanglement of sharp dread and smooth delight.

He had come so close.

Too close!

"Well done, Galantia," I chided myself. I should have known better than to let him taunt me. "Stepped right into his shadow trap—"

"All the hand holding, all those failed attempts at shifting." Malyr's voice, laced with venom, sickened the silence, making me swing around to where he stood before me, his teeth barred. "Yet, you seem *perfectly* capable of finding your unkindness when you're trying to escape me."

Malyr shoved me against the tree, his body pinning mine, his hands grasping at my hips. He crushed his lips against mine in a bruising kiss, all teeth and tongue, possessive and demanding. His fingers dug into my thighs, pushing up my skirts.

Anger surged through me, dashed with a flare of heat that spread low in my belly. "You tried to force a bond on me again in the orchard, didn't you?!"

"And what if I had, hmm?" One hand worked its way between my legs, rubbing, caressing, his touch sending shocks of pleasure through me that were wrong... so wrong.

"For the sake of a somewhat harmonious future between us, I would prefer for you to give it freely."

"And if I don't?"

"I don't know," he groaned, lapping at my ear before he nipped at it. "Don't put it to the test. Bond with me."

"Leave me alone!"

"On my mother's shadowy grave, I wish I was a better man and could do just that." His fingers stroked me, finding the place that made my body writhe in pleasure and betrayal alike. It built around his skilled movements as he circled the little bud through my undergarments, desire coursing through my veins along with revulsion. "I stopped looking for you years ago, *anoaley*. Why did you have to run into my arms, hmm? *Why?*" A lap at the corner of my mouth. "Now I'm like a beast trained on the scent of your blood, utterly, irrefutably, immutably fixed on *hunting... you... down.*"

His teeth pinched my bottom lip, drawing traces of iron. He tasted them with deep moans of pleasure that sent a new wave of heat through me. His hard length pressed against one side of my hip, coercing treacherous tingles into my clit, and... Gods help me, how could I succumb to him so easily? After everything he'd done?

I slammed my fists against his chest. "No!"

Energy crackled through me, splitting me into my unkindness. We dashed through the branches, and behind us, wood snapped and dry leaves rustled as black ravens chased after us relentlessly.

Faster! We had to escape them!

Our muscles burned with the strain of speed, each hurried beat sending a jolt of pain through our wings. We landed on the fence beside a mill, wood creaking under our weight. A creek blubbered past it beneath the ice in some areas, the wheel frozen, resonating the desolate air. Where was Malyr? Still behind us?

We glanced at the sky.

Nothing.

In a surge of exhaustion, we huddled together, letting creamy feathers drift to the snow.

I hopped off the fence, rounded the mill, and pushed through its oaken door inside. Dust particles danced in the rays of pale sunlight that filtered through the open window across, floating around massive wheels and wallowers that slept through winter. Presume I could hide in here, at least until I could regain my composure and—

Ravens fluttered in through the window in a dark cloud, reshaping into Malyr within moments. "Given how you are urging me to give you lessons in flight, let me tell you this: nothing quite exhausts your unkindness like shifting between forms. How long do you presume you can keep up this chase, little dove?"

I backed away until my calves pressed against sacks of stacked grains. "Until you learn to take 'no' for an answer."

"If you confuse a beast for a pet easily commanded off, chances are, you will get yourself bit." Malyr slowly prowled toward me, making me inch back until the grain sacks threatened my balance. His hand shot out, grasping my throat. His long fingers curled around my windpipe just as his mouth lowered to mine in a brutal kiss that ended with a threatening whisper against my ear, "Say it. Say *no* to me."

The moment my lips parted, Malyr slammed his mouth back onto mine. His teeth closed around my bottom lip, nipping hard enough to break the delicate skin. Warm blood spilled into my mouth and Malyr moaned, deepening the kiss, his tongue lapping up the blood.

"You like this... you always have," he groaned into my mouth as he grabbed my hips, lifting me onto the sacks of grain before he quickly gathered my skirts. His hand found its way between my thighs, pushing my undergarments aside and teasing my entrance with his fingers. They dipped inside me, quickly moving from side to side until a wet *smacking* sound resonated in the room. "It must be agonizing, this intense longing for someone you know you should reject. I know all about it. Not a night passes where I tell myself I should send you away, all while I stroke my cock to the memory of your scent."

Shadows once more streamed into me, a dark river of power that my void swallowed greedily. Delight raced through my veins, tingles of pleasure spreading throughout my body from my core. Only something wicked could possibly feel this good.

Something terribly, terribly wrong.

Malyr's fingers flicked relentlessly until pleasure coiled tightly around me, my body responding to his touch against my wishes, letting my shout come out as a moan. "No..."

He kissed a path down my chest, to my scar, where he murmured, "Moan that again. It gets me hard."

He held me in place, pressing his shoulder to the back of my knee as he crouched between my legs. In one swift motion, he yanked my skirt up over my hips and settled it around my waist. He parted me with his fingers before burying his face between my thighs.

My body quivered at the sensation of his mouth on me, sucking and licking like a man possessed. His tongue swirled and spiraled around me, seeking every sensitive spot until I was gasping for breath. Every flick of his tongue

sent shockwaves through me, making me moan louder
with each thrust into my center.

"Malyr." His name escaped my lips in a deep groan, only
fueling his determined efforts to pleasure me.

Pressure began to build between my legs, a liquid
warmth that spread out from my clit and foreboding something I wouldn't give him. Could *not* give him!

I slammed my hand to my chest, digging my nails into
my scars until it hurt, burning through the arousal of this
insanity. "No!"

Shift, I commanded my primal. *Shift now!*

My body splintered into white feathers, my unkindness
swirling around the confined space in a disoriented frenzy.
We crashed into grain sacks, bumped against walls, scraped
against rough wood as we fluttered about in panic. Feathers
bent at awkward angles, cries of distress echoed from our
throats.

Out! Out!

At last, we dashed through the open window. Snow-
flecked wind chilled our feathers as we swooped and
soared. Wings fluttered. Ravens croaked.

But not ours.

One of us glanced behind, little heart startling at the
sight of five pitch-black ravens chasing after us, much
faster than we could beat our aching wings. We swerved
right, skimming so low over a frozen lake that our wingtips
brushed the translucent ice. The ravens followed, mirroring
our every twist and turn, eating away on the distance
between us.

Lungs blazing, we banked left, swirling around the
drooping branches of a frosted pine tree in our haste. The
cerulean field rushed by in a blur, icicles on bare branches
flashing in the pale sunlight. But the black cloud stayed on

our tails, nipping at our feathers and forcing us into harsher winds that burned our muscles. It hurt too much!

A sharp gust caught us by surprise, sending us tumbling into a wild spin. Malyr's ravens swooped in, allowing our weary wings to rest in their slipstream. They guided us down to the rocky ground behind a waterfall curtained with massive icicles of steadily dripping water.

I reshaped into my human form, collapsing onto the stone in utter exhaustion. My body ached, every muscle protesting as I lay there, gasping for breath.

"Are you done running from me now?" Malyr approached, his eyes darker than only a moment ago, the white webbed with black veins. He climbed on top of me, pinning me beneath his body before he slipped his hand beneath the back of my head, lifting it off the hard stone. "Lesson two: exhaust your body too much, and you will no longer be able to call upon your primal."

His other hand tore at the fabric of my dress, kneading and fondling my breast before trailing a sharp nail around my nipple. He rocked his hard cock against my cunt with such strength, the fabric between us offered no cushion, as if he was determined to shatter every barrier that kept us apart.

My body melted into his wild, hurried rhythm, no matter how self-hatred burned fiercely in my veins. "You're awful."

"I know." His hand abandoned the torment of my breast and glided between us, where it shoved my skirts up before he quickly wrenched my undergarments aside, laying me bare. "Every shroud of darkness, every wicked desire, every single fucked-up part of me, I poured into you. You have experienced my depravity, my hatred, those suffocating shadows at my core." His fingers kept on fumbling, more frantically now. "And you liked it. Goddess, help me... please tell me you liked it."

I quivered at Malyr's words, for some twisted part of me had indeed responded to his darkness, his shadows awakening the most depraved desires in me. "You betrayed me!"

"And before I did, did you have love for me? Just a little? Just a day? Say yes. Give Sebian your kisses if you must, but at least give me that." The warm bulbous crown of his cock nestled against my entrance, already slippery with seed, making my breath hitch. "Because if you did, then what could possibly scare you so much that you keep trying to run from me, hmm? If you loved all the shattered pieces that I am, how can the goddess not have made you to be mine?"

I clenched my thighs around his hips, keeping him from entering me. "No. Don't do this!"

"Shh..." His hush came with a wave of shadows that slammed against my imaginary box, seeping straight through the glass and into my core. "Bond with me. Please!"

No. No, no, no.

I clenched my eyes shut. *Shift!*

Nothing happened.

I focused on my primal. *Shift!*

Nothing.

"Malyr!" I shouted, pounding my fists against his shoulders and arms.

It did nothing.

Not until I slapped his face with a force that ripped his head sideways, strands of hair clinging to his mouth, my palm flaring as if I'd touched hot coals.

Malyr's onyx eyes snapped back to mine, his jaws trembling, his lips parting, his teeth barred when he shouted, "You don't get to hurt me!"

Black tears seeped from his eyes.

I shuddered under his pitch-black stare, the darkness that swallowed his irises and the whites right along with it, turning him into something terrifying. Monstrous. What was happen—

He gripped my hair, pulling me up by it while he sat back on his haunches, only for a twisting motion to spin me onto my stomach. Weight settled between my shoulder blades, pushing my breasts against the hard stone. Something slung around my hips. One pull, and my ass lifted high. Pain bit into my knees.

Malyr pushed into me, stabbing through clenched muscles and slamming all the way into my shattering soul. A surge of shadows followed, slamming against my box, sending hundreds of hairline cracks across the glass. Skinny tendrils slipped through—scratching, scraping—curling around something deep in my core. Then, they tugged.

The bond!

I closed my eyes once more, focusing on the box of glass. No, not glass. Diamond! Indestructible. As black as the backdrop of my mind, so dark that the shadows couldn't distinguish it from its own tendrils. Impenetrable.

"What are you doing?!" Malyr snarled in frustration behind me, thrusting so hard, the grit and gravel scratched over my cheek. "One way or another, I will get this bond!"

With a roar, Malyr poured every ounce of his power into an onslaught against my void, in an all-out assault intended to shatter my defenses. But I held firm, my resolve unyielding. I would not open, and he would not enter.

At least, not into my void.

But he did enter my body—violently, ruthlessly.

Tears rolled down my cheeks as I looked over my shoulder back at him. "Don't hold back, Malyr. I beg of you," I bit out. "Never let me forget what you are."

His features contorted into a furious mask, shadows flaring from his eyes. Until he spotted my tears, an unknown emotion passing over his face, darkening his features and causing his entire body to tremble.

He looked down at where he was buried inside me, his gaze lingering there for a moment as the shadows cleared from his eyes, if not completely. Then he pulled out, withdrawing from me entirely before he quickly rose and turned his back on me.

I struggled myself up to sit, brushing my skirts down before wrapping my arms around my knees. Silence stretched between us, tense and heavy. Why had he stopped?

"I hadn't meant to..." His voice faded on a trembling exhale. "It is a poor excuse, I know full well, but I have little agency—"

An unkindness of ravens fluttered in, letting Sebian shift out of his shadows. "I searched *everywhere* for you two, scouting out the— Wait. Why are you crying? What happened?" He turned toward Malyr, letting his shout shatter from the rock. "What did you do now?"

Malyr walked toward the curtain of icicles that clung to the overhang. He glanced back at me over his shoulder, his eyes carrying a sheen I'd only once witnessed on him before —back when he'd learned I had played a hand in his brother's death. Except, this time, there was no hate mixed into it, leaving nothing behind for me to read but... sadness.

I shivered under his unguarded stare. "He taught me how to shift."

With a laughed exhale, Malyr turned toward a gap in

the icicles. "You have until a day before the next full moon to practice flight formations with her."

Sebian scoffed. "So much about having time on your hand."

"I want her in the air at least five hours a day," Malyr simply continued, ignoring the remark. "Every day. She needs to get her endurance up before we leave."

Sebian took a step toward him. "Leave for where?"

Shadows and feathers already swirled around Malyr, bringing about his shift, but one word lingered between the flapping of wings. "Valtaris."

CHAPTER
TWENTY-ONE

Sebian

Present Day, the border of Vhaerya and Dranada

Beside us, Galantia's ravens glided along our slipstream, occasionally flapping their tired wings, our massive unkindness casting small shadows that hushed over the landscape below. The longer we followed the river beneath us upstream, the murkier it became, the water a disgusting, disease-ridden green.

It hadn't improved; if anything, I could have sworn it was worse now than it was a year ago. Smelled bad, too.

Probably from whatever stupid animal had gotten too close for a deadly drink, now rotting away beneath the surface.

"Her muscles are weary," Malyr's voice sounded through the unkindness, something Galantia had still not figured out how to do. *"We will make camp in that copse of trees for the night."*

"We must keep our distance from the river," Asker's voice added. *"There is no saying how far over its bank it spreads."*

We dived, gliding into the copse of trees, our claws dragging through snow. Shadows surrounded me, interrupted only by Galantia, who stumbled several steps forward through the snow, hissing and cursing. Goddess help us, she was a fucking poor flyer. Something to do with her feathers, Asker had explained, which were awfully brittle. Not that I minded preening them...

Malyr grabbed her arm, yanking her straight until she steadied. He frowned at her, then frowned at me. Then, without saying a word, he released her and walked off to survey the airy forest.

I stared after him, my teeth grinding together. Something had happened behind that waterfall, and it sure as fuck hadn't been lessons in shifting. I had my idea, but I couldn't be certain. Whatever it was, the way Galantia had handled it must've done something to Malyr's head, given how he'd barely shown his face since, spending his nights alone on rooftops staring at the ocean.

"Smoother landings will come," Marla said with a pat on Galantia's shoulder before she looked over at Nathiel. "These trunks and branches should make solid columns and rafters. How about you get to work?"

The young weaver—seventeen, from what he'd told me —ran his light brown fingers through his long, black curls, his hazel eyes taking in the trees. Then, with a flick of his hand, shadows streamed from his fingers. Using the trunks for beams and the branches for warp yarn, he wove thick walls of shadowcloth. The shadows formed roofs where branches intersected or touched, creating tent-like structures throughout the forest.

"Stop gaping, sweetheart, or your tongue will freeze to the roof of your mouth," I said with a grin as I stepped up beside Galantia, her brown pelt dress enchanted with shadowthread matching her eyes perfectly. "Did you expect that any of us were willing to roost on a dead tree for a second night?"

She shrugged. "It wasn't so bad."

"Wasn't so bad?" Fuck, it had been so drafty and awful, I still couldn't turn my head to the left properly. "You might be a Raven, but it's alright to enjoy the comforts of having a human form whenever possible. I'll get the fire started." I lowered my forehead to hers, loving the way her lips immediately found mine in a quick kiss. "Help me with kindling?"

"Of course." Using her ravens, she clamped dry twigs from the trees using their beaks, piling them where I dug a pit in the snow.

"I'll go find some halfway decent wood," I said to them before I rose and walked deeper into the forest.

Asker carved spits with his sword to my left, and to my right, Marla assisted Nathiel in weaving blankets. Malyr stood ahead of me, saying something to Lorn I couldn't hear, before she turned away and flew off. To hunt, probably. My aim with the bow had been useless these days.

Probably because I had no arrows...

"I don't like having Lorn anywhere near Galantia," I mumbled as I stepped up beside Malyr, assessing the trees for potential firewood. "Has it ever crossed your mind that she might have put fire to that rope during our attack? We came back without Galantia, and you ordered Taradur to hold back on the siege weapons. Lorn isn't stupid; she knew Galantia was in there."

Malyr's gaze wandered in the direction in which Lorn had left, but he shook his head. "She wouldn't do that. Scare Galantia? Injure? Harass? All that, yes, but not kill."

I scoffed, "Lorn hates her."

"I never said she did not. That does not change the fact that she, against all my efforts to make her see otherwise, thinks she loves me. She would not do this to me."

"I sure hope you're right," I said. "She's not someone I can easily fight off, should it come to that."

"Nobody is easy for you to fight off in your current state," Malyr mumbled, giving me a concerned side-glance. "You think I'm not aware that you cannot conjure arrows? Daggers? Galantia is draining your shadows."

And my amplified senses right along with it, especially with how Malyr had made himself rare, but I'd rather have a woodpecker repeatedly stab its beak into my brain than confess how I struggled to soothe Galantia's void. "Why did you have to bring Lorn?"

He frowned at me for long moments before he looked up and down at the trees. "She is the only other death-weaver somewhat capable of controlling my shadows, and that is hardly a bad thing to have around in Vhaerya. We need her."

"Care to finally tell me why?"

"You will see," he said for the tenth time over the course of nearly two weeks. He jutted his chin at a dead birch, eaten up by woodworms. "That one should do for the night?"

I looked over the brittle trunk, some of the smaller

branches dangling on nothing more but strings of bark. "Definitely."

Malyr lifted his wielding hand at the tree. His shadows shot forward in dozens of black ropes, wrapping around the tree, squeezing harder and harder. Several cracks resonated in the forest at once, sending chunks of wood flying in all directions, but most fell to the ground by the exposed roots.

With a nod, he turned away and flew off, leaving me with a pile of wood as brittle as this quiet truce between us —yet another result of whatever had happened behind that waterfall. No snarky remarks, no backhanded attempts at getting to Galantia. No chest-pounding male aggression between us, and no jealous outbursts over the fact that his fated mate roosted with me at night.

As if he'd given up...

Unlikely.

"That wood will do," Marla said in passing, offering me a smile before she leaned over, collecting the pieces in the gathered train of her dress. "Twice, Malyr went to the healers at Tidestone, requesting a light tea of gray devil bark for the pain." A pound of her fist against her chest. "It's been many, many years, but I still remember how I ached for Asker."

My calves tensed in my boots. "Is this your subtle attempt at telling me you disapprove of me being with Galantia?"

"You are where the goddess wants you to be; it is not for me to judge her plans," she said, and there was no jest in her tone, no sarcasm. "It is simply a sad thing to watch Malyr suffer."

I stacked some of the wood in the cradle of my arm, the weight tugging heavier on my shoulder than it should. Quarrels and betrayal aside, Malyr was my best friend, the brother I never had. Had I wanted him to find contentment in a bond? Absolutely. But I wouldn't feel guilty over my love for Galantia or her choice to be with me.

I turned back toward the fire. "If he's suffering the Endless Ache, maybe he should ask himself if he deserves it."

"Perhaps he does," Marla called behind me. "She, however, does not."

My foot rested on the ground a second too long, hesitation slinking into my limbs. Galantia was in constant discomfort—no matter how she tried to shrug it off—pretending that she wasn't drawn to Malyr, that she didn't still harbor affection for him somewhere buried under her anger and disappointment. If it wasn't for me, would she change her mind and bond? Could she allow herself to fully love him once more? Would he be the better choice?

I pushed through those questions and strode back toward the pit, because only one truly counted. Could Malyr be a good mate and make her happy?

Nothing else mattered.

Not until he stepped up to the fucking task.

A good while later, Asker sat on one of the three fallen tree trunks Malyr had arranged around the fire that now crackled at the center of our group. Night had settled quickly, and luckily, the cold was bearable.

"From what the scouts reported," Asker said, "Lord Brisden did exactly as we anticipated. He is sailing his remaining troops to join forces with King Barat once more, adding several hundred well-trained archers to Ammarett's defenses, as per my account."

Beside him, Malyr shook his head, pulling strings of meat from a spitted roasted rabbit as he stared into the flickering flames. "It does not upset me nearly as much as the ten ships he took to get his men there."

Lorn sat behind Asker in a tree, her back leaning against the trunk. "Something that could be solved with flasks of oil and a few torches."

"As if he would be stupid enough to allow it." Malyr leaned over, his eyes still fixed on the fire, bracing his elbows on his thighs as he continued eating. "He took the ships far out into the ocean. Longer journey, but making it difficult for our ravens to wrestle the wind without tiring."

"There's a reason why ravens don't migrate; we're not built for crossing oceans." I tore a string of meat from the roasted rabbit in my hand and dangled it before Galantia's mouth. "Eat some more."

Fuck me, she smiled so beautifully. The way she ate from my fingers caused such flutters in my chest before she said, "You've been feeding me all night."

"I enjoy doing it." Just like I enjoyed the way she'd started to comb out my hair and tie up my topknot each morning. "You'll need your strength. Valtaris is still half a day flight away, and I know you're sore."

"I'll manage."

I gave a little nuzzle at her temple, but only until I noticed how everyone shifted uncomfortably on their tree trunks. Except for Lorn, who fucking grinned into her piece of bread. Oh, and Malyr, who stared at me through sparks of the fire, as if he was considering how much it would hurt to run through the coals.

Until he sank his gaze to the ground.

That was... not like him at all.

"Yes, well, it is a shame," Asker said eventually. "If only the goddess would have showed me. Unpredictable, like just about any woman."

Beside him, Marla *tsked.* "Enough with this talk of war; no battles will be fought until spring, anyway—too much ice in the bay of Ammarett."

Galantia cleared her throat. "Will the shadow prince finally tell us why we're going to Valtaris?"

"Sweet little girl," Lorn huffed, "don't ask questions you aren't ready to hear the answer to. Wouldn't want you to faint."

Galantia scoffed, "Goodness, Lorn, I had no idea you took this much concern in my well-being."

Lorn dropped one leg off the branch, something menacing glinting in her eyes. "You've been awfully—"

"I want you to try to lift the shadows near Valtaris." Malyr's voice silenced Lorn... and everyone else. For long moments, he kept chewing on his meat before he finally added, "Your void is deep... deeper than even my mother's was."

A laugh bubbled from Galantia's throat, slowed when Malyr ripped more meat off his rabbit, and ultimately stretched into a groan before she said, "Oh gods, you actually mean it."

Looking up, Malyr licked his fingers. "Why would I not?"

Galantia swallowed audibly beside me, running her palms over the train of her dress. "How... how much of these shadows do you want me to absorb?"

Malyr tossed the carcass of his meal into the underbrush behind him. "A kingdom full."

Nodding slowly, Asker gave a long, drawn-out *mm-hmm.* "Yes, her void is very deep and strong, indeed. The idea has merit."

"You want me to... lift a shadowy curse from an entire kingdom? *Me?*" Galantia's breathing quickened along with her heart, which had her placing her hand to her chest. "I've never even lifted the damn lid on my privy."

Malyr's gaze fell to her fingers, watching how she nervously massaged her aching bond before he lifted his eyes to hers. "Lorn and I will help you by controlling the shadows there, funneling them into your void."

"Presume it is worth trying." Asker sat up straight, his glistening gaze losing itself somewhere in the forest's darkness. "By all the stars out there, it would be a fine thing to patrol the Tarred Road once more. I have seen many places in my life, but none as beautiful as our Valtaris."

"Malyr said he wants you to try; he didn't say he expects you to succeed, and especially not right away." I combed my fingers through Galantia's strands, tattered from the wind, letting whatever shadows I currently had at my disposal stream into her void. Not much, not even enough to get her to lower her hand. "It'll be a good opportunity to test your void beyond what you've been doing so far, hmm?"

She nodded, albeit slowly. "I think I'll try to sleep now."

"Get some rest, child," Marla said, then looked at me. "Sebian?"

"Hmm?"

"In my satchel on the nest," she started. "Get the salve from there. It'll help with her soreness."

"I'll be right with you," I whispered to Galantia. "Wait in your tent for me."

TWENTY-TWO

Galantia

Present Day, a copse of trees

I let the shadowy flap of my tent fall closed behind me, my pulse still rushing through my veins. Malyr wanted me to remove those mysterious shadows I knew next to nothing about. *A kingdom full.*

How large even was Vhaerya?

I undid the laces of my dress, let it pool by my feet, and stepped out of it, clad only in my undergown. What if Malyr was mistaken, and my void wasn't nearly deep enough for that?

But what if it was?

It might return the Ravens—*us*—to our home. And wasn't that what Marla said my birth mother might have wanted? For me to fix this? To come home? Valtaris was home, was it not?

Sebian stepped into the tent, its darkness interrupted only by the orange hue that drifted through the fabric from the nearby fires that crackled throughout the camp, the tub of salve Marla had mentioned sitting in his palm. "No doubt you'll wake sore regardless, but this should help some."

"My arms and back are killing me." I sighed, reaching to the black ties on the front of my shift. "Still, I wouldn't have it any other way. Being up there in the sky, drifting over miles upon miles of land. It's... magical."

"Here. Let me do it." Sebian stepped in front of me, one hand skillfully yanking the ties wider, his eyes fixed on mine. "Sit on the blankets. More comfortable."

I slipped out of my shoes, then let my toes search for the cushiony edge before I lowered myself into the ocean of thick shadowcloth. "Why do most of you sleep in these... nests?"

Boots abandoned, Sebian kneeled on the cushions behind me, shoving my shift down on one shoulder. "For the nestlings, sweetheart."

I almost moaned at the way he gathered up my hair, twirling it around his hand before he rested it over my other shoulder. "Nestlings?"

"There's just no telling when a baby will shift for the first time." His thumb spread some of the salve down along one side of my neck, pressed deeper into my skin around the shoulder, then worked the tight, tense muscle. "Even a fall from the height of a bed could seriously injure nestlings if they start hopping around."

"That makes sense."

"You did well today," Sebian praised, his heat blanketing my back. "Never forget to keep your eyes open and always watch the skies, even the winds above you. Too many predators up there."

I let my head drift sideways, mind numbing at the pleasure-pain of his touch. "Falcons."

"Mm-hmm." He pushed my shift lower, letting his hand cup my breast while his thumb gently stroked along the sore muscles above. "Owls are worse. They hunt at night and have much better vision than us, which is why we usually roost when the moon is up."

I closed my eyes in bliss as he kissed behind my earlobe, my body growing heavy with a warm, cozy sluggishness. "There are people outside, and the walls are cloth…"

"There were people in the library, but that didn't keep you from coming against my finger that day." He cupped my breast, kneading the flesh until my blood thickened. "There was no cloth in the bailey, yet you ground your needy little cunt so nicely over the outline of my cock. Why so shy all of a sudden, hmm?"

Teeth raked along the side of my neck. Nails caught on my shift, pulling the fabric down to pool in my lap before Sebian's hand glided between my legs. Fingers stroked along each side of my cunt. Up, down. Up, down. A pinch around my clit. Gods, this Raven knew pleasure, providing it with an eagerness that put a tremble in my breath.

"Lie down." He pressed his erection against my backside, bearing down on me with his weight until I dove into the shadowcloth.

"We can't—"

"Shh." He slowly ran his knuckles up along the muscle to the left of my spine. "Did anybody warn you yet about what will happen come spring?"

I gasped at the way he ground his hard shaft against my ass with the same vigor he dug his thumb into the base of my skull, working out a knot there. "What?"

"That the bay of Ammarett will be frozen isn't the only reason Malyr is waiting with the attack until after spring. Nesting season is having us Ravens feel a certain way, you know," he purred into my ear, rolling his hips against my backside with skilled rhythm. "Once the snow thaws and those first buds emerge on the trees, all you'll hear in Tidestone are Ravens fucking, nesting, making babies. Our heads are so clouded with the need to rut, there's no such thing as shyness or even a concern for privacy."

I failed to contain my raspy breaths, loving how hard he was for me, how his breathing altered alongside mine. "What if they hear?"

"Hear what, sweetheart?" he crooned in that innocent way of his. "I'm just rubbing out that tightness."

The delicious pain continued in rhythmic circles as his hand moved lower. He massaged my waist, kneaded my hips, stroked over my thigh before he hooked into the waistband of my undergarment. Sebian pulled it down with startling restraint—and my shift right along with it—the unhurried motion teasing my nerve endings.

"Sebian," I once more pleaded. "Everyone will be able to hear..."

"They sure as fuck will if you keep talking." His weight

shifted from one side and eased down on the other. Fingers fumbled near my thighs. Leather ties slapped. "Can you be quiet for me once more, hmm?"

His cock pushed between my thighs, spreading warm slickness on my skin. Gods, he was so incredibly hard, pulsing with arousal. Sebian's breath was hot and heavy against my neck.

"Sebian," I moaned, my brain frantically searching for objections as my hips lifted, loving the way he slipped deeper into my thighs.

"Shh... I'm just working your knots out, sweetheart. That's all we're doing here as far as I'm concerned." His hips rocked into me, each thrust letting his cockhead nudge at my wet, needy entrance. His large hand settled on my neck, kneading; his thumb once more digging into sore knots as he lapped at my earlobe. "I need inside you, sweetheart. I need to come, or I swear, I'll lose my fucking mind."

My raspy breaths tumbled into the blanket, my entire being drowning in lust and desire. "Seb—"

He pressed his scarred hand firmly over my mouth, smothering my muffled pleas. He rolled his hips against my ass, taking his time to slide deep inside me, holding the pressure for a moment, making my body quake and shiver under the stretching demand of his thickness. Then he pulled back, only to glide into me again, adopting an unhurried, but no less intense, rhythm.

"I need you to come, fast and hard, for me, sweetheart." His other hand traveled down around my body, slipping through my legs, where his fingers played with my clit. "I want you to drip your cum all over my cock. Get me nice and wet until I'm fucking soaked with it. Come on. You can do it."

His fingers circled and drummed, pushed and prodded, skillfully working my body into heats of pleasure. Tingles thrummed all around my clit, spread through my core, and...

Mmm, it felt so good!

"Are you going to be stubborn or are you going to come for me?" Sebian's words were a harsh whisper against my feverish skin, his breath becoming more ragged, even as he kept up his diabolical rhythm. "Remember, don't make a sound..."

His fingers on my clit hardened, sending spirals of pleasure racing through my body, making me moan into his palm, my entire body shaking on the verge of relief. He kept thrusting, his hips pushing me down on the workings of his fingers. My orgasm tore through me like a wildfire, setting my entire body aflame. I screamed into his palm, bucking against his fingers as wave after wave of pleasure consumed me.

"Oh, I have no doubt they heard *that*, but it's hardly my fault." He chuckled by my ear, his hips faltering into stillness. "Were you a good girl and came all over my cock, hmm? If I put my mouth on your cunt right now, are you going to drip down my throat?"

He shifted his body, pulling out of me before he rolled me onto my back, and pressed himself between my legs. His head hungrily dipped down as he delved his mouth into the depths of my folds, lapping my core with wild strokes. His mouth relentlessly lapped up every drop of wetness from my burning flesh, exploring every inch of me and curling his tongue around my most intimate parts in a relentless drive to consume it all.

My body quivered and writhed, my hands pulling strands from his topknot as I rode out the aftershocks of pleasure. I moaned and gasped as he dutifully continued to lap up every drop of passion from me. When he was sated, he nuzzled his face against my belly before kissing a trail up my body, wedging his hips between my thighs.

"Have a taste." His whisper broke against my lips before his mouth connected with mine, his tongue invading to spread sweet saltiness around my gums. "That's what you taste like after you come on my cock. Delicious. Not fertile, though, so we don't even have to be careful."

He groaned into my mouth on another kiss, his hands tangling in my hair as he thrust into me again, the leather of his breeches that still clung to his thighs slapping against mine.

I reached around him, running my palms over the shifting muscles of his buttocks that hardened beneath my touch. "Your shirt. Take it off. I want to touch you."

"Anywhere you want, Galantia." He reached behind him, grabbing the white cotton before he hurriedly yanked it over his head. "Touch me. I'm all yours."

All mine.

With his mouth devouring mine, I ran my hands up along the muscles coiling around his ribcage, breathing in his masculine scent of leather and sweat. His powerful shoulders, his strong arms that had pulled me from danger many times. He was so perfectly built, all lean muscle and dense power, one side of him beautiful, the other disfigured.

It was the marred side I preferred best.

Broken, like me.

I focused my touch there, mapping every puckered rise, kissing every valley my lips reached. That was where we met, between our scars—naked, vulnerable, and all lies stripped away. It made us real, the feelings between us tangible, in a way that no farce, no deception ever could.

Sebian fucked into me harder with every kiss. His loss of control was an aphrodisiac, making me lift my hips to meet him, beat for powerful beat, rubbing my clit on the honed muscles of his body. The ecstasy of it once more rose closer to the edge of release, my body starting to tighten and clench around him.

Sebian must have sensed the change in me because he suddenly slowed his thrusts and pressed a tender kiss to my forehead. "Let go for me, sweetheart," he whispered against my skin. His hips rolled against mine in languid, lazy circles. "I'll be right there with you."

The tension that had been building inside me began to melt away under Sebian's gentle pace. I relaxed into his body, swaying in time with his rocking hips. Pleasure suffused me in waves, rippling through my limbs and tingling across my skin. When release finally came, it washed over me softly, yet completely.

"I'm coming," Sebian whispered, his cock twitching inside me, kissing me slowly as he spilled his seed. "Mmm, feel me, sweetheart. *Fuck*, the way your cunt is squeezing my cock right now..."

When the intensity faded, I took a long, slow inhale. "That was beautiful."

"It was," he murmured as he rolled onto his back and took me with him, cradling me close to his body until I nestled my head against his chest. He grabbed the nearest blanket and pulled it over us. Beneath it, he continued rubbing my muscles while pressing the occasional kiss to my hair. "One thing's missing, though."

I looked up at him. "What?"

A smirk tugged on his lips. "Put your frigid little toes under my calf."

That lured a soft chuckle from me, making me shift into a better position that allowed me to do just that. "Better?"

"Uh-huh." Another kiss to my head, then he folded one arm beneath his head, and wrapped the other tightly around me beneath the thick, warm blanket. "I love you."

"Mmm," I crooned against his chest, "love you, too."

TWENTY-THREE

Malyr

Present Day, a copse of trees

L ove.

I slammed the back of my head against the trunk of the tree beside Galantia's tent, jaws aching with how I barred my teeth at the full moon in a silent scream. No need to make them aware of my presence. What right did I have to ruin this moment where they enjoyed what they deserved? None.

"Are you warm enough?" Sebian's voice came muffled through the shadowcloth.

Galantia answered with a sigh.

An innocent little sound, full of calm bliss and contented benevolence. A sound I'd never heard from her lips, not knowing how to cultivate it because I was so... fucking... broken.

Darkness shifted at my core.

Scratching. Scraping.

My fingers fisted around the braided blue ribbons resting in my palm until the shards of *aerymel* I'd sewn onto them cut into my flesh, droplets of blood running warm over my knuckles. I needed to get the fuck away from here.

I turned away from Galantia's tent, hurried steps weaving me around trees toward the rushing river. When I reached the riverbank, I cast one glance over the foaming waters, then took three precautionary steps back.

Shadows writhed on the surface, thin tendrils clinging to the rocky soil on each side, fighting against the current that threatened to wash them away. My attention drifted to the dead stunted firs that lined the river on the other side. They had not been dead the last time I'd come here, had they?

Maybe, maybe not.

It was hard to remember, considering we only bothered flying up to Vhaerya... what? Once a year? Nothing but wasted time. I had not seen the temple or even its roof in a decade, all of Valtaris sleeping beneath shadows ever so cruel. I would not see it tomorrow.

Snow shifted with a faint crunch behind me, snapping me from my brooding contemplation. I turned just in time to see Galantia emerge from between the trees, her slender frame wrapped haphazardly in a blanket. She came to an abrupt stop when our eyes met, the shadows of the moon-light illuminating her dread, maybe even fear.

It shamed me.

It aroused me.

I turned to face her fully, and that alone caused one of her feet to shift back ever so slightly. "What are you doing out here?"

"I... I need to relieve myself, and nobody seemed to be in this area."

I let my thumb trace over the blood-damp silk of the bracelet. Why had I made it? To hand it to her and say, *I'm sorry for raping you while I tried to force our bond, so here is a courting gift for you?*

I scoffed.

Fuck, I was pathetic.

"We avoid the river," I said. "The water is polluted with shadows."

Her gaze wandered upstream as she thought for a moment. "Washing in from Valtaris."

Muscles I barely used twitched along my cheeks, too atrophied to form all the way into a smile. Of all the things enticing about Galantia—be it her resilience, her kind-ness, or her curiosity—it was her keen mind that I liked best.

She was smart.

Smart enough to reject me.

I turned back toward the river and shoved the bracelet into the fold of my tunic. It was bloodied now anyway. Ruined, just like my chances to ever bond with her, and was that not a good thing? A righteous thing? A kind thing? To relinquish my claim on her like I had said I would, so she might find happiness in life where all I could offer was darkness?

"Do not succumb to it." Mother's words echoed from the past.

But how could I not have, Mother? It was around me. Inside me. Always with me.

My ears pricked at the way Galantia dared a step toward me. "I'm not sure if my void is deep or strong enough to lift the shadows from your kingdom."

Oh, but it was.

The day I'd chased her?

I had poured such a vast amount of my shadows into her void. Just like I'd noticed in the orchard, there was no resistance, no barrier—only an open chasm that swallowed it with greed. I hadn't held back; I'd simply released, exhaled, and then siphoned everything into her without a care.

Until she'd slapped me.

It hadn't hurt; truthfully, I had barely felt it.

So why had I roughly turned her around? Why had I thrust inside her, fucking her viciously against a ground as cold as the walls of the dungeons where they'd fucked my ass bloody? Why would I do such a thing to my fated mate? The woman I silently loved?

Because I liked things I shouldn't.

And my shadows liked them more.

"I want to help," she said after a while. "If this is what can give the Ravens their home back, then I will give it my best try."

"The Ravens..." I scoffed. "You *are* a Raven."

"I've been a Raven for mere weeks, whereas I've grown up a human all my life. I've lived on both sides, and the war isn't looking pretty on either one. If this can end the war, then I will do everything it takes to lift those shadows."

"Do not disappoint me by suddenly sounding stupid.

This will not end the war." I glanced over my shoulder at her and how the moon cast a blueish haze over her bright hair. Such a stunning creature. Strange, but stunning. "Have you even been to Ammarett?"

"No."

"It stinks." Like human corruption, lies, and betrayal. "I care little about the city—care even less about the lands—but I won't rest until I killed everyone responsible for the suffering of my family."

"You're forgetting that my family suffered, too. Brisden killed my mother. His death won't bother me; however, seeing innocent people suffer will."

People who would kill her on sight, but such was the kindness I loved so much about her, where all I managed to harbor was hate. "Do what you have to do. We will fly early, so you best get back to your tent."

To Sebian.

I barely heard her footsteps in that loud place that was my head, but I sensed the way she walked away from me. As she should. I was not at all the man I was supposed to have become for her. Could Sebian be?

"Mmm…" Came softly from behind me, along with the sensation of a finger stroking along my open strands. "Such humiliation, how she spent the evening in Sebian's arms… and in front of *everyone*." A low, malicious chuckle. "Tell me, pretty Raven boy, how does it feel to be rejected?"

My muscles tensed at the sound of Lorn's voice, at the way her finger continued down my jawline, sending the hairs up along my arms. "What do you want?"

"Nothing, aside from watching you brood and suffer," she hummed in wicked delight as she pressed her hips against my backside, hand sliding down along my throat for her arm to settle across my chest. "Didn't I tell you,

Malyr? That sweet little girl with her freakishly bright hair isn't for you."

A chilling sensation radiated from the pit of my stomach, as if even my guts knew she was right. "Galantia and I are fated."

"Fate," Lorn scoffed, letting her other hand reach around my hip, fingers slipping beneath my tunic before they fanned out, stroking over the length of my cock behind the leather. "Fate is currently sleeping in Sebian's arms, sated on his cock, his sweet words, and those gentle touches that *bore* you. You want to know why? Because fate abandoned us; she tossed us into those stinking dungeons, turning us into their whores."

The shadows beneath my skin pulsed like a living force, crawling and writhing with the energy of a hundred bugs, their tiny legs prying apart my flesh as they searched for a way out. "Shut... up."

"Why? Does it make you angry, remembering how they tied you down? How they pulled your pants to your ankles? How they spit on your asshole? How they pushed their—"

"Stop."

"—cocks up your ass, stroking your hair and kissing your neck until they spilled deep inside you? How they left you behind, dripping, whimpering, *crying*? Or maybe..." Her hand gripped my cock like a vise, her fingers kneading and squeezing the engorging flesh until it was heavy and pulsing. "Mmm, yes, it makes you angry. Because it makes you hard."

I clenched my eyes shut as if I could somehow hide from the degradation, the shame of how I twitched under her touch. "I hate you."

Hated this perverse connection we shared. Hated how she teased the most contemptible reactions from my body.

Hated how I longed to escape the past and the memories of the dungeons, only for her to relentlessly pull me back, her words, her reminders, her touch a chain anchoring me to the darkness.

"I hate you, too," she crooned, releasing my cock with a slow slide of her palm, gliding around my hip and between us.

My ass clenched tight, yet my cock gave a single tingling throb that wrenched a moan from my lips. "I told you in the library never to touch me again."

"Oh, but you like how I touch you," she said with a roll of her hips. "Did she ever touch you like this? Mmm, how silly of me to ask; she's too prude for that. You're too afraid to ask her, are you not? Too afraid—"

"You will not speak of her."

"Too afraid that she will judge you, laugh at you, think you a lesser man." Her fingers stroked along the curves of my buttocks, tracing the indentations of muscle that ran down each side before coming to rest in the cleft between them. "Did you truly think your little void will pull you out of the darkness, pretty Raven boy? Take you from me? Malyr, there has been nothing for us but darkness. There will be nothing but shadows."

Shadows that coiled tighter around my heart each time she rubbed her hand along my cleft, making me moan or whimper, or both. "Why do you keep doing this to me? To yourself?"

"Why? Because you love when I remind you how they made you their woman, all weak and vulnerable. Pretty Raven boy, they called you when they fucked you. And after they forced your cum from your body? They spit on you. They laughed and called you a faggot."

I growled low. "I told you to—"

Shadows clawed their way up my throat where her other hand still rested, digging into my skin, choking me. "Such a pretty Raven boy."

I shuddered at the way her fingers fondled my ass through my breeches, drawing circles around the sensitive skin before pressing against my anus. Yes, I liked things I shouldn't... given the circumstances under which I'd acquired the taste.

Loved the anticipation of what was to come even more, which had a drop of seed emerge, thick and wet, from my crown. This had been our sick game for years. Lorn would try to overwhelm me with her shadows, and I would let her. Allow myself to go back to the dungeons, to the feeling of being utterly powerless while they hurt me.

Next, I would overpower Lorn. Yank her hair, maybe slap her. Call her a filthy whore. Then I would rape her, fast and hard, just like she wanted. Because that was what she thought she was, a whore to be used, worth nothing more than that, and certainly not a bond with her mate.

Just like I was probably not worth a bond with mine.

My chest ached at the thought.

No. No, I couldn't succumb to this.

Slap.

I flinched at the heat that spread across my cheek where Lorn had slapped me, rage pouring hot into my veins. "Stop it."

She fondled my ass faster, harder. "Make me, pretty Raven boy."

"I swear, if you don't stop right this—"

Slap. "Make me!"

Black heat surged through my veins, burning me from the inside out, the simmering resentment giving way to a roaring fury that threatened to consume me alive. My hand shot out. I reached behind me, gripping her hair in an unrelenting fist, yanking her sideways.

I pushed her onto all fours with one hand, while I sank to my knees, then wrenched her trousers down with the other, laying her cunt bare. "You are a fucking disease, Lorn!"

She laughed. "Don't hold back."

Don't hold back.

Those words cut deep and festered. The same ones Galantia had used that day behind the waterfall, their echo making my blood freeze over. What the fuck was I doing? No, no, no-no-no... I couldn't keep doing this. Didn't want to fucking keep doing this!

I grabbed her hair. One hard pull, and she slammed back against my chest. There, I held her tightly, leaning over until my face was inches from hers, my gaze locked on those pitch-black eyes submerged by her shadows. Always shadows. Fucking shadows!

"Tomorrow, you will do as you are bid. After that, I don't want you to speak to me again. Dare to look in my fucking direction again, and I will forget what you and I went through. I will personally tie you down with my shadows until your mate manages to force a bond on you so he can take you and your poisonous, rotten soul to Hanneling Hold."

The moon reflected in her glistening eyes, illuminating that single tear that rolled down her cheek. "You love her, don't you?"

Bitterness spreading across my gums, I shoved her forward, rose, and turned back toward the tents.

"She will never love you back!" Lorn shouted. "You two will never be happy together. I won't allow it!"

My feet stalled, a strange hollowness expanding in my

stomach. *"Has it ever crossed your mind that she might have put fire to that rope during our attack,"* Sebian's voice resonated my mind.

I turned around, grabbed her by her throat, yanked her up, and slammed her back against a tree until a bone crackled. "Stay away from my mate, Lorn. If you harm her in any way... if you so much as break a hair of her brittle strands, I will... kill... you."

I dropped her, then turned and walked off, leaving her behind in the darkness as I headed for the bright fire.

CHAPTER
TWENTY-FOUR

Galantia
Present Day, kingdom of Vhaerya

"I do not understand." Asker stood beside me, donning his black ravenguard armor. His hands rested on his hips, his narrowed gaze fixed on a glinting something that seemed to scrape the wintery clouds far in the distance where it sat on a mountain cloaked in black plumes. "Goddess give me strength, I have not seen the sparkling shingles of Valtaris in..."

"Ten years," Malyr marveled, the Raven prince equally

transfixed by the sight, his thumb mindlessly brushing over the black cuirass he wore under his heavy cloak. "The shadows are moving; something I thought I had noticed last night, but I was not certain until now. They are drifting south down the mountain range, which must have cleared parts of the temple."

I squinted at the unassuming speck on the horizon, whatever curious excitement I'd harbored about venturing this close to Valtaris shriveling in the sour pit of my stomach. There was nothing to see, nothing but shadows that mounted before us like black clouds so heavy with rain, they'd fallen off the sky to pile upon the earth.

"What's south?" I asked.

Malyr turned his head my way, but his eyes never truly found mine. "You."

I must have imagined that breathed reverence in his tone and cast my gaze to the shifting edges of the shadows before us, where they clawed at the snowy ground. They stretched as far as the eye could see to both sides, black tendrils coiling toward us. Or toward me?

"Why?" My void might be strong—or so they claimed—but none of the shadows at Tidestone moved toward me if I kept a healthy distance. This? This was a three-day flight of distance. "I don't understand..."

Malyr took a deep breath, releasing it all on a mumbled, "I fear you will understand soon enough."

What was that supposed to mean?

To my left, Sebian kicked against the corner of a dilapidated farm, the only indicator that people had once lived in this area. "I've never actually seen Valtaris before the shadows."

Marla tugged her black shawl over the lower part of her face. "The city itself spans the entire length of the mountain range. Even when traveling along the Tarred Road, it takes days to walk from the temple plateau to the Winged Keep."

I stepped toward the shadows, crushed seashells and rocks shifting beneath the snow, telling me I stood on a road once heavily traveled. Before me, shadows undulated all the way into the horizon and beyond. How could I ever absorb such a vast amount?

"Do not be afraid, child, for a raven can always rely on its unkindness." Marla's palm settled on my shoulder, warm and reassuring. "Getting lost in the shadows is all too easy, should they somehow close around you. Sebian's ravens will circle above you at a safe distance for guidance. Should something happen, shift and flee upward. Malyr and Lorn will be by your side."

A wave of discomfort washed over me, leeching all warmth from Marla's touch. I braved a glance to the right, where Lorn sat on a field stone, boring her eyes into me with an intensity that felt akin to daggers. She'd done that a lot all morning.

With a deep, steadying breath, I stepped toward the line where daylight met darkness, and raised my left hand.

Focus!

Shadows lunged toward me like a starved animal, seeping through my palm with such desperation, my thoughts clouded. They poured, and poured, and poured... cold and bone-chilling.

Intense. Familiar?

Yes, because they felt like the ones behind the waterfall, almost as if... as if...

My eyes shot to Malyr, immediately locking on his frown. His gaze had been on me this entire time, hadn't it? Watching, anticipating, waiting for me to figure it out.

These were his.

210

That mysterious blast that had thrown an entire kingdom into darkness? It had been him.

The shock of it nearly took my breath away.

So did the shadows.

They rushed into me in thick, relentless plumes, clogging my chest, robbing me of air. I gasped, clutching my other hand to my sternum.

"Control your void." Malyr's hand rose toward the shadows, slowing their voracious flow, strangling it into a thin stream. "Lorn, hold them back to her right. Only let through whatever you can't subdue."

"Oh, I'll subdue them." Taking a wide stance, Lorn shot her hand out, visibly pushing the shadows back a foot, where they split, becoming hundreds of little tendrils, writhing and pulsing in defiance. Her upper lip tugged into a lopsided grin as she said, "Still as stubborn as ten years ago."

Sebian shifted beside me. "What if she *isn't* strong enough for this?"

"She is," Malyr blurted before I had a chance to do so, then his gaze found mine with such certainty sitting in the depths of his two-colored irises, it sent a jolt of energy through me. It was strangely empowering, considering it came from him. "But if you have doubts, little dove, now is your last chance to walk—"

"No," I said, reinforcing my determination. "I can do it."

I had to.

And I would.

"Remember our practice," Sebian whispered against my temple, the tip of his nose nuzzling my hair. "I promise I won't be far. If you need me, all you have to do is call, and I'll be there, right beside you."

I nodded, barely noticing the flapping of wings beside

me as he left, my entire focus on my void—on that obsidian box at my core, opening by a mere inch. The pressure eased from my chest, the shadows flowing in a steady, more manageable stream that allowed me to breathe.

I stepped into the darkness, one foot in front of the other in slow, measured strides. Malyr flanked my left side while Lorn prowled to my right. Before me, the shadows thinned with each step I took, pulled into the hollowness inside me until only skinny fingerlings remained, writhing in vain against the widening swathe of daylight.

Metal armor shifted behind me, followed by Asker's voice that already sounded so far away. "She is doing it. Goddess bless her, she is lifting the shadows."

Energy surged through me.

I was doing it! I was removing—

A shadowy tendril broke from the mass, lashing out at Malyr. It whipped across his face, ripping a hiss from him, leaving bloody streaks across his cheek and chin. Before I could react, it coiled around his wrist, yanking his hand away. His own shadows... attacked him?

Malyr looked at me, his features twisted in pain, his arm trembling. "Focus..."

"I'm sorry." I shifted my absorbing hand toward Malyr, watching how the tendrils around his wrist slowly dissolved. I had to focus. No distractions. "Why are your shadows attacking you?"

"Because only a fourth of them are truly mine."

That man rarely made sense, but now was not the time to solve riddles. I passed the skeletal remains of a broken-down carriage, the vibrant colors still strangely well preserved, the red curtains shifting in the window barely faded.

"You caused the blast ten years ago, didn't you?"

Beside me, Lorn chuckled, a sound too merry, considering we were crossing blighted grounds, sending the hairs up along my arms. "Mmm, the little girl figured out your terrible secret, Malyr."

Little girl...

My pulse quickened. "This little girl is currently clearing a kingdom."

"Mmm, can you imagine what might happen if anybody ever breathed a word of this?" She tilted her head just so, her gaze merely brushing Malyr before she added through a grin, "Who will follow the prince who killed his own people by the thousands? His own father, the king. His mothe—"

Malyr sent a hiss her way. "Were my words not clear last night?"

"A simple misunderstanding, my prince," she crooned in the sweetest of voices. "I blame the way you *moaned* them."

A knot pulled tight in my chest, but I ignored the unexpected surge of... annoyance. Because she was goading me, costing me my focus, that fucking bitch...

Malyr exhaled deeply, his eyes flicking to mine before they lowered to the ground. No denial there.

Not that I cared if he'd fucked her.

I was hardly such a hypocrite, considering I'd been with Sebian, and even that damn ache in my chest wouldn't convince me otherwise. The way shadows once more lashed out? Nothing but the stupid bond strangling my focus.

I lifted my gaze to those five black ravens that somersaulted, dived, and soared, almost as if Sebian was determined to cheer me up when I just needed Lorn to quit talking. To quit distracting me.

"Did I say something wrong, sweet little girl?" Lorn mocked as she pushed back at the shadows once more.

My teeth clenched. "Shut up."

"Stop taunting her and disturbing her bond." Malyr performed a swift, smooth arc with his hand, sending a rippling wave through the shadows that slowed them. "She's losing control."

"I am not," I ground out.

Whyever would I?

I continued forward.

One step. Two. Three.

Crunch.

My gaze dropped to the ground, my breath hitching in my chest. The snow was barely a dusting here, speckling the elongated thing poking out from beneath my boot. Gray and pale, wrinkled skin drew tight over gnarled fingers that splayed out over the ground, the nails discolored to a deep brown, brittle and chipped. The hand was frozen in a claw-like grasp, reaching out from the ground.

A chill went up my spine as shadows crawled over the corpse, from where they spread out, once more thickening over a scene of death and destruction. Corpses littered the road, their final moments immortalized in chillingly grotesque poses.

Nausea swept onto the back of my tongue. "Why haven't they decomposed?"

"I do not know," Malyr said. "The thickness of the shadows might have kept them embalmed. This is the first time I'm seeing it."

My breath quickened, turning shallow as the pungent odor of decay assaulted my senses. The stench, like rotten eggs and dead mice, clawed its way into my nostrils, choking the air around me. It fogged my mind, making the world sway around me. So much death. So much tragedy. So much—

"*Anoaley.*" Malyr's voice broke through my shock, making me blink at the way shadows crept over the corpses, once more thickening. "We should turn around. This is too much for you. I can sense it."

"He can sense it," Lorn crooned, followed by a sarcastic scoff. "I told you she's too weak."

I stiffened at her words, the cold shock of standing on a corpse replaced with the heat of my anger. *Shut up. Shut up. Shut up!*

I kept walking, telling myself the crunch beneath my steps were seashells, the gray objects I wove around rocks, and the dark wisps poking out from the white drifts were nothing but rotten ropes. But no lie could disguise the sickening stench of death that clung to the air.

My knees shook with the effort of putting one foot in front of the other. Each step jolted bones gone brittle with cold. Dull eyes followed my progress, condemning me for walking amongst their remains.

Crunch.

No, *on top* of their remains.

Beside me, Lorn let out an annoyed huff, "Staring at death not quite like gazing at your reflection in a golden mirror, darling?"

My heart thrummed against my ribs.

Too loud! Too fast!

The world tilted on its axis as a wave of vertigo washed over me, every stumble sideways letting bones crunch. *Corpses. Corpses everywhere.* The thought spun around and around in my head. I was walking on corpses. *Crunch.* Bones shattered beneath my boots. *Crunch.* More bones.

Everything began to spin, the monochrome world blurring into a smear of gray and white, the faces of the dead staring at me from every direction. What was happening?

"Galantia!"

I jerked out of my stupor.

Malyr built himself up in front of the shadows that rippled toward us like ocean waves at night. They wrapped around him, slithering and crawling, leaving bloody trails across his face before they burrowed into his skin. Beside me, Lorn fought them off.

Until her eyes caught mine.

Then she smiled.

"Fly, Galantia!" Malyr commanded, ripping my attention back to him. "Get out of here while I'll hold them back. Go!"

Flee. Yes, I had to flee.

My primal croaked.

My body tingled.

Shadows wrapped around me, hot and searing, as if someone bound me with ropes tinged in oil and set aflame. They hurt. Hurt badly!

"Sebian!" Malyr shouted.

The hot shadows retreated the moment black feathers burst beside me. I slumped to the ground. Something hit my head, sending a quake through my brain. Above me, five black ravens fluttered off. Lorn?

"Galantia!" Sebian leaned over, staring at me wide-eyed as he grabbed me by my arms and hauled me to my feet. "What's happening?"

"She's not shifting," Malyr shouted. "Get her out of here!"

Sebian intertwined our fingers. "What about you?"

"They'll drag your ravens down if I let go of them now." Malyr turned to face Sebian, one hand struggling to keep the shadows away, black blood dripping from his chin and little droplets flying from his mouth as he shouted, "Save her! Save her and—"

Malyr coughed up a swell of rotten blood.

An agonizing surge of pain ripped through my chest as though I was being torn apart from the inside, fraying my life threads. A sense of loss, a profound emptiness, gnawed at my insides, as if a vital part of me was about to be violently ripped away, leaving a gaping void that no amount of shadows could fill.

I pulled my hand from Sebian's.

Darkness reached out to me, tendrils of blackness snaking and wrapping around my limbs. They pulled me, tugging with the desperation of a drowning man, pulling me into its ocean of blackness.

And I let it.

I breathed it into my void where it swelled, building, building, building, until—

Darkness blasted from me.

Then... nothing.

TWENTY-FIVE

Galantia

Present Day, a shadowy tent

The scent of blood mingled with bitter herbal tinctures assaulted my nostrils, jarring me awake. Squinting against the blurry haze, I made out two distorted figures, their outlines wavering in and out of focus. What was that slow, faint drumming sound?

No, not drumming.

A heartbeat.

I pushed up onto my elbow, the world tilting as a wave

of dizziness swept over me. I drifted forward but pressed my hand down before me to keep from falling. It was then that I felt it: warmth, along with the disjointed rise and fall of a chest.

Malyr's chest.

He lay beside me, unconscious, his breathing reduced to irregular gasps. Bloody cuts marred his features and black veins webbed under his pallid skin. I lifted my hand to his face, running a finger over his blackish-purple lips, just as my chest tightened painfully. It was strange to see him this... vulnerable.

"She is awake," Asker said, his outline slowly sharpening as he hurried to Malyr's side, where he sank to his knees with the clanks of his armor.

The other figure, who had to be Marla, shuffled toward the flap of the... tent. Yes, I was in a tent. "I will see if Sebian returned with the herbs for her tea."

I blinked Asker into focus. "What happened?"

"There was a blast that sent the shadows back far enough where we managed to drag you and Malyr to safety." He ran a hand over his braid, the entire thing tousled and crooked. "We cannot be certain, but we believe you caused it, echoing Malyr's power in an act of sheer desperation."

"Echoed? I don't remember doing anything." But I hadn't forgotten the surmounting sense of loss I'd felt at the thought of losing Malyr. "Why am I here?"

"We placed you here, in this tent, one beside the other, so your void may draw out his shadows, but..." He frowned down at Malyr, and a somber, almost fatherly look hushed across his usually stern face. "He exposed himself to their vicious lashes much too long in an attempt to hold them back."

A lump formed in my throat, thick and choking, as I struggled to find words that could possibly match the weight of how he'd been willing to sacrifice his life for mine. "Is he... dying?"

"His internal injuries are significant," Asker said with a solemn nod, but it carried reassurance, too. "Malyr will live. All he needs is time to heal."

"Why are his shadows attacking him? He told me that only a fourth of them are truly his. What does that mean?"

He pouted for a moment, the wiry salt and pepper hairs of his beard curling against his lips. "The day we spoke at Deepmarsh, you said you read about the thief who stole the gifts of three deathweavers, did you not?"

Nodding, I lifted my hand to Malyr's face, settling my palm on his cheek so I may absorb the shadows that made him look so terribly pale. "He was a Khysal, and grew strong enough that he took the throne, establishing their long line of kings and queens."

"Kædrin the Unkind, many called him, for the three additional *anoas* he gained through his thievery," he said. "Our gifts, Galantia, are passed down through generations. When Malyr revealed as the most powerful deathweaver since the beginning of our recordings, many at court believed it a blessing. Others, however, believed that Kædrin's shadows had been passed down to him were not a blessing, but a curse."

"Kædrin got killed by those shadows because they weren't truly his." My fingers traced along his cheek, careful around the cleaned cuts, his skin damp with a thin sheen of cold sweat. So that was what he'd meant. Not a riddle at all. A curse. "What did you think?"

"I thought it a blessing... at first." He sighed. "I was there when he was born, you know, standing guard outside.

He came out of his mother without a single cry, the entire chamber filled with nothing but soft croons. When he was a little over a month old, he smiled for the first time. At four months, his laughs filled the Winged Keep with pure joy."

A flutter hushed through my chest, similar to the one at the cliff, when Malyr had told me how he'd tried to steal honey from the larders, telling me about a time when he'd been so different from what he was now. I stroked over his mouth once more, over those severe lips I'd rarely seen smile and never laugh.

"He was a jolly little boy, but it all changed the day his gift revealed itself," Asker said. "That very first night, I woke to Malyr's hand shaking me awake. His shadows had attacked him, but ultimately killed his dog. So afraid was he of his king father's reaction, he made me promise not to tell. And so, I buried the dog. He had run away, we agreed we would simply say, and speak of it no more."

A piece chipped off my heart at the thought of this little jolly boy having lost his beloved pet to his own shadows. "A curse, then."

"One I witnessed taking its toll on him. With each passing day, that jolly boy faded under the weight of his shadows. He no longer laughed, and he rarely smiled. He barely played anymore, hiding himself away between books, much to his father's displeasure." A deep, sorrowful frown. "Every morning, he brought one of his feathers to the shrine at the Winged Keep in offering. 'Please make my mate a void,' he prayed. 'My very own void, who will relieve me of my shadows.'"

"Let me pour my shadows into your void," Malyr's words whispered through my memory to the sinking sensation of my heart. *"I just want to siphon into you."*

He'd struggled under the weight of this curse, hadn't

he? Had desperately sought relief in my void, only for me to deny him. Twice. Maybe more.

"For an entire summer, that boy could not fly properly because he had plucked his ravens bare," Asker continued. "Utterly, wretchedly, unforgivably selfish, his father had scolded him, such a wish was."

My heart gave a strange thud.

"I have three reasons," Malyr had told me when I'd accused him of solely wanting to bond with me to strengthen his power, *"all utterly, wretchedly, unforgivably selfish."*

If his amplified power was one of them, and finding relief from his shadows the other... Then what was the third? Should I dare wonder?

"His shadows grew stronger," Asker said. "Malyr grew... angrier, at times falling into fits of destructive, deadly rage whenever he could contain his shadows no more, his eyes... pitch black."

Pitch black.

My throat narrowed at the terrifying memory of that familiar sight. The day Malyr had ripped through my maidenhead, when he'd found me kissing Sebian, behind the waterfall... Each time, those shadow-infested eyes had foreboded his most atrocious acts.

"They are... vicious beings, eating him from the inside." Asker ran a palm over his braid, his lips pinching until they paled for a moment. "I cannot imagine what it must feel like to carry this plight for nearly a lifetime, only for it to... strip you of your agency, leaving you behind to deal with consequences not entirely of your making."

It caused a twinge in my chest, the way I could relate to having no agency, to being pushed and pulled at the mercy of another entity. "I had no idea."

"Few do," Asker replied, his voice gravelly with a depth of emotion he seldom revealed. "For the sake of his family and the kingdom, he carried his burden quietly. Much is expected of an heir... even a spare."

"It was an accident, was it not? The blast at Valtaris?"

"When your father's—pardon me—when *Lord Brisden's* catapult struck, it buried Princess Naya under rocks and debris. Malyr was... disoriented, having escaped death by mere inches. I still remember how he lifted the rock off her shattered skull, the way he trembled... That was when it happened." He *tsked*. "So much death and misery in one day, causing a lifetime of grief and shame."

My heart clenched painfully, understanding intertwining with my disdain for Malyr, a complex tangle of emotions too knotted for me to unravel. Maybe he was not the monster I'd made him out to be, but its prey.

"This will restore your strength in no time," Marla said as she entered the tent, crossing toward our nest of shadowcloth with a steaming wooden cup between her palms. She reached it to me. "Drink this. Sebian searched the forests for hours in the dark to find what we needed."

"Thank you." I took the mug, letting the sweet broth-like mixture with hints of honey run down my parched throat, emptying it swiftly. "What of Malyr?"

She knelt beside Asker, who immediately took her hand into his. "We took care of his wounds the best we could, but... there is only one who can rid him of the shadows that still infest his organs."

Nodding, I put down the mug and gave a tug on his black tunic. Shadows veined down along his throat, darkening where they spread across his chest, turning nearly black where they disappeared behind fabric. On his face, however, where I'd touched him, they'd faded nearly completely.

"We have to get rid of the fabric," I said. "Help me undress him."

When Marla made quick work of peeling Malyr out of his clothes, I focused on my own, undoing the ties on the front of my dress. If skin against skin was what we needed here, then so be it. Malyr and I had done things together in the past far more outrageous than that.

The moment I shoved my dress down, Asker shot to his feet, spun around, and strode off. "I will stand guard outside."

"Always so proper, my Asker," Marla said with a grin, then pulled the tunic out from underneath Malyr, only for something reddish blue to fall from the fabric's folds.

I lowered myself against Malyr, my chest pressing against his, and pinched the thing between my fingers. "What's this? A... bracelet?"

It had to be with the way several strands of blue silk ribbon had been braided into a loop, the ends fashioned with black clasps. Shards of *aerymel* dangled from it, catching the glint of the flames from the nearby fire basket. It was beautiful, even though stains that could only be blood speckled the fabric.

"Oh, that damn bird of his, and its obsession with ribbons," Marla said as she tugged a blanket over our bodies. "The tree outside his rooms at Deepmarsh hangs full of it, hundreds of colored ribbons dangling from the branches. Blue is his favorite."

All warmth sucked from my cheeks.

Blue ribbons were his favorite.

Not buttons.

Blue ribbons.

There had been a raven at Deepmarsh one night, who'd brought me a blue ribbon. Had it been Malyr's? Had he courted me all along? Or had his *anoa*, sensing more than its master had comprehended? Why had this one been in Malyr's tunic?

"How are you feeling?" Marla asked.

"Fine." Much better than Malyr to be certain, so I wouldn't complain about silly things like headaches or sore muscles. "My skin is burning. Probably because of those hot shadows that attacked me."

Marla stilled, staring at the fire for a moment before she turned and offered a smile. "We will return to Tidestone as soon as Malyr is fit to travel."

I turned my head where it rested on Malyr's chest, watching how the black tendrils sitting between scars from the flogging whip slowly grayed. "My gift isn't powerful enough to save Vhaerya, is it?"

Even with two of the strongest deathweavers by my side, all it had taken me to fail were snide remarks and gruesome sights that would only get worse the closer we came to Valtaris. And we'd been very, very far.

Marla's features softened. "Not without the bond to amplify your void."

The bond. Everything always came back to it, seemingly threading its way through my life.

"I always thought of it as this... ethereal thing of death-defying love," I said. "Something that comes easily."

"All the goddess does is show you the person who matches you perfectly. The one who teaches you, makes you grow, and makes you find your place in this life. It is up to both to nurture love."

I thought back on the day Malyr had sent me to canter across the meadow, making me feel more alive than ever before. How he'd broken my heart, making me regain my tears. How he'd shoved me off that cliff, knowing full well I would find my tears. In a way, Malyr had taught me more than anyone else—for questionable reasons, yes, but the result had always been the same.

Learning.

Growing.

Finding my place.

"I'm starting to feel I understand nothing of love," I said. "What it is. What it feels like. What it is not."

"Love is a mother giving up her daughter so she may live. Love is a father dying to protect her gift. Love is a nursemaid keeping a girl's secret." She stepped closer, squatted beside us, and placed her hand on top of mine where it rested on Malyr's chest. "Love is another mother giving up her life so the girl may escape death."

My throat tightened, tears prickling behind my eyes. Her words rang through me like a bell, echoing in the hollow spaces of my heart. She was right; love had been there all along, secretly woven into the tapestry of my fate with threads of sacrifices that had ensured my life. Just like Malyr had been willing to sacrifice himself today, and what did that say about his feelings?

Though, the more important question was, what was I supposed to do to ensure no death would have been in vain?

TWENTY-SIX

Sebian

Present day, Tidestone

E ven back home on Lanai, where the climate was milder, there hadn't been a single winter where I hadn't cursed being born with ravens. Why not sparrows? At least they headed south, away from this fucking cold.

I wrapped my brown cloak tighter around me as I strode along Tidestone's balcony. Below me, the inner bailey looked like a kicked anthill. Some of the older children scampered around, stringing up garlands made of twigs, moss, shaved bark, and other nesting material, getting the stronghold ready for the *drif*. For years, I'd asked Malyr to announce the courting festival. And now that he finally had, he might be too bloody injured to participate.

I stepped into the chancery, the musty scent of old books hitting me full force, along with a swath of heat from the glowing hearth. Malyr had refused to take up Lord Brisden's old chambers; instead, he'd made himself a nest on the floor here, wedged between towering shelves and framed maps.

He stood by one of the three windows—fully dressed for the first time since we'd returned to Tidestone—with one white-knuckled hand clasping the stone frame. The other, he pressed tightly to his chest, where shadows still infested his lungs. Or perhaps his bond hurt? Maybe both.

The sight pulled at my guts as I walked up to him—I knew that pain all too well. "You're up."

"Mm-hmm..." He acknowledged me with a quick glance over his shoulder, then his gaze meandered back through the window where he looked down at something.

At Galantia, to be precise, who paced a circle into the snow beside the cliff and around one of our younger female deathweavers and Asker. "I didn't know she went outside. Don't like it, either."

"I have been standing here the entire time, watching her."

"She's still not giving up?"

Malyr scoffed, lifted a brow, and exchanged a knowing look with me. "This is the fifth weaver she dragged out there this morning, trying to echo shadows."

"You think she can wield?"

"Hard to say with how fast everything went wrong that day." His entire body tensed beside me, wrenching a pained cough from him, a trickle of dark blood glistening on one corner of his mouth. "What do you need?"

The sight of that black blood slowly running down his chin ate at me. I'd seen Malyr injured plenty of times. We'd sparred, fought... hell, I'd even accidentally stabbed him with a dagger once.

But this... this was different.

He'd decided to sacrifice himself that day so Galantia may live. And maybe he would have succeeded if it wasn't for how she'd done the same for him. If that wasn't a fated connection hard at work, then I wouldn't know what was. Didn't quite know how to feel about it, either.

"Making sure you stopped pissing blood, though there's something I wanted to bring up now that you're on the mend." A tap of my finger at the corner of my mouth. "You might want to clean that."

He lifted his arm, wiped the back of his hand over his chin, and frowned at the black smear. "Shit."

"You should lie down again," I said, and then more quietly, "Guess Galantia will have to spend another night here."

The sixth one where she'd fall asleep beside him, probably not once reaching her fingers to her chest during sleep like she had with me. I knew because I'd been there, beside them, watching them all night in case Malyr got worse. With him, her void was sated.

My fingers lifted to my chest. The Endless Ache wasn't something I would wish on my worst enemy—certainly not on my friend, and most definitely not on the woman I loved. Yet here I was, taking comfort in the fact that Galantia refused to bond to Malyr which, in turn, meant I took comfort in their pain. How fucked up was that?

"It bothers you," Malyr stated plainly.

"As if it matters what it does to me." Malyr was infested with more shadows than even he could handle, and Galantia was the only void strong enough to absorb them. End of story. "Now that you're walking among the living again, what are you going to do about Lorn?"

Malyr sighed, running his fingers over his half-lidded eyes before he pinched the bridge of his nose. "That is a complicated matter."

"Complicated matter?" I barked, anger seeping into my veins at the speed of lightning. "Galantia told Marla the shadows that attacked her felt hot and burning. Yours are cold, always have been. Lorn attacked your *anoaley*, and you're saying this is a *complicated matter*?"

"It is not a problem easily solved." Malyr dropped his hand, his gaze lifting to mine. "In my current state, I am no match for Lorn, should things escalate. At the same time, I cannot draw attention by sending a small army to arrest the fated mate of the Raven bannerman who stores sixty percent of our grains and has soldiers under his command."

"Send her away."

"Oh, because I have not tried? Because I *have*. A dozen times, I sent her away, but she either refuses or returns within days," he snapped. "Lorn is fully aware of Galantia's strength, or she would have attacked sooner. I already ordered Asker not to leave Galantia's side, did I not? I have been standing here, guarding over her."

"Yeah, and nearly collapsing on your ass," I snarled. "And what if Asker looks away for just one moment? If a vision distracts him? If you can't shift quickly enough or not at all? Then what, huh? I told you back in the forest... I told you Lorn shouldn't be anywhere near—"

"Yes, yes, you told me!" He threw his hands up. "Is that

why you came? To ensure I know how terribly I misjudged the situation?"

"Misjudged the..." Goddess, drag his ass through hell. "She could have died! Lorn's shadows could have killed her. And even if not, your shadows might have finished the deed! You fucked up!"

"I know I fucked up!" Malyr unleashed his temper with a roar, shadows drowning his eyes in pitch-black darkness. "I fucked up when I was so blinded by hate, I refused to recognize my *anoaley!* I fucked up when I betrayed her, breaking her heart and trust! I fucked up when I tried to force a bond on her, my mind drunk on shadows and the urge to hurt her! I fucked up when I shoved her to the—"

A cough cut through his words, lancing straight into his lungs until a blob of black blood oozed over his bottom lip. He quickly hunched over, wheezing, letting it drip to the floor. The rest, he wiped away on the sleeve of his robe.

"Fucking shit..." I turned away and grabbed a nearby shirt or whatever hung over the chair and reached it out to him. "Here."

He took it with trembling fingers, wiping it over his mouth as he slowly straightened, but all it did was streak the lower half of his face a reddish black. The sight did something to me. Buried deep into my chest.

"I'm sorry," I said. "I just... got angry."

At him, yes, but maybe also a little at myself. I was one to talk about not protecting Galantia. Fuck, I hadn't been able to produce an arrow in... too damn long. Lorn could sneak up on us at night and I wouldn't hear shit. Our goddess might have been a cunt at times, but stupid, she was not. Malyr and Galantia were perfectly matched, the deathweaver with shadows too strong fated to the void with a hole too deep.

I shook my head at that. "You're a mess."

"I am fully aware of what I am." A wheezing chuckle vibrated his chest. "Why do you think I never, over a decade, called in a *drif*? Never much concerned myself with finding my *anoaley*?"

"Why?"

"Before the dungeons, I prayed to the goddess to let me find my mate," he said, a new pearl of blood pooling on his bottom lip. "When I came out, I prayed to the goddess to never let my mate find me... but she did. That is where Galantia fucked up. And for a while, I hoped that, maybe, we can be fucked up together. But she is... putting herself back together piece by piece. I am the one broken beyond repair."

His words tore through me, sudden and brutal. I had known Malyr for years, fought beside him, lived beside him, cursed him more times than I could count, but I had never heard him talk like that. To openly admit to whatever fucking demons haunted him, aside from those damn shadows.

I stepped up to him and placed my hand on his shoulder. "Malyr, I—"

"Once I am recovered and no longer in need of her void, I want you to take Galantia to Lanai," he said. "Find a decent estate. Many lie abandoned since the local Ravens joined the war here on the mainland, but none have been touched by war's destruction."

My guts pulled tight. "What?"

"I am dismissing you from my service, Sebian." His hand landed on my shoulder, heavy and foreboding, causing my tendons to tighten. "As for the expenses, don't worry. Send a scout to Tidestone, letting me know how

232

much you need to purchase the land, hire servants... whatever it is she wants. I will see it paid."

"What are you talking about?"

His throat bobbed, his black eyes slowly clearing as he said, "I am relinquishing my claim on her."

"You're jesting." He had to be! "How can you—"

"I forced myself on her." He straightened slightly, his gaze locking with mine. "Behind the waterfall. My fated mate. The one I ought to protect, but cannot seem to protect from myself." When I said nothing for long moments, he added, "I expected a punch."

"And you'd deserve it." But I'd carried that suspicion long enough that my anger over it was now manageable. "Tell me your shadows were at play."

"What difference does it make? I did what I did, and I was never one to avoid responsibility by crying *curse*."

"I'm just trying to understand."

"I was... furious the day I found you in the bailey, my shadows already pushing me toward the edge of my control." He removed his hand and turned back to the window. "At first, I asked her to open her void so I may siphon some of them into her, to ease my burden and regain control, but she refused. She did not trust me—not that I blame her. Things escalated when she slapped me, triggering a sort of..." A long exhale. "It does not matter. I thought on this long and hard, and I am firm in my decision." He stared out the window for long moments before he said, "Make no mistake, Sebian, I expect that you keep her happy in Lanai. The goddess knows I can make her miserable just fine without you. She's all yours."

All mine.

I waited for the tension to slip off my muscles, or at the very least, to let go of the room and return some breathable air. Those words should feel like some sort of victory, but they didn't. There was no winner here. All three of us were in some sort of pain while Valtaris remained lost.

I stared at him for a long time. Malyr was relinquishing his claim on her. He'd let her go, selflessly. He gave her to me, probably thinking I was better for her when, in reality, I'd started to wonder if she would be better off with him. How was that for a mess?

"You actually *do* love her, don't you?" Loved her so much, he was willing to give her up to ensure her safety and happiness. "None of it was feigned."

He gave a pat on my shoulder, then turned for the door. "None of it."

TWENTY-SEVEN

Galantia
Present Day, Tidestone

I sat on the wall of the balcony that rounded the inner bailey, my back pressed against a stone column, watching how Sebian aimed his bow at the target near a gate. Shadows flickered around those fingers near the string only to fizzle out—much to the disappointment of the young pathfinder girl who frowned up at him. He didn't have enough shadows, did he?

I let my finger stroke over the blue silk ribbon I'd found on Malyr, letting it circle my wrist. "Sebian."

He neither turned nor hesitated as he helped the girl adjust her bow hand, his senses dulled, his shadows drained. *Because of me.* Because of that insatiable void of mine that no one could sate.

Except for Malyr.

Overhead, the winter sun skimmed over the many garlands spanning between the restored walls, the entire sky dotted with ravens. Would the constant arrivals ever end?

As if to answer my question, three ornate carriages rolled in from the main gate, their glistening insignias signaling the arrival of nobility. Human lords and ladies, no doubt. Had Malyr invited them to the *drif* as well?

My mind went to Marla's words. Every perceived wrong was nothing but an essential right in this thing called fate —a statement I'd first shrugged off, now becoming clearer the more I contemplated it.

Without the capture by the Ravens, I would never have learned the truth about this war. Without Malyr's betrayal, I would not have shifted. Without my true identity, I would never have set out to find my gift, would never have learned of Lady Brisden's complicated love.

All those perceived wrongs had led me right here. So many people had died to ensure that I could sit on this wall... to do what? Soak up the sun? No, their sacrifices had to account for more.

That took a sacrifice of my own, didn't it?

My gaze went back to Sebian, my heart aching in my chest. I thought... I thought I knew what I had to do, but... how would that affect us? Could I bond myself to Malyr and still love Sebian? Be with him? Could Malyr accept such a

CHAPTER

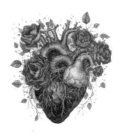

thing, or would the monogamous nature of our kind forbid it? Did I have to give up the man I loved?

I didn't know.

I didn't want to know.

I slipped off the wall, shadowcloth wafting around my ankles, forcing my eyes away from Sebian. One pained look on his handsome features, one glare of a tear in his vibrant eyes, one plea from his lips not to do it, one word about a bond bringing an end to our relationship...

My heart couldn't bear it.

My determination wouldn't survive it.

I all but sprinted along the balcony and toward the chancery. My strides faltered when I reached the stairs that led down to the bailey, but I pushed on. No, I couldn't succumb to doubt.

I slipped into the chancery and closed the door, the metallic sweetness of blood still lingering, even though Malyr had stopped coughing crimson two days ago. The Raven prince lay on his back in the center of his nest, wearing black robes, the book clasped between his hands hovering high above his face.

Malyr shifted the tome merely enough for his eyes to brush mine. "Yes?"

I clenched my eyes shut with such force, green and blue specks floated before me. This was the right thing. No! It was a perceived wrong, guiding me along the path of fate to the essential right.

Taking a deep breath, I opened my eyes, my pulse pounding in my ears. "I won't fight it anymore."

Malyr arched a brow at the speed of a snail crossing a continent. "I have no idea what you are talking about, but I do know you will *most definitely* fight it."

My throat narrowed, letting barely any of my panted

gasps through, my mind clouding. "The bond... I won't reject it anymore."

Flares of uncomfortable heat prickled up along my neck, one for each second he silently stared at me from eyes that held none of the victorious gleam I'd expected. Hells, he didn't even smirk. Had he not heard me? Had I mumbled? Gods, had I *imagined* saying it?

I rubbed my clammy hands over the train of my dress and took my deepest breath yet. "I said—"

"I heard what you said." His eyes disappeared behind the well-worn leather binding of the book once more, the rustling of a page being turned resonating in the otherwise still room. "I will not bond myself to you."

I swallowed past the restriction in my throat, confusion tangling through me. "Not until you are fully recovered?"

"Not ever."

Not... ever?

That heat climbed into my earlobes, itching worse than a head full of lice as if— Wait, what had he just said? "What do you mean, you won't ever bond yourself to me?"

"What could possibly not be clear about my words?" he said with a nonchalance that had my hackles lift. "I decided to relinquish my claim on you."

"Relinquish your..."

My nostrils flared, the heat that spread across my face morphing to first flares of annoyance, anger even. I hadn't come here with much of a plan, but if I had, I was certain it would have looked *nothing* like this.

"Gaining this bond was your objective for weeks," I said, my voice wavering right along with my sanity because this made no sense. "You've tried to force it on me several times, and now that I come to you, you... reject it? Why?"

Another page flip.

Then, unconcerned silence.

Humiliation washed over me, hot and sticky. "For hours, I sat out there, thinking, pondering, working up the courage to come here and accept my fate, and for what? Malyr, you're making me feel like a fool all over again!"

Another page flip.

Gods, this infuriating man!

"What of the shadows?" I took a strong step toward him. "Valtaris? Vhaerya?"

"It will remain lost to us as it has for a decade," he said, his tone flat. "The premise of lifting the shadows distracted me, that much I will confess. A temporary lapse of judgment. My attention once again rests on my priorities, the promises I have given to myself, the vows I have given to others."

"To kill Lord Brisden and King Barat?" I asked. "To conquer Dranada and take the throne at Ammarett?"

His jaws shifted.

Heat tingled my fingers, itching under my nails. "I lost my father. My nursemaid. Both of my mothers. They sacrificed themselves because they loved me. If I don't lift these shadows and return the Ravens their home, then they died for nothing. For that, I need this bond!"

A page flip.

And then another one.

My anger coalesced, a terrible heat building inside me. And the fact that he said nothing? Didn't even look up? Gods fetch that bastard, had he just flipped to the next page in his stupid book?

I stormed toward him, the layers of my dress whipping around me, knocked the book from his clasp, and sent it flying across the room before it thudded to the ground.

"Whatever happened to *you will get this bond one way or another?*"

Malyr shifted in a burst of shadows and feathers, only to reshape right in front of me, his sudden nearness sending me stumbling a step back until he snatched my arm, steadying me. "Whatever happened to *you would rather jump off a cliff before bonding yourself to me?*"

His sudden proximity hit me like a wave, causing an alarming shudder to ripple through my frame. The warmth radiating from him seeped through my skin, winding its way into the deepest corners of my being. I could hardly breathe with the intensity of our closeness, with the blistering undercurrent of desire that suddenly charged the air around us. Gods, this couldn't get any worse...

Then, it did.

Sebian stepped into the room, his eyes going back and forth between Malyr and me. "Did I miss something?"

Only the potential wreckage of his heart, apparently. "Nothing."

Malyr looked at Sebian and released my wrist. "Your sweetheart asked me to bond with her."

My heart plummeted to my stomach, all warmth draining from my limbs. I lowered my gaze to the ground, eyes trailing the gaps between Malyr's naked feet, the grain of the floorboards around them, the specks of dust here and there... Anything that would keep me from seeing the disappointment in Sebian's eyes, the pain, maybe even the betrayal.

Gods help me, I should have told him.

Footsteps resonated as Sebian walked over to us, his hand settling warm on my chin, giving a tug that brought my gaze to meet his. There was no pain in it, no anger, no betrayal. Instead, I saw... guilt?

I gulped. "I'm so sorry."

"There's nothing to be sorry for," he said. "It's not your fault I can't properly take care of you and your void."

"What? But... no." I shook my head. "You always give me your shadows."

"And we both know it's not enough, not nearly. I know because I haven't shaped an arrow in weeks. You know because your void is constantly hurting."

My shoulders turned heavy because it was true. "That's not why I decided to bond."

Two frown lines appeared between his brows. "Then why?"

"What if Lilieth, my birth mother, didn't only see that I would die in Valtaris, but also what I could be if I did not?" It was nothing but an idea, but I clung to the guidance it provided, the connection between a past I'd never lived and a future that was so uncertain. "Marla said that my mother always wanted me to come home. And my home is Valtaris, is it not? I'm just trying to give meaning to the death of all those who sacrificed themselves for me. What if lifting the shadows is my fate?"

The two lines between his brows slowly eased, and his features softened. "Why didn't you come to me with this? Did you think that I wouldn't understand? Would stand in the way if this is what you chose?"

"No." Sebian wasn't like that. "Because I feared that, if I came to you, I would grow doubtful and never leave you again. Would never be able to work up the courage again to bond. I guess I just... didn't want to face the knowledge of potentially losing you."

Malyr turned away from us. He strode over to the book I'd slapped from his hands, picked it up, and carried it over to one of the many shelves.

Sebian thumbed my cheek, a smile settling onto those lips he lowered to mine in a long, gentle kiss, then he straightened and looked at Malyr. "It's time the three of us talked, don't you think, Malyr?"

Sighing heavily, Malyr pushed the book into a gap and leaned with his hand against the bookshelves, remaining like that with his back turned on us. "There is nothing to talk about. My decision remains the same. After the *drif*, you will take her to Lanai."

My mouth fell open. "Excuse me?"

"Malyr is planning to dismiss me from his service," Sebian said. "He wants to send the both of us to Lanai."

"You will have an easy life there," Malyr added.

"An easy life?" When four people had paid with theirs to save mine? "No. I'm not going."

"You will do as you are bid," Malyr ground out. "We might be fated, but I am also your prince. And your prince says that you will go to Lanai."

"Do as I am bid?" Now that I was finally able to make choices of my own? The fuck I would! "Five days of flight from Lanai to Deepmarsh, Sebian once told me. I listened. I remember. Maybe another seven from there to Valtaris. I'm not going anywhere but *home*."

Malyr gave a slow, defeated shake of his head. "She *is* stubborn."

"She also has a point," Sebian said. "Once bonded, she might actually be able to remove the shadows, Malyr."

His words confused me, making me stare at Sebian unabashed. "You're actually supporting this?"

He ran the back of his hand down my cheek before he let his fingers intertwine with mine. "I'm supporting *you*, because I love you."

Warm flutters filled my chest, luring me to soak up his

words, if only for a moment before I had to face the harsh reality of all this. "Am I going to lose you?"

"You will not," Malyr ground out. "Because there will be no bond."

"Why not, hmm?" I threw my other hand up in utter disbelief. "Tell me, Malyr, why would you suddenly refuse our bond?"

"Because I am not good for you!" he shouted. "I am hateful, ill-tempered, cruel... I am all those things you accused me of." He glanced over his shoulder at me, his eyes no longer dull, the slight sparkle they carried bringing out the gray in his eyes. "I would rather suffer the Endless Ache until my dying breath than risk hurting you even one more time."

A shiver cascaded down my neck at the sight of his unguarded stare, the glisten that shone in those two-colored eyes, lending Malyr a vulnerability that took my breath away. They held sadness, regret. They made me question my perception of this man up to this point.

"I still want this bond." It wasn't like I'd come here oblivious to how Malyr could be. "Whatever... conse-quences it might bring, I'm willing to bear them."

The two men looked at each other for a long time, having one of their silent conversations I wasn't privy to.

"We made it work before, didn't we?" Sebian said after a while. "Why not see where it leads us?"

Malyr expelled a long breath. "It will lead you straight onto a pyre."

"Wait..." I looked back and forth between these men, but my gaze ultimately landed on Sebian. "Are you saying I won't necessarily have to give you up?"

"The problem isn't so much you as it is that Malyr is naturally possessive of you. Has been from the beginning,"

Sebian said. "The bond will amplify that. All it boils down to, really, is if he can control his urge to fight me off."

"It is not the control of *urges* that should concern you," Malyr scoffed, "but my shadows."

"What if you siphon them into her? And I don't mean seconds before you snap, Malyr, but every day, so you can keep those vicious fuckers at a manageable level."

"He can siphon his shadows into me whenever he wants to," I said, and then a little louder, as I looked at Malyr. "In fact, I would've let you do it this entire time, if only you'd explained."

"Are you fully aware of what you will be facing, Galantia?" Malyr finally turned, leaning one shoulder against the shelf's frame as his intense gaze found mine. "Your void will deepen. Your longing for my shadows will increase. The physical pull between us will be... intense."

"Meaning?"

"Meaning you can loathe me all you want," he said, his eyes narrowing, "but you will still want to fuck me."

A tingle pattered down my spine. "Oh."

"The desire between bonded pairs is strong, sweetheart, especially after a fresh bonding," Sebian added. "It's why a *drif* is usually held in the fall. Gives people enough time to find their fated mate, court each other, then bond in spring. You remember what I told you about spring, right? Because this will feel damn close to that."

All too well, given that foreboding throb between my legs. "We might be Ravens, but I don't think that spares us the oppressive rules of royalty in this... unusual arrangement." I looked at Malyr. "I presume there needs to be a level of discretion?"

Malyr blew out a long exhale. "Anything else would

potentially endanger any... nestlings that might spring from this. If anybody ever questioned the legitimacy—"

"That won't happen," Sebian said. "I was careful with her so far, wasn't I?"

I chewed on that for a moment, having to forego a child with Sebian. But then again, I'd spend nineteen years expecting no different than to push out titled babies from a man I may or may not have adored, therefore the jar was minimal. I'd once been willing to carry Malyr's child to achieve my goal, and I saw no reason why it should be different this time.

"But can you live like this?" I asked Sebian. "You'd be my dirty secret."

"I don't give a shit what I am out there as long as I get to love and care for you when we're among the people we trust," he said with a stern certainty that caved my chest, but it all faded with his playful wink. "I do insist on it being dirty, though." When I shoved at his shoulder, he smirked. "The more important question might be, can you handle us both?"

"I've done it before," I said and looked back at Malyr. "You shattered me into a million pieces. The least you owe me is your help in putting this final piece back into me."

Malyr stared at me for seconds or minutes. "Does this truly mean this much to you? Enough to bind your soul to me for a lifetime? For an eternity?"

I gave a resolute nod. "It is."

Another second of silence.

Two. Three. Five.

"Tonight, when the moon stands halfway between the bay," he finally said, "meet me where we first met."

TWENTY-EIGHT

Galantia
Present Day, a cliff

I stared at the reflection of a woman I barely recognized, the copper frame of my mirror glinting with the flames from the hearth across. For once, my hair hadn't been forced into those ridiculous ringlets so fashionable at the human court. Instead, intricate braids, each about a finger long, lay tightly plaited along my scalp, the rest of my hair flowing open, wild, and unconfined.

Like a Raven's.

A *bonded* one.

I breathed against the constraints of the bodice set into my gray mink dress, but all it did was provide more room for the quick beat of my heart to echo. "Why such a fuss if it's only going to be the three of us?"

"You only bond once in your life, sweetheart." Sitting behind me on a stool, Sebian ran his nails along my scalp, gathering that final strand that needed plaiting with slow, focused movements. "From here and on, we will keep your hair braided. Show the entire world that you are ours."

Theirs...

My body turned sluggish under his caressing touch, calming some of the disquiet inside me. Or perhaps it was the way I thumbed the blue-ribbon bracelet on my wrist, turning the shards of *aerymel* sewn onto it this way and that.

Beyond my door, Tidestone lay silent, save for the occasional footsteps of guards patrolling the way to my room on the order of Malyr, for some reason. Outside the window, the moon illuminated the gray swaths of snow. Not much longer, and it would stand halfway between the bay.

When Sebian finished the tie on the braid's end, I reached behind me, letting my fingers seek his.

He immediately took my hand, guiding our arms down in front of me while his chest pressed warm and reassuring against my back. Tender lips pressed against the side of my neck, kissing a slow, languid path up to my ear where he whispered, "I'll be right there with you. Yes?"

I nodded. "Yes."

"Good. Now come." He nuzzled my temple, gingerly ushering me to rise before he intertwined our hands and turned me to face him. "Which one is it going to be? Through the flight hole, or the long way around the castle?"

I looked up at those freshly shaved sides, his neat topknot, and that clean brown tunic he wore that I hadn't known he actually possessed. "Long."

"Yeah, I figured as much," he said with a smirk, pressed a kiss to the back of my hand, then led me toward the door.

We strolled through the inner bailey where a group of minstrels sat around a fire, assessing their lutes and other instruments before the *drif*, dimly lit torches casting flickering shadows over the walls. A few lonely snowflakes swirled down from the sky.

"You'll feel better soon, you'll see," Sebian said as he led me out through the gate. "The Endless Ache? It's not going to be like that anymore, so long as you're not separated for a prolonged time. Your void will be sated, too, sweetheart. No more rubbing your chest in your sleep because it's starving."

I drank him in and how the moon brought out his handsome features, huddling myself closer against his side. It took a good man to take care of a woman, but only the best would recognize what she truly needed, even if it meant embracing what he couldn't provide.

Malyr's figure formed where he stood at the edge of the cliff, his back to us, overlooking the black ocean with a line of silver glimmer dancing on its surface. Swaths of shadows wafted around him, seemingly drifting off with the breeze before they melted with the inky darkness of the night.

Then he turned around.

My heart stalled, caught in a moment between beats. He'd put on his finest tunic yet—the black shadowcloth embroidered with golden star alignments and ravens drifting between them—his face freshly shaven, his boots polished enough that they sparkled under the moon. He looked so handsome, so elegant—the very image of royalty, unable to deny his upbringing.

His eyes met mine, and I saw something in them—vigilance, worry, vulnerability—that mirrored the turmoil inside me. He was waiting, just as I was, here on this cliff, where our fates had first crossed. Where they would intertwine, binding us together 'til death and beyond.

"Wait here," Sebian said, letting his fingers slip from mine.

He walked over to Malyr, placed his hand on his shoulder, and leaned into him. Whispers went back and forth between them, unintelligible with how the waves rumbled, biting away at the bottom of the cliff.

Malyr nodded, following Sebian back toward me before he came to a stop a mere foot from me. His eyes took in my braids, and a small but sincere smile curved his lips.

Sebian stepped up beside me, cupped the back of my head, and lowered his forehead against mine. "I might not be able to bond myself to you, but I want you to know that I'm yours until the end... whenever that might be. I will forever treasure you. I will forever provide for you. I will forever fly with you. I will forever care for you."

My breath stuttered in that inch of space between us, the foreboding warmth of tears filling my eyes. "I give you the same promise."

His eyes clenched shut for a moment, then he stepped back, gave Malyr a slap against his arm, and turned away. "Do it right this time."

I watched how Sebian hopped onto a nearby outcropping, where he sat and observed us.

"Nervous?"

The sudden baritone of Malyr's voice had my eyes snap

back to his, my heart pounding against my esophagus. "Yes."

"Me, too."

Just then, the drift of the wind carried the quiet thrums of strings from Tidestone, resonating the cliff with a low, playful tune. It caught Malyr's attention, and he looked back at the castle, his eyes narrowing in thought.

"Must be the minstrels in the bailey," Sebian said and pulled a handful of roasted chestnuts from his satchel, popping the first one into his mouth, chewing around it. "Probably having a mighty good time over wine and old stories."

Malyr's gaze returned to me, softer now, before he extended his hand in offering. "May I have this dance?"

The world seemed to pause, waiting for my response. With hesitation, I placed my gloved hand atop his.

Malyr placed his arm around my middle while I lifted my palm to rest on his chest. He took my other hand into his. Then, with a firm frame around my body and a step ever-so-certain, he guided me into the rhythm of the music.

I matched his stride, our movements flowing seamlessly over the snow, our bodies harmonizing with every spin. "This seems familiar."

"Pleasantly so." His gaze wandered to my hand on his chest, his brows knitting together in a frown. "Is that my bracelet?"

I looked at where the sleeve of my dress had shifted enough to reveal the blue ribbons tied around my wrist, the moonlight glinting off the *aerymel*. "It fell out of your tunic when you were injured and we had to undress you. I... I decided I wanted to wear it."

"I thought I'd lost it." His eyes found mine again. "But it

seems as though it has found its way to the right person all on its own."

I looked down at the golden thread shaping a sparkling star on his sleeve, evading those extraordinary eyes that never failed to cave in my lungs. "It was meant for me?"

"Yes." His thumb brushed over my palm within the confines of our intertwined fingers. "One of the silken ribbons I used, I found many years ago. More than ten, to be precise, right here at the beach. It had slipped off the hair of the most beautiful girl I had ever seen."

Tremors danced around my knees as if they wanted to bend beneath my steps. I remembered that day, back when I'd seen a white seagull...

No. A white dove.

"She spun so fast down by the bay, much to her nurse-maid's frustration," Malyr continued. "When I shifted, right here on this cliff, my unkindness could not help itself. We turned and glided along the water, grabbing it with our claws before we carried it with us for reasons we did not understand. Could not with good conscience."

My fingers curled into the contour of his muscled chest, the warmth emanating from him and his rhythmic heart-beat against my palm. "Do you remember the blue ribbon you cut at the *kjaer?* The one from the strange raven?"

"Mm-hmm."

I breathed past the mounting pressure in my chest and slowly, so slowly, lifted my eyes to his. "Was it yours?"

He pulled me deeper into his embrace, our motions smooth as if we were water flowing down a stream. "Little dove, I think we both know the answer to that question now."

The air grew dense with the scent of him—winter and lemongrass—reminding me of mornings I'd spent on his lap by his desk, practicing to write in Old Vhaer. "If I recall correctly, then you threatened harm to a certain body part of the man who dared to court me. I believe the word *balls* was used... Something about cutting them off and feeding them to your ravens."

The corners of his mouth twitched, twitched some more, then lifted into what had to be the most defined smile I'd ever seen on his face. "I daresay, *anoaley*, you have been doing a mighty good job at castrating me, determined to avoid this bond at all costs."

A faint little laugh escaped me. "Until now."

"Until now," he whispered, our bodies moving as one, the distance between us measured in mere breaths. "There is no telling how fast our gifts will amplify or by how much. I would like to... pour some of my shadows into your void now. A precaution." A beat, and then, "May I?"

"Always."

Shadows swirled into me, caressing my heart before they disappeared into my void. The longer they poured, the tighter Malyr held me against him, his voice shaking with the pummel of his breaths when he said, "Thank you."

"Please make my mate a void," Malyr's childhood prayer resonated my head. *"My very own void, who will relieve from my shadows."* Maybe saving a kingdom wasn't my only fate? Maybe I needed to save its prince right along with it.

"Thank you for agreeing to my request to bond," I said, the blood warming in my veins, thickening at the languid flow of shadows.

"See it as my atonement."

"How so?"

"At first, I wanted to send you far away from me, even if it meant pain from not having you," he said, his hand on the small of my back, pressing just enough to guide, not command. "Only having you by half will bring a different kind of pain. Either way, I am sure to suffer, yet it might never be enough to make up for the pain I've caused you, everything that I am truly sorry for. Therefore, I will bear it gladly."

An act of such guilt, remorse, and repentance, it struggled to co-exist with those last remnants of hate I harbored for him. Not many. Maybe none at all. Not anymore, now that I finally understood the burdens he'd carried, the weight of shadows ever so cruel.

"How long until we leave for Valtaris?"

"I have a thousand men ready to depart at a moment's notice," he said. "Making the city habitable again will require time and hard labor."

"You will need a coronation once you take the throne. What will you call yourself? King Malyr? King of Shadows?" When he only stared at me, I said, "There's still time to come up with something. Do you think I can do it this time? Lift the shadows?"

Malyr's hand wandered from my back to my chin. "If I had doubt in your success, I wouldn't have agreed to bond."

His faith in me sent a bright energy into my core, letting it glint off those shadows that continued to pour into my void. "I think we should do that now."

He brushed his thumb over my lower lip, a gesture so intimate it drew my breath in short. "I believe it is already happening. I feel... something. Do you?"

I listened inside myself. Yes. Yes, I could feel it. There was a pull in my chest, an irresistible tug toward him—and not just physically.

Emotionally. Spiritually.

We became magnets, drawn inexorably closer until the space between us was no more. Our lips were inches apart, breaths mingling, hearts beating as one. The intensity of the moment, the surging heat and raw emotion, ripped a whimper from me.

Shadows rose around Malyr, swathing us in more darkness than the night ever could. They did not slither, did not attack. They merely streamed into me, faster and faster, demanding my void to open, to stretch, to grow.

I held tighter to his chest at the intensity of it, the superb sensation of being filled so deeply, and looked up at those eyes, widened with wonder. "Now I know. King of Darkness."

His eyes slipped to my lips. "Queen of Light."

Sudden heat seeped through me, bringing a quiver to my muscles. "What?"

"What do you think you have just become, little white dove, hmm?" His fingers trailed the line of my jaw, down to the pulse point at my neck, every point of contact burning into me. "My bondmate. My future queen." His lips brushed against the corner of my mouth. "My wife at last."

His wife.

A mix of joy and trepidation churned within me. It was a delicate balance, the urge to succumb to his skilled words and the need to protect my heart.

I chose the latter.

"Thank you, Malyr," I said and stepped out of his embrace, bringing our dance to a stop before I struggled a swallow down my dry throat. "I think I should... should go back to my room now."

His fingers clasped my wrist. "Galantia, I..."

When his voice faded, I held his gaze, my lungs not daring an inhale as I waited. What for, I didn't dare contemplate. For him to tell me that he loved me? Maybe.

"I..." Malyr looked at how Sebian slipped off the rock

and came over, then his gaze returned to me with a nod. "Yes. It's a cold night. You should head inside."

Sebian wrapped his arm around my shoulders and pulled me into the warmth of his body as he spun us toward Tidestone, then glanced back at Malyr. "You coming?"

"No," he said and turned toward the ocean once more. "I think I will stay a while longer."

TWENTY-NINE

Galantia

Present Day, Tidestone

S omething pierced my heart, pulling it up through my throat before it punched against my esophagus. I startled awake to a whimper, blinking through the orange haze the glowing embers cast over my room. What was that noise? Gods, why was I so hot?

"Shh, you were whimpering in your sleep, so I decided to wake you." Sebian's frown hovered right above me, his body tightly pressed against my side in the bed we shared, his fingers caressing my arm through my black shift. "Your void is drawing from my shadows."

Was it?

Another yank at my heart and I lifted my palm to press where a thousand daggers stabbed into the organ, right there in my chest. "It hurts."

"Come here..." Arm wrapped around my waist, Sebian pulled me on top of him, his body bare, save for his cotton trousers. "Let's see if we can get your void placated, hmm? I'll pour more shadows into you."

They trickled into me, my veins flushing with maddening heat. Arousal seared through me, scorching my spirit and setting my soul ablaze as a wave of desire swept all sensibility aside. Oh gods, what was *this*?

My mind clouding, I rocked my pelvis against him, curling my fingers into his hard chest at another pained whimper. "Something is wrong with me."

"Nothing's wrong with you," he groaned, lifting his pelvis, his cock already growing hard beneath me. "This is perfectly natural for our kind." He slipped his hand around my thigh, fumbled my undergarments down, and let his fingers explore my folds. "Fuck, you're dripping wet. How's that void doing?"

"Still hurts," I cried out, even as I kept rocking my clit on his stomach, more fervently when Sebian reached between us and shoved his trousers down enough to free his hard length.

"Shh... I got you." Hands to my hips, he guided me down on his cock, slipping into me with such ease, filling me so perfectly, it ripped a long moan from my throat. "Take what you need."

I pushed myself upright, shifting my hips as I straddled him. He pulled my shift over my head, or maybe I did... it was hard to say. My mind fogged, my senses drowning in the caress of shadows and pleasure where they intertwined at my core. Mmm, Sebian felt so good between my legs, the way his hands kneaded my breasts, letting my nipples harden to aching points.

"That's it, sweet thing," Sebian crooned, his features distorting with pleasure. "Make yourself feel good on my cock."

My body moved on its own accord, pushing against him and feeling his hips rise to meet each of my demanding thrusts. My breaths came hard and fast, every muscle in my body shaking as the sensations in my core grew more intense.

More. I needed more!

Somewhere inside me, my void gaped wide open, yanking all shadows within reach down into its endless maw. Black tendrils lifted from Sebian's skin, swirling into me, his teeth barring at the sensation. The surge of darkness dizzied my mind, sending ripples of ecstasy through my veins, making the pain a distant memory...

Until the flow of shadows slowed.

Slowed some more.

Turned into nothing but a slow trickle, threatening to leave me hollow, empty. So empty...

Dread rose, and I rolled my pelvis faster, rubbing my clit on Sebian's hard body. "More, please..."

"Sweetheart, you have me at the edge already," Sebian groaned. "Can you close your void for me? Just a little to ease the flow?"

"No..." My blood boiled and roared in my ears, drowning out every semblance of focus. I couldn't, I didn't want to! "Please, Sebian, it hurts so much."

"Shh... it's alright. Come here, kiss me." He dove his

fingers into my hair and pulled my lips into a gentle, unhurried kiss before he whispered, "I'll take care of you, I promise." His eyes, vibrant even in the moonlight, sought out mine. "This is what we'll do. Are you listening, sweetheart?"

I nodded.

"Grab the blanket because it's freezing outside. You got it?"

I dug my fingers into the nearby shadowcloth. "Uh-huh."

"Alright, hold on." Supporting my ass with one arm and pulling me against him with the other, he moved to his feet. "I'll carry you to Malyr, do you hear me?"

I wrapped my legs around his waist, which made it near impossible for me to rock against him. "But—"

"No buts. Whatever this thing is between us three, it's not going to keep either one of us from loving you right, do you understand?"

No. I understood nothing with how the cold nipped at my bare soles, my body awkwardly humping against him— chasing pleasure just to distract me from the pain. Gods, the pain...

"It hurts so much!"

"Fucking turn around and look the other way!" Sebian hissed at a nearby guard as he hurried toward the door of the chancery, and... Shadows! They seeped out from underneath Malyr's door, bringing Sebian to a stop. "Shit. This can't be a good sign. Sweetheart, I need you to absorb—"

They swirled up like a twisting storm, surging into my void. I cried out at the sublime sensation, shuddering, my whole body tingling with pleasure. The pain within me melted away, replaced by a sensation so strong, it threatened to shatter me anew.

"Did you just come, sweet thing?" Sebian asked, all but careening through the door and into the chancery.

Shadows.

Shadows everywhere!

They twisted around us like a sandstorm at midnight, all light choked from the room, before Sebian slammed the door. "Malyr?"

My void sucked at the shadows with such force, the gust it caused swallowed all blackness, streaming into me with tingles of utter delight. A chair knocked over and books thudded to the ground.

The fire in the hearth fanned into a bright flare, casting a red hue over that heaving figure that hunched over the nest of black shadowcloth on all fours, naked. Skin webbed with dark lines, eyes pitch black, shadows streaming from the inner corners like ink dripping from a quill.

"Shit..." Sebian mumbled. "Sweetheart, do you still have your head together? Because I need you to get some of those shadows off him."

Sebian carried me over to the nest and kneeled. The blanket fell away from us.

Malyr finally turned his gaze our way. His eyes fixed on where I sat, impaled on Sebian's cock. His entire body began to shake and tremble.

Then he hissed.

Sebian stiffened against me. "I am so done for."

I twisted on his hip and let my upper body fall against Malyr's. I wrapped my hands around his neck, sensing how his tendons protruded under his skin, how his thick veins pulsed with blood and darkness. The latter, I drew into my void until my head spun, trembling in the throes of their intensity.

Malyr trembled harder, his fingers roaming over my

body with a desperation that thickened my blood. "This will take some getting used to."

"Just don't kill me, that's all I'm asking," Sebian said. "She needs you."

"Is that true, little dove?" I was so dizzy from the intake of shadows, so terribly heated, I didn't notice Malyr had sunk to his knees behind me until his hand settled on my throat. One tug, and he pulled me back against his chest, his whisper scathing the thin skin on the side of my neck. "You need me?"

I couldn't stop my body from thrumming, treacherous thing it was. "Your shadows."

His thumb stubbed at my jaw, turning my head until my mouth brushed against his, shadowy tendrils wafting from his dark lips to mine. "Take them."

It was an instinct rather than a choice with how I lifted my arm behind me, digging my fingers into his open black strands before I pulled his mouth to mine. I devoured his shadows, chasing them with my tongue as I trailed along the soft inner flesh of his lips. They bled into me in a torrent of heat that seared my veins, setting my entire body alight with rapturous pleasure.

"That's it, Galantia, fill your void," Sebian crooned, thrusting into me once more. "Fuck, I love the way you're writhing and grinding on me."

Malyr groaned, his breaths fanning across my face faster, hotter, as his hand fumbled behind my back. His knuckles bumped against the bottom of my spine. Warm wetness spread across my skin each time the crown of his cock pressed against me with harsh, quick strokes of his hand.

I rolled my pelvis against Sebian, every thrust sending

splinters of delight through me until my clit throbbed. "Mmm..."

"Fuck, she's already clenching around me again. Are you going to come for us, sweetheart?" With my back supported by Malyr's chest, Sebian grabbed my hips, holding me steady as he fucked into me with rapid pulsations. "That's our good girl, coming so—"

I threw my head back with a scream, my body tensing and convulsing as another orgasm tore through me with a force that shook my soul. That was when it happened again. Shadows swelled... building, building, building, until—

Darkness blasted from me.

Wood splintered.

Parchment rustled.

Something cut the side of my neck, ripping a hiss from me, only for a storm of book pages to flurry past. What... what was happening?

Sebian's hips stalled, his pupils flitting across the room. "The fuck was that?"

Behind me, Malyr tensed, only the sound of his grunts filling the room as his seed splashed warm against my back, which his fingers hurriedly spread across my ass. "She's wielding my shadows."

"Echoing?"

Malyr chuckled. "No. Stealing."

"Fire," Sebian growled, his eyes going to those blazing book pages on the ground before the hearth. "Fucking shit, she's going to burn the entire castle down. Malyr!"

"I got it." Malyr flicked his hand toward the flames, letting a dense blanket of shadows choke them out. His cum-dripping fingers settled wet on my cheek, two of them pushing past my lips and into my mouth, spreading the salty tang across my tongue as he whispered against my ear, "Little dove, are you trying to get us all killed? Do you know what happens to out-of-control thieves?"

"They get tied up." Sebian fisted my hair. He pushed me off him, turned me around by my strands, and shoved me down until my face dove into the velvety softness of Malyr's nest. "Bind her hands!"

I gasped into the fibers. "What!?"

Icy ropes wrapped around my wrists. One pull, and they yanked my arms behind my back. Someone arranged my fingers to intertwine, one palm pressed against the other while shadows bound them.

"Sorry, sweetheart, we'll take care of you, but we can't take chances." Sebian reached across my chest, pulling me up by it until my bound arm pressed against his body and my head rested in the crook of his neck. "If you keep wielding like this, there won't be a single stone left standing once we're done fucking you."

Malyr scooted in front of me, his eyes two black orbs that sent shadows feathering across his face. "Did you come inside her?"

"Didn't get the chance."

"If you think I have it in me to let you back in there tonight, then you are courting death."

"Didn't expect any different," Sebian said. "I'll squeeze myself into this, don't you worry."

"Keep an eye on her wielding hand." Malyr's fingers clasped my chin like a vise before he slammed his lips to mine, letting another gust of tingles storm through my core until I moaned into his mouth.

Sebian wedged his knee between my thighs, forcing my legs apart before he inched me into Malyr's arm with a push of his cock against my backside. "Be good for us and let those shadows stream from one hand into the other. Simple. Safe."

Releasing my chin without breaking the kiss, Malyr reached one arm behind him, bracing against the way he sat and stretched his legs out. He pulled me to straddle him before his hand lowered to the base of his once more hardening cock, letting his damp crown rub against my slit.

Sebian grabbed my hips, pushing me down on Malyr's length. "Take his cock, sweetheart. Feel your mate inside you, hard and so fucking ready to fill you. To put a little baby in your belly."

Malyr released a long, drawn-out groan.

When my muscles tensed, Sebian let his whisper play around my temple. "I swear, he sounds as if he really likes the idea of breeding you. Should I tell him that you're not fertile tonight, sweetheart? Or should we make that our little secret, hmm?"

My body trembled and quaked with each additional inch of Malyr's cock, a savage pulse of pleasure coursing through me. I gasped as my insides stretched for his thick length, the pressure building until it was almost too much to bear, leaving me in a trance-like state between pain and pleasure.

Sebian nudged his cock at my asshole, circling it, spreading the cum Malyr had left there. "Shh... you had him in there before. It's my turn now."

Every single muscle in my body snapped tight at the way he pushed upward, the sting around the clenching muscle too biting. "It's too much."

"It's exactly what you need tonight," Sebian grunted as he forced himself deeper, along the immense pressure of Malyr's thrusting cock, ripping a whimper from me. "Distract her."

Malyr collared my throat. His lips crushed against mine with a ravenous hunger, savoring my bottom lip between his teeth before he chomped down. The metallic tang of blood spread on my tongue, and each moan of pleasure I released was met with a stream of shadows—black whirls that had my clit pulsating.

"I want your ass, sweetheart," Sebian rasped by my ear, sinking deeper into me, the shadow-veiled sting morphing into pleasant heat. "You said you could handle us both. Show me. Let me fuck your ass while Malyr keeps fucking your cunt." At his next thrust, he groaned, a deeply masculine sound that sent little tremors through my lower belly. "That's it. Damn, isn't she being good for us, Malyr?"

Malyr kissed me, deep and drinking, his strong hips thrusting upward into me. "She is perfect."

A passionate embrace swept through the three of us, our bodies moving in perfect unison. Sebian thrust deeper and harder into me, driving me mad with pleasure while I felt Malyr's body beneath me, his rock-hard body pressing against my clit with every stroke. His hips surged upward, raising me on a tide of ecstatic bliss as our lips met in a kiss of blood and shadows. I arched my back, letting out a low moan as I gasped for air, feeling Sebian pulsing deep within me as I sank back down on his cock.

We moved in perfect sync, every shared motion driving me closer and closer to the edge of release. Two cocks moved within me, thrusting at different angles and in alternating intensity, fucking me with an unbridled ferocity that made my bones quiver and my breath catch.

Sebian's breaths grew deeper, louder, and his hand shifted to my breast, where he kneaded the flesh and pinched the nipple. "She's close."

"I know," Malyr groaned into my mouth, his fingers flexing around my throat. "Come for us. Come *now*."

When another surge of shadows flowed into me, a guttural moan wedged from my throat. I came hard, my muscles clenching around them both. They grunted in pleasure and thrust faster, harder, fucking me into oblivion. A black rift tore open inside me.

My wrists released.

My arms fell forward. Another blast of shadows rippled through the room before my hands gripped Malyr's shoulders. Wood cracked. A map fell off the wall. A storm of papers followed.

Malyr tore his mouth away with a hiss, shuddering as he released inside me, his shaft throbbing against my muscles with each spurt of seed. "Grab her arms!"

Another warm wash filled my ass as Sebian grunted, his hips stuttering behind me just as he grabbed my arms and yanked them behind my back, pressing my palms together. "Fire..."

Malyr cupped the back of my head and pulled my forehead against his, then he lifted his hand toward the blazing curtain. "I got it."

THIRTY

Malyr

Present Day, Tidestone

At some point during the night, Galantia's gift must have gone through a spurt of tremendous growth while she'd slept, pulling on shadows many rooms over. Or so Asker had reported about an hour ago, when he'd stumbled in here, finding two Ravens buried deep inside the void responsible for the nighttime mayhem. I'd never seen him bow and back out of a room—one on fire, no less—as quickly as he had.

I turned my head, looking at where Galantia pulled little gasps of air through her slightly parted lips while she slept, her hair so bright, her face so peaceful. So beautiful it ached my heart.

Even though my gift pulsed at my core with newfound strength, it had taken me a tremendous amount of shadows to fill her void. And not even to the brim, merely to a point where she'd managed to regain some control over it, leaving me behind with a sense of... how could I say?

Calm? No, not strong enough.

Serenity?

I'd once erased that word from my vocabulary, but it now encapsulated my entire being. Nothing scratched, nothing scraped. I simply lay in our nest beside the only thief currently known to exist, my chest not infested with shadows, all gloom lifted from my mind. When was the last time I'd felt this light and carefree? Fourteen years ago? Sixteen? Eighteen?

I couldn't even say.

Once we returned to Valtaris, I would pluck a flight feather and offer it at the shrine by the Winged Keep. Nothing less would do, given how the goddess had indeed heard my prayers, gifting me my perfect counterpart—the void to my shadows, the light to my darkness. Galantia was everything I always wanted... even if she didn't fully want me back.

I folded my arm beneath my head, shifting like I had for what felt like hours, unable to sleep with how strangely well I felt. Never again did I want it to be otherwise. Never again did I want to return to that darkness. Now, how to ensure I never again would...?

My heart turned heavy.

I think I knew.

First specks of pink filtered in through the eastern window, but the soft hue did nothing to camouflage the absolute destruction of the room. Shadow ropes, as it turned out, could not hold my *anoaley*. And so, we'd tied her wrists with shreds of cotton from Sebian's trousers, her folded hands resting on the easy rise and fall of her chest. Behind her, only two out of twelve shelves had survived, and probably not a single book. Neither the maps nor the furniture had suffered great losses, but the biting scent of smoke might never leave this room.

The muscles around my mouth twitched into something I liked to imagine was a smile. She would undoubtedly drag one deathweaver after another out onto an open field, practicing for hours to steal shadows and wield them at her will. Most likely before breakfast.

Just as my gaze returned to Galantia, it caught with Sebian's, who smirked at me for long seconds before he finally said, "Maybe we should have water buckets ready next time... just in case."

A low chuckle rumbled in my chest. "I'll bring the rope, you bring the armor."

His eyes shone with jest before his face relaxed into something more serious. "How difficult is it? Sharing your bondmate?"

"It doesn't matter. I profited off her feelings for you. I can hardly complain if there are some dues to be paid now." Maybe one day, I would manage to settle the debt. "What aches me is that, right now, under this blanket, I am sure she has her toes wedged beneath *your* calf, not mine. As much as we may share her body, in matters of the heart, there will always be an inequality."

He held my gaze, a frown forming on his mouth. "Do you remember your very first flight?"

"Of course."

"It was the best feeling I ever had in my life... nothing compared. Until I broke a fucking rib when my unkindness slammed against the face of the cliff," he said. "Ever had a broken rib? It's so excruciating, you can't even breathe without pain. Once it healed, I wanted to fly again so badly. I didn't, though, telling everyone that it really wasn't that great. Because I was terrified of getting myself hurt again." A long exhale. "What I'm trying to say is that Galantia never knew love. And when it came, it was the best feeling, until it broke her heart. Now she's scared of getting hurt again."

My eyes wandered to the broken shelf behind him. "I seem to fail in understanding your point."

"Without love, you would never have managed to hurt her the way you did in the first place," he said. "That urge to fly? It doesn't go away; it's always there. We just do a great job of telling ourselves it isn't. That work? Or do I have to spell it out for you?"

I shook my head. It wasn't that I didn't understand, but simply couldn't imagine that Galantia still harbored any warm feelings for me. Limerence and lust? Yes, but that was the bond, not love.

Sebian let out a long exhale. "You need to tell her how you feel, Malyr."

I'd tried after the bonding, only to realize that my heart wasn't in the condition to brave her potential response. Her rejection. "Words..."

"What do you think? How many times had someone told her *I love you* in her past, hmm? My guess is zero. Maybe that nursemaid of hers, but at the end of the day, those people are hired help. Words happen to mean a lot to your little dove. *Use them.* You know how."

I shoved the blanket off me, rose, and went hunting for my clothes in this mess of singed book pages spilled about the room. "Her void should trouble her no more. Not for a few days, I would assume."

"Where are you going?"

"There is something I have to do." I grabbed the nearest shirt before I slipped into it, along with my discarded breeches. "I won't be long."

"You should stay and take care of her," he said. "You are bonded now, Malyr. You have to do better."

"And I will." Starting now, ensuring that I would forever revel in her light, even if it took the occasional darkness to protect it. "Nobody can know she is a thief, aside from those we trust—too much fear and ignorance about it. Do you understand?"

He gave a curt nod. "Whatever keeps her safe."

I shifted into my unkindness.

We dashed through the flight hole and out into the cold winter morning, spreading our wings. We banked right, circling a castle deep asleep, aside from the few servants setting up for the *drif*. Then, we slipped through the gap between two towers, slowing our speed before we drifted through another flight hole and back into the warmth.

I reshaped in the center of the sizable room, the hearth holding only glowing embers, just about every furniture piece covered in leather corsets of different styles. She'd always been messy, pretending to be unconcerned about how the world perceived her, and perhaps that afforded her a ruthlessness that had always surpassed my own.

My naked soles made no sound as I walked over to where Lorn slept in her little nest beside the hearth. Yet another farce, how she hoarded the softest blankets while she curled a disgusted lip at just about any snot-covered child, pretending that her barrenness was a choice rather than the result of that shift by the cliff when she was pregnant.

I sat beside her, running my fingers through black strands I'd caressed a hundred times. Ardently after we'd escaped the dungeons, more and more roughly after we lost our true virginity to each other, only for it all to rot into yanking it until she screamed.

"Lorn." I gave a little shove at her shoulder. "Wake up."

She blinked her eyes open and frowned at me. "Malyr? What... what are you doing here?"

My ribs curled around my heart at the way she rubbed at her eyes, her movements still uncoordinated, her features soft and void of her usual studied siren's smile. She looked like the innocent girl who'd cried so bitterly beside me.

It lasted but a second.

"The sun is barely up," she said with an annoyed roll of her eyes that brought about that teasing smirk that had started to trigger a rush of anger in me about three years ago. "Aww, the pretty Raven boy can't sleep because his chest is hurting?"

I forced my muscles to relax at the sound of that rotten moniker. Nothing but her attempt at stoking my anger, the aggressive outburst that had always followed in the past, along with darkness.

Darkness. Always darkness.

Never again.

After all the weight my gift had put on me, the misery, the loss spun into my fate, the goddess had finally given me a way out. As much as I hated Lorn, hated what we'd made each other become, I would not leave her behind in the dark like she'd done with me the day of her attack.

Not unless she left me no choice.

"Before the sun rises above the cliffs, I want you to find Aros, who arrived last night for the *drif*," I said. "You will bond yourself to him, posthaste. No delays. No excuses."

Her breathed laugh carried too much amusement, making it clear she wasn't grasping the seriousness of all this. "I'll never bond—"

"You will return with him to Hanneling Hold and remain there for the rest of your life," I continued. "You will never fly north, never seek me out, never come even within a thousand furlongs of my *anoaley*."

"You're not serious—"

"To ensure this, your *anoa's* flight feathers will be clipped once a year." Her unkindness was not likely to leave her gift behind, but I had to take precautions. "Should you leave your mate's territory, even if only once, even if only by accident, I will personally kill your bird."

Her pupils darted across my face in the dim light, as though searching for my sincerity and, when they found it, she struggled down a swallow. "Malyr, please... don't send me away."

My throat narrowed, but I forced a deep breath to fight against the sensation. I owed Galantia so much. From here on out, I had to do better. A lot better. This was a painful, but necessary, start.

"There is joy and a deep connection to be had in a bond, Lorn." Now my throat turned itchy—likely because I had no idea if I could ever find the same in mine—burdened as my relationship with Galantia was. That would not keep me from trying to set things right. "Aros has seen every fucked-up part of you, every black second of what was done to you in the dungeons. And he loves you with all his heart."

"But I love *you*," she whimpered, her eyes the same sparkling orbs I'd looked into many times through the little cutout in the dungeons.

"No, you do not." I'd done the same in the past, finding a sense of connection in our brokenness and confusing it as love. But it had never been that. Never. "What you love is this idea of what we are: bound together to eternal darkness. I am leaving all that behind, and so should you."

"No," she murmured, and then a bit louder, "No." A resolute shake of her head. "I won't let you send me away. You tried it before. You never meant it."

I'd always meant it, but had somehow been unable to sever our ties completely, almost as if I'd been addicted to the familiarity of that darkness she brought to me and me to her. "You will leave and never return to my side. Ever."

A tremble took hold of her lower lip as she sat up. "And if I refuse?"

My heart turned heavy, dragging on its strings. I wanted to get her out of this darkness, but not at the cost of her dragging me back down—or the woman I'd vowed to protect.

Holding her stare, I leaned into her so she may see the determination in my eyes before I whispered, "Then I will kill you, just like I said I would, should you ever harm my mate."

Of course, she only lifted her chin, that single twitch on the right corner of her mouth making my teeth clench. Had I hoped, even for a moment, that she would deny the attack on my *anoaley*? Perhaps.

A haughty scoff puffed from her lips as she reached a finger into my hair, twirling one of my strands around it, her gaze keeping mine with unwavering strength. "Are you sure you want to take me on, pretty Raven boy? All by yourself? You're still injured."

"Yes, courtesy of the way you left me behind that day, gambling with my life for a chance at killing my fated mate." Energy flickered along the side of my neck, a palpable sensation that quickened my pulse, a warning of those shadows that writhed around her fingertips. "Do not make me fight you."

"Fight me?" she asked with a breathy chuckle, shifting her other hand behind her back. "Pretty Raven boy, fighting me won't be enough. You will have to *kill* me. Because if you leave even a single breath in my lungs, I'll use it to shout, telling all the world what you did in Valtaris."

Shadows shifted at my core—scratching, scraping—her threat nothing but a drop of that endless source of darkness she was. "Don't make me kill you, Lorn."

Her lips curved into a smile that tensed all my muscles at once. "The moment you leave me forever, I'm already dead. Might as well take you with me and have you forever."

She slammed her hand onto my chest, sending raw, blistering pain straight into my lungs. Her other hand shot forward from behind her back, the blast of shadows erupting from her palm and knocking me back several feet.

My spine hit something hard as pressure expanded inside my chest. Every breath became a tortured rasp, each gasp a desperate attempt to stave off the blood pooling inside my lungs. Darkness swallowed the edges of my vision.

Always darkness...

"No more!" I shouted and thrust my hands forward.

Shadows burst from both my palms for the first time in

my life. They undulated around each other, two streams combining into a deadly projectile that sent Lorn tumbling backward over her nest, a web of black shadows clinging to her chest.

They penetrated her shift, her skin, her flesh, her bone, all while she struggled to her feet, her wide eyes fixed on my hands before they found mine. Then they snapped to the flight hole. Lorn shifted in a blast of plumes and shadows. Five ravens cawed and fluttered, dashing toward the cutout.

I struggled to my feet and moved my arms outward. A wall of shadows rippled around the entire room, growing tall and taller still, until they blocked the walls and the flight hole right along with it. They curved inward at the top, forcing the ravens back like a massive ocean wave.

It crashed down on the unkindness, leaving nothing behind but a trembling Lorn that swept up before my feet, and looked back at me from frightened eyes. "You bonded."

"I did." I grabbed her hair, yanked her to her feet, and positioned myself behind her. "I warned you!"

I sealed my hand over her mouth and nose, forcing my shadows deep into her lungs. My other arm wrapped tightly around her body, pulling her back against me, no matter how she bucked and writhed, her body so full of this fucking darkness she loved so much that she could no longer shift.

"I won't let you hurt her," I bit out, tears blurring my vision, my breaths nothing but hiccupping trembles as her tossing limbs lost their vigor. "I'm sorry. I'm sorry. *I'm sorry...*" A guttural cry scratched my throat bloody as I collapsed to my knees, her legs listlessly sprawling out, her arms hanging motionlessly by her side. "I'm sorry for not getting you out..."

Lorn's head tossed to the tremble of my body, her gaping mouth nothing but a blackened hole, her face gilded in a dark silver sheen. Not a smile on her lips, not a taunt from her tongue.

Dead.

Gone.

Cold swept over me, a sense of dread driving into my stomach that turned me more nauseous with every whimper, every sob, every wail. How long I cried over her body, I couldn't say, but by the time I quietly carried her outside, the sun had fully emerged. It cast flickers of orange over the pyre I'd already prepared for her before the bonding. After ten years, one knew a person well. She would have never left me, would have never stopped being a threat to my bondmate.

But I'd tried.

Goddess help me, I'd tried.

"There's nothing left of me worth saving," Lorn's words resonated in my head. *"Just promise me you will burn me so my ashes will drift forever on the wind."*

"I gave you this promise," I said and pressed the torch into the wood, the straw catching fire with a hiss. "You are truly free now. Fly, Lorn. Drift on the wind one final time."

CHAPTER
THIRTY-ONE

Galantia
Present Day, Tidestone

The meadows surrounding Tidestone had transformed into a vast ocean of black tents overnight, the nearby trees bustling with massive flocks of ravens. Inside the walls, the air pulsed with life, and my heart right along with it. Sweet smoke curled up from scattered braziers, intertwining with the scents of roasted meat, warm bread, and the tangy undercurrent of drink that flowed all around us.

The *drif* was magical. A *real* festival.

And I was part of it!

Sebian returned from a merchant with a sugar figure on a stick, the pathfinder wearing a fine green vest beneath his brown cloak, his hair pulled into a single, rather loose braid along his scalp by my not-so-skilled fingers. "Ever had one of these before?"

"As a child." I grabbed the stick, licking at the yellowish-brown treat before I held it out to Malyr. "Have some."

No reaction. He only stared at those far away plumes of gray smoke that rose into the sky somewhere outside the walls of Tidestone. Maybe it came from between those tents.

"Malyr?"

He turned his head, looked down at the figure, then up at me. "Hmm?"

"I said, have some. It's good." I couldn't help but frown at the paleness of his face, seemingly exaggerated by those red threads forming roses and vines that adorned his black corseted vest. I wasn't sure if he looked so poorly because he'd extinguished the fires I'd set all night, or if it was something different. "You seem distracted."

He broke off a small piece and placed it on his tongue. "Merely feeling nostalgic."

"Because of the *drif?*"

He nodded. "Do you enjoy it?"

"Enjoy?" This was a childhood dream come true. "I love it."

I looked over at the old, crooked oak in the outer bailey, its naked branches alive with the fluttering of black wings. Ravens landed, perched, and sidestepped on the gnarly wood. Necklaces dangled from their beaks, which they gingerly hung on smaller twigs, the trinkets glinting under the late afternoon sun.

I reached my right hand up for one of them, where it hung from a low branch, running my thumb over the seashells strung onto ribbon, the single feather tied into it, and traced the name engraved on the wooden plaque. *Julan.* "What are they for?"

"We call it a seeker's chain." Sebian stepped up beside me and ran his fingers down the shells. "Unbonded Ravens make them, displaying their treasures, one of their best feathers, and their name, hoping that their fated mate might spot it in the tree, take a fancy to it, and come to find them."

"What a wonderful tradition." I rounded the tree, looking over seeker chains that had to count into the thousands. Oh, how much I wanted to do this! To participate! "How do I get a nice feather from my unkindness?"

"Command your *anoa* to separate from your human form," Malyr said.

"I don't know how to do that."

"Like so..." Malyr broke off another piece of browned sugar, crumbled it in his palm, then reached his arm out to let his *anoa* shape there from shadows and feathers. "At first, you lure them. Then, you command."

I stepped up to Malyr's *anoa*, a majestic specimen, easily one of the largest I'd seen so far, with plumes as black as those shadows in his master's core. Sometimes, hues of dark green and blue hushed across those wings the bird stretched before folding them again.

"I remember you." The moment I reached my hand for his head, he ran the smooth length of his beak along my fingers, all but curling himself into my touch. "He's a lot friendlier than you."

Sebian snorted a laugh. "Smarter, too."

"I never claimed otherwise." The corners of Malyr's mouth twitched ever so slightly, as if they wanted to smile but weren't certain how to. "Try it. Put some food in your palm, commune with your *anoa*, and lure her out."

I broke off some sugar, crumbled it, handed the stick to Sebian, then held out my arm. With closed eyes, I called for that bird of mine. The more I focused on the gift at my core, the faster something fluttered in my chest.

Then, something weighed down my arm.

Claws curled into the sleeve of my dress.

I opened my eyes, the muscles in my cheeks pulling taught at the sight of my *anoa* perching on my arm. "She looks... bigger."

"Uh-huh," Sebian agreed and patted her head. "That little thing sure gained some weight. Feathers are looking better, too."

"Must be all the preening you do," Malyr said with a quick glance at the braid resting on my shoulder. "She's always been very recept—"

My *anoa* hopped onto Malyr's arm. Then, she side-stepped, huddling against Malyr's black bird, their beaks caressing each other's in gentle strokes. They ruffled their feathers, preening at each other's plumage, smoothing any errant feathers into place, unfettered by how the three of us stared at them.

Malyr's eyes met mine above the affectionate display of our *anoas,* his face holding much more color now. "He loves her very much."

My heart pounded a strange rhythm of fear and yearning, words that Sebian had spoken last night creeping back into my memory. "Whatever this thing is between us three," he'd said, "it's not going to keep either one of us from loving you right."

From loving me right.

Either one of them.

Something that hadn't made any sense in the throes of lust now caused genuine hope, rather than guarded skepticism. What if my shattered heart had been much like a cracked mirror, not allowing me to see the truth that Malyr had tried to share with me all along? That he *had* loved me. That he loved me still? Was that what he'd wanted to tell me after the bonding?

With a quick shake of her head that puffed some of my *anoa's* feathers, she sidestepped away from Malyr's bird, all the way to his wrist. There, she turned her head this way and that, staring at the crumbs of browned sugar. She blinked once, twice. Then, she started pecking at it.

It was Malyr's stuttered exhale that drew my attention back to him, a sound that held so much shock and surprise, only to find that he was staring at Sebian. Actually, they stared at each other.

Sebian smirked. "I told you so."

My gaze went back and forth between them. "What? What is it? What does this mean?"

"That's a question for you to figure out. Now close your eyes and call her back before Malyr's arm falls off."

She dissolved into plumes, as did Malyr's bird, easily melting back into my form. Luckily, she'd left feathers behind on the ground, the largest and finest of which I picked up. Still, a few things were missing.

When I turned for the wooden cart beneath the oak, Sebian called behind me, "What are you doing?"

Experiencing everything I'd missed out on. "You'll see."

I greeted the heavyset merchant with a nod and looked

over his display of raven treasures. "How much for these polished stones so I can hang a chain?"

"Here, my lady," the merchant said and reached me one of those wooden plaques, along with a stick of coal. "Write down your name, and I will brand it into the wood for you before I count out how many stones we'll need. With luck, a new Raven will meet you in your nest tonight."

Before my fingertips touched the items, Sebian grabbed me and slung me over his shoulder. "Tell that fucker her nest is full."

"What are you doing?!"

"Are you trying to get your wrists tied up again, sweetheart?" He spun several times, ripping a little squeal from me. "Because this is the way to go about it."

"Let me down!" I pounded at Sebian's back, kicking and writhing, but mostly laughing. "I just want to hang a necklace!"

A deep rumbling laugh echoed in the air.

A laugh that stopped even Sebian dead in his tracks as he slowly slid me off his shoulder. It was a sound so foreign, so unexpectedly soul-stirring, that it seemed to reverberate through my chest, halting my heart for a spellbinding moment.

Because it came from Malyr.

Sebian and I stared at him. There he stood, the unadulterated smile on his face reaching all the way into his eyes, making them sparkle like never before. Gods help me, I'd never seen him this unrestrained, unburdened... happy? The look suited him, how it carved away on his perpetually somber features. I wanted to see him like this more often.

Sebian exchanged a glance with me, his eyes twinkling in a bemused shock that seemed to match mine. "Stop scaring the people, Malyr."

"Malyr!" a shout rumbled through the *drif,* causing the three of us to spin around. "Show yourself, you murdering bastard!"

Lord Aros stomped toward us, his eyes red-rimmed, his soft black curls disheveled and knotted, one hand tightly fisting the pommel of his sheathed sword. Rage poured off him, carving a path through the parting crowd.

Out of nowhere, Sebian thrust a shadow dagger at Aros, which pierced his cloak and pinned a corner to the ground, making Aros stumble back a few steps. "The fuck you think you're doing, storming at us like that?!"

Malyr shoved me behind him. "Take one more step toward my *anoaley*, and you'll be a dead man."

"You killed her!" Aros shouted, the tendons on his neck strung taught. Fine red veins popped across his face as he yanked his cloak free, but made no further advance. "She's burning on a pyre because you put her there. You killed my fated mate!"

"Oh shit," Sebian mumbled.

THIRTY-TWO

Galantia
Present Day, Tidestone

Burning on a pyre. *Burning.*

I looked back at those swathes of smoke that had kept Malyr so distracted, realization settling on me. He *had* killed Lorn. Not that it bothered me, but... why?

"I did what I had to do, and you would have acted no different if the roles had been reversed," Malyr said. "Lorn attempted to kill Galantia. As her mate, I made certain that she would never try again."

My toes curled in my boots. "What?"

"I can attest to it, as can Marla and Asker," Sebian said. "The day we tried to remove the shadows from Vhaerya, Lorn attacked her. She kept her from shifting while the shadows there attacked us before she fled, leaving Galantia, Malyr, and me behind to die."

But of course...

Internally, I scolded myself. I should have figured that out on my own, given how different those shadows had felt, but Malyr's injuries had occupied my entire focus.

"You know it is true," Malyr said. "Deep down, you know Lorn had committed a crime and why. I never intended to rob you of your mate, but neither will I allow *anybody* to rob me of mine."

"Of course, if you have doubts, I guess you can insist on an investigation," Sebian added. "Make it a public spectacle, worse than the one we're having right now, on the first *drif* after a fucking decade! If you want everyone to hear five matching testaments about what she did, that woman *you* couldn't charm into a bond, then go right ahead."

For a brief, agonizing moment, Aros' face twisted as if in physical pain. He shook his head, a tremulous movement that betrayed his internal struggle. But then, almost as if resigning himself to the grim truth, the motion transitioned into a single, reluctant nod. He pivoted as if to walk away, only to swing back around and sink to his knees.

Head lowered, his voice was little more than a mumble toward the ground. "May I take her remains with me, my prince?"

Malyr hesitated but a moment. "Of course."

"There's nothing to see here," Sebian shouted when

Aros rose and trudged away, ushering curious bystanders back into the bustle of the *drif*. "Go have a drink. For the next hour, the wine flows and your prince pays!"

Malyr rolled his eyes in-tune with the crowd's cheers, then his gaze lowered softly on me. "I did not mean to ruin this for you."

"I'm fine."

If I harbored any uncomfortable feelings toward this, it was pity for Aros... and perhaps for Malyr. It couldn't have been easy for him to do that. But he had. For me.

"Nothing's fucking ruined until we allow it to be," Sebian added, equally unfazed by Lorn's death. "Would you look at that." He gestured to tall wooden stakes draped with loops and nets attached to the castle wall, ropes and pulleys extending over a path marked with intricately carved symbols. "I once broke a fucking flight feather on one of those when I was... nine or so."

Eager to help Sebian in his effort to return the joy we deserved to this moment, I turned toward the attraction. "What's it for?"

"It's an obstacle course," Sebian explained, pointing at a piece of black cloth that dangled from a hook high above the ground. "See that? Whoever makes it through the fastest gets the cloth." Just then, one raven out of an unkindness snatched it in its beak, only for a young woman to emerge at the bottom of the course. She held the cloth up high to the cheers of the crowd, turned, and offered it to another young woman. "She's trying to court her, offering it as a gift for her nest. What do you say, Malyr? Are you up for it?"

Malyr crossed his arms in front of his chest, observing the hoops and nets. The corners of his mouth lifted higher, promising another smile—only for them to drop as he shook his head.

"It looks like good fun," I said, wanting to see one of those rare smiles that seemed to light up the shadowed corridors of his soul.

"No, it most definitely looks like broken flight feathers," he said. "And while I do not mind giving one up, I certainly won't do it for plain amusement."

"Well," Sebian scoffed, "that's one way of avoiding defeat."

"What's wrong with plain amusement?" Maybe that was exactly what he needed for those severe lips to remember how to smile, for his lungs to remember how to laugh. "How about this? If you win, I will..."

That caught Malyr's interest, his eyes flashing, finding mine as he drew closer. "You will...?"

His closeness sent a ripple of warmth through me, the shadows that naturally drifted into me tantalizingly intimate, my void pulling them deeper. "Every morning, I will braid your hair."

Malyr's eyes widened for a split second. "Very well."

"It's a deal then." Sebian grinned and gave me a wink. "But you pay."

"Of course..." Malyr strode forward, reaching the woman who had just strung up a fresh piece of shadowcloth on the hook a gleaming coin. "My friend and I will go next."

The woman nodded and quickly accepted the coin. "Of course, Prince Malyr."

"It's Prince Malyr..." The whisper threaded through the crowd before it morphed into an enthusiastic chant. "The prince himself is taking on the course!"

Faces turned, eyes alight with anticipation, cheers knitting together into a fabric of palpable excitement. I couldn't help but get swept up in the moment, a thrill tingling my belly.

Sebian stretched his arms before he swung them in wide circles. "Just try to keep up. I know those *princely* duties have you a bit rusty. Wouldn't want you to break one of your royal wings."

"If we judged the race by the size of your mouth, you'd win every time," Malyr said with a grin, all tension of the last weeks between the two evaporated, revealing the long-standing friendship between them. I liked that, very much so. "Let's see if your wings are as fast as your tongue."

At the woman's call, Malyr and Sebian shifted. Malyr's unkindness dashed into the air, slicing through the first set of hoops at a rapid speed. Sebian's birds turned, swooped, and somersaulted, their acrobatic shortcuts closing any gap between them to the excited claps of the crowd.

"Galantia."

I flinched at the sound of that voice and turned toward Ciel. Of course, the carriages that had arrived that day... I should have known.

"Why are you here?"

"I thought Prince Malyr might have told you," she said, her green dress framed by a golden cloak, her hair, for once, open copper ringlets. "He will make my father the new lord of Tidestone, along with all its holdings."

To make up for the marriage agreement that Malyr had broken. Something I could hardly hold against him, how it would cost me my home. It made my success at Valtaris all the more crucial.

"What do you want?"

"To apologize. I know that you feel betrayed, and—"

"I don't care to hear your apology. I thought I'd found a

sort of friend in you, or at least a confidante, yet you schemed against me behind my back."

"How could I not have?" She clasped my arm, pushing herself in front of me, her glistening emerald eyes finding mine. "You tell me, Galantia, what choices you had in the past when your lord father bid you to marry Prince Domren, Prince Malyr... any man, truly, not of our choosing."

My throat narrowed at the truth in her words, but the betrayal ran too deep to be so easily forgiven. "Not of your choosing? Sebian told me of your disheveled state when you came out of Malyr's private rooms that morning."

Cici's gaze remained a visceral thing that bore into my side. "I know you had love for Prince Malyr. I saw it in the way you looked at him."

I flinched but said nothing.

"For what it is worth, he never touched me," she said. "Unless, of course, one counts the way he grabbed my hair that day, held my face to his hearth, and threatened to melt my skin off should I breathe a word to you about our secret betrothal. How you managed to tolerate his attention has my respect. I never wanted it beyond my family's need to find our place in this new world."

The cacophony of cheering muted to a hum as she walked away. Two sensations warred at my core: the sinking of my stomach at Malyr's viciousness toward her, and the lifting of my chest at the fact that he hadn't touched her, not intimately. My jealousy had been... misplaced.

At least with Cici.

And Lorn? Well, she was currently sizzling on a pyre. How likely was it that Malyr had fucked her one night and killed her a week later? How likely was it that she'd lied to weaken me that day? And how likely was it that Malyr had gotten injured because I'd fallen for it?

But most of all, how likely was it that I'd misjudged Malyr and the heart he carried beneath the shadows? Marla had told me it was up to the both of us to nurture love. Maybe it was time for me to stop fighting it.

But first, Valtaris.

CHAPTER
THIRTY-THREE

Galantia
Present Day, Valtaris

My hips shifted with the slow beats of Liual's hooves clanking on the stone, my body aching with a bone-deep fatigue that had settled in my very marrow, turning my limbs to lead. Still, I held my hand up at those shadows undulating ahead of us, absorbing them into my void as we ventured deeper into Valtaris.

The Tarred Road wound its way through the city with

its black flagstones cut from obsidian, flanked by buildings that loomed in graveyard's silence. No tiny claws scrabbled along the sills of barricaded windows, no sharp teeth gnawed at the carcasses of ravens.

No, the city's rats were as dead as everything else, lying scattered here and there between blackened corpses and bony, withered trees. Soldiers, their faces etched with an exhaustion that matched my own, lifted the dead onto waiting carts, the stench of decay barely masked by the scarf I'd wrapped around my mouth and nose.

I should have felt proud, perhaps happy even. For three whole days, I'd been at this, clearing the city one plateau or main road at a time. But happiness seemed like a twisted emotion to feel when it was steeped in death...

I glanced back at Malyr, who sat behind me in the saddle, his hair put into a single braid along his scalp. "How much longer until we reach the Winged Keep?"

He reined Liual, his black gelding, around a corpse with one hand, his other hand fixed at the shadows ahead. "I want us to go to the Perch first."

"What's there?"

"Naya and my mother. My father, too." A beat of silence. "I want to give them a proper funeral before I dare step into the keep."

That explained the shadows writhing quicker against my back the deeper we ventured, those black tendrils so often a visible extension of Malyr's emotional state. He was... anxious.

"I understand."

"If I remember correctly, the stairs should come up to our right soon," he said. "Asker? You patrolled the Tarred Road nearly every day. How far are we?"

"Another two hundred steps, perhaps more." Asker,

who rode a few paces behind us, assessed the vibrant red banners that wafted from balconies, and wooden signs that hung over shop doors seemingly untouched by time. "Valtaris is as beautiful as I remember."

"If you say so," Sebian said from where he rode beside us on Pius, and not even the cloth covering his mouth and nose could hide that disgusted curl of his lip. "The buildings are in good condition, yes, but the land...? It's completely dead."

"It will recover," Malyr said. "All it needs is sun and rain. Nature will do the rest. Perhaps some good seed that we can cart from Hanneling Hold."

"If Aros feels so inclined to give it up," Sebian added. "I told you we should have slit his throat instead of let him walk away."

Asker *tsked*. "Not advisable. Lord Aros—"

"Yeah, yeah, I know," Sebian groaned. "He has a title, a stronghold, commands a devout army of humans and Ravens, and politics, blah-blah-blah... Not to mention that, *apparently*, he's holding seeds hostage."

"He knelt and returned home with his mate's remains with no further incident," Malyr added. "There might be bad blood between us, but he's a Raven. He's loyal to our cause."

"Good. The last thing we need is a bannerman not easily replaced going sour somewhere in the south," Asker said and glanced over one of the city's lower-lying plateaus. "Much of the borderlands that weren't so terribly blighted are occupied by humans."

"I want them gone," Malyr said. "Send pathfinders out to inform them to pack up and leave. We will require the land by the first thaw if we want to avoid food shortages."

"They're nothing but the poorest of farmers who

couldn't afford the tenancy on Dranadian soil." I raised my hand to the shadows before us, my shoulder, elbow, wrist... every single damn sinew I possessed along the limb burned in pain. "Please tell me you won't just... chase them off."

"You are too kind for your own good."

"Says the deathweaver who needs me to suck out his darkness."

"You and I are symbiosis, little dove." He reached his hand beneath my arm, supporting the heavy limb and allowing me some reprieve. "As much as your void brings me light, my shadows bring you darkness. Balance."

My stomach clenched, but I couldn't deny the logic, and neither could I come up with a smart retort. "Just give the farmers notice and time. If not for them, then for me, please?"

There was an awfully long pause. "For you."

"Thank you."

Around us, other deathweavers worked in grim unison, their hands weaving intricate patterns in the air as they wrestled with the shadows. Keeping my open palm pointed at the shadows, I absorbed their wild swirl into a void filled to the brim, their excess tendrils scraping at my insides. So far, I hadn't been able to wield them again, which was beyond frustrating.

"What in the name of the goddess is this?" Asker asked as he brought his brown mare to a stop, his stare fixed on... something within the lifting shadows.

A corpse? An... animal?

A chill settled against my nape at the sight of the grotesque figure before me. It was unlike anything I'd ever seen, barely resembling a human form with how it distorted into nightmarish shapes, like a broken reflection on a river's rippling surface. Black limbs stretched and contorted into wings and talons, yet remained partially human in a way that defied nature. Black flesh melded with feathers in utter chaos, with no semblance of order or reason, held together only by swirling shadows that felt... different.

"Those are not Malyr's shadows," I said under my breath so the soldiers and deathweavers around us wouldn't hear. "Should I absorb them?"

"The fuck you will." With a tug on the reins, Sebian brought Pius to a stop. "Neither am I going to ride past that thing without knowing what it is."

Sebian reached behind him for his bow. An almost spectral whisper hummed through the air as he conjured a shadowy arrow, its fletching nothing but midnight tendrils. He nocked it, his body a picture of taut concentration. He let the arrow fly.

The figure shattered on impact, unleashing a cacophony of soul-splitting screeches and guttural *kra-kras*. It pierced my ears, sending a shudder through my bones that trembled all the way into my core with how it echoed on the flagstone, bile rushing onto my tongue.

"Whoa..." Malyr wrapped his arm around me, shortening the reins of a nervously dancing Liual. *"Eze nja... Liual. Eze."*

Around us, soldiers scrambled backward, some losing their footing in their haste. Sebian's horse reared, its eyes white with panic, its hooves clattering wildly on the road. One hind leg slipped on the slick surface, and Pius staggered back. With a terrified whinny, he lost his balance and fell sideways, throwing Sebian from the saddle.

The sickening *thud* of Sebian's head striking a wooden column resonated through the chaos. A pained groan followed as he slumped to the ground while Pius struggled to its hooves and cantered back down the Tarred Road, soldiers dodging the panicked horse left and right.

"Sebian!" Asker's shout still echoed as he shifted into his unkindness, which quickly fluttered forward.

Mine dashed faster, having me reshape beside Sebian as he struggled himself onto all fours. "Are you hurt?"

He held his hand up the moment I stepped toward him, gesturing for me to stay back while his shoulders rose and rounded. A heave. A grunt. Then, his entire body convulsed as he retched onto the flagstone.

Malyr walked up to Sebian and handed him a waterskin. "Should have shifted."

"Mm-hmm," was all Sebian answered before he grabbed the waterskin and rinsed his mouth a few times. "Please tell me I'm not the only one who almost shit his pants."

"It must have been a Raven who got trapped in the shadows mid-shift, magic and all," Asker said, his face pale, his eyes trailing to the crumbled creature. "There is no telling how many of these we might encounter this close to the Perch. We would be well-advised to keep our distance from these... screamers."

"We have to leave the horses behind—too much risk should we accidentally disturb more of them." Malyr took Sebian's hand and pulled him to stand, then turned and set his eyes on me. "Can you walk?"

"If you can, then so can I."

We continued on foot along the winding road, past ornate lampposts, intricate tooling that decorated the wooden frames of shops, and elegant facades with shining *aerymel* set into its daub. How strange it was to have such beauty mark the backdrop for new heartaches that waited around every curve: piles of dead birds,

soldiers with their grips still firm on their swords, those...
screamers.

"Valtaris was beautiful," I said where I walked beside
Sebian, removing the shadows several steps ahead where
Malyr strangled them.

"Black diamond, King Omaniel called this city," Asker
said, squinting at a set of alabaster stairs that emerged from
the shadows just ahead. "Its roofs will sparkle under the
sun again soon enough. Once word travels of this, there's
no doubt Ravens from across the realm will return home,
eager to help in the restoration."

Malyr came to a sudden halt at the narrow set of stairs,
his gaze transfixed on the intricately winding, cast iron
banister attached to the bright stone wall that lined the
stairs to one side. His hand reached out, fingers lightly
tracing the cold metalwork, following the elegant curves
and delicate twists that had once been the pride of a skilled
craftsman.

His eyes closed briefly, his touch lingering and jaw set,
before he began the climb. "I remember now."

I followed in silence, the stairs narrow and steep, each
step echoing in the still air. With every footfall, the bond
within me seemed to wrench and jar, like the string of an
untuned lute screeching terribly in my chest.

That couldn't be good...

Finally, the stairs leveled out, leading me onto a plateau
with several airy pavilions, stone benches, and statues of
birds in flight, their wings outstretched. A large fountain
stood at the center of the plateau, its basin long dry, the
dead hedges around it the remnants of a once lustrous
garden.

There was much less death here, much less devastation
aside from the rubble of a nearby watchtower that had

halfway collapsed. That, and the two black bodies that lay on the ground, one male, the other female. Malyr's mother; I could tell by those feather-shaped pins I'd once seen depicted in a book, which still sparkled in her long, dark hair.

Malyr passed his parents' bodies without a glance, his eyes fixed on the pile of rocks and debris ahead, where he didn't so much stop as fall to his knees. He grabbed at rocks, stones, and boulders—fast, faster—tossing them away as shadows flared up around him.

Asker appeared beside me, pulling an intake of air through his barred teeth with a hiss, watching Malyr's shadows grow, swell, expand. "My prince, maybe we should return in the morrow?"

Malyr showed no reaction, his movements growing frenzied, his body consumed by an urgency that bordered on madness. Each clank of rock against rock seemed to send a strike into my chest, the shadows it stirred there matching the ones that undulated around him.

"When was the last time he poured his shadows into you?" Sebian asked.

"Two days ago, since I was too exhausted from clearing our way up here," I said, and there was no denying how Asker's balance shifted onto his heels. "I need to help him."

Akser's hand landed heavily on my shoulder. "We do not know the limit of your void, but my guess is that you might have reached it."

I exchanged a look with Sebian for no more than a second, but it was all that was needed for me to spot the commitment in his eyes that coursed through my veins. The commitment to us: three souls connected by fate, friendship, and the feelings we harbored for each other.

Sebian jutted his chin toward Malyr. "You handle his

shadows; I see how I can handle him."

He matched my stride as we hurried over to what had turned into a volatile wall of shadows that flicked and writhed. Hand outreached, I absorbed them, carving us a way through the darkness. And there, on the ground, Malyr heaved and sobbed, frantically grappling at whatever rocks he managed to lift off the small body that lay beneath them.

I knelt before him and clasped his face between my hands, my mouth turning dry at the sight of him. "Malyr, pour your shadows into me." When he showed no reaction, I lifted his pitch-black eyes to mine, black droplets running down his cheeks like spilled ink. "Malyr?" No recognition. "Malyr!" Nothing. "*Anoaley!*"

His fingers slowed, his eyes finally settling on me in the dim darkness. "I have to get her out."

"We'll get her out. Look, I can already see her." Sebian grabbed the first large boulder in reach, carefully lifting it off a splintered grayish rib that protruded from Naya's smashed corpse. "Can you tap into his core? Suck them out?"

"I... I don't know."

I tortured my upper lip for a moment until a distant memory from the orchard came to mind, when Malyr's eyes had been black one moment, then clearing the next. I pressed my absorbing hand onto his chest the way I had done that day.

His eyes lightened.

My chest darkened, like an eternal eclipse that slowly settled over my mind as a strange sensation swept through my core. A... tingling? No. Scratching and scraping, like claws threatening to tear me up from the inside.

Shadows ever so cruel.

THIRTY-FOUR

Galantia
Present Day, Valtaris

The black shingles that crowned Valtaris easily soaked up the warmth of the winter sun during the day, keeping the city pleasantly mild. A large triangular scarf knitted from shadows was all I needed as I crossed the Perch, the fox-lined dress I wore beneath matching the setting sun's deep orange rays.

In front of it, Malyr stood at the edge of the plateau that overlooked all of Valtaris, a large clay vessel clasped between his hands. To the right, black stairs a furlong wide led up to the Winged Keep. The city itself spread out along the hill chain in several areas of different heights, most of them connected by narrow stairs. Left of us, too far for my eyes to see, lay the Temple Plateau.

I wasn't allowed there.

Not yet.

A sight too gruesome for me to stomach, Malyr had said, since the temple was where the women and children had taken refuge during the siege. The shadows hadn't killed them, only trapped them, leaving them to die slow deaths fueled by panic as water and food, perhaps even air, grew scarce.

For three more days, I'd cleared the most important parts of the city, allowing us to rest at ease within the sparkling ruins. Rooms had been cleaned and assigned, foods had been carted into the kitchen and larders, and servants had been hired and instructed.

I watched how Malyr tilted the vessel ever so slightly, his black robes drifting left with the breeze—as did the ashes he'd collected from his family's pyre, spiraling downward like a storm, only to dissolve in the looming dusk.

"I know you are there," he said as he tossed the vessel to wherever it may land and shatter. "I can feel you."

Arms wrapped around myself, I walked up to stand beside him. "I'm sorry if I interrupted... or if you wanted to be alone."

A slow shake of his head. "Sebian?"

"He went to help Marla clear out the chimney in the home you assigned them."

He nodded, then turned to look at me, his eyes neither red-rimmed from pain nor glistening from grief, but calm.

"Can I show you a special place? The only way of reaching it is by flying."

A tingle rose in my chest at the idea of exploring. "I'd like that."

"Follow us," he said through the burst of feathers and shadows.

It took but a thought for me to shift. We beat our white wings, leaving the plateau in pursuit of those black ravens ahead. They dashed through narrow alleys, dove to a lower level, then rounded the face of the mountain on which sat the Winged Keep. We followed, slipping into a sort of wide cavity that looked as though a giant had bitten into the mountain, ripping a large chunk of stone out and leaving behind a pool of water.

I reshaped near a rock-carved, gold-painted column that supported the overhang, the steam that rose from the water's surface seasoning the air with minerals and sulfur. "What is this place?"

"It is a natural spring that, at some point in the past, carved itself to freedom and created this," Malyr said where he stood on the damp rock on the opposite side of the pool, first wiggling out of one boot, then the other. "The spring is vast and powerful. The pressure of the heat causes the obsidian in the mountain to compress, which creates *aerymel*."

Pure awe trickled through my veins as I looked back at the entrance, many of the lower areas of Valtaris sprawling out before us. "It's why this place has so many different plateaus. The compression made the ground shift and sink over time."

He stared at me for a long second, nodded, and pulled his robes up over his head. "Not much escapes you, does it?"

Warmth flushed my neck when he pulled at the ties of the cotton trousers he'd worn beneath his robes, which he quickly removed. "What are you doing?"

"Bathing," he said simply, as if he wasn't naked out in the open, following the natural edge of the black pool toward one of the columns, his body a picture of masculinity with strong legs, a perfectly-sculpted buttocks, and shadowed valleys that lay between his shifting muscles. "My father came here often after he sparred with Asker. There's nothing quite like it for soothing your bones and muscles. Try it; I know you're sore." He lowered himself into the water, sending a ripple across the surface. Then he leaned his back against the edge, rested his elbows there, and smirked up at me. "Surely, you are not going to act coy now, considering how it took two grown men, their cocks, and a lot of cotton shreds to handle you the night of our bonding?"

I tilted my head and arched a brow. "I cannot swim. Mother never allowed me to learn."

"Then I shall have to teach you." Malyr pushed himself off the edge, swam over, and reached his hand up. "But until then, let me hold you."

That aching knot at the base of my skull decided for me, having me quickly strip out of my clothes and boots. I sat at the edge of the pool, then slowly let myself slip into the embrace of his arms, the soothing heat of the water, the caress of bubbles tingling along my skin.

"This feels wonderful," I all but groaned, easily settling into the draping hold of his arms as I slung one of mine around his neck. "And to think that winter is still all around us."

"Spring is nearly here." Malyr slowly waded toward the outer edge of the pool that seemed to flow into the horizon, the water only reaching his mid-chest. "The pool, however, is not what I wanted to show you."

"No?"

"No, it is this." Guiding my hands to the rocky edge for hold, he turned me toward the sprawling city beneath us, one arm wrapped around my belly, his body pressing into me from behind. With his other hand, he pointed at the lit windows that speckled Valtaris here and there in the quickly falling night, his lips pressing against my earlobe as he whispered, "Whenever you look about the city, remember that it sparkles because of you and only you. Every Raven who calls Valtaris his home is in your debt, but none so more than I. Without you, I could not have given my family a proper burial. You are... a miracle, my little white dove."

Not worthless.

A miracle.

My chest expanded wider against the slick wall of the pool, pulling the fresh air deep into my lungs where it mingled with those swirls of joy and pride I hadn't allowed myself to feel for days. "Valtaris is my home now, too."

"And it will receive you with all the honor that is due to you," he said. "Asker is already busy planning my coronation now that we recovered the crowns. I requested that our coronations take place together, during one unified ceremony, so the world may see what you've done for us."

Confused, I glanced over my shoulder back at him. "My... what?"

His gaze slipped to my lips for a moment before it found mine again. "You don't know, do you? Ravens have neither king nor queen consort, not among bonded couples. Little dove, you and I are expected to rule side by side."

A shudder played along my exposed shoulders, making

my gaze snap forward as wave of dizziness hit me. I went from Domren's betrothed, to Lord Brisden's hated daughter, to worthless Galantia, to Malyr's betrothed, to betrayed, to Raven, to void, to miracle... all in the span of less than half a year. But queen? I couldn't say if I was ready for that.

"Can I ask you something?"

Malyr let a scoop of hot water run down the side of my neck, languid heat soaking into my skin. "Anything."

"You said you had three reasons why you wanted this bond," I said. "To strengthen your gift. To find relief from your shadows. What is the third?"

"To make it impossible for you to run away from me." A gentle kiss against my nape. "That leaves me with a lifetime to show you that I can do better. With you by my side... I can. And maybe, with prayers, I can regain your heart."

That heart he wanted shuddered in my chest, as affected by this man as it had been when he'd first kissed me. He'd had it then—something I'd struggled so hard to obscure even from myself, drowning my feelings for him in heartbreak and hatred.

I shook my head. "Seems to me there would've been no running regardless. You need me; I need you."

"I don't want to be needed; I want to be *wanted*." His warm whisper caressed the side of my neck, making my breath hobble. "What is it?"

"Nothing." At least nothing that I could put into words in a way that would make sense even to myself right now. "I'm just... confused, I guess."

Somewhere, wings flapped.

"About?"

"My own thoughts?" My heart and how it pounded faster at this strange intimacy between us, with how openly we spoke, and how different he was when not burdened by shadows. "Bonds. Relationships. Fate. Love."

His breathing altered, his inhales turning into shallow gasps that he held for a second before he exhaled, as if it took him great effort to continue breathing at all. "You are bonded to me. You are in a relationship with Sebian. The three of us are where fate wants us to be. As for love..." a faint, short inhale, "Sebian loves you deeply." A quivering exhale. "As do I."

My breath caught.

My eyes clenched shut.

His words resonated deep inside the cave of my chest, flooding a heart I'd carefully put back together. I braced for the torrent to rip away the pieces, reopening wounds barely mended. Instead, they seeped into the thousands of cracks that webbed the organ, filling each fissure with a warmth that spread like molten gold.

Not breaking.

Strengthening.

"I have loved you since you came to my chambers that night." Malyr's tightly-paced breaths ghosted along the damp side of my neck as he slowly opened my braid, combing my strands out with his fingers. Then, they settled on my cheek with light pressure. "Loved you when I told myself I did not. Loved you when I told you that nobody ever would." A tug on my cheek. "Please, look at me."

The tenderness of his touch caved my lungs, choked my words, and froze my limbs. For a moment, I was trapped in what we'd been, everything we were now, and the tantalizing, *terrifying* possibility of what we might become.

I shook my head. "I fear that it isn't real."

"My love is not gentle, or tender, or easy. But it is real, grown from hate and pain deep inside a chest sullied by shadows. It is cutting and biting, leaving behind scars as unfading as my love for you." His warm lips scathed my jawline. "And once we are gone from this earth, I will continue to love you among the stars. I will be the night, the darkest patch of sky around you, just to ensure that everyone can see how you sparkle. And once your light starts fading, I will take you into my black embrace, and that is where I will love you beyond death."

A pulse of warmth radiated from my core, trembling through my soul before it washed over me like the first light of dawn. I had waited, hoped, *longed* for this kind of love, a pledge of such unequivocal fortitude that not even death could impose conditions. Once again, it had been around me all along...

I breathed past the lump in my throat. "I... I don't know what to say."

"Your *anoa* has already told me everything I need to hear for now. *Vinja a meh, shå,*" Malyr whispered between kisses along my jawline, his damp fingers settling on my chin, urging me to turn my head. "Look at me, please."

I turned in the frame of his embrace and looked into those eyes that seemed brighter than ever before, bringing out the gray swirls of his irises. The tension pulled taut between us, a palpable energy that begged for release but was too sacred to hurry. For a beat that stretched into eternity, his lips hovered mere inches from mine.

Hesitant.

Uncertain.

Asking for permission.

With my next inhale, as if guided by some unseen celestial pull, my mouth lifted just a fraction. And like the first brush of starlight across a night sky, our lips met. It was the softest of touches, a whisper against the roaring cacophony of emotions within me.

Malyr's hand glided down my sides, fingers curling into my thighs before he slung my legs around his waist, trapping his hard length between us. "Tell me you want this."

My head fell back as his mouth trailed down my neck, his tongue flicking and tasting, thickening the blood in my veins. "I do."

We weaved and tangled together until the taut muscles of his abdomen pushed against mine. With uncontrollable need, he surged upward, entering me with an exhilarating force that sent a chill up my spine.

His groan rumbled through his chest, putting a little sway into his body before he tangled his fingers in my hair, pulling my mouth back to his. Our lips moved in trembling synchrony, each brush and retreat, each glide and pause like the mating breaths of two souls finally united.

My breathing quickened as we ground against each other in the watery depths, our movements sensual, our panting breaths matching our deep longing for each other. "Malyr..."

"Anoaley..." Clasping my thighs, he pulled me away from the edge. "Nothing on me is gentle anymore. However, I shall try."

He waded toward a natural feature of the basin that I hadn't noticed before—a gentle incline in the rock floor that formed an underwater plateau of sorts. It was as if nature itself had sculpted a cradle within the pool, subtly sloping upward where it melted with the edge, the water there merely a silken veil over the rock.

Malyr slowly lowered me onto the smooth rock, guiding my head to rest against the ledge, as if it were a carefully prepared pillow. Hot water lapped at my skin, washing into

309

the valley between my breasts while my exposed nipples hardened against the chill of the air.

Until Malyr lowered himself down on me, bringing a wash of heat with him as his skin pressed against mine. Back hunched, his mouth moved hungrily over my nipples, sucking them, squeezing them between his lips, pulling them.

I grappled at his back, letting my fingers explore the contours of his strong shoulders, those shifting muscles beneath them. "I want you."

"You have me. You've had me since I was born." He pushed back inside me on a groan, his powerful thrust amplified by the smooth but ungiving stone beneath me. "Goddess help me, nothing compares to you. Nothing."

He moved with a force that was both controlled and passionate, his powerful body brushing against my core as he thrust into me. His hips boldly rolled in a hypnotic rhythm that sent reverberations cascading across my quivering flesh, as if he touched me in a million different places all at once.

Because he did.

Shadows as thin as feather vanes billowed from his skin, sending icy fingers to whisper across my body, stirring up a sensation that left me breathless. Malyr's kiss burned into me, more passionate than before. He nipped at my lips and tongue, sending jolts of pleasure and pain through me, spiraling me into a sea of pure euphoria.

"This is what happens when a shadow and void come together, my little dove," he rasped. "I can only dare do this when we're alone now. They will not tolerate someone else near you."

I trembled as his shadows coiled around my nipples, kneading and teasing my sensitive flesh until an unbearable ache spread across my nerve endings. They jabbed and thrummed around my clit, stroked and pried at my asshole, before finally wiggling deep inside my cunt, filling me with exquisite pleasure that burned deep in my core.

A primal scream ripped from my throat as I clawed at the hard strings of muscle that shifted on each side of his spine. "Malyr..."

"I love it when you allow yourself to moan my name," he crooned. "Take my shadows. Let them spoil you."

My fingers dug deep, likely drawing blood, but all it did was lure a masculine groan from his throat as he fucked into me harder. Scratching my nails down his back, I desperately searched for hold as my mind threatened to drown in the rapture, until they sank into the depression of his taut buttocks. Gods, the way those muscles clenched each time he thrust into me...

I palmed his ass, pulling him deeper into me with each thrust. At each retreat, I ran my hands over those relaxing cheeks. The closer I came to the dip between them, the louder he moaned, his cock turning impossibly harder, throbbing inside my clenching cunt.

Surrendering to impulse, I grabbed his cheeks, kneaded them and spread them apart. Loved how an edge of desperation laced his panted moans and how his entire body trembled against mine. How his cock pulsed—

Malyr stiffened against me so suddenly, so completely, the weight of his body seemed to triple. He squeezed all the air from my lungs, but only until he slipped off me, jumped to his feet, and stared down at me with glistening eyes.

"Why did you do that?!" His sudden shout came with a black swell of shadows that cast over his eyes, sending a shudder through me. He was all anger and vibrating rage. Furious. "Why would you touch me like that, huh?"

My throat seemed to loop into a knot, not letting a single gasp of air into my lungs, amplifying that confusion that quickly settled onto my thoughts. "I... I thought you liked it."

A flinch went through him, head jerking back as if I'd physically slapped him. He gasped, swallowed thickly, only for yet another gasp to tumble from his quivering lips.

Then he shifted and flew off.

CHAPTER
THIRTY-FIVE

Sebian

Present Day, Valtaris, throne room

Something was wrong.

Malyr sat on a throne as dramatic as the man himself—a monstrosity with ten massive wings carved from *aerymel* spreading out behind the hard seat—looking rather lost with how he sank his head in his palm on an exhale. "You are doing it wrong."

"Clearly." At the center of the throne room, Galantia stared at the polished black floor in her shadowcloth dress, her shoulders slouching after a dozen failed attempts at wielding his shadows. "Maybe I wouldn't be doing it wrong if you told me how to do it right?"

Malyr's jaws shifted, the grinding of molars against molars sending gooseflesh across my skin. They'd done that for two days now, hiding their frustration behind calm voices and lackluster conversations. Either that, or they didn't talk at all, which was damn uncomfortable when one shared a nest with them. There was only so much awkward silence I could take at night before they finally fell to sleep, returning some fucking air in the room to breathe.

This shit needed fixing.

My attention drifted to the servant girl who carried a bowl of fruits. When she passed by, I plucked a goldenberry they must've brought from Lanai, and popped it into my mouth.

The girl turned to look at me, her cheeks flushing a peachy pink as she giggled and curtsied. "Lord Sebian."

I lifted my hand and pointed at those three braids Galantia had weaved together down along my scalp this morning. "I'm no lord."

Cute, how she flushed even harder, almost tripping over her feet as she hurried off. As far as I was concerned, I was bonded. Maybe not by soul, but by heart.

"Watching dough rise is less strenuous than watching them tiptoe around each other," Asker whispered as he stepped beside me. "Do you know what transpired between them?"

I shook my head, unable to twist my brain around this, same as him. I'd found them at the grotto that evening, just when Malyr had finally told her that he loved her. *I will be the night, the darkest patch of sky around you?* What man came up with that stuff when his cock was undoubtedly already throbbing in the water? I'd bet three coins that he'd fucking studied that line for days!

And then he'd... fucked it up. How?

On instinct, my hand lifted to my side, scratching an itch there. I'd left when they'd kissed. As much as I usually enjoyed being with both of them, I loved my time with Galantia alone just as much. Like this morning, after Malyr had left to do princely stuff, and we'd stayed in the nest a while longer to make love. Not all moments needed sharing. Surely, Malyr had enjoyed having her emotionally closer to him than ever before... until he'd fucked it up.

How, exactly, had he done that?!

Another itch on the side of my neck, like a faint tingle when someone stared at you. Like the way Asker was...

"Do I owe you money?" I glanced at him and shrugged. "I told you, I don't know what happened."

Asker's gaze lingered on me for several beats too long, each passing second layering the air with an almost palpable density, like the weight of something unsaid. For a moment, he looked as though he was about to speak, his lips parting slightly above his beard.

But then, just as quickly, his expression shuttered closed. "Thank you for helping Marla with the chimney."

As if helping people I'd once considered my family would ever require a 'thank you'. "Of course."

His balance shifted from one plated leg to the other, where I'd only ever seen him standing stiff and still. "Marla wants you to—no, I am saying that wrong." He clenched his lips, letting the bristles of his beard noisily scrape against each other. "We would like you to come and visit us one of these evenings. For supper. Like it used to be."

Like it used to be.

Every muscle in my body strung tight, turning me into

the one who couldn't quit staring at him. He'd spoken more with me in these last few weeks than he had in those last five years combined—and not one degrading remark uttered. Why? To make peace? To reconnect? Why bother now?

I crossed my arms in front of my chest, not knowing what to make of this. "I'll think about it."

"Very well," he said and turned his attention back to the squabbling couple before us.

"I am not a thief," Malyr said. "All I can do is offer up my shadows for you to practice, but harnessing your gift is on you." He stretched out his hand, casting tendrils of shadow that slithered down the stairs, blackening the red carpet beneath. "Absorb, then wield."

"Focus." Galantia's whisper was likely too quiet for anybody but me to hear as she raised her absorbing hand, her eyes intently fixed on the tendrils. She lifted her other hand toward the wall to avoid accidentally killing someone. "Absorb and mirror. Absorb and mirror. Absorb and—"

Shadows oozed from her fingertips like molasses in winter—sluggish, heavy, and so fucking uninspired. They dripped onto the ground, forming a black pool there that wouldn't kill any enemy... unless he happened to step on it, slip, and conveniently break his neck.

Not fucking likely.

Galantia sighed, the way frustration carved itself onto her forehead in deep frowns looking more adorable than it should. "Isn't there a single thief out there who can help me?"

"I am afraid not, my lady," Asker said and hinted a bow. "You are the only recorded one. If there are other thieves, then they chose to remain hidden."

Malyr slouched deeper into his throne, thumbing his

temple as if warding off a headache. "Perhaps you should visit my mother's old chamber. Look through her personal writings and see if we can find something, *anything*, on voids that went unrecorded. Since she revealed late, she kept journals about how she found her power. See if you find them."

Five ravens soared in through a flight hole along the wall of stained windows. They landed at the bottom of the stairs to the throne, morphing into one of our younger scouts—a pathfinder boy, barely older than a fledgling, with sparse wisps of hair sprouting on his chin, his black hair cropped short. He acknowledged Asker with a nod, then shifted his focus to Malyr.

Dropping to one knee, he said, "My prince, the human farmers near the western fields and meadows didn't vacate their homes. They report that their—"

Malyr slammed his hands down on the armrests of his throne, shadows surging through the sparkling black metal until the wings behind him seemed to shift and move. "I could have driven those humans off our lands the way they have done with us. Instead, I have given them notice and time... and this is how they repay me?!"

"Without spring seeding, Valtaris will face a grain shortage with the next winter to be certain." Asker folded his arms behind his back and straightened. "My prince, I will personally fly down there and see to the issue."

"Take fifty deathweavers and ten pathfinders with you," Malyr commanded. "If they will not leave on their own, then you shall *make them.*"

"You cannot seriously contemplate to drive them off the land by force." Galantia gaped up at him, those furrows between her brows deepening further. "You told me you would give them time."

"I *have* given them time."

"How much was that? Six days? Seven?" Galantia scoffed. "Malyr, you can't expect those people to uproot their lives within a week. With snow still on the ground, no less. These farms are their homes!"

"No, they are *our* home," Malyr snapped with a bump of his fist against his chest. "For ten years, they have paid no tenancy. I want them gone by the morrow, or they will repay with their lives."

Galantia lifted her chin in that stubborn, proud way of hers. "They are innocent farmers."

"They... are... *humans*," Malyr ground out.

Something in Galantia's expression shifted. The anger receded like a tide pulling back from the shore, leaving only... disappointment.

"Like I was once," she said softly, her words a lingering echo in this massive room before she turned away, her dress billowing as she left the room with purpose in her stride.

Malyr immediately rose, reaching out his hand as if he could physically grab hold of her despite the distance. All he caught was empty air. He threw his hands up, letting them drop to his sides with the sound of his exhale.

Damn his fucking temper...

I hurried after Galantia, because this needed patching before I lost my damn mind. I caught up with her in the great hall, where servants scurried about, polishing silver and replacing candles in the massive golden chandeliers that dangled from the ceiling's tarred crossbeams.

I grabbed her arm and pulled her against me, a jab piercing through my chest at the sight of her glossy eyes. "Come here, sweetheart."

Curling her little fingers into my shirt, she sank into my

embrace, her entire body turning sluggish as if she'd held in too much tension for too long. "I'm so exhausted."

"I know." She'd gone from not knowing who she was, to the thief who'd lifted a curse within a matter of weeks. Then there was her frustration over not being able to wield shadows. "Care to finally tell me what the fuck he did now?"

She blinked up at me, her lips parting and closing about as many times as she shook her head before she said, "He didn't do anything. It was me."

That... was not what I'd expected her to say. "What do you mean? What did you do?"

"I don't... I don't know." Her voice wavered, the corners of her mouth twitching. "One moment, everything was fine. But then he just... stiffened. He got angry."

"You know he has a temper." Something that Asker and I agreed had improved drastically, otherwise Malyr would already be on his way to those farms to take care of the issue in one deadly sweep. "He's trying to control himself better, now that he syphons into you."

"That's what made it so bad," she all but whimpered. "I expected his shadows to lash out that evening, but they didn't. He was a different kind of angry. I don't know how, but... it felt terrible. Pitch black and... sad."

"And that happened in the spring?" When she nodded, I cupped her beautiful face. "Did you say something to anger him?"

She shook her head. "No. All I did was... well, touch him. I thought he liked it; he sounded like he liked it."

A foreboding tightness settled into my stomach, making me scan the great hall for pathfinders, then ushered her into an empty corridor for good measure. "Touched him... how?"

"I..." Her voice faded, and her noisy gulp had my ears prick. "I touched his... buttocks. Grabbed it, and kneaded it, and just fondled—I really thought he liked what I did. I don't understand why he got so angry."

That tightness twisted my guts, putting a bitter taste on the back of my tongue. No, of course she didn't understand. She had no fucking clue that he'd been so viciously raped in those dungeons that he'd bled from his ass when I'd found him. The worst part? How he hadn't moved an inch when I'd pulled his bloodied trousers down to tend to the tears and cuts. He'd just... laid there, his soul so fucking crushed that he hadn't even questioned a stranger feeling him up down there.

I tortured my upper lip for a moment. How did one explain that kind of depravity to a soul as sweet as Galantia?

Ten years. Ten years of friendship with Malyr, and not once had he brought it up, and neither had I. It was silently understood. If he would ever tell her... well, I doubted it. That didn't make it my place to do it for him, but neither could I shrug it off and say nothing.

"Do you remember how angry you got the night of the feast, hmm? When he let his shadows play with you, getting you dripping wet?" I tilted her head back a little, then lowered my mouth to her forehead in a long, gentle kiss. "Do you remember what I told you in that corridor?"

Her pupils flitted across my face for a moment before she nodded. "That I was just angry at myself."

"Sometimes, we lash out at others when, in reality, we're just mad at ourselves for liking something we think we shouldn't." I thumbed those lips I couldn't get enough of kissing good morning, kissing good night, and kissing a dozen more times in-between when nobody was looking.

"Or maybe we simply don't want others to know because... because it shames us that we feel that way. Or how we got to feel that way. Maybe it's something that was once so unpleasant, it's shameful for us to find pleasure in it now. Do you understand?"

Her frown suggested that she didn't, but all I could do was try to help them overcome this. "Will you walk with me? I'd like some fresh air."

"Go grab a cape or something because they opened the wind barriers, so it's chilly," I said. "Let me go back in there to check on Malyr. I'll come to our chamber and get you."

THIRTY-SIX

Malyr
Present Day, Valtaris, throne room

I'd inspired all sorts of reactions in Galantia over the last few months. She'd feared me, despised me, loathed me, but that look of somber disappointment just now?

It had gutted me.

"Does she not understand?" I asked Asker, who'd moved to stand at the bottom of the stairs to a throne that had always seemed so imposing, but now turned out to be quite uncomfortable. "With the risk of Aros withholding grains, Deepmarsh sitting in a marsh, and Tidestone already eating up resources for its restoration, how am I to feed the hundreds of Ravens that are returning to Valtaris each day? Am I so wrong to want those humans gone? After all the atrocities we've endured from them?"

There was a long string of varying vowels, nothing but noise before he finally mumbled, "It is said that a bonded royal pair ought to rule together, not because one of them is likely right, but because they are both likely wrong, and—"

"The right way is somewhere in the middle," I said on a sigh. "My mate is smart, resourceful, and quick at figuring things out. But she is also still very naive about war and the hardships outside a castle's walls. What am I supposed to do?"

"Not slaughter a bunch of unarmed farmers." In a burst of shadows, Sebian's unkindness dashed forward, only for him to slump himself on the stairs to my throne, looking so enviously comfortable with how he eased himself back onto his elbow and sprawled his legs out. "Unless, of course, you preferred to roost outside on one of the dead trees all along."

Sick of this hard seat, I rose and moved toward the stairs, then eased down on them beside Sebian. "You are my advisor, Asker. Advise me on how I can avoid my mate kicking me out of my own chambers without having to watch my people starve as a result."

I waited for some sage advice.

None came.

Sebian gave a bemused scoff that had his lips twitch. "I will be the *night*, the darkest patch of sky around you," he mocked, but it wasn't like I hadn't heard his unkindness back at the spring. "How many days did it take you to come up with those lines?"

"Five," I said with a slap against the back of his head that had him coughing up a laugh and actually brought a twitch of a smile to my face. "Three for drafting, two for revisions."

My smile didn't last.

Heart dragging downward inside my chest, my thoughts wandered back to that evening. How fast Galantia's heart had pounded upon those words, making her spine vibrate against my chest. How passionately we'd kissed. How close her soul had been to mine, until she'd touched me...

...there.

No doubt she'd read my outburst as anger when, in reality, it had been shame. If she knew that many men had made me their whore, would she think me filthy? If she knew that I had somehow developed a liking to it—an act that had once been forced upon me with pain and violence —would she think me tainted? Sick? More twisted than I had already proven her to be?

"You were right," I finally confessed, and not for the first time when it came to Galantia. "Words do have an impact on her."

"Yeah, well, if only you wouldn't have such a talent for saying the right thing one moment and ruining all your efforts the next."

Yes, that was my forte. "Meaning?"

"Meaning that it took you weeks to convince her of your feelings," he said. "The prince who allowed himself to fall in love with what he thought was a human woman, but can't bring himself to extend a shred of kindness to those human farmers."

That observation cut deeper than I wanted it to, sending a stabbing pain through my core. For nineteen years, my mate had lived as a human. Naturally, she would continue to feel pity on their behalf. As much as I understood that, I wasn't sure if I could ever bring myself to do the same.

And why would I? Had they not slaughtered my family, destroyed our lands, desecrated our shrines? Where had humans' pity been for those Raven farmers they'd cut down? The fledglings they'd set aflame? Where had their kindness been when they'd—

"My prince," an unfamiliar voice said, making me lift my gaze to the guard who suddenly stood at the center of the throne room. "This man refused to be turned away. He said he has urgent information on the western farms, but refused to supply it, even after we gave him ten lashes, stating that he will only share it with you."

I didn't bother to straighten, let alone endure another minute on that hard throne by taking on a more presentable position. Certainly not for the likes of him.

My eyes fell to the man beside the guard. Brown, tousled hair. Rags for clothing. A back that had probably been hunched, even before those ten lashes. Beside him, an auburn-haired woman fisted her dirty brown dress, her gaze on the ground. Between them stood a young boy, nine, maybe ten years old, his blond hair such a stark contrast to the black floors.

My upper lip curled all on its own.

Humans.

I gave a wave of my hand that had them shuffle forward, stopping several feet short of the first step. "And what urgent information might you have about those farms and the trespassers who dare to disobey my order?"

"Your Highness." The man took another step forward, his bow as crooked as his spine, showing the bloodied threads on his back. "Please forgive me, but I had no other choice, I did not. I've got no information, I don't. It was... it was all a lie just so they'd let us in here."

"Humans telling lies." What a surprise. "Are you one of those farmers from the western fields?"

Another half-bow. "Yes, Your Highness. One of the farmers, I am. It's not a large plot of land, but we were content."

And yet, too large for his kind. "You must have walked for a long time."

"Five days on the road, Your Highness."

"There are less strenuous ways to die," I said. "And yet, you chose to come here, to a place where you are not wanted, with nothing of value."

Sebian gave me a side-glance, raising a brow at me as if I was about to let my shadows swallow them whole. And maybe I would have a few weeks ago, but not anymore. My shadows were... calm enough.

The woman beside him, his wife, presumably, swatted at him, but didn't dare lift her eyes. "Tell him, Oscar. Just tell the Raven king."

"It's true, we have nothing of value. The little we had, we put into buying seeds for the spring, but they'll now never be planted, they won't. The only thing left precious to us is our son here. Come and bow." When the boy remained stiff and still, his father gently ushered him half a step forward. "Bow."

"Come on now, bow," his mother said with a nod of encouragement and more of her swatting motions. "Just like we practiced at home. Do it."

The boy lifted his blue eyes to me, gulped, then bowed.

"I surely hope you do not expect that we will take him in," I said. "Valtaris is not an orphanage for abandoned human children. The goddess knows we have enough children of our own who have lost their parents."

"No, it's nothing like that, Your Highness." The man knelt beside his son, looking up at him with a gentleness I never remembered receiving from mine. That made me envious, too. "Show him, lad. Show the Raven king what you can do."

A blink of his teary eyes, then the boy lifted his hand, only for white shadows to stream from his fingers. Thousands of hair-thin threads cascaded forward and down, weaving into what barely resembled a blanket.

"Goddess bless us," Asker said, his mouth momentarily standing open. "A whiteweaver."

"Well I'll be fucking damned," Sebian mumbled.

All warmth left my cheeks and fingers, leaving behind a strange tingle. A white Raven boy. How was this possible?

I rose and slowly descended the stairs. "How did you come by this child?"

"King Malyr..." The woman gave a curtsy, or something that wanted to be one. "We found him when he was maybe two, when we heard a child cry inside a farm near a road. There was nobody there; he was all by himself, soiled up to his neck and gaunt. We took him but we didn't steal nothing. Twice, my husband went back to look for his parents, but nobody ever came back to that farm."

"We have no children of our own," the man continued. "So we took him in. Raised him as our son."

Pain stabbed into my right temple, announcing a headache at the most inconvenient of times. They had... taken in a Raven boy? Raised him as their own? Protected him?

No. No, what they'd protected had been their own skins when they'd found out what he was. It couldn't have been any other way.

I squatted before the cloth the boy had woven, and took in those pale strands as nuanced as Galantia's. "Surely, it must have come as a shock to you when he shifted? Weaved shadows?"

"Shock?" The boy's mother pressed a palm to her sternum and slowly shook her head. "No, Your Highness. We knew what he was when we found him."

"There were white feathers everywhere," his father said. "I've never seen no white Raven, only black ones. But when I tried to pick him up, he... his body twisted."

"He was too hungry to shift," the woman added. "But we knew."

Another stab into my temple, as if this information collided with everything I'd known to be true about humans and their never-ending hatred for my kind. "Why did you take him?"

"Well..." The woman exchanged a confused glance with her husband, as though her answer was supposed to be clear to me, where I could barely line my thoughts up straight anymore. "He was a child, abandoned, crying, and hungry. What were we supposed to do?"

Stab him. Cage him. Burn him.

I lifted my hand before the boy, letting the shadows between my fingertips shape a horse close enough it brought a shy little smile to his face. "What is your name?"

He looked at his father and, when it was met with a nod, he looked back at me. "David."

"He's not the only one, Your Highness," the man said, and goddess help me, this was getting worse with each word he spoke. "We never speak of it out of fear if King

Barat ever sent soldiers through our farms, but... there are more."

More Raven children.

Saved. By. Humans.

"Our cart is frozen into the earth," the man said. "My wife and I will be on our way just as soon as we managed it free, we will. But..." He bit back a sob. "We cannot take David with us, not where we're going. It's too dangerous, so we were hoping, Your Highness, that you would—"

The boy threw himself into his father's embrace. "Don't leave me here, Father. Please."

My molars ground together until they ached at the roots, amplifying that headache, cleaving through years and years of my screwed perceptions. Back at Deepmarsh, Galantia had put her prejudice aside, extending us Ravens her kindness. And if I managed to fall in love with what I'd thought to be a human woman, how could I not make an effort and extend kindness in return?

I rose and gestured the man to do the same. "Have you always been a farmer? Or have you learned another trade?"

The man rose and bowed. "I've worked fields, mines, and stones."

"All useful skills," I said and turned toward Asker. "Find them a home near the Winged Keep. Supply them with provisions. I want a guard to remain close to them while we find a way to avoid animosity or violence against the humans currently living on Vhaeryan soil."

THIRTY-SEVEN

Galantia

Present Day, Valtaris, Winged Keep

I n the hushed stillness of Queen Elnora's chamber, a sense of trespass weighed on me, yet my fingers tingled with curiosity and excitement as they rummaged through remnants of the past.

And what a lovely past it had been.

Rose-scented air filled the room, the aroma lingering, even after years of disuse. Tapestries of gold-threaded shadeweloth adorned the walls, their intricate weavings a cele-bration of Raven history, ever-so elusive to me. The towering bookshelves seemed to whisper as I ran my fingers along the leather- and vellum-bound spines, one wrist carrying a blue ribbon, the other a chestnut bracelet, searching for some-thing, *anything,* that could help me wield shadows.

"She loved to read." A trait she must have passed on to Malyr as he, too, enjoyed surrounding himself with books. "But I'm thinking she loved nothing quite as much as her children."

A love that reflected itself in various artifacts that filled the room. Children's drawings preserved like sacred texts, simple wood carvings embodying a son's adoration for his mother, bundles of tiny black feathers wrapped in embroi-dered cloth... The love this place must once have harbored created an atmosphere of nurturing warmth that I'd never known.

"I couldn't find information about voids or thieves in any of them." Tjema carefully looked through folded linens, her movements slow and respectful, her black strands braided down the burnt side of her face the way I'd once showed her. "Her gift revealed late. Maybe she never learned much about being a void?"

"The way Prince Malyr spoke of her made her sound powerful." My gaze shifted to the dressing table beside the tall window that overlooked Valtaris' central market, my pulse quickening. How likely was it to find what I was looking for among jewelry and powders? Would it be wrong to peek into those drawers? "Have you looked under the bed?"

Tjema yawned since she'd only arrived at Valtaris a few days ago by carriage, but that hadn't kept her from tending to me the way she'd done it at Tidestone and Deepmarsh. "There was nothing."

Hesitation tingled through my muscles, pulling my gaze back to the dressing table adorned with delicate trinkets. After a lingering moment, I took hesitant steps toward it. The cushioned stool felt soft under me, like a welcoming embrace, urging me to unlock the secrets that lay hidden within the wooden drawers.

I pulled at them.

Locked.

Locked.

Locked.

I kept tugging on the golden knobs, my hope dimming with each unyielding click. Until the seventh one opened with a reluctant creak. Inside, a square wooden box lay hidden beneath a layer of lavender sachets, their scent faint but lingering. My hands trembled as I lifted the box, setting it before me on the table.

A deep breath. Then I opened it.

Stacks of letters looked back at me, each sealed with black wax, their address of onyx ink elegantly dancing across parchment yellowed by age... in Old Vhaer.

"Tjema, can you read Old Vhaer?"

"No."

"Maybe they are farewell letters?" I went through them, squinting at writings I couldn't decipher, my arms tugging heavily on my shoulders. "It would be easier to understand what I'm holding here, if only I could—"

My hands stilled on the next parchment, my heart clanking against my throat at the words it held in the common tongue: *To Malyr's fated mate.*

The seal broke with the cracking of brittle wax, revealing Queen Elnora's ornate handwriting.

Dear daughter,

If you read this, then I am gone from this world, never having had the chance to meet you. But if I had, I would have asked you to take good care of my son. Do not shy away from his darkness... embrace it.

Understand that shadows cling to crevices and secret corners, thriving in the unseen, the hidden, the unacknowledged. If you fully embrace my son's darkness, welcoming every aspect of him without reservation, then those shadows will find their domain reduced, having less surface to cling to.

I entrust him to you and hope that you can be the light in his life, as I pray you will find your missing piece in him.

With all the love that words can carry from one heart to another, even across the veil of time and death,

Your mother-in-law
Elnora

A tear ran down my cheek, curved away from my smile, and dropped onto the parchment. I wiped it off on my shadowcloth dress, folded it, and carefully placed the letter into my sleeve. The others, I returned to the box, and rose with it clasped in my hands.

"We should give these—"

Malyr leaned in the doorframe, one hand in the pocket of his breeches, the other thumbing the silver buttons on his black vest. "Did you gain anything?"

Yes, a third mother, or so it seemed.

"We found farewell letters that I thought you might

want." I walked over and reached him the box. "I'm sure there's one for you in there."

He took the box, looking over its intricate carvings for a moment before his eyes found mine. "I was hoping you would come to the parlor with me. The dressmaker is waiting there for us."

"A dress for...?"

He pulled his hand from his pocket, reached it up to my face, and wiped away a tear that I must have missed. "That coronation you feel so uneasy about."

I let my eyes trail over that utterly crooked braid I'd put into his hair this morning, but he seemed to carry it with pride, regardless. "A coronation I can't refuse."

"You can." Malyr stepped closer, looking down at me with a tenderness that put tiny flutters into my chest. "But you won't."

I scoffed, "How very bold, granting agency with one sentence, only to strip it away with the next."

He *tsked*. "I'm coming to you with a proposition you cannot resist."

That caught my interest. "Oh?"

"Agree to sit beside me as our queen for all of Vhaerya to see, and in return..." His fingers pulled a blonde strand from my braid, which he twirled around his fingers, the tip of his nose giving a little stub against mine. "I will allow the humans in our kingdom to remain here, unbothered, if they so choose and—"

"I'll do it!" I blurted in a burst of pure relief and... yes, joy. "I'll put that crown on right now."

It looked beautiful, the way he chewed away his grin, chomping his face back into something princely. "There are conditions. From now on, they will pay tenancy. Thirty percent of the food they produce will go to our granaries, which is slightly higher than what Ravens are to contribute, and their right to remain here will be relinquished if they sell their produce to anybody who is not a citizen of Vhaerya."

"Sounds fair."

Malyr's eyes twinkled, reflecting both relief and a happiness so pure, it seemed to emanate from him like a soft glow. Carefully, as though I were a fragile piece of glasswork, he leaned down to me and his lips met mine, moving with an attentive sweetness I hadn't known he possessed.

"I don't want there to be discord between us," he whispered between featherlight kisses. "I'm no easy man—I know this—but I am irrefutably yours, heart and soul, left with a lifetime to strive to walk in your light."

Warmth spread through me. No, no more discord. Hate, lies, deceit... it all lay behind us now.

When he finally pulled away, he gifted me one of his smiles that wasn't quite so rare anymore and took my hand into his. "Come. I have a surprise for you."

"Another surprise?"

Malyr handed Tjema the box, gesturing for her to follow behind us into the corridor and back toward the more formal rooms. "The mines are being worked. The first tenancies are coming in. Raven artisans and merchants from all over the realm are returning to Valtaris. Nothing's holding me back now from spoiling my mate a little." Malyr led me into the lavish parlor, a stately sitting room filled with a sense of grandeur, yet imbued with warmth. "You remember Darien, I presume?"

"My future queen," Darien said with a deep bow, the dressmaker once more donning a fine gown of black shadowcloth, woven with parts of a fox pelt. "I hope you can forgive our last encounter. That red-haired thing never looked good in that black gown... not much of a waist, while yours is just right! Too pale a complexion and too stark a contrast to her hair, too. Downright sickly. But you..."

As if I didn't know that he'd merely acted on orders. "All is forgiven, but you better make this gown the most fabulous."

"Nothing else will do!" he said with a flamboyant wave of his hands that shoved the long black strands off his shoulders. "And how rare a beauty it will be, created together with my new apprentice. David, how did we practice you would greet your future queen?"

A scrawny blond-haired boy wearing lovely white robes stepped out from behind Darien, bowing so deeply, he stumbled forward, having to paddle his arms to regain his balance. "Your Highness."

I looked back and forth between Malyr's strange smirk and that boy's big blue eyes, not understanding any of this. "Apprentice?"

A... human?

Darien knelt before me and gave David an encouraging pat on the back. "Show Her Highness what I taught you this morning."

David took a deep breath.

With focus carved between his brows, he extended his arms in front of him. With a flick of his wrists and a graceful curling of his fingers, mesmerizing swirls of white fog emanated from his fingertips. The plumes danced in the air, twirling together into threads of the most radiant silk I'd ever seen. It wove together right before my eyes, its surface so luminous, it caught and reflected the sunlight streaming in through the windows, casting a softer, brighter glow across the room.

A gasp escaped me. I looked at Malyr, finding his eyes already on me, a smile curving his narrow lips. And then he did something I hadn't expected his muscles capable of.

He winked.

The lightness of the gesture sent a ripple of warm elation through me, and for a moment, treacherous flutters settled into my stomach too intense to be ignored. And why would I? With my name washed away, my identity revealed, our souls bound, and no more hate to keep us apart, what stood in the way of our hearts?

Nothing.

When David swayed on his tippy toes in an attempt to weave a white sleeve over my dissolving black one, I knelt down and offered him a smile. "I thought I was the only white Raven."

His eyes gleamed. "You're a white Raven, too... um... Your Highness?"

"Yes."

"I've never seen another white Raven," he said as Darien pointed out where exactly he needed to continue with the swift movements of his hands. "Actually, I've never seen any other Raven before. Not until yesterday."

I frowned at that. "What do you mean? Where did you come from?"

"My father has a farm, but he's human," he said with a shrug. "My mother, too. But now we live in Valtaris. Prince Malyr said that I need to be close, or I can't be Darien's apprentice."

My eyes flicked to Malyr, searching his face for some explanation, some sign that I hadn't heard correctly. All he offered was a playful tilt of his head and an arched brow that seemed to mimic his renewing smirk.

Something unfurled deep within me, a tight knot loosening in my chest before I returned my attention back to David. "Did you teach yourself how to weave like this?"

He nodded. "What is your gift?"

"I'm a thief." At Malyr's reprimanding cough, I added, "But that's our little secret, yes?"

David's eyes widened, making it clear his adoptive parents had taught him about our kind. "You can steal gifts?"

"In theory." Given the slow progress I made on tapping into other's shadows and wielding them, I had no hope in stealing anyone's gift anytime soon. Even then, I would never *not* return it—something I read in a book was possible, same as storing them within salt like mine had been. "Did you read about thieves?"

David's hands seemed to have long stilled, his eyes fixed on something behind me. No, not something.

Someone.

I looked back at Tjema, the girl shifting from one leg to the other with the wooden box in hand as though she didn't quite know what to do with the boy's attention, so I helped her along. "That's Tjema, my maid. Tjema, why don't you say hello to David? You look to be about the same age."

Tjema dropped her gaze, shyly shoving the tip of her boot over the dark red carpet. "Hello."

A motion twitched in my periphery.

David had tilted his head in much the same way Malyr had done it the day in the forest, his eyes wide, but not with shock at her appearance. "Hello."

"That will do for now," Darien said, who'd been busy

taking my measurements with threads of woven shadows. "The boy has been practicing since before the sun was up... He even skipped his porridge. I'll have David work on the frame until his weaving is accurate enough to work on the finer details."

Malyr moved to sit on one of the intricately carved, velvet-upholstered chairs that adorned the room, the dark wood standing in stark contrast to the ease of his soft expression. "If I wanted nothing but white shadowcloth for the entire dress, how long do you believe it might take?"

"My Prince," Darien said with a respectful bow, "if you can give us thirty days, we will create a gown more breathtaking than any before."

"I give you twenty."

"Why, of course," Darien said and turned away.

"Tjema," I said with an ushering wave. "Why don't you take David to the kitchen? I'm sure he's hungry. Just leave the box here."

She hesitated for a moment, then put the box on a table and gestured David to follow her.

When the room was finally empty, I strode over to Malyr in a black dress with half a white sleeve. "Did you notice how David reacted to Tjema's voice?"

"I had."

"Do you think they could be fated?"

"It's very well possible, but they can never bond since she lost her anoa." He thought on that for a moment, then smacked his lips. "But they can love each other and make each other happy."

"Everything you proposed, you have already put in place, have you not?"

He took my arm and gave a little tug, but I remained where I was. "I have."

"Why?" I asked. "Why change your mind and bring his human parents to live here?"

"Because I knew that the kindness you so generously extend to others would never let you say no. And then, of course, there is the fact that—" He gave a yank on my arm, pulling me onto his lap just as his arms wrapped around me, taking me into a deep embrace. "It was the right thing to do. If my mate is able to let go of her hate for me, then how can I not follow her lead and try to do the same for humans?"

His words eroded the last fragments of doubt and reservation that had lodged themselves into the crevices of my heart. The walls I'd constructed, built of distrust and fear, seemed to crumble into inconsequence. In that moment, it was so easy to confess my feelings for him. At least to myself...

I lifted my hand to cup his cheek, my fingers lightly grazing the sway of his brow. A sense of deep satisfaction filled me as he leaned into my touch, his eyes closing for a fleeting moment, as if to savor the sensation. That was when I did it.

I closed the distance between us, pressing my mouth against his. His eyes snapped open in surprise for a split second before they fluttered shut again with mine. My lips parted, inviting him to explore further, and he obliged. His tongue slid into my mouth, meeting mine with a deep, masculine groan.

Malyr's hand moved up into my braid, fiercely tugging as if to unleash the energy that resonated between us. His other hand pressed firmly against my hipbone, sending a tingle of pleasure rushing through me before curling around my buttocks with an intensity that demanded to be felt. I melted into him, my hands eagerly exploring his back and gripping tightly, willing him to make me his own in the heat of the moment.

"I want you," he growled into my mouth, our skin humming with desire that threatened to overflow. "I love you."

For a moment, my vocal cords vibrated as if gearing up to reciprocate his declaration, a wave of panic and thrill surging through me at the thought. Instead, I moaned, the tension between us, the sheer need, reaching an unbearable peak.

Until a knock sounded.

Asker poked his head into the parlor. "My prince, I am afraid there is some trouble afoot that requires your attention."

Malyr's throat vibrated with a sound of utter annoyance. "Is it very important? *Very?*"

"Very."

When Malyr sighed, the sound nearly taking on the qualities of a wail, I chuckled. "Sounds like you have to go and do princely stuff."

"Yes, princely stuff," Malyr muttered with a chuckle before he quickly placed another peck on my mouth, then slipped me off him. "I will see you later."

THIRTY-EIGHT

Galantia
Present Day, Valtaris

I ran my fingers through Sebian's black strands where they sprawled out beside me in our nest, his familiar scent clinging to the shadowcloth, black mink, and embroidered pillows surrounding us. He smelled soft and sweet, like the honeyed pine needle tea one cozied up with by a fire after a hard day.

Safe and nurturing.

Warm and grounding.

Sebian was my protector, my haven, my sanctuary. He was my home in the truest sense: not a place, but a feeling of love and belonging; a knowing that wherever he was, I wanted to be.

He was my choice.

Between the three of us, he was usually the last to wake. It would be no different this morning, given how he'd joined us late last night after having spent supper with Asker and Marla.

I looked to my left at Malyr, his breathing even, his eyes still firmly shut. He was usually the first of us to wake, often slipping out of our room with the first rays of the sun. I lifted my hand to cup his cheek, sensing the first stubble beneath my touch.

Malyr sealed his hand over mine, and his lashes fanned open, blinking lazily a few times before his eyes locked with mine. And what extraordinary eyes they were, shimmering in that delicate space between sleep and wakefulness, revealing a landscape of unguarded emotions.

Love and affection.

Curiosity and hope.

It was as if dawn itself had found a place to reside within them, illuminating the shadows that often clouded his gaze. Here, in this transient moment, he showed me his heart, his soul, and the truth within.

Yes, he loved me.

I knew that now.

Scooting closer until mere inches remained between our faces, he silently guided my hand onto his bare chest, letting my fingertips glide over every puckered rise of a scar, every smooth valley between them. His movements slowed and the weight of his hand lifted some, all guidance quickly diminishing.

A question.

An invitation.

A hope that I would touch him of my own volition.

I traced his firm pectorals, the gap between them, and the furrow that trailed down along the muscles on his stomach. "I didn't mean to wake you," I whispered.

"Wake me like this more often." His fingers dove into my hair and cradled the back of my head. "Any day. Any time."

His lips feathered around the corner of my mouth, the sensation bringing my lungs to an abrupt halt before he pressed his forehead to mine. A rush of shadows flowed over me like liquid night, seeping through the fabric of my nightgown, enveloping me in a sensuous caress. Every inch of my skin tingled with an energy that left me heated.

I moaned, the sensation intoxicating, each shadowy tendril dancing over my nerve endings and leaving a trail of tingling warmth. "I need you."

"I told you once before, *anoaley*," he whispered, the weight of his hand lowering to the sway of my hip, "I don't want to be needed; I want to be wanted."

I nuzzled his temple, taking in the crisp scent of winter and those undercurrents of lemongrass. He smelled cold but alluring, like a fresh blanket of snow that hid the first buds of spring.

Treacherous and beautiful.

Tempting and elusive.

Malyr was my tormentor, my paradox, my teacher. He was a million painful lessons, shaping me into who I had always meant to become.

He was my fate.

I ran my hand down between us to the hard contour of

his cock, squeezing his throbbing crown through his trousers. "I want you."

Malyr's masculine groan echoed like thunder through my body, setting my skin ablaze. He held me tight, pressing his body against mine until I could feel every hard plane of him. His lips crashed down on mine with a fervor that sent sparks of pleasure through my body. I clung to him, my leg desperately wrapping around his as our bodies rocked against each other.

"Get rid of your gown," he rasped as he shoved his trousers down beneath the blanket. "Absorb it."

I opened my void, hungry after a night with no shadows, letting it tug and pull on the threads. They frayed into black plumes that rushed into my core with such desperation, my nipples hardened with my moan.

Malyr captured the needy sound between his lips, his tongue breaching the barrier of my teeth. His hand clenched around my thigh with possessive force, lifting it, spreading me to take him. He thrust inside my wet center on a gasp, spinning and twirling his hips until they were locked tight within mine. With one last lunge, he filled me completely, sending an overwhelming wave of pleasure through my body.

I clawed my fingers into his back, bracing against the intensity of his thrusts, the animalistic desperation with which he fucked into me. "Oh gods, mmm—"

My moan died on my lips, suffocated beneath the collar of his hand on my throat. Waves of bliss rippled through me, my pulse pounding wildly against his fingertips, the room around me melting out of focus at the thrill that raced through my veins.

It lasted but a second.

Malyr eased his grip, his features taut with pleasure, his

eyes clenched shut with each passionate thrust, giving nothing away. His fingers did, however, curl ever-so slightly around my throat, caressing, pressing, never quite choking.

But they wanted to.

I sensed it in their tremble, and how it seemed to spread through his entire body, stiffening his muscles as though he didn't trust what they might do otherwise.

Wicked things.

Deranged things.

Painful things.

Things I'd once rejected out of anger, shamed by how much pleasure they held. Whatever shame Malyr held, for whatever reason, what better way was there for me to encourage him to let it go than to show him that I had done so with mine long ago?

I placed my hand atop his where it rested on my throat, squeezing it in encouragement as I said, "Do it. I want you to."

A dozen emotions flitted across his face, from guilt, to awe, and over lust, then back to guilt again. "I don't want to hurt you."

"Yes, you do." Maybe he wanted to hurt me because he'd had so much pain inflicted on him when he was young. Maybe I wanted to be hurt because I'd had none. "If there's love in this pain, then I want it. I just don't want there to be any pain in this love."

His hips slowed, eyes narrowing at me for a moment before his grip tightened on my throat, sending such lovely white floaters across my vision as he whispered by my ear, "Your heart is safe with me, *anoaley*. Never again will I cause it pain. *Never*. As for the rest..."

One quick move, and he caught my bottom lip between his teeth. Then he bit down.

I yelped at the sudden sting, my breath coming in short gasps as pain and pleasure collided in my core. It burned its way through my veins, setting every part of me ablaze with such energy, such thrill... such life!

"I love you," he ground out, his thrusts almost violent in their intensity, making me dive my fingers into his hair, fisting it for hold. "You, little dove, were made for me."

I shuddered under the scratch of teeth on the inside of my bottom lip as our past flitted in my mind's eye. He was made for me. In him, I'd found my missing pieces.

A gentle whisper of a touch settled on the side of my neck, warm and damp, so at odds with Malyr's rough grip on my breast that it lured a gasp from me.

"Shh, it's only me, sweetheart," Sebian crooned against my ear. "I wouldn't mind waking up to this more often. Watch how good Malyr's cock makes you feel."

I glanced over my shoulder back at Sebian and saw the way he stroked his hard length. He must have for a while, running his fist up along the heavily veined shaft before he rubbed his fingers over his cum-glistening crown.

Fingers that he brought to my mouth, painting my lips with those first traces of seed. "Open up. Have a taste of me."

I licked my lips in anticipation, then opened my mouth, inviting the way he stroked his fingers over my tongue. I curled it around them, savoring the salty taste before I spread it across my gums.

With his hand tight on my hip, Malyr braced me against his next, hard thrust, only to keep at the very end of me, making me writhe and squirm. "Kiss him, little dove."

I reached behind me and slung my arm around Sebian's neck, pulling his mouth to mine. Our lips melted in a slow, languid kiss, my tongue sharing his taste.

A groan vibrated in his naked chest. "Goddess help me, I swear I want to load you up with my cum and lap the taste of us straight out of your cunt. Reach between your legs, sweetheart. Gather some of that mess you two made down there and feed it to me."

I did as I was told. My fingertips grazed Malyr's shaft—which seemed to swell even more at that innocent touch—then I brought it to Sebian's lips, a shudder cascading across my body with how he devoured the two fingers like a starving man.

He looked at Malyr and shook his head. "Missed it by a few days."

It took me a moment to realize what they were talking about, then my eyes snapped to Malyr's. "You were fucking me just fine without knowing that I wasn't fertile."

"And why would I not, hmm?" Malyr rocked into me, pushing himself so tightly against me, my clit throbbed beneath the pressure of his body. "I have no intention of preventing a child. If nature requires patience, then so be it. But if you end up carrying my son or daughter? I'd be overjoyed."

At my gasp, Sebian's chuckle tickled along the side of my neck. "Why's your heart racing, sweetheart? Isn't that what you tried to get from him that night at the *kjaer*, hmm? A baby?" A kiss behind my ear. "Fuck, sweet thing, you have no idea how much I want to see your belly grow round with a little nestling. You'd look adorable."

"Look at me." Malyr gripped my chin like a vise, turning my focus back on him, just as he pulled his cock out of me. "I want you to look at me while he takes his turn fucking your tight, wet cunt."

With my face trapped in the grip of his hand, I kept Malyr's stare as Sebian let his cock nudge at my entrance.

Even blind, I could always tell the difference between these two men from the shape of their cocks. Sebian's gently tapered wider the deeper he sank into me, oh-so gently, so excruciatingly slow, the slight curve in his shaft stroking my inner walls until I shuddered.

He moved at an agonizing pace, each unhurried thrust accompanied by tender kisses behind my ear, gentle tugs on the lobe, and laps of his tongue along the shell. It was torture. Sublime torture, teasing the slowest ripples of pleasure from my body, but never allowing it to crest while he took his time with me.

"Does that feel good?" he whispered by my ear while he rolled his hips against my backside, pushing my clit straight into those fingers that Malyr circled around it. "Are you going to come for me?"

I couldn't answer.

The sensation was too much, and my breathing came in sharp gasps that might have been a yes or it might have been a plea for him to never stop. He didn't. Sebian kept going, driving me with his even thrusts. Sparks of heat tingled around my clit, building and building, until—

Sebian *tsked* just as he pulled out of me, all heat fizzling out to the sound of my whimper. "Take her."

Malyr lifted my thigh higher. In a single thrust, he plunged back into me, his fingers curling into my flesh with bruising strength. He hammered in and out of me with quick, rough pulsations, letting the sound of skin slapping against skin echo in the room.

The frenzied pace, the desperation of Malyr's panted breaths, the brute power of his muscles... It drove my mind straight into a haze, clouding more each time he sealed his other hand over my mouth and nose, robbing me of air, making my head loll back in a daze.

Air rushed into my lungs. "Uh-uh, stay with us." A measured slap at my cheek sent a lovely chill across my heated face and an ungodly throb into my clit. "Do you want to come, little dove, hmm?"

"Yes," I croaked, writhing like a madwoman.

Malyr slowed his pace, his movements shifting from hard thrusts to a rolling motion that caressed my clit straight into a new wave of heated tingles. "Tell Sebian that you love him."

I arched my back, my nipples two hard, aching points, and looked back at Sebian. "I love you."

A hand cupped my breast and roughly lifted it, but that had nothing on the sting of teeth clamping around my areola as Malyr growled through his bite. "Take her."

Malyr pulled out, taking with him the tingling pleasure and the sparks of heat, letting the throb around my clit fade to the sound of my groan.

"No..." I whimpered.

Sebian chuckled, which was a mean thing in itself. But the way he merely teased my entrance with his cockhead...? How he slid his hard shaft up and down along my slit, pressing against my clit, only to retreat?

It was torment.

Glorious, soul-rending torment.

"You want to come, sweetheart?" Sebian crooned by my ear, his arm reaching around for his hand to clasp my chin, bringing my gaze to Malyr before he whispered ever so quietly, "Tell Malyr that you love him. Tell him that, through all this, you never *stopped* loving him."

A rush of emotions surged through my chest, crashing against my heart like a wave against a cliff—each droplet an unspoken truth, each thinning rock a crumbling deception. Remnants of my defenses washed away, allowing the current to flow into my heart and fill it.

"I... I love you," I said and slowly, so slowly, allowed my eyes to find Malyr's. "I never stopped loving you. Not even for a day, not even a little."

Malyr's eyes widened, as if my words had unlocked a realm of possibilities he'd dared not hope for. His lips slightly parted with a sharp intake of breath, the sudden gasp echoing the weight of the confession as it seemed he'd momentarily forgotten how to breathe. Even the hand that rested on my hip quivered.

And then, with a resolve that seemed carved from the same steel as his soul, he gave a tug on my thigh and pulled me flush against him. His lips found mine in a searing kiss that left no room for doubt or hesitation—a kiss that was the sum of all the yearning, all the hope, all the love that had been silently accumulating between us.

Malyr sank his cock back into me, tenderly now, reigniting the tingles between my legs one loving stroke at a time. My skin prickled with desire, every subtle shift of his body sending a wave of ecstasy coursing through my veins, my body trembling with a sudden onslaught of need for release.

Until something prodded at my cunt.

Sebian's cock.

Right. Beside. Malyr's.

Malyr stilled, his narrowing eyes going to Sebian. The two men looked at each other for a long moment, neither one saying a word.

It was Sebian who finally spoke. "You decide if this works for you or not. Either way, we'll manage."

Another second.

More glaring silence.

Until, after what felt like an eternity, Malyr nodded and continued to rock into me, and... what... what did that mean?

Only when Sebian's cock prodded at a hole already thoroughly filled did realization strike and wrench a gasp from me. "What—"

"Shh..." Sebian hushed where he lay on his side behind me, wedging his cock into me with hot-stinging pulsations. "You can handle us both, sweetheart. Just... relax. Let me in."

I let out a deep groan as both men slowly thrust into me, with Sebian lapping the sensitive skin behind my ear while Malyr devoured my mouth. The sensation was intense, stretching and burning in places I'd never felt before. But the sting soon faded into a deep, filling pressure, bringing an overwhelming sense of bliss that seemed to wrap around us like a blanket.

"We love you so much, Galantia," Sebian whispered, making my body quiver and shudder between them as waves of ecstasy flooded over me again and again—each wave stronger than the last. "Do you hear me, sweetheart? Right here, between us, you are so very loved."

"Say that you love us both," Malyr rasped against my bottom lip before he nipped the swollen flesh. "Say it, and we'll let you come this time."

My senses heightened, one arm reaching behind me to grab Sebian's neck while my other hand dove into Malyr's hair. "I love you. Both of you."

I threw my head back against Sebian in pleasure, my moans echoing in the room as both men increased their thrusting pace. Taking complete control of my body, they spread me wide with their passionate movements, sending me into new heights of pleasure that had me quivering and shaking uncontrollably. Their cocks filled me perfectly, each thrust pushing me closer to pure rapture as the sensations between my legs intensified until I couldn't take it anymore.

My release came in a blinding wave of sheer delight, amplified only by the way how, first, Sebian lost his rhythm, groaning as he released deep inside me. Malyr followed mere seconds after, his chest rising and falling rapidly at those panted groans of pleasure.

We stayed connected for a long time afterward, our breathing still labored and our skin slick with sweat. And when I nodded off once more, I did in a protective embrace of arms and legs, my entire being encapsulated by love.

So much love.

CHAPTER
THIRTY-NINE

Galantia

Valtaris, throne room

My heels clicked softly in the eerie quiet as I crossed the throne room, the black stone illuminated by fractured rainbows from how the moonlight streamed through the massive colored windows. The dancing flames from the sconces flickered as if trying to compete, sending shadows to skitter across the blood-red walls that cast the room in a mysterious glow.

Lowering the white scarf David had made me from my heated neck, I continued past the left of the throne, following that faint rumble of deep voices. I loved spending my nights between both Sebian and Malyr. Only one of them was acceptable if the other was busy, but having none of them beside me?

That wouldn't do.

"Several wagonloads of grains have left the granaries at Hanneling Hold, but the thaw and mud make for slow progress," Asker mumbled somewhere behind that stone archway that led to the map room. "Lord Aros himself left for Valtaris so he may attend the coronation. Perhaps he is already in the city?"

Malyr let out a long, audible exhale where he stood over the map chiseled into the stone table before him. "That he obeyed and sent the grains without delay is a relief, indeed. It could have gone differently."

Sebian scoffed, the northern territories apparently inconsequential to this war, because that was where he lay sprawled out on the stone table, his arms folded beneath his head as a pillow. "Maybe he realized that you've done him a fucking favor."

Malyr arched a brow at Sebian before he turned his attention back to Asker. "What about the other bannermen? The human lords?"

"All will attend the ceremony, and scouts have spotted the first carriages coming north-east."

"Have them closely watched. Once the ground hardens, I want them all to gather so we may discuss the attack on Ammarett," Malyr said. "I am looking forward to slicing off the heads of Barat and Brisden before we install human governance we can trust and rely on."

"Nobody touches Domren." There was a dark quality in

Sebian's voice he so rarely showed. "That bastard is mine to kill."

When nobody said anything for long moments, I cleared my throat.

"What's wrong?" Malyr walked up to me, his black vest as unbuttoned as the white shirt beneath was untied, and he wrapped his arms around me. "You cannot sleep?"

"No," I said and looked back and forth between him and Sebian, who'd lifted his head to grin at me. "If you lend me some of your shadows, I'll try to knit myself a blanket. The gods know I'd have more company if I curled up with it here between carved figurines of ravens and horses."

"Is this your way of saying that you're missing us, sweetheart, hmm? Malyr, our woman's feeling neglected." Sebian chuckled, thrust himself up, and slipped off the table before he strode toward us. "How about we take good care of her?"

Asker cleared his throat. "The hour is late, I know, but there is still much to discuss."

Sebian shrugged and looked at Asker. "The war has been going on for over a decade. The way I see it, it'll still be raging on just fine tomorrow, not giving two shits about what you scheme tonight. Might as well enjoy a clear night like this while we can. Live a little."

"Live a little," Asker echoed quietly into his beard, staring at Sebian for another moment before he did the unthinkable; he nodded and turned away. "I will take my leave and see to the preparations outside."

Malyr placed a kiss to my forehead. "What would you like us to do to entertain you, hmm?" His lips trailed kisses down along the side of my face, only for his tongue to lap at my jawline. "Would you like us to... go to the spring together?"

I all but melted into his embrace, loving those gentle touches he now generously offered between the rougher ones when he fucked me. "I already bathed there today."

"And yesterday. And the day before that. Sweetheart, I'm starting to think you're actually a duck in disguise." Sebian pressed himself against me from behind, running a finger down along my braid until it tugged and tingled my scalp so nicely. "I have a better idea. Let's walk through Valtaris. Shadows, coronation, politics... we've been so damn busy this entire time, I haven't had a single chance to enjoy this place."

I gleamed back at him, pure excitement radiating through my core. "Yes!"

"It is settled then," Malyr said, intertwining his fingers with mine before he guided me out the room.

Sebian followed beside me, wearing nothing more but brown breeches and a white shirt, the climate in Valtaris gentle enough where not much more was needed. With the two men framing me, we strode out of the throne room, our footsteps resonating in unison against the stone as we crossed the great hall.

Malyr pushed open one of the heavy double iron doors that lead out of the Winged Keep, its creak the only remnant of the city's long dormancy. Fresh night air greeted us, tinged with the scent of ale and hearty meats, the plateau sprawling out before us transformed into a hive of bustling workers.

They draped cloth of... maybe purple, along the rafters of stores that flanked the stairs down into the city. Others arranged large wooden structures down by the landing that looked much like a frame of ladders.

Malyr pointed at it. "They'll allow as many ravens as possible to roost there and watch the coronation ceremony.

Something similar was done during my father's ascension."

I strode between them along the Tarred Road, marveling at the many candles now dotted windows here and there, offering the warm glow of a home to whichever Ravens had returned. "Are you nervous?"

He wrinkled his nose and looked up at the plumes that weaved through the city, no longer consisting of shadows, but smoke from chimneys. "Being the spare, I didn't receive nearly as much instruction on governance as Harlen."

"I think you will rule well." I knew he tried, assigning new advisors on the daily and listening to their guidance every night before he joined Sebian and me, exhausted yet still attentive to me.

"We," he corrected. "Whatever I may lack in kindness, you bring in spades."

"And I'm pretty sure Malyr will manage just fine to corrupt your sweet heart every now and then, if needed," Sebian added, then jutted his chin toward a dark alley where I wouldn't want to be found alone at night. "There's fun to be found at the end of this one, I'm certain."

I grinned at him, my heart brimming with affection. "Are your senses telling you?"

"No," he said with a grin. "My years of experience in staggering from one tavern into the next is."

With a laugh and a sense of bliss energizing the air between us, we veered off the Tarred Road, trusting Sebian's uncanny instincts to guide us toward fun. And how spectacularly it opened up before me right around the next corner...

The very air shifted, suddenly alive with the intoxicating blend of laughter, song, and the smoky aroma of a fire that roared at the center of a lively square framed by rustic buildings. People danced around it, young and old, their faces flushed. Many held cups of wine, the evidence of their revelry visible in the occasional red spills staining their cotton kirtles and trousers.

My eyes widened, taking in the spectacle before me—unrestrained joy I had always craved but never thought I'd find. "What are they celebrating?"

Malyr chuckled. "You, little dove."

"Come here, sweetheart!" Sebian grabbed my arm and pulled me against him, one arm slinging around the small of my back, the other taking my hand. "Dance with me."

"But—"

Sebian pulled me into the chaotic tangle of limbs, our bodies instantly lost amidst the wild swirl of people. The lutes and drums seemed to thrum from every direction, a discordant melody that defied any sense of rhythm or structure.

"This makes no sense," I said as I stumbled over my own feet, finding no pattern in this frantic dance around the fire. "I don't know this dance."

"Neither do I." Sebian simply grinned and dragged me along, his grip firm but his demeanor completely carefree.

A laugh bubbled out of me—only for me to trip again, nearly tumbling into a couple who sidestepped us with giggles. The more I stumbled, the less it seemed to matter, each misstep nothing but a bump in the rhythm of joy. And then... I simply gave in.

And in this carefreeness, my movements melded with Sebian's like two creeks intertwining. Each curve, each swirl, each burst of laughter sent us forward with more fervor. The lutes and drums, the flames and faces, all faded into a warm, radiant blur as we picked up speed, dancing—

No, rushing around the fire.

My eyes found Malyr's, who stood nearby and clapped, his smile as radiant as those eyes he kept on us. "This is so much fun!"

No rules, no expectations.

Just joy, pure and uninhibited, flowing through my veins the way I'd been deprived of for so long. For the first time, I wasn't tripping over my steps; I was dancing with them, each misstep a part of this beautiful, imperfect tapestry of life.

Fate.

Right here.

All around me.

After a while, the music halted, the musicians pausing to gulp down cups of hard-earned drink. The square erupted in cheers and hollers, a cacophony of joy that seemed to resonate from the very stones beneath us.

Sebian pulled me tightly against him, the happiness gleaming on his features threatening to spill over, the corners of his mouth almost touching the laughter in his eyes. "That's not a night you'll ever forget, is it?"

I grinned back at him, my chest heaving nearly as fast as my heart drummed. "Never."

"That's good." With a tenderness that contrasted the rowdy energy around us, he reached over and gently wiped a stray strand of hair from my sweat-dampened temple. For a moment, we were the only two people in that square—our eyes locked, our hearts pounding to a rhythm that needed no music to sustain it. "I never said this before, but... thank you for bringing me back to life. Thank you for giving a chance to redeem myself in my own eyes. Even just a little."

The sincerity in his eyes seemed to magnify, and I felt enveloped in a warmth that went beyond the physical closeness of our bodies. For the first time, it struck me how reciprocal we had been to each other. In me, Sebian had found someone to care for and protect. And in him, I'd found that care and protection when I'd so desperately needed it.

I reached up with both hands, letting my palms run along his sheared sides, loving the way it tingled my skin. "I love you."

"And I love you," he whispered, his eyes going to something behind me for a moment before he cupped my cheek. "This is what you'll do now while I go find us some decent wine. Turn around and show our prince what this farmer's son taught you about midnight dances around bonfires, hmm?"

With a smile, I turned around, immediately stepping into the frame of Malyr's arms, just as a new tune resonated in the night. "Did you pay attention to the steps?"

His lips parted, his mouth standing agape for a moment. "There were *steps*?"

Hanging the entire weight of my body to his arms, I used all the force I could muster and, with a sidestep, yanked him into the whirling, frenetic, chaotic dance that was life. It was happy. It was joyful...

It did not last.

CHAPTER
FORTY

Galantia
Present Day, Valtaris

The morning light trickled through the windows, casting golden rays across our chamber and adding a touch of radiance to the obsidian of Malyr's hair. How perfectly straight it was. So soft, I loved combing my fingers through it each morning.

I sat behind him in our nest, my fingers parting away a strand. "One braid or three?"

"One. No doubt Asker is already pacing the throne

room." He gave a nudge at Sebian's side with his foot. "Do you intend to get up at all today, or...?"

A soft groan was Sebian's initial answer, but then he stretched his limbs before he finally sat up, his eyes still half-shut. "You're not making it sound as if I have a choice."

"Not on the day before the coronation."

I picked up a section of Malyr's hair, weaving it into a pattern that had taken me many days to master, his muscles lazily giving in to our morning ritual. "It'll be a spectacle."

As if on cue, Sebian knelt behind me, his hair already tightly braided from last night. "How do you want it done, sweetheart?"

"Not at all this morning," I said, finishing the last weave of Malyr's hair and securing it with a silver clasp.

"Ouch..." Sebian let himself fall back into the nest, pressing a fist to his chest in the most dramatic display. "Oh, bitter rejection, how you wound my heart."

"No, you're just trying to find an excuse to crawl back under the blankets," I said with a smile. "I want to bathe in the spring and wash my hair. Tjema can braid it for me after."

"I don't like it when you go to quiet places on your own," Malyr said.

"Well, Tjema lost her ability to fly, and that's really the only way of getting there," I said. "I doubt that some human assassin scaling a mountain for hours to get to me will go unnoticed. Besides, sometimes, a quiet place and some time to myself is exactly what I need."

Sebian grinned at that. "Be honest, which one of us is the one you need a break from? I *have* to know."

I grinned at that. "That's simple: you're both equally annoying at times."

"Ha! That remark deserves a spanking, but I'll leave that to Malyr." He executed a backward somersault in all his naked glory, cock slapping against skin, only to spring up onto his feet with an agility that defied the sluggishness he claimed to feel. "Where do you need me today?"

As Sebian began to clean his teeth by the washstand, Malyr finally rose, giving his braid a squeeze of approval before grabbing his attire for the day. "West, probably. I want to know exactly how many of King Barat's scouting parties are hiding out there, now that they know the *curse* has been lifted from Valtaris."

Malyr dressed, each layer of his fine ensemble bringing out the straightness of his spine. Then, he turned around and leaned down, placing a soft kiss to my lips.

"I will see you later, *anoaley*," he whispered, then straightened and strode out.

"I love you." Sebian's kiss followed before he hurried behind Malyr, all while simultaneously trying to hop into his breeches. "Meet me at the market later, sweetheart, and I'll treat you to some fresh berries."

I rose and walked over to the small satchel I'd prepared earlier. Nothing more but a comb and soap, light enough for my unkindness to carry.

In a burst of feathers, we unfurled our wings. One of us curled talons into the burlap of the satchel, then we fluttered up and through the flight hole. We drifted on the morning chill along the rock wall, lower, lower, until we slipped into the spring hidden inside a cavity not yet touched by the sun.

With a whisper of shifting energies, I returned to my human form. The satchel, dropped by my unkindness, lay beside me on the ground. I picked it up and carefully set it by the edge of the steaming water just as the wind howled around the columns supporting the overhang.

My skin tingled, the pebbling of gooseflesh a stark contrast to the heat rising from the spring. It didn't matter; the water would heat me up soon enough.

I took a deep, appreciative breath, savoring the fresh scent of moss and minerals. Casting my gaze over Valtaris, I marveled at how the morning sun glinted off the black roofs, not a single shadow in sight.

My ears pricked.

Footsteps. Behind me.

I swung around. Something slammed into the side of my head with a dull *thud*. Pain exploded around my temple, spreading across my skull as I staggered sideways. White floaters dotted my vision. My ears rang.

At my next step, my foot slipped on the damp rock. The ground pulled out from beneath me and I paddled my arms, flailing for balance until—

Slap.

My body hit the hard ground. A jerk went through my head just as a sting bit into my tongue, metal seasoning my gums. Something heavy wore down on me.

"No..." I mumbled just as panic flooded my heart, sending it galloping through my chest.

Shift.

We needed to flee.

Energy cleaved through me, parting us into five. We wiggled and writhed, hopped and hurled. We fluttered our wings, only for our feathers to break against the ropes wearing us down.

Trapped!

I found back into my form, filling out the weighted net so completely, I could barely move. "Let me out!"

"Scream as much as you want. Not even that pathfinder puppy of yours will hear you down here." The dark outline of a figure knelt in my periphery. "You have no idea how many times I've waited here for you to show up... I knew you would."

One hand reached through a hole in the net, squeezing my mouth with a brute force that pried it open. Another one shoved little pieces of something, bark or reeds, into my mouth. They scratched at my gums, bittered my tongue, choked the back of my throat.

I coughed, my entire body shivering against the ice-cold fear numbing my veins. "No—"

A hand sealed over my mouth. "Shift. I need you in your unkindness."

Because there was no pathway to or from the spring, no opportunity for this man to carry me off.

A spark of hope.

I focused on breathing through my nose, no matter how my brain clouded with each tiny intake of air. Malyr would look for me; Sebian would hear me if I screamed loudly enough. Until then, I wouldn't let this one take—

"Shift!" The shout came with the chill of metal pressing against my cheek. A burn followed, searing along my skin as a blade cut a pathway of pain through my skin. "I told you to... Yes, there we go."

We emerged from a burst of pain, flapping our wings in panic. Flee. We had to flee. We had to fly. Away. Away!

But our wings soon turned heavy. Our heads drooped to the cold stone to the twitching scratches of talons over rock. Then we stilled, our beady eyes blinking the man in front of us in and out of focus. Handsome. Black hair. Trimmed short.

Lord Aros.

He shoved us into sacks.

～

Ocean.

It was my first thought as traces of salt and algae climbed into my nostrils, a caress of familiarity that, for just a moment, cradled me in a sense of safety—wasn't it for that burn on my cheek, the pain second only to that jarring tug in my chest. Where was I?

With my cheek pressed to the damp wood on which I lay, I blinked my heavy eyelids, my surroundings cast into a veil of fog. Actual fog, its swathes blurring the shadowed figure sitting in front of me to the splash of oars coming up from the water.

Muscles burning from the weight of the net that kept me trapped, I turned my head toward Aros under its tight constraint. "Where are you taking me?"

"As far away from Malyr as possible," Aros said, his attention drifting over the water. "It hurts terribly, you know, being physically separated from your bondmate. I'd say Ammarett should do."

Straight to the enemy.

Dread struck my chest. "You're taking me to Ammarett? On a boat?"

"There's a ship waiting for you farther out to sea. The king himself is expecting you."

A whole-body shiver worked its way into my flesh, but it was the wintery chill out here that drove it into the marrow of my bones. "This is why you came to Valtaris so early, isn't it? To get close enough to me for your visions to work. You saw me going to the spring. Alone."

"A duck in disguise, isn't that what your lover called

you?" He gave an unhurried turn of the oars. "It's a strange gift, and the goddess rarely showed me anything helpful. Quite the opposite, really. But this...? *This* was helpful for once."

"Why are you doing this?"

"Is it not obvious?" Scoffing, he locked the oars, patted down his brown outfit, then brought forth something that sat on the palm of his hand, which he reached through a hole in the net. "Chew on this. It'll keep you sedated enough, making it impossible for Malyr to tell where your bond calls him." When I hesitated, he smacked his tongue. "I am no violent man. I'd rather have you just take it like I asked, but make no mistake... I will do what is necessary to make it so."

I opened my mouth, allowing him to let some of the pieces—bark, from what it looked like up close—tumble onto my tongue. The rest, which was a generous handful, he tossed into his mouth to chew away on it... sedating himself?

"For years, I had to watch how he kissed my mate right in front of me. At night, my visions made me watch how he fucked her. You want to know what was even worse?" He unlocked the oars and kept rowing, slower now, with a slight sway in his upper body. "Watching how he slowly rejected her. I would have tolerated a lifetime of Malyr being with my mate, so long as he made her happy and gave her what she needed. But no, he had to break her heart —that last thing of her that hadn't already been destroyed in those fucking dungeons."

My heart fought the effects of whatever I was chewing, wanting to thresh in my chest... only to be forced into a slowing rhythm. "And to avenge her death, you're handing me over to the very people who have done that to her? How is this fair?"

"Fate's not fair, Galantia. Besides, it's not about you... it's not about you at all," he said to the sound of the oars lifting from the water before he slowly pulled them in again. "I think we're here. Anyway, I want Malyr to suffer. I want him to hurt the way he hurt Lorn, and the only way to achieve that is by taking away his bondmate."

The shadow of a ship fell over me, cooling the air by several degrees to the sound of men shouting commands. "If you do this, you're hurting your own kind. How can you betray us like that?"

"We have Valtaris now," he said and carefully rose, balancing the boat toward me. "Even without you by his side, Malyr is strong enough to take Ammarett. It'll merely take him longer. But then... I'd assume the king will use you as leverage to make sure Malyr stays put. Guess he'll have to decide what is more important to him: keeping you alive or getting his revenge."

"He'll kill you," I spat. "Malyr will find you and kill you."

With a chuckle, he grabbed another handful of those wooden pieces from his breeches and tossed them into his mouth, swaying on his legs as he grabbed one of the wooden cleats of the ship. "I doubt that."

Two men climbed down the rigging, the thud of their boots on the boat putting a rocking sway into the small vessel. One of the men, a soldier donning the red colors of King Barat, grabbed the net which held me and slung me over his shoulder.

The other soldier gave me a quick glance before he turned his attention to Aros. "The king thanks you for your cooperation." In one swift movement too fast for my heavy eyes to follow, the soldier stabbed a knife into the side of Aros' neck. "Stupid Raven scum."

Aros swung a hand to the hilt protruding from his neck, stumbled back a step, then fell and crashed onto the boat's seat. A cough of blood gushed from his mouth, staining those lips that curled upward into a crimson smile. Almost as if he'd known. And perhaps he had, finding solace in the knowledge that, tonight, he would illuminate the sky with his fated mate.

I watched him bleed out in that boat while the soldier climbed the rigging with me. Kept my eyes on it until the fog swallowed it whole, and the soldier hoisted me over the gunwale and onto deck.

A groan wrenched from my lungs as I hit the ground.

"We took care of the Raven, Your Highness," the soldier beside me said.

Blinking my heavy eyes, I looked up until my gaze caught on a metal cuirass. The eyes of the wolf tooled into it stared back at me. To each side, golden clasps attached a heavy red cloak that swayed in the breeze. Strapped to the chest, silver daggers lined in a sort of broad leather belt.

"And so we meet at last, Galantia of no house."

The man stared down at me from a face that robbed his features of all handsomeness: nose too elongated, the lower part stretched much too long, and then there was his slight underbite.

Righteous fear cooled the blood in my veins. "Prince Domren."

"I left Ammarett a prince and will return a king, or so a message has recently informed me," he said. "Put her under deck with the rats. If she shifts, whip her until she can shift no more."

FORTY-ONE

Malyr

Present Day, Valtaris

As expected, Asker was already pacing the thread off the blood-red carpet in the throne room, but I couldn't bring myself to hurry. Not after a night of too much wine, even though half of it had spilled during our graceless stumbling around the fire. A night to be forever remembered, to be certain, shared with the two people I loved the most.

"My prince," Asker said the moment he spotted me,

bowed, hurried over, and pushed a book into my hands. "This is the current ledger that lists all the expenses for tomorrow's coronation ceremony."

I stopped beside the throne, flipping through the pages in the back on a long exhale. It was a good thing that Deepmarsh Castle had been stacked to the ceilings with riches. This event would cost me, but I wouldn't have it any other way. This was more than just a coronation; it was the resurrection of House Khysal, the Ravens I ought to protect, and the kingdom which we called home.

"What of the tenancies from Tidestone?" Yet another annexed stronghold that owed us taxes, now that it was under Raven control. "It should fill the coffers and hold us over until our attack on Ammarett."

"Lord Taradur is still re-assigning plots, taking into account those of us who chose to settle there instead of around Valtaris."

"Any animosity between the humans and those Ravens who are making themselves a new home there?" I'd assigned enough guards to ensure peace in and around Valtaris, but Ravens and humankind hadn't exactly been known for co-existing well these last couple of years. Pains of change ought to be expected, but not tolerated. "Wars between two kingdoms are bad, but wars between the people of one kingdom are worse."

"I spoke to Lady Cecilia last night after she arrived for the coronation, and she assured me that there have been no such reports. I did receive word from a scout just earlier about the farms west of Valtaris, saying that—"

"Of course there had to be trouble." I let myself slump onto my throne, head sinking into my palm. "Please tell me there were no murders."

"There was no such thing." Asker shook his head as he

grinned into his freshly trimmed beard. "The scout reported that the Raven farmers who settled on their new plots struggled to prepare the soil for seeding, blighted as the grounds were for a decade. It was the human farmers who came to their help and taught them how to handle the soil, having years of experience farming near the shadows."

I lifted my head, tilting my gaze at Asker, as if I needed to physically change my perspective to keep up with this upside down world I suddenly found myself in. *Did you hear that, Mother? Humans raising nestlings as their own and working alongside Ravens.*

"In return," Asker continued, "our people helped the humans with the seeding, using their ravens to plant the grains deep and well the way we have always done it."

Beside me, Sebian chuckled. "Didn't see that coming, Malyr, did you? Guess that's the toll of the princes and the titled stock: being oblivious to the fact that farmers don't give a rat's ass about the quarrels of the powerful, so long as they got food in their bellies."

I scoffed, and perhaps a little too hard, because something scratched in my lungs, making me rub at my chest through my shadowcloth robes. "What about the other Raven children?"

"We found two more who have been orphaned, one boy and one girl," Asker said. "Both wish to remain with their human adoptive—"

Pain shot through my chest and straight into my shoulder, and I grabbed the armrest of the throne, bracing against the sudden sway in my upper body, lest I would fall forward and hit the floor. *Goddess, what was this?*

Asker grabbed my shoulder and pushed me against the backrest. "What is it? Are you ill? Should I call for a healer?"

Shaking my head, I rose more in instinct than choice,

holding one of the carved wings for balance. The pain faded as quickly as it had appeared, leaving nothing behind but a strange sort of... dullness beneath my sternum.

"No healer." I didn't catch sicknesses often, and nothing these last few days had indicated that I had caught one now. Just too much wine the night before, maybe. "A brief spell."

Sebian smacked his lips. "He didn't eat yet, and neither did I."

Unless Galantia's cunt counted. And while delicious, it wouldn't hold us over, so I agreed with a nod. "I may have forgotten supper last night as well, with the dozens of meetings I had to attend."

Sebian glimpsed into one of the nearby corridors. When a young maid shuffled by, he let out whistle loud enough that she startled and looked at him.

"Get your prince something to eat. Keep it simple and make it fast." Pleased with how she curtsied and ran off, he turned his attention to Asker. "Malyr said he probably wants me west? Any particular area you need me to look at?"

Asker took the book from my hand. "The northern forest right on the border."

"Too far," Sebian said, probably because he'd promised Galantia some time spent over berries, and I could not hold that against him, the bliss we both experienced with her. "Send another pathfinder who flies faster."

Asker eyed him for a moment, but no reprimand came as his attention drifted to the maid who hurried up the dais.

She held a large silver platter out to me and curtsied. "My prince, is this to your taste?"

I couldn't help but smile at her concern as I looked over

the steaming bread, the boiled eggs, and the cured sausages. As much as I'd always been a prince, I'd also been a prisoner and a fugitive, stripped of pride and food. She could have brought me a stale piece of bread, and I wouldn't have taken notice.

I reached for the egg and gave her a nod. "This will do just—"

Pain once more lanced through my chest, intensifying as it settled somewhere near my heart. My torso buckled, and for a heartbeat, the room blurred into flecks of red and black. My balance drifted forward, further, further, until—

Metal clanked against stone.

My head hit the ground, sending a stabbing vibration through my skull as the world turned around me. But it had nothing on the agony that came through my bond, yanking and pulling as if it meant to snap.

"Malyr!" Asker shouted.

An unkindness fluttered around me, Sebian reshaping beside me and somehow staring down at me. "What happened?"

An excruciating, unyielding pain clenched my chest like an iron fist, each heartbeat a torrent of unbearable anguish that seemed to crush my very soul. I gasped for air, but no breath came, as if I was endlessly suffocating but never dying.

Galantia.

My *anoaley's* name sat on my tongue—a primal instinct, a warning—my mouth gaping but no sound making it past my lips. Something was wrong. She needed me. I had to... had to...

My shift surged through me, the five of us emerging to the sound of our anxious croaks. We dashed through one of the flight holes, our hearts pounding faster with each roof we passed before we banked right, rounded the wall of the mountain, and fluttered up.

Anoaley, we cawed among us. *Anoaley!*

I all but stumbled into the cavity of the spring, nearly crashing into Sebian, who must have read the panic from my eyes and sprinted off into the first shadowed area as he shouted, "Galantia!"

"She's not here."

I couldn't see her.

Worse, I couldn't *sense* her.

But she had been here, I realized with another struck to my core when my eyes landed on her bathing satchel on the ground. I picked it up. Dry. Untouched.

"Something happened to her." Righteous fear filled my entire being. "I can feel it."

"Where is your bond pulling you?"

"I don't know. I don't... I don't—" A gulp severed my voice. "I feel as if someone poured ice into my chest, making it hurt and dulling it at the same time."

Five ravens fluttered in, only for Asker to shape beside us. "Where is she?"

"Not where she's fucking supposed to be," Sebian growled. "Has anybody seen Tjema?"

Rage flooded my veins unfiltered. I would kill whoever dared to touch my *anoaley!*

"Find the girl!" My shout shattered against Asker's shift. "Send every pathfinder in all directions of the sky. Search every dark corner in the Keep. Every narrow alley in Valtaris. Leave no building unsearched, no meadow unscouted!"

"Maybe it's nothing," Sebian said, but I saw the gulped swallow that bobbed his throat. "Maybe she's with Tjema after all, and somehow she got hurt."

"No, she never even took the soap out." I slammed the satchel onto the ground with a shout that sent a brief burst of shadows up around me, letting the wooden comb inside noisily snap before the burlap slipped over the stone. "She never even got into the— What is that?"

Eyes locked on something beside the satchel, I hurried toward it and knelt down, only for my trembling fingers to reach toward...

Goddess, no. No...

Sebian squatted beside me and dipped his fingertips into the small smear of blood tinged with something else on the stone, maybe saliva. Even without bringing it to his nose, a shudder went through him, telling me everything I needed to know.

My mate was injured.

Bleeding. Dying?

With a growl, I shot up, five ravens dashing to the edge of the spring where I reshaped only for my primal shout to shatter from the mountainside. "*Galantia!*"

Several ravens fluttered into the cavity—one of the headscouts, as well as Asker and Marla, who shaped beside me.

Asker took in those restless ropes of shadows around me that whipped at the air before he said, "She never reached her maid."

"We already know that," Sebian muttered and rose, holding out his bloodied fingers. "This is her blood. She was attacked."

"I'm going to kill them. I'm going to *fucking kill* them!" My threat still echoed the cave when I reshaped where they stood, my aorta pounding in my neck. "Who did this? Where is my bondmate?!"

"Let me try for a vision." Marla gripped Sebian's fingers

and led them to her mouth, her eyes slowly falling shut, only for her eyelids to twitch rapidly at the first lick of blood. Then, her eyes ripped open wide. "He took her."

"Who?" My hands balled into fists that barely contained those deadly shadows building in my core. "Who dared to touch my mate? Taradur? One of Brisdon's minions? Another lord?"

She looked at me, her eyes filling with tears. "Aros."

Aros.

That name hit me like slap to the face, putting a sway into my upper body that sent me stumbling sideways. I barely caught my balance as I braced my hand against one of the stone columns. Not Taradur. Not Brisden. No human at all. But of course not. They couldn't even have come up here.

Aros.

A Raven.

A gray veil settled over my vision as a chuckle vibrated somewhere in my chest, amplifying the pain there. A lifetime of distrust and a decade of hate toward humans, and what had it gotten me? My bondmate, taken.

By. My. Own. Kind.

I breathed against the shadows building in my core. I'd done a great many regretful things in moments of anger, when my thoughts were sullied by darkness. This could not be one of them. *Think, Malyr. Think!*

"If he'd wanted to kill her, he could have done so here." Was there blood? Yes, but it was little and diluted. She might have hit the ground and bit her tongue. "Neither does he have the means to keep her from me... not for long." He might have betrayed me, but the Ravens surrounding him would rather slit his throat and return her than bring my wrath down upon them. What then? What? "Where is he taking my mate?"

Asker first exchanged a glance with Marla, then with Sebian, before he finally looked at me. "Ammarett."

"Ammarett." A stronghold not easily taken, keeping me away from her, compromising the power of my shadows, unleashing constant agony on me. The perfect punishment for all my failings—of which there were many. I should have tossed Lorn's body into the ocean years ago. "He conspired with our enemies. For that, he will pay, but not until I have my *anoaley* back. We have to find her before she reaches the city."

"Malyr..." My name from Asker's mouth never failed for my arms to double in weight. "He could be taking her north where the ground is still covered by snow. East, across the ocean. South, under disguise. West into Dranadia, where Barat's scouts have been roaming. The possibilities are endless."

"Not to mention that he probably sedated her," Sebian added. "Malyr said his bond feels dull, which makes it pretty unreliable given the vast territory where she may or may not be. Malyr, the chances of finding her are slim."

I clenched my eyes shut, the sudden understanding of how Sebian must have once felt over failing to protect his *anoaley* like a dagger between my ribs. "What do you advise me to do?"

"We cannot abandon the search, but I daresay that fate calls us to Ammarett," Asker said. "However, we are in no shape to take the city and hold it, stretched thin as we are, with siege weapons undergoing repairs at Tidestone. It will take weeks for us to assemble a proper siege... months if rains come."

Weeks.

Months.

I turned away and looked over the city for a moment, my entire body trembling with fury and fear. They would hurt her. Over and over again, they would hurt her, the way they'd done to me. Days. Weeks. Months.

Eternities.

In darkness.

"Announce that every Raven with a gift for war has to be ready to depart for Ammarett in the morning." I'd never cared about the city. In the face of losing my little dove, I couldn't bring myself to care about those men hiding inside it, oaths and promises be damned. "We're not going there to conquer; we're going there to get back what is *mine*."

CHAPTER
FORTY-TWO

Galantia
Present Day, the belly of a ship

Time no longer passed in seconds, but the rocking ups and downs of the ship's hull while I cowered, ensnared on a floor dampened with my own bile. The constant nausea had finally abated, not so much the rancid stench of my vomit and urine—none of which the men holding me captive bothered to clean.

No, they only ever came down here to offer me ladles of water, and once a tiny piece of hard bread. A handful of times, they'd lifted me up by my cage of knotted ropes, only to drop me onto a spot where I may or may not have retched my guts out yet. Then they disappeared, leaving me behind in the darkness.

And a good thing they did.

Joints stiff from lack of movement, I wiggled my hand past my torso, letting my fingers follow the hemp ropes. Where was it? Somewhere near these knots had to be—

There!

My pulse thudded in those fingertips I pressed into the depression of the worn rope, the last section I needed to cut through for my ravens to fit. But could I even still shift? In an attempt to preserve energy, I hadn't put it to the test, but there was nothing to be done about that uncertainty.

Assuming I could, leaving the netting in the corner beneath the stairs might make it look as though I'd rolled there. They would come to investigate, and the hatchway may remain open long enough for my unkindness to escape.

Where to, I didn't know, but any place was better than this. As long as we found islands, rocks, or even icebergs to rest our wings—depending on the ship's course—we could make it to the mainland. And if we didn't...? Well, the man I was heading to, and *especially* the one on the deck, made death look like a friend.

What precious little remained of Malyr's shadows at my core, I weaved around the ropes in tangles darker than my prison. They squeezed, chafed, and tugged the already worn section, fibers snapping like strands of hair.

My lungs expanded wider, perhaps my only notion of hope that remained in this place, pulling the foul stench deep into my chest. A chest that caved, a sudden stab radiating from my core like a newly mended wound pried open to bleed anew.

"No..." I whimpered against the roar of waves hitting the ship's belly, sensing the shadows fade from my shaky fingers, leaving my void empty. "No, no, no, *no*."

I leaned in and clenched the corner of my teeth around the rope, jaw muscles straining as they chewed on the fraying section. The coarse fibers scratched against the tender insides of my mouth, but I gritted through the discomfort, gnawing with fervor.

The salty tang of my saliva mixed with the musty flavor of the sisal. With a final agonized jerk of my head, the last fibers snapped. It was a small victory, but in a world bereft of light and hope...?

It was everything.

I didn't waste another heartbeat and clenched my eyes shut, communing with my primal. Energy sliced through me.

We struggled onto our little legs, beaks lifting the rope and pushing toward the hole. We wriggled through the frayed hole one by one, each of us unfolding our wings as quietly as the air around us, carefully stretching them as not to alert our captors.

With a silence borne of urgency, we took positions around the net. Then, we tugged as one, pulling with all the combined strength our small forms could muster. The rope slithered across the damp wood, scraping softly as we maneuvered it under the stairs.

We darted over thick, heavy ropes, our talons quietly clattering over the wooden floor. We slipped behind something white and elongated, a rolled-up sail, perhaps. There we waited, and waited—feathers ruffling at every creak of wood, every stomp of a boot, every murmur of voices—a tight cluster of dread and anticipation. Our little hearts beat frantically as time stretched thin, yet we kept patient, our muscles tensed, ready for what would come next.

After something that had felt like both a moment and a lifetime, the hatchway creaked open. A man descended the stairs, his boots thudding heavily with each step, a lantern swinging in his grip.

"Where's that wretched bitch?" he grumbled, reaching the lantern this way and that. "Beast's supposed to be right here."

He took another step down, peering into the darkness, the lantern's light swinging like a pendulum as he turned. Above him, a swathe of daylight beckoned, promising freedom.

We had to flee! Now!

The tension in us snapped, and we shot forward. The man swung around just in time for our talons to scratch at his face. A shout erupted from his mouth as he lost his footing, tumbling down the stairs.

Glass shattered.

A flame roared.

Up, up, up we spiraled, feathers barely missing the licking fire below. The scent of salt filled our nares. Waves roared, loud, louder. Almost there! Freedom was within our grasp!

Until it wasn't.

We slammed into something, like the web of a spider spun from hundreds of finger-thin ropes. Our wings bent, our feet tangled, our feathers broke. The more we struggled, the tighter the contraption squeezed us, wrapping around us with an almost sentient hunger. Our little hearts sank into a pit of despair. *Trapped!*

"Cut the net before she shifts back and breaks her

neck," Domren said, the authority in his voice unmistakable. "Don't let her escape. You and you, put out the fire down there."

Several men sprung into action. Knives glinted in their hands as they deftly cut the net where it was attached to the frame of the hatchway. They tied the ends of the net into tight knots, securing our prison once more. With a heave and a coordinated motion, they tossed us onto the deck.

Pain shot through us on impact, ripping a caw from my lungs that slowly morphed into my groan, failure settling like a rock in my stomach. How was I supposed to make it off this damn ship?

Black boots embellished with golden clasps thudded inches from my face. "And to think that I almost wedded and bedded this *animal*."

Communal laughter.

Anger flaring in my veins, I strained my neck and looked up at Domren. "It would have been the least of your monstrosities."

He folded his arms behind his back, the ends of the elegant red frock he wore shifting with the chilly ocean breeze. "Secure the net to the gunwale. Throw her overboard."

My lungs collapsed. "No!"

Calloused hands grasped the edges of the net, lifting me as if I were a piece of cargo. The men wove additional rope through the netting that entrapped me, their knot meticulous and tight. With a grunt, they secured the end to a large iron hook jutting from the gunwale.

"For a swim you go..." one of them called out.

He tossed me overboard.

The ship rose above me for a split second before I

plunged into the icy abyss below. The cold was a beast, gnashing its teeth into me. I tumbled and rolled in the throes of the ship's speed until the rope strung tight. Then, I drowned, the ocean swallowing me whole, sealing me away from light and air.

A surge of panic shot through me, stabbing straight into my core. Wings flapped frantically, fighting against a current that seemed too viscous, too watery.

No. Please, no!

Another surge.

Hands pushed at the net, a sharp *crack* resonating through my bones and a hot stab of pain lancing my knuckle until feathers once more unfurled. Talons tore desperately at the ropes, finding no purchase. Feet kicked out, my lungs burning as if I'd swallowed fire.

My vision grew dark. Darker.

The darkness receded as a violent jerk yanked me upward. Air rushed into my lungs. Water cascaded off me, the cold air nipping at my drenched body. They pulled me up, but instead of tossing me onto the deck, they kept the net sitting on the gunwale.

"Not much is better at robbing a Raven of his wings than burning them, but alas, we are standing on wood." Domren stepped up to me, his boots tapping against the wood as if he was barely amused and almost bored by the spectacle. "The next time you consider an escape, know that I do not need you pretty, Galantia. I do not need you entirely intact. Come to think of it, I do not even need you... unbesmirched." His upper lip gave a twitch, the sudden attention it conveyed driving a shudder across my body that had nothing to do with the cold. "However, I do need you alive. Send her down."

I cried out.

They hurled me back into the abyss below. Again. And again. And again. Up. Down. Up. Down. A merciless cycle that blurred together, each dunk stripping away a little more of my strength, a little more of my resilience.

How many times they pulled me up, only to plunge me back into the brine, I couldn't say—but enough to rob me of my ability to shift. When they finally hauled me up one last time, I hung there, my body retching up salty water, shivering in uncontrollable spasms.

Domren approached, his eyes searching my face as if gauging how much spirit I had left. "Take her to my cabin."

With swift cuts, they severed the thin ropes. I collapsed onto the deck, a heap of utter exhaustion and lingering despair. Before I could catch a shuddering breath, two men grabbed my arms, dragging me across the deck.

Every fiber of my being screamed in fatigue, each bump and scrape over the wooden planks sending a fresh wave of pain into my muscles as righteous fear clawed at my throat.

Not his cabin!

Anywhere but there!

"No!" I shouted, kicked, and writhed, but I was quickly subdued.

With a rough shove, they pushed me into the monster's den, making me stagger forward one unreliable step before my legs snapped. I collapsed into a shivering, heaving heap between a flickering oil lamp on a wooden desk and a small, but ornate bed.

They didn't bother closing the door as they left, their thudding steps overpowered by those slow, deliberate strides of boots I knew held golden clasps. Every grind of his heel seemed to pulse with unspoken threats, leaving me with a terror I could not shake.

He would rape me.

387

The thought resonated my head clearly, neither conjured by panic nor suspicion. It wasn't needed after what Sebian had told me about this man and what kind of barbarity he was capable of. It wasn't fear... it was a fact.

That knowledge, that sense of preparedness, offered me a sliver of strength. But with the weakness of my body, I couldn't escape. Maybe I would scream. Maybe I would tear. Maybe I would bleed.

But I wouldn't let it break me.

My heart punched against my esophagus to the sound of the door falling shut, pupils darting across the room until they fixed on Domren. "Are you sure you don't want to put me back into a net? What if I shift?"

"That is quite simple: you cannot shift when you are unconscious," he said and stepped up beside me, his boot coming to a stop on strands of my drenched hair. "We're on a ship to Ammarett, and we will be for quite some time. Entertainment is... scarce. They say womenfolk bring sailors bad luck, but I don't agree with the notion. I daresay they are the only thing capable of making such a journey somewhat worthwhile."

"I'm afraid I won't—"

He grabbed my hair right then, yanking me up by it. "That Raven traitor of yours told me that you bonded to that usurper. I hope he can feel just how you're going to *entertain* me."

"Let me go!" I snarled, thrashed, and flung my fist around, fighting every inch he manhandled me toward the desk. "They'll kill you! They'll kill you, and they won't make it swift!"

"Neither will I, if that's what you were hoping." He forced my arms behind my back, gripping my tender wrists in his hand. With the other hand, he once more gripped my hair. Then, he slammed my face down onto the desk, the impact burning like the hissing flame in the trembling lantern beside me, turning me dizzy, making everything spin. "Unless you feel so obliged to scream... I happen to like it that way."

Blood flooded my mouth and mixed with the salt of tears, my entire body so exhausted, I couldn't come up with the energy to spit it out. Neither could I find the strength to fight how clammy fingers pulled my soaked skirts up, the way I squirmed, quickly overwhelmed when he pressed his naked groin to my ass, his slimy cock sullying my thighs.

My legs quivered when he shoved himself inside me with a violence that crossed the border of discomfort and crashed straight into pain. I closed my eyes, whimpering with every aching thrust that pinched, tore, and stabbed.

If I'd thought I'd been acquainted to pain, then I'd been mistaken. There was no moderation in this, no restraint. Only constant anguish as he brutalized me, sometimes slamming my face against the desk to disorient me, other times squeezing my throat until I lost consciousness.

But I always woke with his weight still bearing down on my body. Or again? Perhaps I could have saved myself some agony if I'd screamed.

I didn't.

It must have angered him, for the longer I kept at my little whimpers, the more he hurt me. "I heard he cried and screamed like a woman," he said at one point, my mind dazed, my ears ringing. "Maybe you're more man than he is."

Eventually, he gave a final grunt, lifted off me, and turned away, leaving my body behind shattered, yes, but my soul intact. Until he opened the door and said, "Go have your turns."

CHAPTER
FORTY-THREE

Sebian

Present Day, kingdom of Dranada

Rain pelted down on me where I stood, my boots sinking into the soil with a drawn-out smack, but not even this fucking downpour could clean the air from the stench that drifted here from Ammarett. From a distance, you might feel yourself into thinking it was just another fortress—big, imposing walls, sure, but still just walls. The harder I looked though, the more the city revealed a big fucking issue here.

My gaze wandered over those windows set into the

damn mountain itself, too colorful, even under the veil of rain to indicate anything else but wealth. "Where exactly is the keep?"

Asker exhaled a long breath to my right, the water conveniently running down along his bushy brows. "Carved into the mountainside that serves as the backdrop to the city before it. It is quite impenetrable, the windows barred with tightly-woven chains, the gates heavy iron."

Yeah, that was what I'd thought. "And that dungeon where our scout said they dragged Galantia to after they unloaded her from the ship?"

A ship Malyr and I had tried to reach several times after a scout had found Aros' dead body in a boat that had drifted aimlessly near our coast, or so reports had said. That bastard had probably rowed her to the large vessel, only to conveniently get himself killed. In any case, reaching the ship had been impossible, the winds too strong and our wings too weak. We were fucking poor fliers over open water.

"Beneath it," Malyr said, who stood to my left, the rain dripping into his eyes clear, only to run down his cheeks as black droplets with no way for him to syphon. "Unless things changed, which our informants suggested they have not, that particular dungeon can only be reached from inside the keep."

A keep behind an iron gate, walls of rock, and caged windows. Getting inside that thing would be tricky. But actually making it to the fucking gate? Past net catapults and highly trained archers? How?

I wiped the rain from my face and back over a braid that clung to the last of the tousled strands Galantia had put there, but I'd be damned to open it—it might very well be the one I'd be burned with. "Since you two knew exactly what we'd face, I assume you came up with some smart strategy on our way here?"

Malyr and Asker tortured their lips.

So... no smart strategy then.

With Taradur's army pushing here from the southeast to keep us safe from smaller attacks within the kingdom, getting to a good twenty furlongs of the city had been easy. Getting inside was the problem.

"Our options are limited," Asker said, the rain drumming off his black armor. "Without siege weapons, we cannot take down the catapults and battlements. If we waited for Taradur to—"

"No," Malyr said, his face gaunt, torment chiseled into his cheeks in shadowy valleys. Three times, his ravens had nearly fallen from the sky, the pain coming through their bond costing him every ounce of strength. "Any second I stand out here is a second she suffers in there. We cannot wait for Taradur."

"That's all well and good, Malyr, but as things stand, we won't even make it in there, let alone through the keep and down into the dungeon." Shadows nervously flickered around my fingertips, matching the desperation that ate me from the inside. I couldn't fail. Not again. Not this time. "How do we get her out of the dungeon?"

Malyr stared ahead for long moments before he finally said, "We don't have to get her out."

I arched a brow at him. "What?"

"There is no need for us to make it any farther than the keep itself." Reaching his arm out, he let his *anoa* shape there, the bird immediately ruffling his feathers even though the rain pearled off easily. "Not if she manages to make her own way out of the dungeon."

"You're not helping, Malyr." Galantia might have been

resilient and resourceful, yes, but she was no match for steel, swords, and who knew how many soldiers. "She's a void."

He stroked a knuckle down along his bird's puffed-up chest. "No, she's a *thief*. That makes her anything she wants to be, even a deathweaver. All she needs is my gift."

Realization stabbed me straight in the guts. "She has never stolen a gift before."

"But I believe she came close." His attention settled on me. "I once went to find her in the orchard before Tidestone. You were there, but you neither heard nor smelled me."

"Because she depleted my shadows."

"Which explains how you couldn't conjure arrows," he said. "Should your senses have suffered?"

A shudder spread down my arms. What if he was right, and she'd gotten closer to stealing my gift than any of us had realized? I wouldn't know what that felt like. Nobody knew much about thieves anymore these days.

"None of that changes the fact that she never wielded your shadows," I pointed out. "Not successfully."

"Successful enough to set a room on fire."

"Not controlled, then."

"Out of control might just do. One big blast might be the only thing we need to get us in there."

"They would not see such a thing coming," Asker murmured slowly. "It would take them by great surprise, scrambling their focus and whatever strategies they have set into place."

The more I thought on it, the more promising it seemed, except for one terrifying problem... "What if your shadows attack her?"

"Are you going to attack that white raven female you

love so much?" Malyr asked his *anoa* and, when the bird cawed and spread his wings as if offended, he absorbed him back into himself and lowered his arm. "She cleared an entire kingdom from my shadows. If anyone can handle them, it's her."

"She was born to bring balance to his shadows." Asker cast a final gaze over Ammarett before he looked at me. "This might very well be our only viable option. The dungeon they keep her in is small, reserved only for the most prominent of prisoners. If she can make it to the keep, then you can help her shift, should she no longer be able to, and escort her to safety."

"That's all well and good, but how do we get the damn bird to her? You said that there's only one way to that dungeon, and that way is through the keep."

"It is ventilated by a single shaft set into the wall of the mountain, close to the ocean," Malyr said. "It's too narrow to fit even a child, and constantly pounded by waves."

"But a raven will fit," I finished for him. "Your *anoa* flies well enough, he should avoid the waves."

"My *anoa* can slip in there with a note tied to his leg. All we need is a distraction while he approaches from the ocean. Something that looks like an all-out attack from the southeast without carrying all its risks."

"That can be done," Asker said. "But the question that concerns me the most is how do you intend to fight without your gift?"

Malyr gave a tap on the pommel of his sword. "Only until we have her. It is too much a burden for her to carry long-term, but I will let her borrow it." Whatever it was that he spotted, maybe the way I shifted from one leg to the other, had him lift his hand to my shoulder. "She will come out of this alive."

My lungs slowed. I knew that. The both of us would make certain of it, each in our own ways laid out before us by fate.

"I will ready myself for the attack," Asker said and strode toward one of the shadow tents. "The camp will need to be moved back after to give the impression of retreat. That, coupled with her distraction, should allow us to fly through their defenses and storm the keep."

The moment I turned, Malyr tightened his hold on my shoulder. "I need you to promise me something."

I stopped and faced him, the deathweaver who'd been with me through some of my worst and best memories. "Anything."

"Should something happen to me, I need—"

"Nothing will happen to you." Not if I could help it—and I very much intended to help it. "You made it this far. Don't give those bastards the courtesy of dying now."

But he didn't relent, his stare as somber as his hand was heavy. "Promise me that you will take care of her. Forever, Sebian."

"That you think that needs a promise makes me want to fucking punch you." Same as I didn't need a promise from him that he would make her a good mate, should I end up dead. I knew he would. "It also needs no damn promise because nothing will happen to you. I won't let it."

"You're a good friend, Sebian. A good brother." A final squeeze on my shoulder, then he turned toward his tent. "I will prepare the message and get my *anoa* ready to deliver it."

Which reminded me that I had to check the string on my bow, so I headed toward my tent. When I passed Marla's tent, my strides slowed. Would she want to see me off? Should I rather just keep going?

Asker stepped out of the tent, momentarily staring at me, motionless, before he walked up. "Ammarett."

"Ammarett," I echoed, silent understanding passing between us before I jutted at the tent. "Should I...?"

"You know how she was when Ravenna died. The thought of losing you, too... she barely stopped crying ever since that coward Ares set all this into motion."

I'd thought as much, so I gave a nod and looked back toward my tent. But I didn't manage a single step forward.

Asker's hand landed strangely light on my shoulder before he said, "You are a good man, Sebian."

A good man.

My nose turned stuffy and my vision blurred. Fucking rain. Cold as winter, too, making me tremble.

I turned my head and glanced at that hand that moved on my shoulder, fingertips slowly patting, which was about the biggest display of closeness I'd ever seen that man exchange with someone other than Marla and Ravenna. "So are you."

With that, I kept walking. Goddess damn it to hell and back, in just one day, I'd been called a good friend, a good brother, and a good man. Only one thing was missing.

A good mate.

I wouldn't fail this time.

CHAPTER
FORTY-FOUR

Galantia

Present Day, Ammarett dungeon

I propped my arm under my head, the cage around me nothing but a square iron frame with walls of something similar to chainmail—rusty, tight, unyielding. No window, barely any air and even less light, with nothing for company but the echo of my memories.

"I heard he cried and screamed like a woman."

Domren's echo.

"Sometimes, we're just mad at ourselves for liking some-

thing we think we shouldn't. Maybe it's something that was once so unpleasant, it's shameful for us to find pleasure in it now."

Sebian's echo.

"She can never give you what I do. Do you know that, little girl? The things he likes done to him? Do you know that he likes his vent tickled?"

Lorn's echo.

"Why would you touch me like that, huh?"

The worst echo of them all. Malyr's.

None of it had made sense in those moments. Now, in the stillness of my dark prison, with nothing to distract me, clarity settled into my mind. Malyr had been raped in the dungeons, hadn't he? A despicable act that leaves many women feeling tainted and ashamed, I understood full well —now more than ever. Why would it be different for a boy? A man?

I reached my hand between my legs, past the tatters of my clothes, and stroked over my tender flesh. How the sting of that touch could still make me flinch was beyond me, considering how they'd brutalized me on the ship. How they—

No! I wouldn't go back there. It was bad enough that I'd been forced to take Domren and his men into my body, but I wouldn't allow them a single inch of space in my mind, in my heart, in my life.

When I sensed the viscous wetness I'd been hoping to find after restless sleep interrupted by cramps, I brought my bloodied fingertips to my face. No foul smell, no infection from internal injuries. Only my menses.

There would be no child.

It was a small flicker of relief that illuminated my core for a second as I wiped my fingers on my dress. Nobody had touched me since I'd been locked up in here, with guards roaming the dark passages of this dungeon.

Commotion sounded from the passageway ahead of the room where my cage stood. The firelight there—its orange hue the only color in this black void—danced, flickered, and writhed where it usually remained still in this stagnant air. How curious.

Boots thudded.

Armor clanked.

Silence followed, interrupted only by the crackling of fire. That, and the faintest little *tap-tap-taps*, like claws drumming on stone. The scuffling grew louder, closer.

My breath caught, the already sparse air growing thin in my lungs as I edged toward the wall. Heart pounding, I pressed my face against the iron curtain, squinting to glimpse through one of the small openings. The coarse rust scratched against my skin as my gaze locked onto the darkness ahead, probing, searching, desperate for whatever clue the flickering firelight could offer.

And then, a shift in the blackness on the ground—a subtle movement, a breaking of shadows. Mice? Rats?

My heart stumbled over a beat.

A raven!

And not just any raven with how he hopped toward me, bobbing his head up and down all the while. A scroll had been wrapped around one of his legs, tied to it with two blue ribbons.

"Malyr..." My mate's name all but breathed from my lips as I struggled two fingers through a gap, relief and joy flooding my senses. "Can you push your little foot in here?"

The raven's head turned this way and that, scrutinizing the woven barrier that separated us. Eventually, he ran his beak over the metal, probing here and there. He merely let out a low crooning sound, as if acknowledging our shared dilemma.

Maybe not so smart after all...

"Just sand still." My fingers strained through the tight gap of the chainmail, knuckles aching, my fingertips barely grazing the silken material. "Come on. Come on."

On the third tug, the last ribbon came loose, unraveling the scroll some as it slipped down the spindly leg. The raven let out a flustered caw, hopping back in a mixture of surprise and annoyance. He shook his foot, dislodging the ribbons and sending the parchment rolling... out of reach.

"No," I groaned. "I need that. Bring it to me."

After a couple of beady blinks, he hopped over to the stray parchment and nudged it with his beak, pushing it back toward me. Slowly but surely, the paper slid across the stone floor until it rested close enough for me to grasp. Would it tell me that they were nearly here? That I only needed to hold on a little longer?

With renewed hope, I stretched, my fingertips pinching the parchment. I pulled it inside, my grip shaky but firm. My heart drummed a frantic beat as I unrolled it, tilted it toward the meager light, and squinted at Malyr's handwriting.

Anoaley,

I am writing this from our camp right outside of Ammarett, where every deathweaver, pathfinder, and fate of fighting age is waiting on my command to breach the keep, but we cannot do it without you. We need a distraction from within. Steal my gift. Wield my shadows. Unleash my darkness on them and show them how you sparkle as you make your way from the

dungeon to the keep. We will come through the main gate for you.

We love you. Come back to us.

P.S.: Do you remember what I told you the night at the kjaer, when you and I spoke by the creek?

A chill crept into my fingers, stiffening my knuckles until the parchment noisily crinkled in my grip. They wanted me to... steal Malyr's gift? Wield his shadows? Fight my way up to the keep?

I'd never done any of those things!

Ignoring my rioting nerves, I took a deep breath. What had he told me by the creek? We'd spoken about a great many things. Sebian's scars. The night his family died. Trust. The salt amulet that he'd—

"You are not the damsel in distress you make yourself out to be," Malyr's voice resonated, as if whispered right beside me, his belief in me like a caress to my soul. It always had been.

I clenched the parchment, grounding myself in the urgency of his words. How long ago I'd been taken, I couldn't say, but I knew it wasn't enough time to organize a successful siege. They probably couldn't get through Ammarett's defenses without great losses—and likely not for the wanted outcome.

This was on me.

A shiver of doubt invaded my nerves. I was no warrior; had never held a sword, had never killed. Had never truly lived through the hardships of war.

But I had endured pains, scars, and injustices all the same. Had survived the attack on Tidestone when others around me had died. Had fought for myself when I hadn't even known who I was. I had lifted a curse, saved a prince, gained the admiration of many... and the hearts of two men.

I glanced back down at the note.

We love you.

Come back to us.

Focusing on my void, I raised my absorbing hand toward the *anoa*. The more I communed with the shadows within the raven, the more his feathers ruffled. Two dissolved into black plumes, making my heart give a whomp against my ribcage. Yes, that was it! They slithered through the metal curtain, streaming into me, deeper, deeper—

A sharp, unyielding pain flared up in my chest, like claws tearing across my internal organs, scratching and scraping. I recoiled, pulling my hand back as if burnt, breaking my focus entirely. Such pain...

The raven suddenly cocked his head, attention going to the pathway from which he'd come. Then I heard it.

Footsteps.

With a hurried gesture, I shooed him away. "Go. Go and hide."

If he understood the situation or merely the urgency in my voice, I couldn't say, but he hopped away. Retreating into a dim corner, his black plumage blended seamlessly with the enveloping shadows.

I quickly tore up Malyr's letter. Hands shaky, I stuffed the pieces into my mouth, desperately chewing the dry, pulpy texture. Each shred scraped down along my esophagus, making me choke, making me cough, but I managed it all down.

The orange hue of the fire once more flickered and elongated along the wall, making my heart race. Until one of the two men I wanted dead the most stepped into the small cavern that held my prison.

Then, my heart stopped.

Lord Brisden stood before my cage, his chin held impossibly high, considering how his eyes had to strain as he looked down at me where I sat on the floor. But he wasn't alone. A jailor walked up beside him, putting a bowl on the ground before he pulled a knife from the sheath on his belt.

I peeked into the bowl. Ash.

My stomach clenched.

"Hurry up," Brisden commanded. "The dirty lot of them will think twice about sending their deathweavers in again once we start giving her back in pieces."

My fingers curled into my palm, a slight chatter settling onto my teeth. Once they chopped off one of my fingers, who knew if I could still come up with the energy to use my void? To absorb anything, let alone an entire gift? Wield it?

The jailor limped over and sank to his aged knees under groans, blade in one hand, gripping tongs in the other. "Your finger, girl. Push it through, else we'll bring the fire."

I didn't move an inch—not that I was so stupid to believe that obstinance would spare me the potential mutilation. They hadn't brought that ash to keep infection away for nothing...

"I have no time. Drive her toward the wall with torches." Brisden sighed. "Get in there. She's just a void. If she was capable of doing damage, she would have done so already."

Just a void.

Just a girl.

Worthless. Insignificant. Expendable.

My next swallow went down my throat like sand. I was none of those things. I was Galantia, the future queen of

Vhaerya, bonded to Malyr of the royal House Khysal, only living thief known to exist.

But yes, I couldn't do any damage.

Not unless I stole that gift.

Bringing my hand behind my back, I shifted so my palm would face in the direction where Malyr's *anoa* huddled. Shadows slithered through the darkness ever-so-concealed, tingling through my fingertips.

The jailor rose with a grunt, reached the gripping tongs up, and set to work on something outside the metal frame. "Aye, she might still shift."

"She'll do no such thing," Brisden said, his gaze pinning mine down through those rows of chains that slowly seemed to loosen. "The gods know you have caused me too much trouble already, have you not, *daughter?* And to think that, all these years, I raised the void capable of lifting that damn curse under my own roof. You could have given me a kingdom; instead, you gave me chaos, you and that lying bitch of a *mother* of yours."

His words stoked those first embers of ire inside my veins, which clashed painfully with the coldness of the shadows that streamed into me. This man had taken so much from me, from Malyr.

"I am going to kill you for what you did to Lady Brisden," I ground out through the anguish that once more clawed along my insides. Gods, the pain of that gift... "You hung my mother."

When a wide enough part of the chains lowered, Brisden stepped into my cage, making me scramble back quickly. But not quickly enough to dodge that kick of a boot that struck my temple.

"Even her primal seems useless," Brisden said with a kick against my side that sent me rolling over the ground, like a dagger puncturing my kidney. "It took a lot more to beat the ravens out of Malyr. Even after he couldn't shift at will anymore, at times, his ravens did it for him when he was unconscious, so they could peck at his brother. Disgusting beasts."

Grunting in pain, I rolled over the ground, all focus on the shadows lost. My chin hit the ungiving stone, sending a shockwave through my skull that ripped me onto my back. Weight came down on my chest, heavy, heavier...

"No," I croaked.

"For good measure." Brisden loomed over me, pushing his boot down on my chest until all air whooshed out of my lungs. Only then did he shift the tip of his boot enough for it to press against my esophagus. Beside it, my pulse pounded in my aorta, adopting a frantic rushing sound. "Hurry up, man."

Something touched my numbing finger. The jailor?

Panic hurled my mind into a fog, all blood receding from my cheeks. *The gift! I needed it. Now!*

Pinned down as I was, my vision throbbing around the edges, I shifted my absorbing hand toward the shadows. Any shadows!

Pain slammed into me right then, scratching and scraping, shadows carving at my ribcage, ever so cruel. *Do not shy away from his darkness,* a woman's voice sounded from somewhere in my head. *Embrace it.*

But they hurt!

"And what a vexing affair that was, hanging that faithless bitch," Brisden snarled down at me. "*What have you done*, I asked her before I kicked the crate out from beneath that smiling cunt. And do you know what she said? *Loved her the way I should have all along.*" All weight lifted off my chest. "Finish, and bring me her finger."

Loved me.

She'd loved me.

Anguish clawed its way up from the depths of my soul, so raw and savage that it tore through my heart. My body convulsed, as if trying to expel the unbearable heartache that seared through every fiber of my existence.

My void gaped open.

A dark torrent rushed into my core. My breath caught as the pressure in my chest grew to an unbearable ache, the shadows like a living beast inside me that paced my ribcage.

Scratching. Scraping.

Something sharp nipped at my finger, making me hiss and yank my hand from the jailor's grip. "No!"

A surge of shadows burst forth from my palm, an eruption of dark energy fueled by the anguish, the wrath, the heartbreak. The force of it sent the jailor flying backward, his knife clattering uselessly to the floor.

He hit the wall and slid down, but there was no pain in his eyes, only widening horror as fingerlings of shadows slithered over his body. His scream was nothing short of blood-curdling as the tendrils wound tighter around him. His skin turned ashen, then gray, then black, desiccating and tightening over his bones like a mummified corpse.

How easy it was.

Killing.

The sight tingled at my insides—creeping, crawling—shadows convoluting my chest with the same force they blurred my mind. Pitch-black darkness settled onto my thoughts.

I will fucking kill them. I will kill them all!

I stepped out of the cage and rolled my shoulders, following the narrow pathway toward the clanking of armor and bellow of shouts. They must have heard the commotion.

When those first guards appeared ahead of me, I smiled. Marla once told me that only I could know who I truly was. I was Galantia, the only living thief, the strongest recorded deathweaver. I could bring light.

But right now... I very much wanted to bring darkness.

I lifted my palm at them.

CHAPTER
FORTY-FIVE

Malyr
Present Day, a forest

I stood on the slope at the edge of the forest, my gaze locked on the keep embedded into the mountain like that tumor it was. *Where are you, anoaley? I need a sign from you. Now.*

Sebian shifted beside me, his arms folded in front of his chest, one boot nervously tapping at the squelching ground. "What if she can't steal your gift? What if she stole it, but she can't wield it?"

My fingers tightened around the pommel of my sword, my pupils going from the keep, to the setting sun, and back to the keep, searching for the faintest swathe of shadows. Something all the harder to spot once night settled. Time was slipping through my fingers like water, every thud of my heart a drumbeat of growing unease.

She could, I was certain.

But what if she was not?

Asker braved another step forward, up from the low-lying forest we'd retreated to. "We could send pathfinders to scout the area of the keep. Maybe they will see something?"

Behind me, at the bottom of the slope, tents of shadow-cloth billowed softly between trees, shrouding the wounded who groaned with the occasional grind of a bone saw. The stench of cauterized wounds clung to the air, mingling with the scent of blood, sweat, and ash from the healers. Earlier, we'd launched a diversion so my *anoa* could slip into the dungeon undetected before hiding ourselves away in this forest.

It had cost us.

"None of those pathfinders will make it back while the sun is still up, not until they call their troops to the keep." I tightened the straps on my *aerymel* gauntlets, my thoughts clear, my body lithe. How strange to be without them, my shadows, my curse. "Maybe she needs more time."

Or maybe my *anoa* was dead, lying somewhere in the gutters for some child to poke with a stick. My options had been limited to begin with, but what if I'd chosen the wrong one? No, they would do anything to keep Galantia alive. Fuck, the only thing that had kept me from flying in there and bury Ammarett in a grave of shadows alongside me was the fact that, as long as I stayed out, she would remain alive. But what good was staying alive if one's soul rotted away on the inside?

I couldn't let that happen to her.

I would not!

Sebian's hand slammed into my leather cuirass, jarring me from my spiraling thoughts. "There!"

I squinted, focusing on the keep again. Saw nothing. But then, Sebian was a pathfinder; his sight keener than any of my ravens'.

"I see shadows," he confirmed, his voice tinged with a cautious kind of hope as he stepped forward. "It's faint, but... I swear I see shadows drifting from some of the windows of the keep."

"You have to be absolutely certain," I said, "or I'll lead hundreds of Ravens to their—"

A deafening crack rent the air, its force vibrating through the earth beneath my boots. My eyes snapped toward the city, watching as an entire section of the mountain had sheared off, as though cleaved by some divine blade. It slid away and down in a billowing cloud of stone dust until—

Crash!

Chaos erupted.

The fragment smashed into the city below, fracturing upon impact into a hailstorm of projectiles. Stone shards, large as boulders, slammed into the wall, each collision sending tremors through the fortifications. One tower shattered on impact, its debris triggering a chain of collapse that reached its neighbors. Within moments, two more towers buckled, their stones giving way as they were reduced to rubble.

Sebian let out a low whistle beside me, his eyes wide with disbelief. "But you did see that, didn't you?"

The very core of me quivered in savage delight as I clamped down the urge to laugh, but a grin split my face, promising violence and retribution. "That's my little dove…"

The clang of a bell that rang out in the distance. Two bells. Three. It carried over the wind, melding with the brash cry of a horn.

"Ammarett is calling its defenses to the keep," Asker said. "She did it!"

"We have to get to her. Now!" I gave a tug on the sleeve of my black chainmail that I wore beneath my cuirass. "Any last-minute visions about this attack that you care to share with me, Asker?"

He exchanged a quick glance with Sebian, then shook his head. "I will fight beside you. May the goddess guide my visions, and my visions our swords."

Sebian grabbed my shoulders, turned me toward him, and pressed his forehead against mine, the bloodlust already rimming his eyes. "We see this through, don't we, Malyr?"

"Until the end." I turned and looked down over the other Ravens. Deathweavers, pathfinders, those fates with swords quicker than their visions… they all looked at me from faces alight with anticipation. "If you value the home she has returned to you, then you will value her life. Save your future queen! Show them what we do with those who dare harm the unkindness!"

The camp erupted into a chorus of battle cries and the clangor of weapons just as Asker shouted, "Avoid the arrows. Stay away from the rubble or it might bury you. Breach that gate and flood the halls with the cries of dying men until she is safe. Unleash a darkness onto them that not even their nursemaids have warned them about in nighttime stories about Ravens."

"Fly!" Sebian screamed.

Hundreds of shifts ripped through the camp in a torrent of shadows and feathers that whirled through the trees like a surging tide of darkness. For a moment, the world ceased to be anything but plumes and wings, caws and feathers, shadows and chaos.

My shift surged through me. We dashed into the sky and took our place at the head of the formation, our collective unkindness a swelling tempest, a dark maelstrom that spiraled up and forward. Below us, one massive shadow eclipsed the land, a moving night that crept toward the city, swallowing the light.

The horn sounded again, ripping through the orange hue of the setting sun. Arrows followed, hissing through our flock. We veered, swerved, shot upward. Most arrows missed, but not all. A dull *thud*. A guttural *caw*. A nearby raven plummeted from the sky, a feathery mass hurtling toward the ground.

Split and spiral, I commanded through the unkindness.

We fractured into smaller clusters, each spiraling in opposing directions. It was like watching paint drops scatter in water, unpredictable and hard to aim at. Arrows sliced through the spaces we'd just vacated, finding only air where ravens had been a second before. Then, as every Raven learned from a young age, we converged back into a unified mass, banking toward the gate of the keep.

Deathweavers, let your shadows breach the gate! Asker's shout vibrated through all of us. *Fates, clear the plateau and protect the weavers!*

We swooped low, our shadow stretching over the plateau before the keep's gate, darkening the faces of the soldiers below. Whistles of swords filled the air as we cut through, dodging metal as energy spliced through us.

Feathers still drifted around me as I pulled my sword, its cold *aerymel* singing, slashing through the air.

"Right hand!" Asker shouted.

A soldier lunged at me from there. The clang of metal against metal rang in my ears as I parried, harmonizing with my pounding heart. I ducked under a wild swing, spun, and drove my blade through another soldier. I yanked my sword free as he fell, narrowly dodging an arrow that zipped past my ear.

"Archers above the gate," Sebian ground out where he stabbed one dagger into the thigh of a soldier, while the other slashed across another's throat. "Malyr!"

"I'm with you!" With no time to waste, my form disintegrated into a rush of feathers and darkness. We soared high and darted through one of the narrow arrow slits in the stone.

Sword in one hand, I lunged at the nearest archer, while Sebian skewered another with his daggers. A quick parry, a spin, and the archer's screams joined the cacophony below as my blade found its mark. Sebian moved fluidly beside me, his daggers sprinkling arcs of red on the stone each time he pulled the blades from another corpse.

I glanced down through one of the arrow slits, the plateau outside a field of chaos as the fates tried to fend off the masses of soldiers storming up the stairs. "We have to help open the gate from the inside or they'll slaughter us before we even set a foot in there."

Sebian grabbed his bow. "I'm right behind you."

We dashed to the entrance of the stairwell that led down to the gate, my sword singing with every stroke as I cut down any enemy soldier daring to block our path.

Sebian nocked an arrow and let it fly, even as we took the steps two at a time. Each shot found a target among the soldiers braced against the gate below us, creating momentary openings in their defenses.

"More soldiers coming from somewhere," Sebian shouted.

We had to hurry.

I glanced at the gate, where a massive wooden beam, reinforced with iron, wedged into brackets on either side of the doors. Tendrils of shadow wound around it from outside, slipping through the cracks of the gate.

It wasn't enough.

On instinct, I lifted my hand at it.

No shadows came.

Gritting my teeth, I charged forward. "Keep them off me!"

Sebian's arrows whistled to my left and right as I used my sword as a lever. I wedged the blade beneath the beam and pushed with all my strength. The shadows from our deathweavers gripped tighter, adding their dark pull to my efforts. With a groan of wood against iron, the beam started to lift.

"More soldiers coming from inside the keep!" Sebian shouted. "Open the fucking gate or we'll be done for!"

With a final heave, the beam dislodged, thudding to the stone floor. I yanked my sword free just as the gate burst open, our soldiers surging through in a wave of steel, shadows, and pitch-black birds.

"Inside! Everyone inside!" Asker shouted. "Then cut them down and close the gate! Split their forces in two!"

The threshold erupted into chaos.

Fates held the line, staving off the surge of enemy soldiers still pouring up the stairs from the city, buying precious seconds for the rest of us. Meanwhile, others struggled to push the massive doors closed against the outside onslaught, ravens flitting in through the narrowing gap. Amidst the disarray, deathweavers wove tendrils of shadows to hoist the massive beam, their faces twisted in concentration as they guided it back into its brackets.

Through the renewed clashing of metal and the screams of the injured, I listened to my bond, but my chest remained silent with no *anoa* to guide me. *Where are you, little dove?*

"Asker!" I shouted. "Where to now?"

He turned from the massive gate, finally closed shut, and blinked around the dimly-lit room hollowed into the mountain. "It does not look like twenty years ago... I believe it lays—"

More Ammarett soldiers stormed into the chamber, flooding from doorways and passages like a wave through a burst dam, the sight sucking all warmth from my limbs. So many soldiers, so many corridors... yet not a single idea as to which would lead me to my *anoaley*.

Until a shout shattered from the rock. "Protect the king! I'll have the balls of whoever lets one of them slip through!"

A shudder ran down my spine.

That voice...

I swung around, finding Brisden with his sword drawn a distance from me that seemed both too far and too close. My eyes locked with his, and my vision narrowed. The room, the chaos, all faded into the background of this very moment.

"Malyr..." Sebian said beside me. "Some of the soldiers beside him carry shadowmarks. Wherever she is, it's behind them."

Another smile curled my lips. And here I'd feared for a second that I would have to let Brisden go once more. And I

415

would have... to spare my bondmate even a moment more among these monsters? Yes, I would have.

But alas, I wouldn't need to.

I locked eyes with Sebian for a split second, a silent agreement passing between us. Then we charged.

Sebian darted forward, his daggers slicing through the air. Soldiers fell, clutching their throats or their guts, darkness oozing from their wounds as the daggers found their mark with uncanny precision.

Asker moved in tandem with me, his sword meeting the enemy's in a harsh cacophony of metal and grunts. "Above, left!"

I immediately raised my sword to intercept a descending blade. The force of the blow reverberated up my arm, but I held firm, my eyes scanning the chaos for Brisden. *Where is he?*

"Behind!" Asker's voice broke through again.

I pivoted just in time to sidestep a lunging spear, slashing across the soldier's chest as my eyes locked onto that familiar shade of brown hair. *There you are!*

Pure, unadulterated rage surged through me, guiding my sword with a deadly focus. It became an extension of my fury, every stroke fueled by years of torment. One slash to sever a man's arm, another to pierce a lung. Bodies fell in my wake as I carved a blood-soaked path, each step bringing me closer to the reckoning that had been years in the making. I was almost there.

"Brisden," I growled, my heart beating wildly in my chest.

He widened his stance, his chest heaving, his forehead glistening with the sweat of too many easy years and too little training. "Ah, the young Raven boy came to end me."

"End you?" A laugh echoed in my empty chest, deeper and more freeing than ever before. "No. No..."

With one swift swipe, I clashed my sword against his. And again. And again. His blade wavered, barely parrying my strikes, each one delivered with a decade's worth of shame. Like that, I drove him back into a corner.

He grunted, tried to counter, but his blows were slow, clumsy, his breaths coming in ragged heaves. "This is hardly an honorable fight. I'm old..."

"And I was young." Not a child anymore, but not yet a man, stripped of all honor, decency, and anything that had been good about me. "Innocent." Another swing of my blade. "Pure." I kicked his chest, sending him reeling back before he fell onto his back with a groan. "Helpless."

I booted his sword out of his grip, sending it with sparks across the stone before. Then I knelt on his chest and pressed my bloodied blade to his mouth, watching how it sank into the corners, creeks of blood running down his cheeks. Oh, and how he gargled, his choking sounds making bubbles pop at the back of his throat as I slowly cut through his face.

But no... I would not end him.

Not yet, not like this

Where was the fun in that?

I jumped off him, running behind Sebian toward the corridor where Brisden had emerged from. "Tie him up with shadows! Whoever lets him die will die with him!"

He would feel my hatred later.

Right now, love took precedence.

FORTY-SIX

Galantia

Present Day, the royal keep

Ears ringing, I stared down at the rubble and shadows that piled upon the dungeon stairs from which I'd emerged. A hand that had tried to grab me only moments ago now jutted out from the debris, its fingers frantically scratching at the rock as it blackened. Its knuckles contorted, curling into a grotesque, gouty freeze.

The sight should have been vile, repugnant even, but the shadows inside my chest writhed in savage delight, demanding more death. And I might just comply if I couldn't find my way to Malyr and Sebian, adding my own right to it. A deathweaver I might be, but still very much mortal, obviously lacking the finesse with this gift. I'd merely wanted to push him back, not cause... whatever it was that I'd done here.

Coughing the dust from my lungs, I followed along a corridor, glass crunching beneath my steps. The wind cut itself on those strange metal webbings that clung to the broken windows to my right and howled, mixing with the...

Was that... a bell?

The weight of dread lifted from my chest. Were the Ravens attacking? Where was the main gate? How long until they would breach it?

Chaos echoed from nearby rooms and corridors, the *thuds* of boots and *clanks* of armor driving up my pulse. More soldiers?

Shadows throbbed between the fingers of my right hand as if matching the gallop of my heart, spinning inky tendrils toward my left palm where they absorbed back into me. They swirled in my core—scratching, scraping—clawing along my ribcage like a beast determined to crack through my bones. And to think that Malyr had carried this with him for years...

Something moved in my periphery.

I froze.

Two maids scurried toward me, one holding a silver platter to her chest, their faces flushed and terror-stricken. They clutched white bonnets to their heads, glancing back over their shoulders, as if expecting a demon to be in pursuit.

Or Ravens...

One of the maids tore her gaze away and looked ahead.

Her eyes met mine and they widened. Letting out a scream, she lost her footing, stumbled sideways, and fell onto her rear, the silver platter clattering loudly beside her.

The other maid careened over her, scrambling for balance as she stared at me from panic-rimmed eyes. "Mercy! Mercy, please!"

Shadows nipped at my fingertips with such viciousness, sweat broke on my forehead, but I folded them into my absorbing hand. "The main gate. Which way?"

The fallen maid scrambled to her feet, shakily pointing down the corridor from which they'd come. "Through the throne room."

Both maids broke into a flurry of pleas, nearly tripping over each other as they made a swift, terrified escape around the corner.

I took a step toward the abandoned platter, now lying askew on the floor, and looked down. Face webbed with black veins. Shadows sweeping through blonde strands. Eyes dipped in tar. Yes, I'd run, too...

I hurried into the corridor and straight into chaos. A stampede of frenzied servants shot past me, so focused on their flight that most took no notice of me as they mumbled and prayed. Those soldiers shoving themselves through the masses and toward me, however...?

I lowered my gaze and kept to the right of the wall, turning my body outward just a little to hide my shadows as well as I managed.

"Check the dungeon!" one of them shouted. "Make way!"

Armor clanked louder, louder...

... then clattered past me.

I exhaled a long breath and pushed on. The corridor eventually cleared, giving way to a gold-wrought archway.

A rich blue carpet rolled out beneath it, leading into an opulent, vault-like structure where a dais of polished white marble led up to... a throne, presumably. I couldn't really see it.

Not with all the soldiers camping before it, deep in conversation. Too many to fight off? Maybe. I had no desire to find out and be proven right.

I assessed the room. Each side of the dais gave way to passages that most likely lead to private rooms, or perhaps map rooms, just like at Tidestone and Deepmarsh. The only other obvious exit lay directly across from the corridor I had emerged from. The main gate had to be that way. All I had to do was cross without drawing attention to myself. *Easy.*

My bladder twinged.

I extended my right hand, fingers splayed, and shadows poured into the room. They unfurled like black fog, guided by the flicks of my wrist like I'd seen other deathweavers do. The ones that drifted too far left, risking detection by those soldiers, I thinned-out with my other hand. Just enough to camouflage my movements if I stalked deliberately, but not too much to catch eyes.

Holding my breath, I staggered forward, each step a calculated risk, each second stretching into an eternity. A knot tightened in my stomach, a visceral twist of tension that mirrored the mental strain of the moment. But I shoved that feeling into the background of my consciousness. *Almost there!*

Stealing into the corridor, I cast a wary glance over my shoulder at the throne room. The soldiers remained with their attention fixed elsewhere, their backs a wall of oblivious steel. A pulse of relief surged through me, but it was a fragile thing, easily shattered.

My ears pricked at the faint sound of metal clashing

against metal. Fighting. Nearby. *Malyr and Sebian!* My heart hammered in my ears as I turned back toward the corridor. They couldn't be far. If I managed to get there without running into more—

Something slammed into me.

Thrown off balance, I stumbled backward into the throne room and crashed onto the floor. My spine hit the ground with a crackle. Waves of pain reverberated through my body, culminating in a sharp stab at the back of my head. A vibration rippled through my skull, sending a moment of blackness through my vision.

Light returned, and with it, a dread that stabbed into my bladder with such force, I wasn't sure if it would hold. Because the snarling visage of a wolf looked right at me.

Stunned, I locked eyes with Domren.

No. Not him!

A moment of mutual shock hung suspended in time, then shattered as he bellowed, "Get her!"

Soldiers materialized from behind him, pouring from the corridor. At the same moment, the ones by the throne turned, their swords hissing from their sheaths. Oh no!

A soldier chanced a grab for me.

On instinct, I swept my arm up over my head. Shadows lunged from my fingertips like tendrils of a thorny vine, latching onto his neck and yanking him down with terrifying force.

"Ah!" he screamed, gasping and clawing at his throat as he hit the ground.

Several gasps moved the air.

A flicker of something—Fear? Disbelief?—crossed Domren's face, then he pulled his sword. "Kill the deathweaver!"

My heart exploded in my chest as the room detonated

into violence, every soldier lunging, swiping, charging at me.

Fight. I had to fight!

I thrust out my arms. Shadows spiraled from one hand, only to create frenzied arcs that pushed some soldiers back before they seeped into my other hand. A blade whistled by my ear, another grazed my arm.

I yelped and rolled sideways before I scrambled to my feet. Shadows. I needed more shadows!

Retreating toward the wall, I bought myself time and focused on my void. On that obsidian box surrounded by even blacker darkness. I closed it. Locked it. Gave the shadows nowhere to go but outward.

I wasn't a void.

I was a deathweaver.

Feared by all.

Shadows writhed in my core—scratching, scraping, clawing their way through my ribs with cruel nips and bites. Violent heat rushed through my veins, turning me hot, turning me itchy, making my skin pulse as if I no longer fit my casing. Unbearable!

Seething darkness burst from my seams, billowing out from the tatters of my dress. Whip-like ropes of shadows lashed out from me, reaching for necks, pulling legs from beneath bodies, yanking weapons from grasping hands. They killed, slashed, and slayed, each terrorized scream bringing another lift to the corners of my mouth.

I was powerful, invulnerable.

Until I wasn't.

"Fucking die already!" Domren shouted just as he, in a blink of an eye, thrust something at me.

A whistle cut the air.

One if his daggers embedding itself in my thigh.

A guttural scream tore from my lungs, more wrath than agony. It wasn't pain that flooded my senses when I pulled the blade from my body, it was rage, hotter and more consuming than before.

He'd raped me. He'd whored me out. He'd hurt me.

Well, I was doing the hurting now.

Starting with him!

Domren, his face twisted in a snarl, lunged at me, sword arcing down toward me. My shadows met his blade, a screech of dark against steel echoing in the air. He was strong, but the shock of the clash traveled up his arm, ripping a pained scream from him.

Summoning every last reserve of strength, I lunged forward, ignoring the remaining soldiers closing in on me from all sides. I grabbed his face, fingertips finding purchase in the socket of an eye, the corner of his mouth, around a cheekbone. Shadows slithered into every cavity, the fine blood vessels on his skin going from maroon to purple to black.

Beautiful!

He howled, letting his sword clank to the ground before he yanked my hand off him. Staggering, burying his face in his palms, he collapsed to the floor. Black offshoots spread across his entire body, squeezing tighter the more he twitched...

Until he stilled.

My breath stopped.

Had I... had I killed him?

A violent jerk snapped my head back. A handful of my hair clenched in a soldier's fist, who looked at me from a shadow and blood-streaked face. Cold steel pressed against the vulnerable flesh of my throat, lethality poised inches from my jugular.

This was it.

I was dead.

Strangely, even with death mere breaths away, a sense of detachment washed over me. I had done it; I'd killed Domren. Had exacted my revenge on behalf of so many. Sebian's sister. His family. Ravenna. Not a bad death by any means.

Something speckled my face, warm and wet, seasoning my lips. Metal. Blood? Was I bleeding out already?

I blinked the viscous blur from my vision. No, the soldier who'd grabbed me was bleeding, blood dripping from that gushing socket where a reddened blade had replaced his eye. The sword must have entered through the side of his neck and torn through his aorta, gushes of blood pouring from his mouth in slowing intervals.

My knees buckled.

"Shh..." a voice hushed, a strong arm wrapping around my middle and keeping me upright. "It's just me, *anoaley*. You're safe now. We're here."

I sank into Malyr's chest and looked up at his face, black renegade wisps sticking to the blood that painted his face here and there. "You came..."

"Of course we came. I'm never letting you go." With a kick, he dislodged the twitching corpse from his sword. "By the throne!"

"Saw it!" Beside us, Sebian pulled back a shadowy arrow, sending it through the skull of a soldier who'd drawn his bow beside the throne. Just as quickly, he hoisted his bow and let two black daggers form in his hands, which he sliced through the attacking soldiers. "Footsteps behind you!"

Malyr spun us around, holding me tightly against him

with one arm while cleaving through the head of a soldier with the other. "Can you still shift on your own?"

I shook my head, my muscles suddenly like lead. "No."

"I'll help you," he said. "But first, we have to get rid of these soldiers. Return my gift, little dove. Pour it all into me."

"I've never done that before."

"I'd wager you've done a great many things today that you have never done before," he said with a tense chuckle. "You can do this, too."

He was right. I'd come this far.

I could do this. I had to!

Closing my eyes, I placed my hand onto his black cuirass and focused on the gift at my core—the one that wasn't mine, shadows pacing the closed borders of my void. I tapped into them, luring them from my chest, down my arm, into my hand, and through my fingertips from there.

Malyr tensed, a pained groan rumbling in his chest as shadows ever-so cruel returned a burden that... He pushed me away. "Take her!"

I stumbled sideways as Malyr gripped his sword with both hands, fighting off two soldiers at once.

"I got you, sweetheart." Sebian pulled me against him, throwing a dagger at a soldier who stormed out of a corridor, conjuring a new one before the old embedded itself in the enemy's throat. "We're going to get you out of here, I promise. We just need to cut back some of these bastards before we can dare a shift."

Malyr and Sebian worked in tandem, deflected and countering the soldiers storming toward us. All the while, they kept me shielded, their backs to me, their bodies my fortress in a sea of chaos and death.

"Three o'clock!" Malyr shouted.

Even before Sebian spun around, I sent a blast of shadows toward the soldier, sending him to slam with his spine against the throne before he folded and moved no more.

"That's my girl," Sebian praised, throwing another shadowy dagger that took a soldier in the eye, dropping him instantly. "We can't keep this up. There's a fucking nest of them somewhere in there. We have to get back to the others."

"Get your bow and keep them at a distance!" Malyr shouted, then turned to face me, his hands settling on my arms. "My gift, little dove. Give it to me."

I reached to Malyr's chest once more, my fingers trembling at the sensation of his gift abandoned my core. How empty I was without it, without him.

Something shifted, a movement to my right caught my eye. I turned my head, meeting Domren's cold, deadened eyes as he thrust one of his daggers.

My heart stuttered to a standstill while time lazily crept behind, my gaze searching Malyr's. Our eyes locked, and in that single moment, I saw so many things that hadn't happened yet...

A crown sitting on his head. Tears in his eyes upon the birth of our first child. A handful of white strands weaving through his black hair—like a lifetime of shared memories not yet lived that unraveled before my mind's eye. I wanted them so badly!

Malyr stared at me.

He understood.

Eyes widening, he whirled around, dropping his sword and raising one hand. With the other, he shoved me behind him, positioning his body as a shield between me and impending death.

The dagger turned, and turned, and turned, silently slicing through the air as it grew large, larger. Shadows sparked into existence around Malyr's outstretched fingers. Slow, too slow.

The bond within me spasmed, shrieking out a visceral alarm that resounded through the very marrow of my bones. "No!"

Sebian hurled himself against Malyr's side with a savage grunt. Shoulder collided with shoulder, sending Malyr stumbling sideways.

In a fleeting heartbeat, Sebian's spine straightened right before me. His shoulders broadened. He drew his arm back, releasing a single arrow before a jerk went through him, splintering him into his unkindness to the clank of metal hitting stone.

Every inch of me trembled as I looked down at the bloodied dagger. Over to Domren, who lay sprawled on the ground, an arrow protruding from his face. Back to the blade.

"No!" Malyr whirled around, letting himself fall to his knees where Sebian came into view at the center of shadows and plumes. "Why did you do this? Why did you do this?!"

Ignoring the numbness in my limbs, I stumbled over to where Sebian lay amid a storm of scattered feathers, blood swelling from the slit in his cuirass. My knees hit the ground with a dull *thud*, the world narrowing to those beautiful green eyes—like pines, and grass, and everything alive.

"Did I do it?" Sebian's mouth opened and closed as if gasping for air. "Did I... did I save her?"

Malyr's glistening eyes found mine before they snapped to the soldiers streaming in. Slinging one arm around Sebian's neck, lifting his head up some, he slammed his other hand onto the ground. A circle of shadows rippled away from us, only to rise and crest into a black wall.

Everything dimmed.

Everything turned silent.

I reached out, trembling fingers brushing away a stray feather stuck to Sebian's brow. "You did."

"Galantia?" He looked around disoriented, his eyes grazing mine several times before they narrowed on me. "Can't... can't see you."

"I'm right here," I said and leaned over, my eyes burning and, at my next blink, unleashing streams of tears that dripped onto his brown, scuffed cuirass.

Sebian's smirk tugged impossibly higher as he finally looked at me, only to waver when blood swelled from his mouth, ripping a gargling cough from his throat. "Take... take it. And my bow. You teach her, Malyr, right? Teach her?"

Malyr nodded. "Of course."

"What?"

"He wants you to steal his gift," Malyr said, cradling Sebian's head in his arm, gently rocking from side to side as he brushed the sweaty strands from his forehead.

"But... no." Shaking my head, I took Sebian's fingers into mine, so cold. "You'll need it. Malyr and I, we'll... we'll get you out of here. To a healer. Right, Malyr?" I looked up at Malyr. "You have healers at the camp, don't you? They can take care of him?"

Malyr's gaze dropped to the wound in Sebian's chest, then to the way he gaped for air like a fish out of water, then back up to me. He shook his head.

"I can't lose you." A sob broke from my lips, and in that moment, the world broke with it. "I love you."

"And I... I love you. Don't cry, sweetheart. It's fated," Sebian said, his fingertips twitching against my palms as if he meant to hold me tight just one last time. "Take it. Keep something of me. You have to... have to hurry."

My nose turned stuffy as Sebian's outline blurred behind tears that came faster than I could blink them away. Then I rested my hand on his cuirass, right beside the slit, sensing his shadows rise into my palm. They swirled into my core easily, making themselves a home there.

My nose wrinkled at the smell of blood. My tongue curled at the taste of fear. But mostly, my ears pricked at the rush of blood that flooded Sebian's lungs. That, and the beat of a heart that slowed, slowed some more.

Stopped.

FORTY-SEVEN

Galantia
Present Day, a tent

Water trickled down Sebian's black silky strands, each blood-tainted droplet echoing through the silence of the tent as it fell into the bucket on the ground. After we'd left Ammarett behind in confusion and chaos, we'd broken up camp and carted our dead eastward. With Valtaris several weeks away by road, the decision had been made to hold the fire burials beside a beautiful forest of white-speckled birches and evergreen junipers.

Malyr's jagged exhale scrubbed against the side of my neck where he knelt behind me, his trembling fingers combing the knots from my tattered hair ever so carefully. For hours, he'd held me, patiently letting me cry into his chest until my tears ran dry, leaving nothing behind but a parched landscape of grief.

But he was growing restless now, I could sense it in every second's hesitation before he touched me. As if he wondered if I would shrink away, giving him any indicators as to what had been done to me, saving me uncomfortable questions I knew full well needed asking.

Shadows clung to crevices and secret corners, Malyr's mother had told me, thriving in the unseen, the hidden, the unacknowledged. I would not give them more domain than they already had on him.

When his fingers brushed over my thigh, where a healer had sewn-up my wound, they clenched only to stretch out with a tremble. "Did they... did they rape you?"

I took the wooden comb Marla had let me borrow, running it down along the sleek strands with ease. "They did."

He shot up on something between a shout and a whimper, grabbed onto the braids running along his scalp, and yanked until his knuckles yellowed. "How many times?" Left and right he paced in short, violent strides, swathes of shadows following behind him. "How many times, Galantia?!"

I flinched, not at his shout, but the way his face contorted with a dozen emotions at once under speckles of dried blood. Shame. Guilt. Anger. As if he was imagining all sorts of horrors I must have endured, seeing them vibrantly because he'd endured them, too.

I shook my head. "It doesn't matter."

He spun around and collapsed to his knees beside me, gripping my arms and shaking me, staring at me with such devastation carved into the depth of his gray-brown eyes. "How can you say this? How can you say it *doesn't matter*?"

"Because I refuse to let it matter." I placed the comb on my lap and took Malyr's face between my palms, several minor cuts and scrapes marring his ashen features. "I refuse to give the perpetrators of my past any control over my life by letting this sully my thoughts, my feelings, any part of my life going forward. Shame and hate are heavy burdens, Malyr, and I won't let them drag me down." A deep breath. "And neither should you."

Something fractured in his eyes. A noisy gulp tore from his throat as he pulled back from my touch, knowing that we weren't just talking about me anymore. *Yes, I know what they did to you*, I didn't say, *and I love you no differently for it.*

His gaze sank to the ground as if weighted down by the very shame I wanted him to let go of. I couldn't make him; all I could do was show him that there needn't be any, not between us.

He slid his hand to the back of my head and gently nudged my forehead to sink against his. "I failed you. Damnit, I failed both of you."

I closed my eyes, ignoring the tang of metal while focusing on the faint remnants of lemongrass that still drifted from his hair. "You couldn't have known."

"I should have," he whispered. "Goddess help me, I was so focused on human's wickedness, I failed to protect you from the treachery of our own kind."

"It's in the past now." Yet another perceived wrong that

had cost us Sebian, making it difficult to see the right in it. Maybe it would reveal itself, maybe it wouldn't. "The sun is almost up. We have to get him ready."

Malyr shifted back, nodded, then turned his attention to Sebian. "Do you want me to shave his sides?"

"Hmm." I reached for a section of Sebian's damp hair, where he lay with his head toward me on a makeshift cot. "If we could ask him now, what do you think he'd say?"

Malyr's scoff brought a new glisten to his eyes, but he blinked his tears away. "I'd wager a coin he'd say that he doesn't give a shit."

"No, he wouldn't." *I'm just a farmer's son, sweetheart,* his voice resonated in the quiet space. Oh, but he'd never been simple. "I much prefer him like this. A little bit ragged, a little bit rough around the edges."

My fingers parted five strands, the way he'd liked it best, his lingering scent grounding me in my resolve— earthy, like the wet loam beneath us with a hint of leather coming from the brown cuirass Malyr had already wiped down. I would miss it so much. I missed him!

I bit back the sob building at the bottom of my throat. At least for now. There would be time for grieving, but this moment was for something else—something meaningful between two souls whose lives had been as entwined as the braid I slowly wove into his hair, each twist a silent farewell.

"Here." Malyr removed the silver clasp from the bottom of his braid, and gingerly worked it around the end of Sebian's. "Is there anything else?"

I brushed my thumb over that single stray wisp of hair on Sebian's cold forehead, down a cheek I'd scrubbed clean earlier, and over those plump graying lips that had done nothing but shower me with kisses these last few weeks.

Why had the goddess taken him from us? Could there have been another way? Was there anything I could have done differently to prevent his death?

I would never know.

I shook my head. "I think he's ready."

Asker must have waited nearby, because he announced himself with a clearing of his throat before he stepped into the tent. "I came to help carry him."

Malyr rose and, together with Asker, he carried Sebian's limp body out of the tent and only a brief stretch toward the pyre that had been built, singled-out from the others. He deserved no less recognition, the pathfinder who had taken a dagger through his chest.

To save me. Or Malyr?

Maybe he'd saved us both.

They carefully lowered him onto the pyre, Malyr arranging his limbs while Asker inspected the straw and dry moss between the wood. Here and there, smoke already billowed into a morning sky streaked with pinks and purples. Beautiful.

Marla walked up beside me—her eyes puffy, thin red veins webbing across the white of her eyes—and took my hand into hers. "Only the deepest love is capable of bringing about the deepest pain."

"You just had to be the heroic one, did you not? Damn you, Sebian." Malyr took the torch Asker handed him, bringing the fire to the corners before he shoved it into the center of the pyre. "Fly, brother. We'll meet again among the stars."

Flames roared up with a whoosh, making Asker and Malyr step back as they devoured the pyre. And with it, one of the two men I loved.

As the flames leapt higher, something inside me crystallized—a chilling, absolute stillness. Reality buckled and distorted, like one's reflection when standing too close to a mirror. And I was left on the threshold between what had been and what could never be again, suspended in a moment that was too brutal to absorb fully.

My emotions felt dulled, as if they'd been sanded down to almost nothing; the jagged edges of grief and disbelief smoothed into a kind of emotional numbness. There was nothing more to say, nothing more to feel—just the echoing emptiness where Sebian had made himself a home in my chest. Where he *had been* my home.

How long Malyr had stood behind me, hugging me while he nuzzled my temple, I couldn't say. Each time a hiccuped gulp shook my body, he hushed me, telling me that everything would be alright. That he would take care of me. That I could cry some more if I needed to.

At Marla's nudge, Asker walked up in front of us, pulled a letter from the satchel on his belt, and held it up before us. "He... asked me to give this to you after he... after he—" He took a deep breath, and pushed the letter into my hand. "Sebian wanted you to have this, both of you."

I took the letter, watching how Asker and Marla turned back to their tent before I glanced up at Malyr, strange tingles flickering inside my chest. What did he mean, Sebian had wanted us to have this?

Why? How?

Fingers shaky, I broke the black seal of House Khysal. I unfolded the black scribbles, holding it against the light of dawn as I started to read out loud:

Sweetheart,
   If you read this, then I am dead.

If you read this, then I succeeded.

I am writing these words to you both, sitting at Malyr's desk in the middle of the night, with a candle for company. Every now and then, I gaze over at our nest where the two of you are currently sleeping in a deep embrace. Not much longer, and I will join you, relishing every second I get to spend between now and whenever Asker stands by his word and hands you this letter.

How I died, I can't say. If it was fast or slow, numb or painful, bloody or boring. Did I spit blood and cry, or did I have the chance to tell you how much I love you, Galantia? Was my head clouded by the fear of death, or did I manage to tell you that, right here, right now, with my thoughts clear, that I died gladly?

No doubt you're confused as hell. I hope you already burned me because there isn't much I wouldn't give to smirk down at the two of you just one last time. See, I've chosen to die a long time ago, back when I shared supper with Asker and Marla. That night, I wandered along the Tarred Road...

CHAPTER
FORTY-EIGHT

Sebian
Past, Valtaris

I wandered along the Tarred Road, with its obsidian stone polished by centuries of marching feet, imposing buildings to each side too opulent for a farmer's son like me, and shops selling trinkets too rich for my blood.

My friendship to Malyr aside, I felt strangely out of place.

So much so, my eyes kept jumping to those dark alleys,

their air filled with cheap wine, cheaper sex, and all sorts of trouble. But alas, I kept heading straight until I reached Asker and Marla's home—a two-story building close to the Winged Keep.

Once at the door, I lifted my fist, hesitated for a second, then knocked. Sure, Asker had called me irresponsible, a fool, a good-for-nothing drunk for years, but I was none of those things. I understood that now. And if he could bring himself to invite me, then I sure as fuck could sit through a shared supper with him.

The door swung open almost immediately, as if Asker had been waiting just behind it. His black-and-silver-streaked hair was pulled back from a face lined by age and grimness. He looked at me for a second, two, three— Goddess be damned, had I gotten the day wrong? The time? Did he suddenly remember that I hadn't protected his daughter and actually didn't want me in his home after all?

"Sebian," he finally broke the silence, his voice reluctant, "glad you could make it. Come in, come in."

My joints locked up.

Ignoring it, I stepped inside and straight into a swath of warmth, scented with fried onions and... possibly rosemary, creating a familiar taste that had my tongue curl against my gums. Nobody cooked better than Marla, not even Mother had—not that I'd ever dared to say that out loud or she would've smacked me until daybreak, as if I were eight again.

My gaze trailed over the rich tapestries hanging from the walls, the wooden table at the center of the main room already set with wooden bowls and spoons. "Is the chimney still giving you troubles?"

"After how you had your unkindness climb in there and

tug apart the old bird's nest that clogged it?" Marla said with a jest in her tone that somehow wavered at its edges, steering a ladle around the iron pot that hung near the fire by the hearth. "The chimney is working just as it should now."

"Still too much ash and soot that is sitting everywhere," Asker added, running a finger over the grayed daub on the wall beside him.

He stared at his blackened finger. Then he smudged it against his thumb as if he didn't know what else to do with his hands... like shake mine. Or usher me over to the table. Or smack me.

My molars pressed together all on their own, biting back that sarcastic chuckle tickling the back of my throat. This was going to be a *long* night...

"Asker!" Marla hissed under the breath of her tense smile.

"Hmm?" He startled, looked at her, then nodded and finally gestured me to the table. "Yes, yes, of course. Please, have a seat."

My back had barely touched the chair's backrest when Asker reached for one of the pitchers on the table and started pouring into the wooden cups. Ah, the solace of wine—a loyal friend when it came to making the most awkward situation bearable. At least in that regard, Asker and I were of one mind tonight.

When Asker slid the cup toward me, I took it without hesitation, bringing it to my lips with a quickly mumbled, "Thanks."

The wood pressed against my lips. The first drop hit my tongue, bland and stale and...water. Just water.

My chuckle echoed inside the cup before I took a sip,

then placed it back down on the table. "No wine for me, huh?"

Across the room, Marla stared into her pot with trance-like focus, merely a hint of a shake moving her head. "Just give the boy some wine."

"Old company breeds old habits," Asker said, his words as firm as the pressed shadowcloth of his shirt.

"As if it matters..." Marla mumbled.

What was that supposed to mean?

"Do not make me regret asking him here," Asker bit back.

My veins heated. This was a mistake; I shouldn't have come here. Why the fuck had I bothered coming here?

The chair legs beneath me groaned over the wooden floor as I rose and turned back toward the fucking door. "Don't worry, old man, I'll fix that real quick for you."

"No!" The ladle clinked against the pot as Marla rushed over, cutting my escape short with how she planted herself in front of me and took my hands into hers. "Stay, Sebian. Please! If you can't do it because of him, do it for me."

The longer I looked down at those soft eyes of hers, her fingers frantically gripping mine, as if she feared I might dissolve into feathers at any moment now, the more my muscles tightened. And I just... couldn't see her like that, her features edged with the same pain I'd seen when she'd wailed over Ravenna's charred body.

Nodding, I gave her hands a squeeze before I turned back toward the table and sat my ass back down in the chair. "Weather!" I said, grabbed my cup, and took a sip of my water. "You know, Malyr told me about how the *aerymel* stores the heat and, together with the wind barriers, keeps the temperatures mild even in winter. Still, I didn't think that I'd come here at night in the beginning of spring without a cloak."

Marla returned to stirring her pot, but not without mumbling, "You promised me."

Asker sighed, then he gave me a nod. "Yes, very pleasant, mm-hmm."

"Mm-hmm." Fuck, this was going to be so painful. "Hot in summer?"

"It can be," he said with another stiff nod. "But only if there is no wind, which is not often the case. We open the wind barriers at different heights, which creates a draft throughout the city, except for lower lying alleys."

"Interesting." Not in the slightest, but if it took two hours of talking about sun, wind, and rain to get us through this, then so be it. "I can't wait to, um..." *Get out of here.* "To see if it reminds me of Lanai. I saw mango trees on the Perch. They're dead now, of course, but it reminded me of home. I thought about taking Galantia to Lanai in summer. I'd love to show—"

A sob.

From. Marla.

The hairs on the back of my neck stood up, a shiver crawling up my spine as if the temperature in the room had dropped. "What's wrong?"

The moment Marla's eyes found mine, she gave a dismissive swat at the air, turned her back on me, and stared into her pot. "Oh, don't mind me. It is just... so good to have you here."

"Yes, yes, this has been long overdue." Asker cleared his throat, shoving around in his chair as if he couldn't get comfortable, no matter how he sat. "Malyr and Galantia seem to be reconciled? Happy, even?"

I thought back to last night, when I'd woken for a

second, only to find her lying sprawled-out between Malyr and me, one toe wedged beneath a calf on each side. "They're finding their way..."

"He adores her." Marla poured some of the stew into a large clay vessel, which she clasped between her hands before she turned toward us. "I see it in many visions, the way he stole secret glances at her, utterly mesmerized by the girl."

"Do you know if this... finding their way may result in a child soon?" Asker asked, a thick swallow trailing down his throat before he added, "A *legitimate* heir?"

"Legitimate," I echoed. "Malyr and I are taking measures, if that's what you're concerned about." Rightfully so. Ambitious lords, be it human or Raven, lurked around every corner. "Aside from the fact that we know there can't be a child with questionable lineage, I don't think I would survive it if I lost another one. Doesn't mean that I'm not excited about rocking the little thing, teaching it how to use a bow, or how to—"

Crash!

I startled, eyes first flitting to Marla's empty hands, then down to the puddle of splattered stew and broken pottery pieces in which she stood. Fingers trembling, shoulders bobbing, her face distorting as thick tears ran down her face...

What the fuck is going on here?

"*Anoaley...*" Asker shot up. Clasping her shoulders, he carefully led Marla around the mess before he ushered her onto a chair. Then he sank his head. "I ought not have allowed this. This was a mistake."

I clenched my fists, muscles coiling in readiness to storm out of here. And yet, something kept me in my chair —like a ghostly hand that settled on my shoulder, once more letting the hairs rise at my nape. Until Asker lifted his gaze to me, then that cold shudder spread across my entire body.

Because he was crying.

Nothing more but a lonely tear running down his cheek, that single drop holding an emotion I hadn't seen in him since Ravenna's death.

Sadness.

That shudder clawed its way into my stomach, gripping at my organs. My mind dizzied, going back to the way Asker had stared at me in the throne room. How his lips had parted, as if he'd meant to tell me something, only for him to choke it back down.

The burden of the fate who saw the future...

"I see," I said on a scoff and leaned deeper into my chair, each heartbeat in my chest deafening; no longer a mere rhythmic function but the tick-tock of a mechanical clock. "I'm not going to Lanai this summer, am I?" Would never show Galantia where I'd grown up. Would never touch her growing belly. Would never watch her hair turn gray. "Neither am I going to hold their child. Ever."

Marla cried harder.

Asker said nothing.

Combined, that said just about everything I needed to know. "Did you see how I die?"

Asker's lips trembled. "Visions are... capra—"

"Just fucking tell me!" I shouted, a million fleeting pictures popping into my mind, from how a human soldier would shoot my unkindness from the sky to how I accidentally stumbled and hit my head on a rock, and everything in-between. "Stop beating around the bush when it's damn obvious that you saw my death. How am I going to die?"

"A dagger to your chest," he said, and damn, that was a

fucking painful way to go, the idea alone putting a tremble into my bones. "The goddess showed me how you will throw yourself in its trajectory, taking the blade for Galantia."

The tremble stopped, all tension fading away from my muscles as if, suddenly, death didn't sound so bad anymore. "I... I save her?"

That was...

Yeah, that was a good way to go.

Asker pressed his lips into a grim line for a moment before he said, "Maybe."

"Maybe?" If I had to die, I'd settle for nothing less. "The fuck is that supposed to mean? Do I save her, or do I not?"

"You have to tell him," Marla said.

"Tell me what?"

"I have said too much already," Asker choked out. "It should never have come to this. Knowing when one's death is coming... it is a knowledge too heavy for us to burden."

"Old man, I should have died on that winter night," I said. "I'm not afraid of death, but at least let me make sure that it accounts for something."

Asker closed his eyes for a moment, took a deep breath, then set his gaze on me. "The goddess shows me a throne room. Ammarett, I believe."

"Why would Galantia be in Ammarett?" I asked. "Malyr won't let her anywhere near the actual fighting."

"I can only tell you what I see," Asker said. "Over and over again, the goddess has showed me this vision. It will come to pass. Always the same place. Always the same event. However, the person taking the blade... keeps changing."

"What do you mean?"

"I had the same vision of Malyr."

The shadows in the room deepened, or maybe my vision was just going to shit because darkness rimmed the edges the longer I stared at Asker. "So, when that moment comes, one of us will die?"

Another tear ran down his cheek. "Yes. One of you has to die for her to live."

CHAPTER
FORTY-NINE

Malyr

Present Day, Valtaris

I told Asker and Marla tonight that I would make the fuck certain that it will be me. It was an easy decision, and looking at you two now gives me nothing but resolve and strength to be the one who takes that blade.

Fate rarely gives you choices, but I was given so much more: a chance to set it all right. Ten years ago, I lost my mate. I would not have survived watching you

447

die, sweetheart. Neither would I want you to go through the pain of losing Malyr.

Galantia, it was never my fate to find a second chance at love and life with you. Instead, it's my fate to ensure that you have all that and more with Malyr. I cannot change my past, but I can make certain that the two of you get to share a future.

As for the both of you...

Don't cry. Don't be sad.

I died happily and gladly, I'm sure of it. Don't let it be in vain by allowing it to cast a gloom over your long lives. Get drunk. Dance like we did around the fire. Fuck like it's spring. Do it for me, yes?

I love you. Both of you.

Sebian.

P.S.: Brother, I got you back on that one, didn't I?

"You did." I stared down at Sebian's letter where I slouched in the chair by my desk, that smile tugging on my lips bittersweet. "Fucking bastard fooled me good. Guess we are even now, are we not?"

I thumbed the parchment the way I always did when I read over his scribbles. Unembellished. Pragmatic. Just like him, and that thought echoed in the hole he'd left in our lives.

It had gotten better over the last weeks, of course. Each day that passed softened the grief, more efficiently when the hours were spent watching Galantia practice her archery, teach her how to saddle her own horse, or show her the first wheat seedlings out in the fields. Still, it would never fade entirely, time had taught me, flaring up now and then.

Like today.

"Are you ready?" Galantia stepped out from behind the privacy screen where Tjema had helped her into her gown, the white shadowsilk flowing around her like winter, dawn, and sunshine all at once. Her keen eyes landed on the parchment between my fingers, a soft smile curling her peachy lips as she gave me a scolding look. "He would've wanted you to be happy on this day."

I was happy, very much so. What pained me was the fact that I couldn't share this happiness with the man who'd greatly contributed to get me there. He'd saved my life. He'd saved my relationship with Galantia.

He had saved *us*.

"I know." I let the letter disappear back into the wooden box in one of the desk drawers, then gave a tug on the high collar of my black, tailored jacket, the buttons simple, the shadowcloth holding no embroidery for once—like I'd requested. "I just wish he could be here today."

She walked over to me, her gaze going to the specks of purple and pink beyond the window before she lowered herself onto my lap, the train of her gown eating up space. "The first stars are already glinting on the dusky sky. He was never one to turn down fun, so I'm sure he'll be watching."

I observed the upturn of her lips, the quivering muscles that she ordered to sustain it. The moment she'd heard Sebian's heart stop, she'd grown hysteric, crying and clinging to him, shouting assurances of love, begging him to come back. Until she'd burst into her crying unkindness.

But after the letter?

Every day, she rose with the sun, taking in the beauty of another day granted. Every day, she honored Sebian's sacrifice and final wishes by living it to the fullest, be it by taking Pius for a canter across a meadow, soaring her unkindness through the sky, or enjoying a cup of sweet red from Lanai.

I reached up and ran my fingers over the intricate nest of braids pinned atop her head, careful as not to disturb the masterpiece Tjema had created, and pulled a stray pine needle from between her strands. We did that sometimes, disappear to one of the nearby forests for long strolls. To be with Sebian for a bit, as she called it, allowing us both to spend time with our memories of him, and add our own ones to them. How we talked for hours about our childhood, the things we feared, the things we were looking forward to. It was always blissful.

Calm.

Serene.

She cupped my face, giving an approving swipe of her thumbs over my freshly-shaven cheeks, then lowered her face to mine. "You look very handsome, *anoaley*."

Her breath kissed my lips, making me curl my hand around her waist and pull her closer against me, warmth streaming into my groin. "Nobody will notice. In fact, I wouldn't be surprised if I will be a fleeting mention in whatever books they may write about the day when you were given your crown, Galantia, breaker of curses."

An adorable grin twitched on her mouth at that. "And mountains."

"And mountains," I echoed on a chuckle. "Void of mayhem."

"Thief of shadows."

"Queen of light," I whispered against the corner of her mouth, my breathing coming faster, my heart beating violently at the closeness between us. "I love you."

Her features softened, the few faint scars she'd gained

lending the sweetness she emanated a subtle warning. "I love you, too."

The most gentle of caresses whispered through my core, flaring up the brightness that sat there, allowing it to illuminate more of my shadowed soul. Running my fingers from her cheek to her neck, I pulled her closer. Our lips collided, ripping a groan from me that resonated in her mouth with how my tongue sought out hers. Galantia tasted like berries, summer, and everything that was bright and joyful.

I lost myself in it, heat spreading into my veins as I dug my fingers into her shapely waist. My hips lifted against her all on their own, letting my cock swell and harden against her thigh in such an intense rush of blood, my mind dizzied.

I didn't like it.

"Everyone is waiting for us," I mumbled between kisses, my skin pulsing with shadows and lust alike. I hadn't touched her since... since *they* had hurt her. "Tjema is right over there."

"Tjema left minutes ago," she whispered and shifted to sit astride me, rocking herself over my hard length in search of friction. "As for everyone else... let them wait. I want you."

And I wanted her, the sheer force of how I desired her putting a tremble into my tensing muscles. Those first blossoms out on the trees weren't helping, getting my *anoa* into such a state at my core, I wanted to drag her into our nest and keep her there for however long it took to get her pregnant. To fuck her with abandon, to slap her, choke her, bind her with my—

A warning shuddered through my lungs, making me inhale deeply until that spring fog cleared some from my mind. Maybe at the end of the season, once I had more control over my urges.

I gave a gentle push at her hip. "We have to—"

Her lips devoured mine with abandon, intensifying our kiss. Goddess help me, how she arched her back, rubbing her clit on all the fabric bunched up between us. But I couldn't—

A sting shot into my bottom lip.

Had she just... bit me?

Her lips hardened as if in answer when her mouth narrowed into a smile. "Don't tell me you're going to let that stand."

My entire body shook uncontrollably as I fought the urge to hang her over my lap and spank her. "Little dove, we really ought to—"

Another nip.

Raw skin and the promise of blood seasoned our tongues, sending such a surge of lust through me, I shot my hand up and collared her throat. I bit back all the harder, clamping my teeth around her plump bottom—

She let out a moan.

Or was that a yelp?

Every muscle in my body snapped tight as I released her and pulled back. "I didn't mean to hurt you..."

"Yes, you did." Head tilting, she stared at me with too much empathy and not nearly enough anger. "And I want you to, Malyr. It's alright."

But how could it be? After what she'd endured at the hands of men? They had raped her. They had undoubtedly struck her with no measure. Choked her, probably.

Fuck like it's spring. Well, Sebian, what if fucking her like spring meant that I would do all these things to her? Sully our lovemaking with the memories of these men, hmm?

"We are desperately late," I said and rose, letting her slip off me before I strode toward the door in something that felt too much like panic. "We've delayed this for weeks. The least we owe the people out there—"

I stopped short of the doors and glanced back. There she stood, my beautiful little dove, beside the chair where I'd left her. Looking at me. Confused. Maybe even hurt, as if I'd botched this all over again, achieving exactly what I'd wanted to avoid. What if she thought I rejected her because she appalled me?

I hurried back, took her into my arms, and kissed her. I was not good with words, not when it came to things too close to my past. So I poured everything unsaid into this one kiss. *I desire you. You are not filthy to me. You are not sullied, or tainted, or worth any less of my love and admiration. Perhaps even more.*

When my lips parted from hers, my chest heaving, I took her hand into mine. I stared at her for just a second too long, my skin pulling taut at the way she looked at me, into me, right through me. As if she knew.

"Shame and hate are heavy burdens, Malyr. I won't let them drag me down," her voice resonated my thoughts. *"And neither should you."*

My jaws clenched. I was letting go of my hate, slowly, making room for more love and joy in my life each day. But the shame...

A knock sounded on the door, followed by Asker poking his head through the gap. "The crowd is drunk and merry, but the lords are growing rather restless."

Finally, a worthwhile interruption.

"We are coming," I assured him with a nod, then took Galantia's hand into mine, brushing a white feather back into place on the collar from which it swayed. "Are you ready for this?"

She wiped a fine sheen of sweat from her temple, her neck so wonderfully flushed by the effects of spring. "No. But I'll do it anyway."

That statement resonated like no other as I led her out of our personal rooms, along the silent corridor, and toward the gate. For nearly eleven years, I'd struggled to avenge my family, make a home for my people, and take my rightful place as king. Now that it was near, fear, doubt, and anxiety framed my every step out onto the plateau.

My boots met the black flagstone of the Winged Keep's outer expanse, where two makeshift thrones waited for us. Raven and human aristocrats lined our sides, including Lord Taradur—presume I had to call him *King* Taradur now. After all, King Barat had decided to die weeks before our attack on Ammarett, as I'd later been informed.

After much discussion, my advisors and I had agreed that placing Taradur at the head of what remained of the kingdom of Dranada was in our best interest. Fewer chances at revolts and quarrels among humans for power, which would only have destabilized the lands further. Not to mention that it put an official end to the decade-old war.

Considering that Taradur had stood by his word and helped me take Tidestone, he had proven trustworthy enough. As a precaution, his son was given Hanneling Hold —as a bannerman of mine, obligated to wed a Raven lady —which lay too far south, should he ever grow too ambitious. Lady, or rather, Princess Cecilia, was ordered to marry Lord Thalios, a pathfinder with no living mate...

... until Galantia had insisted to allow her to choose among the Raven lords available, undermining my decision. Something that would take some getting used to, but the end result was the same, ensuring peace.

I took a moment to let my gaze sweep over the scene below, a sea of Ravens, though I could spot the occasional blond, copper, or brown shroud. Murmurs, whispers, and merry guffaws blended into a chorus of collective anticipation that thrummed the air. In the gaps between it all, ravens perched on ladder towers, gathered in flocks on rooftops, and clung to the stone parapets.

I led Galantia to the edge of the stairs, and that was all it took for the masses to explode into a roar of cheers and excited caws. Not a single colorful thread on my black outfit distracted from her white dress as I positioned myself behind her. Like that, I became darkness that framed her, extending through the night that slowly settled on Valtaris.

Above us, stars sparkled.

But none brighter than my little white dove.

FIFTY

Galantia
Present Day, Valtaris

Fanning a hand at my face, I strode along the red-carpeted corridor that led to our personal rooms. It did little to alleviate that cursed heat that followed me, getting worse with every emerging bud outside on the few trees that came back to life. How could I make Malyr understand that—

Giggles.

My steps slowed, attention going to one of the rooms

where servants kept goblets, the door ajar. Beyond the gap, a guard's naked buttocks clenched, his breeches lowered halfway down his thighs. With each thrust, he pinned a giggling maid to the wall, both so engulfed in their love-making that they didn't even notice my hushing by.

I continued, my fingers turning clammy. Sebian hadn't exaggerated, given that this was the third couple I'd spotted in the throes of passion today. Everyone in this keep was under the spell of spring, spending their free time making love.

Everyone but me.

I stepped into our sleeping chamber, finding it empty, but the scent of lemongrass and rose told me that Malyr was nearby. Moisture clung to the air, so easily distinguished with my amplified senses. He'd had Tjema draw him a bath, hadn't he?

Rounding through the nearby archway confirmed my suspicion. Malyr sat on the bench in front of the wall of windows that overlooked the upper market, the trees in front of it naked, though he refused to have them cut down just yet. Knife in hand, he broke the old wax seal of a yellowed scroll, his sweat-glistening chest bare, his breeches untied.

I looked over at the large metal-cast tub, the water not even steaming anymore, then back at him. "Did you let yourself get distracted again?"

There was a heavy sigh, but that didn't keep him from meeting my gaze as his lips lifted into a smile. "Every day, I try to read over at least five accounts that my father left behind. Still, at this rate, I won't be done before I sprout my first gray hair."

I held on to his shoulder, picked up the train of my green silken dress, and sat astride his lap. "Watching you grow old was one of the many things I dreaded I might never experience in that throne room. Read more scrolls. Maybe they'll sprout faster."

Scroll and blade lowered onto the red cushion beside him, he ran his palms along my waist. "Did I neglect you today, *anoaley?*"

"Yes." Spring seedings. Ravens returning to Valtaris with century-old claims to lands or homes. Plot divisions and assignments. Kingly things kept him busy while I looked after the human affairs—none of which was the source of my frustration, though. "Did you notice that the hallways are strangely empty and the servants' quarters quite noisy at the moment?"

I lifted my arms and ran my fingertips through his open strands, loving the way it caused him to release a long, freeing exhale. Then I kissed him, deep and drinking, rolling my cunt over his engorging flesh unabashed. I wasn't usually this forward and lusty, but then again, I'd never suffered through spring with my *anoa* intact before.

As expected, Malyr grabbed my waist, his hands trembling as if tempted to push me down on his hardening cock... only to stall my motion completely. "I should get into the water before it gets cold."

I tried rocking my pelvis, but his hold on me was solid. "It's gone cold already." I knew it; he knew it. "How much longer are you going to do this, *anoaley?* The rejecting?"

"I am not rejecting you. Look at me." His hand shot up to my chin, forcing my gaze to meet his gray-brown stare, which was a promising start. "I am *not* rejecting you. It's just... you are still healing."

"I meant, how much longer will you reject yourself, keeping me at arm's length out of fear that you'll hurt me." Denying his urges. Denying my needs. Denying us the intimacy of our bodies coming together in pleasure and pain. "I've been healed for weeks."

A breath barreled out of him, his face bleak, as if he was coming to the realization that I wasn't as oblivious as he'd hoped me to be. "It is spring..."

"As we all know." I ran my fingers down along the chiseled line of his jaws, over his throat, and lower to where a soft sheen glistened on his scarred chest, even though he'd already bathed once today. "All the more reason for you to abandon the premise of cold water and take me to our warm nest. I miss you. I miss feeling you against me. Inside me."

"I am... worried that I might not be able to control myself," he said. "Not to mention that I haven't syphoned into you for days now."

Three, to be precise, since I'd been *'feeling weak'*. "Who says that I want you in control?"

An excited glint flickered across his eyes, here one second, extinguished under more shame and doubt the next. "You don't know what you're asking."

Oh, I knew.

I rocked my pelvis as much as he let me, which was enough for my neglected, needy clit to throb. Goddess help me, the way he pulsed beneath me, eager but holding back. It had been so long since I'd had his hard cock inside me, driving me wild with pleasure!

"Stop," he said quietly, as if he didn't dare speak up out of fear his voice might break, revealing his crumbling resolve. "It's difficult for me to be gentle on my best days, and today is not one of those days."

Yes, I'd made certain of that by closing my void to him, letting his shadows accumulate. If I'd learned one thing about Malyr, it was that his temper grew shorter in direct relation to the increasing amount of shadows he had to contain. How to get him to unleash it? To smack me, choke me, bite me... and see that I would come out of it alive, satisfied, and filled with bliss?

My eyes wandered to the knife.

That might work. Of all the things I'd witnessed strip him of his control, little was as effective as causing him pain.

"The thing is, Malyr..." I took the knife, the tapered bone handle thick and smooth in my palm, and brought the blade to his chest. "I don't want you gentle. Never did."

"That was before..." *They hurt you*, he didn't say as he glanced down at the knife, his next inhale lifting his chest higher, letting the blade press precariously into his skin. "Whatever enjoyment you might find in it now will forever be tainted."

No, because I wouldn't let it.

He let his past make *him* feel tainted.

"I have no interest in denying myself the joys of life or the pleasures of love over a few people dead in the ground, Malyr." It was surprisingly easy, gliding the blade slowly down his chest, letting blood rise from the cut before it collected and ran in a crimson droplet down his stomach. "Why would you let them rob you of the things you enjoy, hmm?"

He let out a hiss, but he didn't flinch, didn't move an inch, aside from how he stared down at the bloody cut. "What are you trying to achieve here, little dove?"

Oh, he knew, I could tell by the way he smirked when his gaze met mine once more, but I only shrugged. "A flower, maybe. I would promise you to make it pretty, but I'm afraid I'm not nearly as artistic as you are."

"Mmm. How about a dove? Surely you can manage a

faint likeness?" He leaned back, lowering his arms to his left and right on the bench, as if offering himself up as a canvas. Calm, entirely too calm. "Go ahead. I have dozens of scars, but this one, I will treasure."

With my other hand, I tugged on the already deep neckline of my dress, revealing my scar: a spread-winged raven on a skull, framed by bite marks.

His breathing came faster, harder, his hand lifting to let his fingertips trace the outlines of the mark he'd left on me. More promising were those black hairline threads that webbed across his forehead and down toward his eyes.

I gingerly moved the blade across his pectoral. Wings here. A beak there. Lines beneath it for the waves behind Tidestone, by which we'd first met. It wouldn't be a masterpiece, but it masterfully caused his skin to pebble around his hardening nipple.

"I know what you're trying to do, little white dove," he whispered at the pummel of his breath, his voice as shaky as those fingers that slowly clawed into the scar between my breasts. "You're not going to get the reaction you seek."

"Do not provoke him, sweetheart."

Smiling at the sound of Sebian's voice, I lifted the knife from the oozing wound on Malyr's chest and pressed the flat side across one corner of his mouth. Oh, I had every intention of provoking my hot-headed bondmate to let the past be the past.

His lips parted, his eyes capturing mine before he carefully spoke beside the sharp edge, his cock throbbing and pulsing against my cunt. "Let me guess... you want me to lick it?"

I parted my lips, holding his gaze as I leaned forward, bringing my mouth to his. I pressed my tongue against the blade. In one, slow, languid motion, I slid it upward, moaning at the familiar burn of the cut, the taste of blood, that pleasant chill that clashed with the heat between my legs.

Malyr stared at me, transfixed, a noisy gulp tearing from his throat. The thinnest coils of shadows extended across the white of his eyes.

"You forgot, did you not?" With one quick move, he grabbed my wrist and skillfully maneuvered the knife out from between us, though the hilt remained solidly in my palm. "Only *I* get to hurt you."

His mouth clashed onto mine with a groan. Our teeth collided before he forced his tongue into my mouth, lapping and suckling, letting the tip search for the throbbing, burning source on the side of mine.

I shifted. The room turned.

"You want me to hurt you, hmm?" Arms slung around me, he rose and carried me into our sleeping chamber. There, he lowered me to our nest of black mink and onyx silk. "I should spank you for cutting me up like that, making me bleed all over myself."

"Yes!"

Dropping the knife, I kicked my shoes off, only to shove his breeches down with my feet where he knelt. Gods he was hard, his crown swollen red and positively throbbing, each vein on his shaft protruding.

"You sound entirely too eager about this." Hands to my hips, he flipped me onto my stomach, then ushered me back onto my knees. "If you think I'll let you come anytime soon, that I'll let you have even an ounce of pleasure from this, then you are severely mistaken, *anoaley*."

Fingers fisted my hair, only to shove my face into the mink. Fabric shifted around my thighs, lifting and bunching over my waist. A swat came down on my rear with a thundering smack, sending such a ripple of heat through me, it flared my breaths straight into panting. Yes! This was what I wanted. This was what we enjoyed.

Except... nothing else happened.

For long seconds, I knelt there with my ass throbbing, the mink caressing my face as I turned my head and looked back at him. Why had he stopped?

Malyr knelt behind me, his hard cock bouncing with every ragged breaths as his darkening eyes found mine. "I need to syphon into you. Get myself back under control."

Disappointment, heartache, and too much heat coursed through my veins. No, I'd gotten him to this point, and I wouldn't allow his mind to retreat into the dungeons again, the shadowed parts of his soul, the darkest crevices of his imagination. Shadows clung to secret corners, thriving in the unseen, the unacknowledged. But if we fully embraced it...? They would find their domain reduced, leaving more room for light and love.

I turned around, sat up, and pressed my absorbing hand onto his chest. With no leather for a filter, not even a shred of fabric between our skins, I sucked his shadows straight into my void.

And I did not stop.

"What... what are you doing?" The more the black glaze faded from his eyes, his upper body swaying at the force, the wider they grew. Then, his hand launched at my arm. "No!"

I didn't need to slap his hand away.

The shadows at my core did it all on their own—scratching, scraping—winding like ropes around his wrist. First one, then the other, and a band across his chest for good measure. At my command, the shadows lifted his arms up over his head.

I rose and let my dress pool by my feet, my undergarments, too. Then, I gave a little nudge with my toe on his torso, sending him backward under curses where he sank into the cushions, bound and helpless.

Angry, too.

"Unbind me!" he spat through gritted teeth, the tendons along his neck bulging. "Give me my gift back! Get those bonds off me!"

Naked, I knelt beside his legs, removing his breeches where they still hung around his ankles. I climbed to sit astride his lap, arching my back and rolling my hips as I let my cunt search for his cock.

"I will punish you for this," he said, as if that was a threat and not my goal. "Stop thi—mmm..."

I pushed back onto his cock, a shudder spreading across my entire body with how his girth filled me, stretching neglected muscles to accommodate him. "You were saying?"

His eyes fluttered shut, his expression pulling taut as he lifted his hips. "Just... just get these shadows off me."

"Isn't this the perfect solution?" I whimpered when I sat more upright, carefully rocking on his length as I breathed through the demand of it. "You can't hurt me like this, can you?"

He groaned, planting his soles and angling his legs, allowing him to lift me slightly with each of his thrusts. "Unbind me..."

They'd tied him down in the dungeons, hadn't they? Had stripped him of all control, leaving him exposed and helpless. And yet, he pulsed inside me—the way my clit had when he'd cut me, bit me, choked me, revealing a truth not easily reconciled with one's mind.

He *did* like it.

Or perhaps it was the building of his anger he enjoyed. The memory of being at someone's mercy, only to unleash it all in an act of sheer dominance? How to get him there, hmm? Maybe if...?

I rubbed my clit over the hard plane of his body, riding him as I reached one hand behind me. Back arched with a slight twist to it, I let my fingers roam down along my ass, wetting them on the creamy mess between us, and to his taut testicles. I fondled their smooth skin, cupped them, felt their weight on my fingertips. Fingertips that I stroked lower, lower...

Malyr's deep, masculine groan shook the air, and tremors settled into those legs he shifted. He spread them wider, gave me better access. Knowingly? Instinctively?

Scattering caution and reluctance to the wind, I explored the area with my wet fingertips until they met soft, puckered skin. They circled it, stroked over it... dipped slightly inside the tight hole.

A grunt gulped from his mouth. Chest heaving, his shocked eyes found mine just as he writhed, every muscle in his body pulling taut beneath his skin. With how the shadows held him down, he only ended up bucking upward into me with quick, uncontrolled pulsations.

His lips curled into a snarl, but all that came through his barred teeth was another guttural groan, his face distorting into one of overwhelming pleasure. Probably because of the way I'd started to tease his ass, curling my finger, orbiting along the sensitive skin.

I wanted to push deeper, but... I couldn't reach. Not without slipping off his cock, and the premise of that alone ripped a whimper from me as I bore down, seeking more friction.

Ivory. Smooth. Tapered.

I didn't realize that I'd been staring at the knife until my other hand grabbed my discarded dress. Haphazardly wrapped around the blade, it created a soft hilt by which I held it, bringing it to my face. Could this reach?

Malyr stared up at me, but his eyes didn't widen until I spit onto the polished bone handle. "Put that knife down, Galantia."

I couldn't help but grin as I once more arched my back, bringing the handle down behind me. When he fought anew, I dipped my finger back into his ass as deeply as I could reach, teasing the little hole, drumming it from the inside. Gods, how hard he grew inside me, his eyes once more clenching shut as he all but whimpered at the ceiling.

That was when I brought the end of the handle to his ass, rubbing it over the puckered skin. The more I teased it, the more he shook beneath me, panting heavily, sweat breaking on his forehead. At his next moan, I pushed inside, letting the sound swell into a deep, throaty groan.

The deeper I pushed the handle, the longer and harder his cock seemed to grow inside me. A cock he thrust upward under trembles that ransacked his entire body, his face contorting in pleasure like I'd never seen on his face. I adopted an even rhythm, thrusting the blade into him whenever I rocked forward, retreating some when I rolled back. Then I pushed it back in, turning it some, wiggling it.

"Please..." Malyr moaned as he shook his head, his eyes looking at everything but me. Everything but me. "Goddess, help me. Stop. I'm going to... I'm going to come."

And whatever was wrong with that?

I kept going, fucking into him with more abandon, feeling how he twitched inside me. His testicles tightened against my wrist. His cock grew painfully long, his shaft pulsed.

Everything on Malyr convulsed—sinews, muscles, tendons. It all tightened, pressing against his skin as if it no longer fit whatever was building inside him. It burst with an upward thrust of his hips that seemed to roll back through his spine. He released inside me, rope upon forceful rope, which wrenched a pained shout from his mouth and a few stray tears from his eyes.

Eyes that finally looked at me, wide and glistening. He didn't move, didn't speak. Almost as if he was waiting for my judgment. Who was I to judge, the woman who enjoyed pain? Who was anybody to judge the way we enjoyed each other?

I simply removed the handle, tossed the blade somewhere into our nest, and rocked my pelvis while he was still hard inside me.

"Remove my bonds." He swallowed audibly, a slight waver in his voice when he added, "Return my gift."

Palm to his chest, I let his gift stream back into him. The bonds dissolved all on their own, the way his eyes flooded with pitch black darkness letting my muscles tighten. Would he grab my throat? Choke me until my vision speckled?

When he reached up for me, I expected a slap, but his fingers merely curled around my neck. Malyr pulled me down until my mouth landed on his. He kissed me, his palm stroking my ass and pushing me down on him, intensifying the pressure right where I needed it.

"I love you," he whispered between kisses as he rolled his pelvis in tune with mine, sending those first flickers of energy into my clit.

When I came, he wrapped his arms around me, pulling me tightly against him. We stayed like that until night fell. Nothing needed to be said, all lies stripped away between us, our truths resonating silently. He had me again that night, roughly, letting his smacks on my rear and my choking sounds make our room sound like spring.

And when I finally drifted to sleep on his chest, I did so to the sound of Marla's words. *"Only the deepest love was capable of bringing about the deepest pain."* Love and pain. Truth and lies. Light and dark. Fate and choice. None of them were adversaries; none of them could exist without the other.

Together, they were life.

FIFTY-ONE

Malyr
Present Day, Valtaris

Muscles sluggish from the heat of the *aerymel* shingles beneath me, I stared up at the clear night sky, a skin of wine in my right hand and my mate in my left arm. "Tired?"

"Yes, but too lazy to shift." Galantia propped herself onto her elbow, grabbed the skin from my hand, and took a healthy swallow of the sweet red from Lanai. "I wouldn't mind sleeping out here on the roof."

The largest one that crowned the temple beneath us. "It is tempting, I know. But I do not recommend it. Nothing quite scares the soul out of you like accidentally rolling off in your sleep, waking during the fall."

Another swallow of wine, then she handed me the skin back with a shrug. "I'll shift."

"And perhaps right in time for your unkindness to hit the ground in an explosion of feathers." I brought the waterskin to my mouth, letting the sweet red run down my throat and lighten my thoughts. "Trust me, *anoaley*, you wouldn't be the first one to wake with a broken bone or two."

Her head shifted where she'd lowered it back onto my chest, allowing her to grin up at me. "Speaking from experience?"

I smirked at that. "Harlen once fell off this roof when we were young, after he nodded off one fall afternoon. Broke an arm. You should have seen my mother. She was furious enough to smack him but couldn't bring herself to do it since he was groaning in pain already."

She chuckled and held me tighter. These were the moments I loved best. The quiet ones, where little was spoken but much was said, like when we braided each other's hair, enjoyed a good meal together, held each other while we both drifted to sleep. Mundane things. After all, there were more mundane moments in one's life than special ones, and I was greedy. Greedy to spend them all with that little girl who had gained my heart upon first sight.

"I have something for you," she said.

"You do?"

"Uh-huh." Shifting just enough to reach into the satchel attached to the belt on her dress, she pulled out a bracelet

—no, a necklace—which she dangled in front of me. "My *anoa* keeps bringing me shards of *aerymel*, so I made this for you. To replace the amulet you kept for me all these years."

That warmth from the shingles soaked deeper into me, straight to my core, flooding me with the sensation of feeling loved. I ran my fingers along the shards of *aerymel* tied into sockets of... copper, maybe, which dangled from a string of leather. *My first courting gift.*

That alone made it the most precious thing ever received, but she gifted me something else in that moment that took my breath away: she shoved her naked little toes beneath my calf, and not even the leather of my breeches could keep their damn chill away. And I didn't want it to.

I took the necklace and let it slip over my head, then pressed my leg down to warm her. "It's beautiful. Thank you."

She huddled closer against me, the roof warm from a sunny spring day, yes, but the breeze up here was still chilly. Beside us, at the edge of the roof, our *anoas* huddled together in the same way, a white female framed by two black males, one to each side. Both preened her gently, letting out soft crooning sounds. Until a large bird moved in the darkness nearby, an owl, probably, making them dissolve and return to us.

Galantia flared her nostrils. "Do you smell that?"

I couldn't help but grin at that, mostly because that question now came several times a week as she still attuned herself to her amplified senses. "Can't say I do."

"Mashed apples with brown sugar," she said and gazed back toward the keep, even though it was impossible to spot from the distance, no matter how Valtaris once more sparkled, not a single window going unlit by night. "Do you think Marla made mashed apples again?"

"Only one way of finding out," I said.

She slowly rose and looked down at me, slipping into her shoes. "Are you coming?"

"Shortly," I said. "I'd like to stay a while longer, if you don't mind."

"More mashed apples for me." She shrugged, her voice lingering between a mix of white and black feathers, then she flew off with Sebian's *anoa* in tow.

I stared behind her unkindness, the black raven struggling to keep up with five white ones, and grinned at the sky. "I hope you saw that just now. I'm sure she pushed her toes beneath my calf a hundred times already while I was asleep. I'm glad that I was awake for it once, but brother, how did you handle it? Her toes are bitterly cold."

Sebian didn't answer.

But it didn't matter.

I knew he was listening, watching, probably laughing his ass off whenever Galantia and I argued over the most ridiculous things, only to end up fucking five minutes later.

Sometimes gently.

Most of the time rough, leaving her ass red, her voice a bit hoarse, and her cunt sore. But I was not Domren; I always kissed her in between, telling her how much I loved her, assuring her that I would take care of her after. And I always did, bathing her, putting salve on whatever marks my love had left on her. Then I kissed her, held her as she drifted off to sleep in my arms.

She always fondles my ass now if the position allows it. And I let her, taking the pleasure from it that she wanted to give me. And sometimes, just sometimes, I let her penetrate me with her fingers or whatever nearby object proved smooth enough. There was no more anger after it, no more shame. Because she was not a Brisden.

There was nothing wrong with me.

There was nothing wrong with her.

Or maybe, there was something wrong with both of us, but who cared? Even if we were both broken, then put together, her cracks matched up perfectly with mine.

"I made her cry, you know," I mumbled. "Two weeks ago, she suddenly couldn't shift anymore, making us all think that she was with child. Obviously, she blamed me for taking her ability to fly. It was hard not to laugh with how overwhelmed she was, tears streaming down her face as if she hadn't been very eager in participating."

I took another sip of wine. "It got us talking about names. For a girl, Valora. A boy, Quaelin. Sounds familiar, doesn't it? It's what you would have called your first child, or so Asker told us, had it lived. She isn't pregnant, so maybe it was stress. Still, it showed me that a child will have to wait, and I don't mind. There is still so much she wants to see. After how isolated she grew up, I can't keep that from her. So we decided to *live a little*. I hope you don't mind that we did settle on those names for when the time comes."

I slowly sat up, almost wanting to groan with how quickly the heat left my spine, and tossed the water-skin off the roof. "Once the winds calm, I will take her to Lanai. Show her where you came from." I rose and readied myself to shift, but not without tilting my gaze skyward once more. "Thank you for all you did for us."

My shift came about slowly, courtesy of lazy heat and perhaps a bit too much wine, taking us up along the Tarred Road. We rounded the perch, then dove down along the cliff. One swoop to the left, and we reached the dungeons set into one of our old, defunct mines. Something Galantia hadn't discovered yet during one of her many excursions. Luckily.

A single guard bowed as I shifted and strode past him, and even that precaution was probably unnecessary. One of the few things I appreciated about humans; they couldn't fly, making them easy to catch and even easier to keep locked up. No need for tightly woven steel, iron nets, or tangles of rope.

Only three hooks and crows.

I strode into the last cell to the right, grateful that I wasn't a pathfinder. How the jailor could breathe through the stench of urine, shit, and infection was beyond me.

My gaze wandered over the motionless lump of meat that dangled from chains at the center of the room. "Is he dead?"

"No, Your Highness," the jailor said, who was stirring up a new paste of ground seeds and tallow on a candle-lit table. "Merely passed out from the fever."

Something that would have made me grin a few weeks ago now just... annoyed me. For years, I'd imagined the many ways I would torture Brisden. How satisfying it would feel, to make him a whore to things far worse than what I had endured. And it had been oh-so satisfying...

... for a day or two.

Until I'd come here to quench my hate by watching him suffer, only to return to the keep and find out that I'd missed how Galantia had finally hit the target with Sebian's bow. Or that one night when I'd returned to our nest, only to find her awake because she'd had a nightmare, and had waited for me to hold her before daring to fall back to sleep. Along with another bunch of mundane, but all the more precious, moments.

And I'd missed them.

The light. The joy. The love.

I covered my mouth and nose with the sleeve of my shirt as I stepped up to Brisden, the skin around each of his shoulders visibly inflamed even in the dim light. It couldn't be avoided, given how most of his weight hung from the hooks embedded into his flesh. The third one disappeared into his asshole, only to come up again around the area where his penis was.

Or rather, where it had been...

With a swat of my hand, I shooed off the crows that perched on his thighs and buttocks. I'd tried ravens at first —leftovers from someone's unkindness—but alas, our wingspan took up too much room. Crows were much smaller... more fond of carrion, too!

That was what his asshole looked like, the stench of rot and the maggots crawling around the pecked opening, sending a wave of nausea up my throat. Brisden was nothing but dead meat, and he would have long died if I hadn't instructed the healers to keep him alive. But what for? Right this moment, Galantia might enjoy a bowl full of mashed apples in good company.

I could be there.

Yes, I could be there, holding her, listening to Asker's stories about how I did this as a boy, or how he'd taught me that. Instead, I... looked at Brisden's asshole. If it could even be called that anymore...

When the jailor walked over with the leather funnel he'd filled with the mixture of tallow and seeds, I squatted beside Brisden's reddish face. I stared at his closed eyes, expecting a rush of delight when the funnel was pushed into his ass. Or a sense of justice when Brisden's eyes snapped open, and he released a grunt when the jailor squeezed the mixture into his rectum. At the very least, a hint of vengeance when the crows all came fluttering back, digging their sharp beaks into his rear to make him a meal.

But nothing like that came.

What if Marla *had* made mashed apples?

"This is starting to bore me," I said, holding Brisden's gaze, although I was pretty certain his mind was too far gone to understand who was doing this to him as he screamed in pain. No, not scream; he mostly grunted. Probably because I'd gagged him with the salt-dried remnants of his cock. "For ten years, I thought that this would bring me joy. It doesn't. There is only hate to be had here, and that has started to bore me, too." I gave the jailor a curt nod. "No more healers. Once he's dead, dispose of his body. No need to inform me." I brushed a strand of Brisden's brown, greasy hair behind his ear the way he'd done it with me. "This pretty Raven boy is going to eat some mashed apples now. *Caw. Caw.*"